A PRECIOUS MEMORY

"Marcellus, don't do this to me."

"Don't do what . . . want you? Too late. I've wanted you since the moment I first laid eyes on you, and I don't believe I ever stopped. In fact, I know it for certain. Call it my precious memory, if you will."

With dark, snappy eyes reflecting in the mirror, she replied sharply, "How dare you?" She spun around to face him headlong, hands placed belligerently on her hips. It hurt just to remember his distrust, her vision shaded in gloom with the memory, but she plunged on. "You have a lot of nerve, claiming to want me, all the while believing I've been sleeping with your best friend. You've got a lot of nerve, you bastard," she spat out in pain-singed anger.

"You think I came all this way to lie to you . . . for what reason? What do I have to gain by baring my soul to you if I didn't need you in my life? I'm not blind or stupid to the fact that other men, my best friend included, would be attracted to you."

"But Don is . . ."

"Don is what . . . white? And you think that makes a difference? That that would somehow make you less attractive to him? Hell, he's still a man, and you're still a desirable woman. When are you going to get that through your head?"

CONSPIRACY

Margie Walker

Pinnacle Books
Kensington Publishing Corp.
http://www.pinnaclebooks.com

PINNACLE BOOKS are published by

Kensington Publishing Corp.
850 Third Avenue
New York, NY 10022

Pinnacle, the P logo, and Arabesque Reg. U.S. Pat. & TM Off.

First Printing: April, 1997
10 9 8 7 6 5 4 3 2 1

Printed in the United States of America

Chapter One

Pauline's anxious gaze was riveted on the swinging double doors at the end of the white corridor, as if willing Dr. Reuben Hawse to appear. She desperately needed to hear the doctor declare that his patient would live.

Donald's heart had stopped beating, while hers had gone into overdrive. Within minutes of performing CPR on him, though it had seemed like hours, his heartbeat resumed. Although she had worked on him with expedient skill, she wondered if she had performed well enough to save his life.

She wrapped her arms around herself and scanned her surroundings. She felt as though she were trapped in a tableau of surrealism. Everything was familiar, yet alien: the sustained whine of an ambulance siren fading in the background, the aromatic blend of antiseptics and pine cleanser stinging her nostrils, the steady buzz of efficiency as doctors and nurses moved swiftly back and forth between the cluster of rooms. Yet, she had never been on this side of the emergency ward before.

Pauline stepped from the spot where she had seemed rooted and began to pace the white tile floor. As she walked, her mind darted about the recent past, and how she had come to be here. Though she knew she had done everything possible to ensure Donald Wellsing a fighting chance at life, she yielded to her misty doubt about the quality of her performance.

It was her first day on the job and, conceivably, her last. Even before she had settled into her new office, she received a panicked call from Donald's secretary. *"Would you please come up? And hurry?"*

Pauline shuddered, then shook her head free of the harrowing memory. She had experienced nothing like today since she joined the agency that placed nurses in temporary positions. Her present assignment was at Cav Well Space Industries, known as CSI. Located in Clear Lake, NASA's home in Houston, the company designed inventions for use in space.

She had thought the job would include nothing more strenuous than applying band aids to cuts or compresses to minor bruises. But nothing like this. Even more ironic was that Donald Wellsing was one of the most health-conscious people she knew: he was young, 38; he balanced the stresses of his job with daily exercise, careful attention to his diet, and he didn't smoke. For him to suffer a heart attack was the last thing she expected.

Her eyes slid to the regulation clock on the wall. The emergency waiting area had been full when they arrived hours ago. It was five o'clock, Friday evening. Except for Don's wife, Sarah, who'd gone off to the ladies' room, she was the only one remaining.

Time ticked off slowly while Pauline's uneasiness grew. There were few people she called friend, and Donald was definitely in that category. He was the only one who knew, she mused, staring into her private space. She could think of no one else for whom she would risk confronting her past on a daily basis. Just imagining *his* shock at seeing her again sent a chill up her spine like mercury rising in a thermometer. Despite the circumstances, she prepared herself to expect an unfavorable reception.

Marcellus lowered the collar of his all-weather coat as he strode through the automatic doors. He left the wet and dreary evening air behind him; the warmth of the hospital's sterile atmosphere greeted him. He was tired, he had a sore throat, and a raging head cold. Covering a cough with his hand over his mouth, he followed the red arrow pointing the way to the emergency ward.

He had been in D.C. on a lobbying mission for CSI when he got the call about his business partner and longtime friend Donald Wellsing. When he arrived in Houston, he found the weather as bad as the news that contributed to his hasty return.

Dread joined the fever tormenting his tired, aching body. Walking was a chore that required concentration. He couldn't help hoping that it was all a terrible mistake . . . that instead of a heart attack, Don had simply suffered a severe case of indigestion or something like it.

As Marcellus walked into the reception area of the emergency ward, he slid his arms from the all-weather coat to wear it loosely on his shoulders. Spotting Pauline Sinclair, he halted in his tracks and nearly choked on the next cough erupting from his chest. Suddenly, he felt delusional, though his skyrocketing pulse confirmed that she was no mirage.

He stood spellbound and feasted his watery gaze on her. Warm sensations—very different from the fever burning his insides—seared through him. He promptly forgot the reason he was there as his eyes roamed her striking, slender profile. She was an autumn color, her smooth skin golden brown, but she had the even temperament of spring.

Stylishly dressed in a forest-green sweater ensemble, she held herself tall. In actuality, the top of her head barely reached his chin. She sported a popular new "do," a smooth shag of auburn hair that molded her perfectly oval head like a hood. She had used to wear a single French braid that fell just below her shoulder blades, where she had a small black mole on the left side of her back, he recalled, time threatening to wash away reality. Small pert breasts protruded the button-down top that was tucked into the slim waistline of the slacks that hid her fine, filly legs.

She looked across the distance toward him. Her face was small and oval, its features as delicately defined as her exquisite body. Her intoxicating eyes, light brown like fine scotch, connected with his and lingered there. His heart flip-flopped in his chest.

Pauline had pivoted to return to her seat when the corner of her eye was caught by a piercing, black glare. Slowly, as if externally compelled, she turned toward the dynamic force, unable to tear her eyes away. The noise of urgent activity receded. She touched his name in her mind, her lips parting as if to speak it aloud. Her heart was thudding with incredible velocity in her bosom, as she stared fixedly into her past.

Over six feet tall and weighing two-hundred-plus pounds, a monolith of virility stood roughly a yard and a half away. Tired, red-rimmed eyes and a rumbling cough betrayed his physical condition, but Marcellus P. Cavanaugh was still by far the most majestic man she had ever laid eyes on. The woman she had thought dead inside experienced a rebirth as her feminine senses came to life.

No matter how civilized he looked, in an expensive pearl-gray suit with a white button-down Oxford dress shirt, a gray London Fog thrown over his shoulder, a quality of animal assurance emanated from him. King of the jungle, she mused, as familiar with his lion-hearted qualities as she was with his worst.

Yet knowing didn't retard the mounting excitement she felt. Her body conspired against her, remembering, tingling, and wanting anew. Savory memories, not only of the depths of his sexual largesse but also of his tenderness, threatened to join the conspiracy.

"Dr. Walls to Room Three. Dr. Walls to Three."

The loudspeaker voice jolted Pauline from her foray into the forbidden. She realized soberly that she'd made a drastic mistake by accepting this assignment. How could she have let Donald talk her into this? she wondered, disconcerted by her reaction.

Marcellus presented a staggering challenge, an inducement to dream. And she was too old for fairy tales, she upbraided herself, paying particular attention to the emotion on his handsome face.

Marcellus was dismayed by the accuracy of his memory. Another recollection followed on its heels, and an enveloping flush of embarrassment invaded his mind. Summoning disgust from a cool spot in his hot body, he started off toward Pauline Sinclair. A sneeze preceded him.

"Marcellus."

Hearing a familiar soft-toned voice, Marcellus halted, then turned to face Sarah Wellsing. His demeanor softened toward his partner's wife of seven months, who had just emerged from a side door marked "Women." She had the kind of face synonymous with sincerity; long, narrow, and elegant, with a camellia-like complexion. Torn, he wanted to deal with Pauline first, but, noting distress in Sarah's tear-stained green eyes, duty took precedent. He ambled toward her with his arms opened, and they shared a compassionate embrace.

"I didn't expect you to make it back so soon," Sarah said. Her voice was muffled against his chest, but relief was prominent in her tone. She withdrew to examine him from arm's length. "I'm glad to see you, but you look absolutely horrible." She managed a wee smile.

"I feel it, too," he replied laughingly, before a cough bolted from him. "How is Don? Any word from Reuben?"

Sarah shook her head in a negative fashion, and trepidation slipped back into her expression before she spoke. "I'm afraid I haven't even talked to Reuben. He was already with Don when I arrived, and he hasn't come out, so I really don't know what's happening."

Reuben Hawse was not only the physician who attended CSI's employees, but was also a mentor to Don and him. Reuben was utterly likable and competent, and Marcellus could think of no one else he trusted with his partner's life.

"Do you know what happened to bring this on?" he asked. He hadn't forgotten Pauline. He felt her gaze boring a hole in his back. Just the thought sent an unexpected tremor through him. He planned to deal with her shortly, he thought irascibly. Sarah's chin quivered, then tears flooded her eyes and a sob cracked her voice. Marcellus pulled her back into his arms.

"Shhh," he consoled softly. "It's going to be all right. You'll see," he promised, wishing it were so.

"I got second-hand information from Miss Sinclair," Sarah said, sniffing. "You need to ask her for the details. She was there," she added, tilting her chin toward Pauline.

More than the information Marcellus picked up a hint of truculence in Sarah's voice. He angled his head, following the direction of her gaze, with his handsome face rearranged into a scowl. He fully intended to pursue the reason for her tone. Ever more anxious, he said, "I plan to do just that," stalking off, leaving Sarah to follow.

* * *

Pauline schooled her expression to return Marcellus's insolent stare with a bold lie of self-confidence on her face. Watching his long-legged, stalking approach, she felt the acidic quality of anxiety burn the walls of her stomach.

"Marcellus," she said weakly.

"You're out of your jurisdiction here, Miss Sinclair."

She flinched inwardly at the unwelcome of the words, issued in his balladeer's velvet voice, deep, rich, and mellow. She knew he couldn't carry a tune: the humorous reminder quelled her eagerness to escape. "I didn't realize your family owned the hospital, Mr. Cavanaugh," she replied.

He tramped right into her space, the fire of his temper filling the minute distance between them. Almost imperceptibly, she inched back a half step.

"If you don't leave on your own, I'll have security throw you out," he threatened before a raspy cough wracked his body.

Haughtily, Pauline tilted her chin to look up at him along her straight, narrow nose before she spoke. "I have as much, if not more, right than you to be here; I'm the nurse for CSI."

Flabbergasted, Marcellus sputtered. His head whipped around to look down at Sarah, who had appeared at his side. "What—?" he said, pointing an agitated finger back and forth between Pauline and Sarah. "What is she talking about?"

A look of disbelief marred Sarah's expression. "Didn't you know?" she asked, amazed. "Don hired her."

There was a look kindred to contempt in Sarah's eyes before they slid back to Marcellus, Pauline noted. But he commanded her attention.

"That's impossible," Marcellus exclaimed. "When did this happen?" he demanded to know, glowering at Pauline.

From the corner of her eye, she saw the white-coated Dr. Reuben Hawse heading their way. In his late fifties, he was a tall, erudite-looking man with dark, wire-rimmed eyeglasses on his narrow face and a skirt of white hair fanning his bald head. She flashed a dissuasive glance at Marcellus, which he promptly returned with a snarly look.

"I asked you a question," he reiterated in hot demand, "and I expect an honest answer this time."

"Marcellus, please. Keep your voice down," Dr. Hawse said. "What's all the ruckus about?"

The tension between Pauline and Marcellus was palpable. She noticed that even the doctor sensed it as he looked back and forth between Marcellus and her. With the butterflies swarming in her stomach safely hidden from view, she flashed a look of ignorance at the curious glance the doctor cast her way.

Dr. Hawse examined Marcellus critically from his bespectacled gaze, determining, "You should be home in bed."

Pauline concurred, but knew to keep her counsel.

Marcellus erupted in a fit of coughing and began searching his pants and coat pockets. Pauline walked to the chair where she'd left her purse, pulled out a small pack of tissue, then returned. She held the pack out to him. Her eyebrow lifted meaningfully as she watched the debate on his face.

"Thank you," Marcellus said grudgingly, taking the tissues from her hand. Making use of them, he cleared his throat before declaring, "I'll be all right."

"I'm glad everybody is here. Now I won't have to repeat myself," Dr. Hawse said. He angled his head to take Pauline in his sight. "Marcellus, apparently you have no idea that Miss . . ."

Cutting him off, Marcellus asked, "What is Don's condition?"

Positioned between the two men, Pauline felt the warmth of Marcellus's nearness, teasing her senses into forgetting it was merely the heat from his hostility. She wanted to move. It was only because she knew he would derive satisfaction from her retreat that she held her ground. Still, it took all the inner strength she could muster to keep from fidgeting.

"We've been able to stabilize his heart rhythms with morphine," Dr. Hawse replied.

Sarah's hands flew to cover her mouth, but a whimper of relieved gratitude escaped her lips nevertheless. Pauline heard the unspoken "but" and caution in his tone.

"How could this happen?" Marcellus asked incredulously, then turned a disapproving look on Pauline. "Don is the healthiest person in the world," he insisted.

Whether he was accusing her of being responsible for Donald's present condition, or simply making a point, Pauline didn't know for sure. Even though it was ridiculous, she knew for certain that the former supposition was not farfetched coming from Marcellus. She looked at him emotionlessly, hiding her resentment with indifference stamped on her face.

"Don works in a pretty stressful environment," Dr. Hawse replied.

Pauline thought his answer too pat to apply to Donald, who thrived on pressure. The doctor then launched into a lengthy discourse on factors contributing to heart disease, of which she was all too familiar, as a nurse of five years. With her mind free to idle, she stole stealthy glances at Marcellus, who dwarfed them all with his broad-shouldered, brawny build. He sniffled, and frequently coughed into the tissue balled in his hand. She was familiar with his disdain for weakness and knew he would make a horrible patient in his present condition.

Warm brown skin, the color of butterscotch, stretched over the elegant ridge of firm cheekbones and chin which clearly marked his temperament and magnified the pearl black eyes that peered out from under his thick brows.

Wavy black hair in need of cutting edged the square wall of his forehead, creating a certain sensuality about his stubborn, arrogant face. Pauline felt her pulses tremble like a dulcet sigh.

Marcellus sneezed as if on taunting cue. In his company for only a couple of minutes and she felt like a puppet already, Pauline chided herself. She diverted her thoughts elsewhere, succumbing to amazement as she reviewed how she had come to be in this awkward situation.

Despite her separation from Marcellus, Donald never abandoned her. They talked on the phone every three months, or met when he had business in Houston. This time, she had accepted an invitation to lunch with him.

It was one of the better March days they had had this month—cool enough for a run on flounder, yet clear, bright, and a little windy. She sat across the table from Donald in the *Crab Hut Restaurant* overlooking the waters edging Seabrook, one of nine communities that comprised the NASA/Clear Lake area. Fishermen in protective wading gear were out fishing for trout or anything else that would bite in the foamy white surf.

She was reminded of how much she used to enjoy the water for its calming quality, as well as fishing. She hadn't done the latter in a long time, and it had been far longer, it seemed, since she had felt at peace with herself. Not since her split from Marcellus. It was then that she realized how much of life she had suppressed. She had been merely surviving, keeping busy with work: existence disguised as living.

While eating from platters of messy cracked crab legs, the subject of her next job had come up. Donald knew she worked temporary nursing assignments and requested her services at CSI. Initially, she had objected vehemently. Donald understood completely, but proceeded to assure her that he was acting only in the best interest of the company.

It was then that she believed something was wrong. Scoffing at her worried inquiry, he explained that because the company was intensifying its research, he simply wanted an old friend, someone he trusted to be available should an accident occur. He didn't want one of the scientists babbling, even innocently, about the company's secrets, to strangers, he had told her with a chuckle.

Though she had thought the picture he painted more comical than plausible, she understood his concerns. The excitement NASA once generated with its space launches had become commonplace. Besieged by scandal, economic pressures from Congress, and waning public confidence, the agency existed on tenterhooks. The tenth anniversary of the Challenger explosion last year, in which fingers of blame were even pointed at the late President Nixon, hadn't helped matters. Likewise, companies contracted to provide services to NASA were put on that same tightrope. CSI was one of them.

Still, she had been intrigued by the offer. In hindsight, she thought, she should have been more suspicious. Looking sidelong at Marcellus, she felt certain she should have declined altogether.

". . . potassium as a precaution. We're also going to run a sample of his blood through a chromotograph," Dr. Hawse was saying.

The mention of blood work caught and held Pauline's attention. Though Dr. Hawse did not elaborate, she was familiar with chromatography, of which there were several methods to measure, separate, and identify concentrations of various substances. Of the three, one seemed applicable, but she wondered what he could be looking for. Though curious, she held her tongue.

"Did Don complain of abdominal cramps, nausea, vomiting, or any other intestinal problems?" Dr. Hawse asked both Pauline and Sarah. Both shook their heads no. The doctor sighed inconclusively. "Sometimes, these things just happen," he said in summation. Focusing his gaze on Marcellus, he said, "Take you, for instance."

Defensively, Marcellus replied, "What about me?"

"Next to Don, I'd say you're in pretty good shape for a man who eats, sleeps, and drinks his work. Yet, you've contracted the flu. I suspect you're aching all over and your temperature is over one-hundred-two, maybe even one-o-three."

Coughing, Marcellus said, "I'll be fine. Just the sniffles."

"Why don't you follow me to my office and I'll give you something before your sniffles get worse?" Dr. Hawse replied, a trace of amusement in his voice.

"In a few minutes," Marcellus replied. "I want to see Don."

Staring amazed at him, Pauline shook her head. It was just like him to barrel his way through like a bull, putting his impulsive, insensitive desires before the welfare of others. He hadn't changed.

"There's no way I'm letting you past those doors," Dr. Hawse replied. "You're contagious, my friend. Don is much too vulnerable. If you expose him to your virus, that would be something else he'd have to fight."

"Marcellus, why don't you let Pauline drive you home?" Sarah said. "I'll call . . ."

"I can take care of my . . ." Marcellus interrupted her decisively, then cut himself off with a fit of coughing.

"You need to go home as well, madam," Dr. Hawse said compassionately to Sarah. "There's nothing you can do for Don now. Trust me."

"You know I can't leave, Reuben," Sarah pled in a tone that matched the liquid look in her eyes. "Don't even ask me to."

Dr. Hawse turned to Pauline, asking, "What do you think we ought to do with these two?"

Although neither could be of help to Donald, Pauline understood both their needs to stay. Empathy coursed through her as she took them both in her sight. "Sedate them both, then strap them in bed," she said at last.

"What a wonderful idea," Dr. Hawse said laughingly. He looked at them as if seriously considering the suggestion.

In the tense, pregnant silence, Marcellus stared pointedly at Pauline with displeasure. She refused to shrink under his harsh look, though she didn't know how long she could keep up the bold facade. Inexplicably, it hurt, knowing he loathed her enough to want to act on it.

"I need to run by the office," Marcellus announced to no one in particular. "I got off the plane and took a cab straight to the hospital." Running his fingers over his hair, "I'm sure the staff could use some reassuring."

"You need to run home to bed," Pauline said. "In your condition, you couldn't assure a doorknob." The words were out before she could stop them, and they continued to run unchecked. "What are you trying to prove? That you're some super he-man."

"If I were that powerful, you wouldn't be here, that's for sure," Marcellus retorted.

"I'm here because Donald requested my services," Pauline said, feeling compelled to defend her presence. However, since learning Dr. Hawse was the primary caregiver to CSI employees, she wondered why Donald really wanted her on staff.

"And that's something else we need to clarify," Marcellus said in a retaliatory tone.

With his hands raised like a referee separating boxers, Dr. Hawse scolded mildly, "Children, children. Need I remind you that this is a hospital?"

She and Marcellus were both gnawed by worry and fear for Donald's life, Pauline thought, abashed for losing her temper. She also realized she was fighting the pain of his rejection. At the same time, she couldn't stand to watch him drive himself into the ground. Why did she even bother to care?

"Ms. Sin . . ." Dr. Hawse said before correcting himself. "Nurse Sinclair is right, Marcellus. And if that fever weren't frying your brain, I know you'd realize that."

Sarah chimed in as well. "Please, Marcellus. Let Reuben give you something. The sooner you're well, the sooner you can take care of the company. Besides, it's after six, and I'm sure everyone has gone home by now anyway."

Pauline noted the wheels of reason spinning in Marcellus's expression; wrinkles lined his forehead over long, thick brows arched into triangles. Acquiescing, she knew, was still a fifty-fifty proposition. A proud man, he would do just the opposite to save face.

"All right," Marcellus said grudgingly. "I'll take something. But I won't go home," he said with stubborn recalcitrance.

Stripped to his underwear, Marcellus looked down absently at his socked feet, dangling in the air from the hospital bed, while Dr. Hawse took his blood pressure. For all his doctoring, Reuben couldn't cure the source of his irritation.

He was forced to admit that he didn't despise Pauline, as it would appear. And that was the problem, he thought churlishly. He was over her. Pauline was nothing but one of those bad choices one makes in life, he told himself philosophically. It was simply that seeing her again refreshed his memory of more than the love he once felt. He winced just thinking of his reaction to her rejection eighteen months ago. She hurt him so bad he had cried— bawled like a baby. Though no one knew but him, it was humiliating just remembering his utter loss of control.

But he'd gotten over her, he echoed silently with resolution etched in his expression. Her reappearance was but a mere jolt to his senses. That was all. Now that he was over the shock of her presence, he could concentrate on what was really important.

"Reuben, has Don been in touch with you?"

"Not lately," Dr. Hawse replied. "Why?"

"It just doesn't make sense," Marcellus said with an expletive in his tone.

"If you're talking about your condition," Dr. Hawse replied, "you're quite right. You should take better care of yourself."

"No," Marcellus said. "I'm talking about Don. I can't figure out why he felt we needed a nurse on the premises. We never needed a nurse on staff before. The most serious accident we've ever had required only a Band-Aid at the most. We always called you."

"Well, I'm not offended," Dr. Hawse replied. "And from the look of things, I'd say Don's decision was prudent. If Nurse Sinclair hadn't been present, I shudder to think what would have happened."

Marcellus didn't hear the ominous tone in Dr. Hawse's voice; his thoughts were elsewhere. Even if Pauline was telling the truth about Don requesting her services, he wondered why she had accepted. Certainly she must have known she was the last person in the world he expected, or wanted, to see. Still, he couldn't get over the changes in her, he thought, trying to calm his own altered state when Reuben lifted the base of the stethoscope to his chest. He sucked in a deep breath.

"Being the perceptive fellow that I am," Dr. Hawse said with a hint of mirth in his voice, "I'd say there's some warm blood between you and Nurse Sinclair."

"As far as she's concern," Marcellus coughed through the air he exhaled, "the blood between us is ice cold."

Dr. Hawse arched a curious brow at Marcellus as he listened to his heartbeat. When he was done, he rapidly pressed a finger against his ear as if to restore his hearing to normal. Marcellus ignored the silent taunt, knowing

Reuben heard his heart beating like rocket boosters in his chest at the mere mention of her name.

Adjusting the stethoscope around his neck, the doctor wrote on the bedside chart. "Was Don aware of that little tidbit?" he asked casually.

Marcellus paused to ponder the notion that sprang to his mind. Was it possible that Don hired Pauline in an attempt to get them back together? Sometimes his partner was more humanist than scientist and wanted everybody to be happy, he mused. But Don knew how he felt about Pauline, even though he didn't know the real reason behind their separation. "Nah," he decided out loud: Don playing Cupid in a romantic conspiracy was impossible.

"There, you see," Dr. Hawse replied. "Don must have known or foreseen a need for her." He unwrapped the band from Marcellus's arm. "I'll be right back," he explained, heading from the room.

Marcellus stared after him quizzically. His brain was slow to process Reuben's explanation. Then, realizing he'd given his doctor and friend the wrong impression, he shook his head, pinching his lids together, the point of pain spreading through his brain.

Dr. Hawse returned with a needle and a warning. "Close your eyes," he said. "I know how you are about these. Just don't look."

Marcellus grunted as the needle pricked his hip.

"All right, you can get dressed now," Dr. Hawse said, placing the needle on the nearby tray table.

"Damn, Reuben, not only did you hurt me," Marcellus complained, rubbing his hip, "but that shot you gave me is making me dizzy. What was in that needle?"

Making notes on the chart on the bed, Dr. Hawse replied, "That's your illness working, because the shot of Benadryl I gave you hasn't kicked in yet. I want you to come in next week."

Stepping into his pants, Marcellus asked, "What for?"

"Your blood pressure is a little high, pulse rate a little too fast. I want to be sure it's nothing serious," the doctor replied reassuringly. "Meanwhile, go home and get in the bed. A few days of bed rest, along with the medication I prescribed for you, will be the best thing to work that flu out of your system. Don't forget to eat."

"You'll have to do better than that," Marcellus said stubbornly, getting his shirt from the back of a chair to put on. "I took your shot, so . . ." He tried to hold back another cough, but it burst through. Clearing his throat, he said, "Just get me a room here at the hospital. I'll be fine." He tucked his shirt in his pants.

"No can do," Dr. Hawse replied. "The hospital's nearly full. There's a strain of flu attacking babies and toddlers. I could barely find a room for Sarah. You'll have to convalesce at home."

With protest in his voice, Marcellus said, "I'm too dizzy." Stepping into his loafers, "I know you're not going to insist I drive myself home in this condition."

Helping Marcellus put on his overcoat, Dr. Hawse replied, "You're right. It's already taken care of; I've found you a driver." He flicked a piece of lint from the back of the coat, then escorted Marcellus out the room to the elevator across the hall. "They have the medication I want you to take."

Within seconds, the elevator arrived, and they stepped on. "I thought you were my friend," Marcellus said, leaning against the back wall of the elevator as it descended.

"I am. When we get on the racquetball court in a couple of weeks, you'll thank me. Though heaven knows I could stand to beat you once in a while." The elevator doors opened, and they stepped off. "Your ride is waiting out in front." Guiding Marcellus by the arm to the front doors of the hospital, he added, "A highly skilled and talented individual, I might add. Calm under stressful situations. Knows how to deal with people like you," he chuckled.

"Ha," Marcellus chortled, amusement slipping into his voice. "Sounds like you're trying to sell me something."

Winking, Dr. Hawse replied, "If I were, I'm sure you would agree the product is top of the line." As he patted Marcellus on the back, he said, "I'll call you when I get something concrete on Don."

Marcellus said, "Thanks, Reuben. I really do appreciate all you've done."

Watching Dr. Hawse return to the elevators, Marcellus braced himself for the cold. He pulled the collar of his coat up around his neck and rushed through the automatic doors. He looked at the small car idling at the curb curiously. The horn blew. Guessing this was the ride to which Reuben had referred, he opened the car door and looked in.

"You!" Marcellus shouted scornfully.

Pauline calmly replied, "Get in the car, Marcellus, and fasten your seat belt."

Chapter Two

The damage from one sighting of Marcellus left Pauline's emotions raw. Separated eighteen months from him, she should be immune. It appeared she wasn't.

Pastry ingredients and baking utensils littered the counters in the elegant corridor-kitchen-turned-bakery. Mouthwatering aromas of freshly baked breads and sweet cakes wafted through the air. Flour was everywhere—on the floor and in the sink. A streak of the white powder was even on the baker's face as she grumbled under her breath with displeasure.

"The hell with him," Pauline exclaimed as she pounded a ball of sticky dough on the counter, stirring up a wind that sent a dust of white powder flying. Every time she thought about Marcellus walking off from her car—dozens of freshly baked chocolate chip cookies and three loaves of bread later—she felt like screaming.

"Ooh," she growled between gritted teeth, trembling with outrage, as she kneaded the dough with her knuckles. She should have known better than to let Dr. Hawse talk her into driving Marcellus home. Likewise, she never should have let Donald talk her into working for their company.

"Ungrateful, arrogant ... !" she said, recalling Marcellus's refusal to get in the car. She pulled the one lump of dough into two and tossed one onto the counter, stirring the thin bed of flour. Re-wetting the dough with drops of water, she sprinkled a stingy portion of flour over it and began to knead it like an artist molding wet clay. As if the damp clump of bread were Marcellus's neck in her hands, she squeezed the pasty dough, and it oozed through her fingers like soft mud. A grin teased her lips with a satisfying thought, then the phone rang.

Pauline rasped a curse, looked up at the dark gray wall phone, then down at the goo on her hands. Quickly, she washed them in the sink, dried them on the apron she wore over her clothes, and answered on the tail end of the third ring. "Hello."

"Hello, Pauline, this is Katherine Lacey. Do you remember me?"

Though she hadn't heard that husky voice in ages, Pauline recognized it instantly and her expression brightened. "Remember you?" she said with laughing fondness in her voice. "Of course I remember you. How are you?"

Katherine Lacey used to be Marcellus's secretary at his family's savings and loan, where he once worked. She remembered her fondly as a plump, motherly woman in her late fifties with a bubbling disposition, who treated her like she was someone special. She used to wonder what Mrs. Lacey thought about her sudden disappearance from his life.

"I'm just fine," Katherine replied. "I hope I didn't catch you at a bad time."

"Oh, no, not at all," Pauline replied, quirking a brow at the mess she created. The timer on the oven rang, and she stretched the phone cord to the other side of the room to turn it off. "I was just doing a little baking," she said, opening the oven door. "What can I do for you?" Using the glove she pulled from a pocket on her apron, she folded it over the side of the hot pan in the oven.

"Pauline, I'm in a terrible . . ." Katherine said.

"Ouch!" Pauline yelled, snatching her hand from inside the oven. "I'm sorry, Katherine, hold on a second." Holding the phone in the crook of her neck, she put the glove on properly, then slid the loaf of bread from the oven and set it across the grill on the stove adjacent to the oven. "Now, what were you about to tell me?" she asked, sucking on her burned finger.

"Well, I'm here with Marcellus," Katherine replied.

"Marcellus?" Pauline echoed warily. Both hands gripped the receiver and her heart stopped beating. She was afraid to know the answer, but asked, "Has something happened?" Damn! she swore silently, pulling the apron string behind her back. *I should have made him get his butt in the car.* Her heart resumed beating at a galloping pace. "Is he all right?"

"No," Katherine replied hastily, "nothing's happened. He's just down with this horrible, godforsaken cold." She enunciated the words with emphasis as if each was a deadly virus.

A tsk of disgust escaped Pauline's lips. Still, she was relieved. "Oh, that. He'll live, Katherine." Then a calculating frown outlined her expression. "Katherine," she asked perplexed, "what are you doing at Marcellus's?"

"Well, you know I'm his secretary at CSI," Katherine replied hesitantly.

"No, I didn't," Pauline said, lifting an astonished brow. Don never mentioned it. "I guess I should have realized it, but I never thought about it, to be perfectly honest."

"I had planned on going down to the clinic and surprising you today, but things started happening so fast that I never got a chance," Katherine replied. "How is Mr. Wells-ing, by the way?"

"He was holding his own when we left," Pauline replied with the same note of caution Dr. Hawse had used. She didn't want to raise anyone's hopes for Donald's survival. However, she was shamed to admit she had been so preoc-cupied, thinking about Marcellus, that she hadn't given him any thought since leaving the hospital. "They're still running tests."

"I hope he pulls through," Katherine said. "He's not only a great boss to work for, he's a nice man." Following a slight pause, she said, "I was really calling about Marcellus. He's really sick, Pauline."

Pauline schooled the emotion from her voice before she spoke. "I know."

As silence loomed between them, Pauline didn't know whether it was in agreement or censure. She offered to help Marcellus, he rejected it, and she was not going to put herself in that position again. "Katherine, why call me?"

"I didn't know who else to call," Katherine replied inno-cently. "And I figured since you were the company nurse . . ."

Pauline tried to ignore the twinge of responsibility that crept into her consciousness. "Why don't you call his mother? I'm sure she'll be more than willing to come nurse her baby boy."

"I phoned, but neither she nor Mr. Cavanaugh was in, and the maid didn't know when to expect them. He's really in bad shape here and, unfortunately, I can't stay with him any longer. He's been coughing and sneezing ever since I picked him up from the hospital."

"You should have let him catch a cab," Pauline snapped and then felt instantly contrite. Katherine was innocent in the emotional war she fought with herself. Torn, unsaid screams of frustration scratched the back of her throat. She pulled the glove off her hand and flung it across the room toward the counter. It hit the edge, then fell to the floor.

"Well, he wanted to do that," Katherine said in his defense, "but he sounded so miserable that I didn't have the heart to let him come to this big old . . . cold . . . house alone. Before he dozed off, fully dressed I might add, he mumbled something about some medication Dr. Hawse prescribed, but I can't find it."

"Oh, no!" Pauline groaned, slapping herself on the forehead. "It's in my medicine kit. Dr. Hawse gave it to me, and when . . . Oh, never mind. Katherine," she wheedled as she twisted the phone cord around her hand, "please don't ask me what I think you're going to ask." With hope sinking, she wondered if the Fates were conspiring against her.

The sky bawled, pelting the glass shield persistently with windblown rain. No sooner than the wipers had swiped the black night's tears away, more fell to take their place. Like a game of tic-tac-toe, neither reigned dominantly.

Pauline felt similarly fated as her thoughts waged a repetitive ritual that was endless. With each slash of the wiper blade across the car window, she denied being lured back into Marcellus's life. She preferred to attribute the rapid beat of her heart to an eagerness to get out of the terrible weather.

This was only a one-time occurrence, which would leave no ill effects on her, she told herself. She didn't want anything to do with Marcellus, nor he with her. She had walked away before, and she could do it again.

The rain didn't let up. Lulled by the deluge, she felt each gang of raindrops wash away the bitter memories of time—the lonely months, the wretched days, the agonizing minutes she'd suffered second-guessing the decision she made eighteen months ago. Despite the pain she brought upon herself, the decision had seemed the best at the time.

Still, she couldn't help wondering whether things would have been different had she stayed with Marcellus.

Following the directions Katherine had given her, Pauline finally arrived at the exclusive Clear Lake address. She slipped into her raincoat, pulling the hood over her head. If she had any common sense, she told herself, she would set the medicine outside the door, ring the doorbell, then get back in her car and drive off.

Though ready to face the downpour, she couldn't make herself move. She sat in the idling car, holding onto the steering wheel tightly.

"I'm being ridiculous," she scolded herself. Okay, she nodded resignedly, Marcellus could make her mad, but that was the only emotion he provoked in her. She was stronger now, more confident with who she was, and that included being a professional nurse. She would deliver the medication—definitely staying no longer than it took to administer one dose—then she would leave.

Bolstered by her strategy, Pauline grabbed her black leather medical kit from the back seat, got out of the car and raced to the front door. Before she could ring the doorbell, the door was opened with a flourish.

"Come in, come in," Katherine said. "I saw you drive up."

Standing in the dramatic high entry foyer, Pauline took in the lavish, expensive surroundings as Katherine fiddled with a little box behind the door. If just the little she saw of the outside of the house was impressive, the interior was more so. The floor was white marble, the walls mahogany-paneled. A family of hand-painted Egyptian figures was displayed atop the hall table, covered by a royal-blue velvet cloth.

She wished for their poise, though they reminded her of the wide gulf between her and Marcellus, which had been part of the problem that led to their physical parting. He could trace his family lineage back to Ethiopia, where his great-great-grandfather was an esteemed member of Haile Selassie's cabinet. She could trace her history back to the dumpster where she had been found by a grocery store employee emptying the trash.

"Now," Katherine said, facing Pauline, "let me have a look at you."

Alternating hands that held her valise, Pauline shrugged out of her coat. "I was really surprised to hear from you," she said, forcing a cheerfulness she didn't feel. What she felt was apprehension. Recalling Marcellus's hostility at the hospital, she wondered about his reaction to her being in his house.

"No more surprised than I was when I heard Mr. Wellsing hired you as the company nurse," Katherine replied with a grin rounding her plump cheeks. "It's so good to see you again." She held up Pauline's hands and inspected her from face to foot. "You've changed hairstyles, cut off all that pretty hair. But I like it. Even put on a little weight. It all looks good on you."

"Thank you."

Katherine took her coat and hung it in the hall closet. "Come on, let's get you settled in."

"Settled?" Pauline replied uneasily. "Katherine, I can't stay either. I just came to deliver this medicine," she said firmly, holding up her kit.

"I just hope what you have in there will do him some good," Katherine said, undaunted.

Wearing the expression of the condemned, Pauline felt as if she were following Katherine to her doom as they passed a sunken room with a high, vaulted ceiling. She gulped down her awe. Although it begged for warmth and lacked a lived-in feeling, the room made up for it in loftiness, majesty and grandeur. Another reminder of the

Great Divide between Marcellus and her, she mused, feeling an odd twinge of regret.

Blue and white were the mainstay colors of the oversized room with its expensive decorative accessories. Multi-leveled marble tables, fat-based brass lamps, and a blue-velvet sectional sat atop a plush navy carpet. The walls along the mahogany spiral staircase were covered with a bluish-gray fabric. In the center of the fourth, white-bricked, wall was a marble fireplace, surrounded by white porcelain statuettes of animals and people. A waist-high counter ran along the south of the room, providing a view into the darkened kitchen and breakfast area.

"A professional decorator did it," Katherine said, her arms spread out to encompass the room. "It's great for entertaining, but a little too much like a mausoleum for my everyday taste."

"Where is he?" Pauline asked. She wanted to hurry and get this over with.

"This way," Katherine replied, walking up the stairs.

They reached the top landing and passed several rooms off the dimly lit, carpeted hallway before Katherine changed directions. The door to the room where she stopped wasn't really a door, but a large entry-way into a bedroom that was roomy enough to house a sitting area and fireplace. Between the floor lamps was a semicircular black-tiled fireplace. A stack of starter fire-logs and two bushy plants of potted ivy—both looked badly in need of water—rested on its apron. The linen upholstery and furnishings of two cushiony wide chairs with footrests were done in shades of gray, and the walls in a deep terra-cotta paint.

Pauline was marveling at the cozy setting when Katherine tapped her on the shoulder, pointing in the opposite direction. She turned toward the sound of a rumbling cough.

"See what I was telling you," Katherine said in a whisper. Despite the coughing, Marcellus didn't stir. Curled under his all-weather coat, he lay atop the bedding of the king-sized bed. As she studied the breadth of him, an unconscious smile softened the set of her mouth, and she likened him to a big, cuddly teddy bear in hibernation. The operative word was cuddly, springing loose the dreams and memories that had filled her lonely days and nights. The dusks and dawns welded together and she felt a vesper's bell summon yearning in her.

Sensing Katherine's gaze on her, Pauline was grateful her color didn't lend itself to a telltale blush. She pasted an impartial look on her face and walked to the head of the bed, which sat on an unusual wooden frame, off the wool-carpeted floor. It was angled between two walls to accent the triangular-shaped headboard. Above it was a large mirror which reflected a window wall and a sliding glass door across the room. She opened the white pharmacy bag and set three bottles of medication on the lamp table next to the bed.

"I'll leave you to do your thing," Katherine said. "Don't bother coming down to lock up. I'll do it on my way out. Call if you need me."

Staring intently at Marcellus, Pauline didn't hear Katherine leave. He cocked open an eye to look up at her complacently.

Pauline's whole body tightened; she didn't even breathe, as if lack of motion would make her invisible to him. A flicker of disbelief flashed across his pinched expression, then the lid closed over his eye. He mumbled unintelligibly, turned over to his other side, and went back to sleep.

Pauline freed her lungs in a sigh of relief that she had escaped his wrath. There was time before his next dosage of medicine was due: she should be able to get through unscathed until then, she told herself, as she looked down at him. Even in repose, she was aware of his masculine appeal, as a wave of awareness infused her with warmth.

She knew it was not from heat in the room. Deciding not to awaken Marcellus, she set out to light the fireplace.

Teased from the ashes of his dreams by a cough, Marcellus stirred, peeking open one eye. If he didn't know better, he would have sworn Pauline was staring down at him, her hands in her pockets. She always used to put her hands in her pockets. Pity. They were such nice hands, and skillful, too.

A pleasant murmur on his lips, he turned over to his other side, folded his hands together under his cheek and closed his eye. With recollections rising and falling like waves, his dream took him on a fitful journey.

The meeting with Congressman Dennison had gone poorly. He was having a strategy meeting in his hotel room with the CSI attorney who lived in Washington, D.C. He was downing aspirin like candy. Then he was in a plane, flying into Hobby Airport; finally, hailing a cab to the hospital. He was bone weary and couldn't remember the last meal he'd eaten. Always tired. Then he saw Pauline.

An indecipherable sound escaped his lips. It could have been a sniffle, except for the smile tilting up a corner of his mouth. And as naturally as winter turned to spring, his manhood became tumescent between his legs. A warm coziness covered him in dreamland as his sleep deepened, regressing back in time.

It was late at night, pitch black, except for the intermittent splashes of light from street posts. And it was hot and sticky. After putting in long hard hours, going over the papers for the partnership he and Don were forming, he was heading home. Driving was boring to him under the best of circumstances, for his mind had a tendency to wander. That—coupled with the fact that he could barely keep his eyes open—was his undoing. His lids were heavy, and he blinked, nodding off behind the wheel. When his eyes opened again, his reflexes demanded instant action. But it was too late; the street post was already upon him.

Marcellus flinched in his sleep.

Shortly, anxious voices were shouting at him, as strong hands pulled him from the wreckage. Then he remembered nothing, until a small beam of light was shined into his eyes and a white-coated doctor was asking him childish questions.

"How many fingers do you see, Marcellus?"

"Two."

"Touch my fingers, Marcellus," instructed the doctor.

After several attempts, he gave up trying. Then he slept. For twelve straight hours, he later learned.

He was in a hospital room, the steel protectors raised on both sides of the bed. Dawn peeked through the heavy curtains on the lone window in the room. His eyes were closed in sleep, a slumber light enough for him to detect someone entering the room.

Her scent first alerted him. It was faint, but against the antiseptic odor of the hospital, its sweet flowery fragrance aroused his drowsy senses. She moved soundlessly, as if floating. He must have been dreaming. Opening his eyes, he gazed into radiant pale brown eyes. She looked ethereal, unreal in the dim light. Beautiful. He thought he was looking at an angel.

"Am I dead?" he asked.

"No, Mr. Cavanaugh," she replied laughingly. "Don't fret; you're very much alive."

She was soft-spoken, yet her voice rang with a rich, full-bodied tone that reminded him of Hubert Law's fluting. Standing five feet five inches in her bare feet, she was slim, skinny almost, with a tiny waist, shapely hips, and a nice round bottom.

"Oh, I wasn't fretting," he said, his eyes closed again, a smile on his lips. "I was just thinking that if I were dead,

then you must be my angel, and death was the best thing
that could have ever happened to me."

With a jolt, Marcellus sat up in bed. An entranced glaze
over his eyes, he simply stared, turning his head one way,
then the other, sweeping his field of vision with thorough
intensity. He felt a strange familiarity as he wrestled with
memories that came in bits and pieces. Serendipity lurked
in the depths of eyes that sparkled like precious stones of
topaz. They were oval, heavy-lidded and luxuriously lashed
as if to see out, yet not let anyone see in.

Not that the new style was unflattering, but he wondered
why she had cut her hair. More puzzling was how he knew
that. His gaze lowered to examine the sensuous symmetry
of her body in a delicate green sweater and jeans that
hugged her slender frame, and approval teased his senses.

He felt thoughts of desire for an incredibly desirable
woman: his pulse shot up and his hormones followed,
shocking him into full awareness. He realized he hadn't
been dreaming. Pauline Sinclair was actually standing at
the foot of the bed, holding a thermometer.

Nervous fluttering plucked at Pauline's chest. She stood
stature-still, anticipating the explosion. As seconds ticked
off, the threat of it lessened. In that small space of time,
her senses awakened. Her breasts tingled, her pulse accel-
erated, and a flush of warmth flashed over her. Then, from
the sudden silence alive with tension, it came.

"You," Marcellus exclaimed hotly. "How the hell did
you get in here?"

"Katherine . . . "

"Katherine called you? Where is she?" he demanded
vexed. He searched the room frantically and located the
source of the warmth; a fire was crackling in the fireplace.
He swung his legs over the side of the bed, setting his feet

on the floor. The effort took a lot out of him, and he had to pause to catch his breath.

Pauline counted to ten. She was dismayed to discover the unsuspected shadows of attraction she felt. Marcellus was ranting, yet her awareness of him refused to dissipate. It was as if he were hot-wired into her senses.

"I didn't give her permission to call you or anybody else," Marcellus rasped. "Just wait until I see her again; I'm going to fire her."

"I don't want any nonsense out of you, Marcellus," Pauline warned with an authority she was far from feeling. "Be quiet."

She backed up the command by slipping the thermometer into his mouth, then took his wrist to check his pulse. She felt him sizing her up with cold, watery eyes, and wondered if it was just the fever or his burning rage at her that quickened his pulse. She released his wrist, took the thermometer from between his lips and read it: his temperature was a hundred three. She masked her concern with rote work: shaking the thermometer, then setting it in the glass of clear liquid on the bedside table.

"Now, I want you get out of those clothes and into some pajamas," she said, expecting her orders to be obeyed. He looked at her contrarily.

"Are you going to stand there and watch me change?" he asked, grumpily.

Patiently, she replied, "Call me when you're finished, and I'll come back to give you your medicine."

Looking back and forth from her to the medications on the table, he asked, irritated, "I have to take all that stuff?"

"Yes," Pauline replied on her way out of the room. She was grateful for the brief respite, needing the distance and time to regain control of her senses. Pressing a thumb to her inner wrist, she counted the beats of her pulse. She took deep cleansing breaths until it returned to normal, then sauntered back into the room.

Marcellus had lain down again, still fully dressed. She exhaled a weary sigh. Shaking him lightly, she said, "Marcellus."

"Leave me alone," he mumbled.

Pulling him upright, she said with a nurse's command, "You have to get in your pajamas. Where are they?"

Running a hand across his face, he replied drowsily, "In the drawer in the other room."

"Okay; I'll get them. Don't you dare lie back down," she instructed as she headed for the adjoining dressing room.

Looking through the dresser, she located pajamas in a bottom drawer. From the neatly folded assortment of sleepwear, she chose a gold flannel nightshirt. She couldn't help remembering that Marcellus used to sleep in the buff until she bought him a nightshirt as a sort of gag gift. She had thought they would have a good laugh over it and that would be the end of it.

Enough of her mental wandering, she told herself, and returned to the bedroom. Marcellus was sitting up, but he hadn't moved an inch from the spot she had left him. "Here's your nightshirt," she said, holding it out to him.

With a snort, Marcellus nodded for her to drop it on the bed alongside him, as if he couldn't bear to touch her for fear of contracting a contagious disease. She watched dispassionately, with her arms folded across her bosom, as he proceeded to fumble with the buttons on his shirt.

"These stupid buttons won't act right," he said agitated, then he let his hands fall to the bed as he breathed short-winded.

"There's nothing wrong with the buttons," Pauline replied, leaning over him. "Here, let me."

Slapping her hands away, he bristled. "I can do it. I'm not a baby."

Pauline felt as if she had been kicked in the stomach by the mindless reference. She thought she had stopped punishing herself for the cruel turn of nature over which she had had no control.

"Either help or get out of the way," Marcellus snapped, tugging at a button. It popped off the shirt and fell in his lap. "Damn!" His attention to the button was diverted by a loud sneeze, and he reached inside the drawer of the bedside table and pulled out a tissue to blow his nose.

"Well?" Marcellus said, glowering up at her. "Are you going to help me or not?"

A warring second passed before Pauline suppressed her anger and took over the simple act of unbuttoning the shirt. Unintentionally, her fingers grazed the curly dark hairs sprinkling across his firm chest. Pleasure prickled from her hands and shot up her arms like sparks of electricity; they sent a shudder through her. Steeling herself inwardly, she acknowledged the sensation grudgingly, then shoved it aside. As soon as the nightshirt was over his head, she stepped away from him to draw fresh air into her lungs.

"You do the rest yourself," she said. She wasn't about to take off his pants, too.

"Can I get a glass of water?" His tone was more demand than request.

Out of his sight beyond the dressing room, Pauline chided herself for overreacting. She filled the glass that was on the counter next to the porcelain face bowl and its brass-plated fixtures, then delayed her return by examining the area with forced interest. It was as lavish as everything else she'd seen in his house so far. A glass shower divided the bath into a grooming area and an L-shaped dressing room. The deep-based shower featured multiple heads and controls. Just across the shower was a hot tub of enameled cast iron. It was large enough for two people, and an image of what two people sneaked into her thoughts.

She shivered, shook the romantic picture from her mind with a scolding rumble in her throat, and returned to the bedroom. Marcellus was sitting up, propped against a stack of pillows, with his arms folded across his chest. He looked like a dictator king, waiting for a servant to meet his imperious demands. *Not nearly as helpless as Katherine had professed to me in order to elicit my cooperation,* she thought. *That should teach me to play Nurse Nightingale.*

Mechanically, he accepted the glass of water, emptied the contents, then passed it back to Pauline.

"You're welcome," she said, her voice dripping with sarcasm.

Succumbing to a brief spasm, Marcellus turned his head from her and coughed in his hand. It spurred Pauline into action and she filled a spoon with dark, syrupy liquid.

"Open up," she said, holding the spoon near his mouth.

Marcellus breathed deeply to stem the rattling echo in his chest before he replied. "I don't want it."

"You can take it like a man, or I'll inject it in your hip like we do little people," she threatened sweetly. Smiling to herself, she watched him weigh the alternative, disgruntlement plastered on his face. Finally he parted his lips, and she poured the cough suppressant down his throat.

"Ugh!" he exclaimed, making a bitter face. He pushed his tongue out of his mouth as if to get rid of the taste.

"Now, you may lie down," she said, putting away the medication. As he adjusted the bed covers, she asked, "Are you hungry?"

"If I were, it wouldn't do me any good," he replied. Lying down as he pulled the covers up to his neck, he said, "There's nothing in the refrigerator. I've been out of town."

Backing from the room, Pauline said, "I'm sure I'll find something."

She didn't know with whom she was more disgusted, Marcellus or herself. She was surprised he hadn't tried to throw her physically out of his house, but she knew she hadn't faced the last of his warmongering. The only thing going in her favor for now was that he was too weak to put up much of a fight.

And if she couldn't control her own wayward reaction to him, she would use up all that fighting energy on herself.

Seconds later, she surveyed the ultra-science dine-in kitchen done in a powdery gray and blue. In the center of the room was an island with a built-in stove, complete with burners and a grill. At a lower level on three sides of the island were place settings and stools. There was more than a generous amount of cabinet space in the wide rect-angular-shaped room; shiny little knobs protruded from cabinets and drawers at all levels.

Mindful of her purpose, she examined the contents on both sides of the big, double-door refrigerator. Though the contents were meager, she was confident she could rustle up a decent meal.

Within a matter of minutes, she was standing over the stove, slowly stirring soup while sprinkling a variety of sea-sonings into the pot. Satisfied with her creation, she pre-pared a lap tray and returned to her grizzly-bear patient. Lying on his side, Marcellus didn't move when she reen-tered the room and stood in his sight.

"I guess you found something," he said, unimpressed.

"Did you doubt that I would?" she replied, saucily.

He grumbled deep in his chest before he spoke. "I don't feel like eating."

With a piqued look, Pauline squashed her irritation. "You can always heat it over. Do you need anything before I leave?"

"Turn off the light on your way out."

"Yes, sir," she replied with a salute.

It was useless getting angry with Marcellus, she reminded herself, backing from the room. Besides, in a few minutes she would be gone, never to set eyes on him again.

She returned the tray to the kitchen, then prepared to leave. Just as she reached the door, she realized she didn't know the security code. She eyed the box as if it would provide instructions. She sighed a frustrated sigh, accepting that she had no choice but to disturb Marcellus.

Marching back up the stairs, she scolded herself at every step for not getting the code from Katherine. In his room, she tiptoed to the side of the bed and clicked on the soft white lamp light.

Marcellus looked to her as if he were just beginning to rest; the medication was finally doing its job, she thought. In sleep, she could see the man her heart remembered, and it caused a fluttering in her bosom. She debated waking him.

Chapter Three

Wood crackled and embers flared and faded among the ashes in the fireplace. Scented by burning pecan wood, the soft sough of slumber ruffled the sense of peace that pervaded the atmosphere in the room.

Pauline dosed fitfully, awakening throughout the night to check on Marcellus. Resigned to her fate, she had selected a green and while silk nightshirt from his drawer of many. Though it fit like a balloon, its length fell modestly to the calves of her legs.

During one of her nursing visits, she noticed Marcellus had squirmed out of the bedding. As she retucked the comforter up to his chin, her hand brushed the side of his face. The incidental touch was light, yet it was potent in its effects on her, unfurling streamers of sensations. Even as she advised herself against the medicinal value of the contact, her hand lingered to gently stroke his slightly damp, warm flesh and, in return, to bask in the tingling delights transmitted through her body.

Out of the tranquillity in the room and into her befuddled longing, Marcellus shot straight up. Pauline cried out, a startled gasp, and instinctively jumped back from the bed.

"Pauline! You let me oversleep," he said harried. "I need to get to the office early. I have a meeting at 8:15. What time is it?"

Momentarily stunned, her heart pounding, Pauline could only stare. She peered into his dazed look and noticed with amazement that Marcellus was asleep. Rallying quickly, she replied, "Oh, it's still too early." She touched his forehead with the back of her hand. He was burning up with fever, which undoubtedly accounted for his delirium. "Relax," she said as much for herself as for him. "You have a few more hours."

"Good," he sighed, relieved. He pulled at his nightshirt. "It's hot." He started to cough.

"Let me get you something cooler," she said, vanishing to the other room. Out of his sight, she took a deep breath punctuated with several even gasps, in an attempt to restore her pulse and heart beat to normal.

When she returned with a bath towel and another night-shirt, she found Marcellus sitting placidly in bed. He had already pulled off the damp nightshirt and looked totally void of inhibitions and his previous hostility. She clutched the towel like a life preserver, her heart thudding like a drum. The covers barely covered his waist, revealing a peek of white briefs and a stretch of a long, strong thigh. Bronze and awesomely muscled, a physical monument of power, he looked like a god.

She touched his bare shoulders, tentatively at first, forbidding her gaze to drop lower as she began to dry him off with the towel. A nice hum of enjoyment slipped past his slightly parted lips, the corners fondly tilted, his eyes closed. As if taking confidence from his reveling disposition, the pressure of her touch roughened gently to match the fine-toned thickness of his chest, the sculptured biceps of his shoulders, and his wide back tapering to his slim waistline. Her senses throbbed with the strength and feel and scent of him under her ministrations.

"Yeah, that feels good," he mumbled with swooning in his tone.

She tried to look upon her task with professional detachment, she tried to steel herself against the tide of desire that was threatening to carry her away, she tried . . . these measures of self-protection against tenderness futilely. Caught up in his pleasure, his explicit trust of her, feelings of an erotic nature swirled through her veins. A cough burst through his murmurs of content and jolted her. Shaken and deeply ashamed of the sexual awareness strumming through her, she hurried herself along. Tossing the soiled garment onto the floor, she tugged the fresh nightshirt over his head.

"Hmm," he sighed, rubbing the front of the shirt.

Pauline's hands were trembling when she picked up the bottle of pills. She had to concentrate fiercely to prevent spilling the entire contents as she shook a capsule into his open palm. She replaced the bottle, then extended a glass of water to him. While Marcellus downed the capsule, she fluffed his pillow and turned it over to the dry side.

Setting the empty glass on the bedside table, he asked, "Did you remember to get my dark blue suit from the cleaners?"

His subconscious had gone back to a precious memory in their relationship. Even as Pauline cautioned herself, a feeling of happiness rose wonderfully inside her that he remembered there had been good times between them. She wet her lips nervously before she replied. "Got it," she said, humoring him.

"Thanks," he said, snuggling under the covers. "Don't let me oversleep, babe."

Though she knew the endearment was falsely induced, it wrapped around her heart like a warm blanket. She could barely speak for the exalted tears clogging her throat. "I won't," she whispered.

"Marcellus."

Drifting in and out of sleep, Marcellus didn't want to leave the soft darkness. It was a comfortable place . . . primrose warm and picnic cozy.

"Marcellus."

His mind searched for a reason behind the persistent intrusion, a familiar timbre, like a wind chime whistling in his ear. He reached blindly, found what he wanted, and pulled the covers over his head.

"Marcellus, it's time to wake up."

"What?" he mumbled, groggy and agitated as he sat up in bed. "What's wrong?" Adjusting to wakefulness, he looked at Pauline as if expecting the worst. "Is it Don?"

"No. I haven't called the hospital yet, but I suspect Dr. Hawse or Sarah would have called if there had been any changes."

Nodding, Marcellus passed his hand across his face. Regarding her quizzically, he noticed that in addition to holding a thermometer in her hand, Pauline was wearing one of his nightshirts. As he concluded it was very becoming on her, he was assailed by an oddly primitive yearning. Disgusted with himself, he asked curtly, "Didn't you bring your own clothes?"

"I couldn't wake you to get the code to get out of this vault you live in," she said crisply.

"One-two-three," he said. In answer to her puzzled look, he explained, "That's the code. One-two-three."

"Oh," she replied. "Then I'll take care of that right away," she said, spinning to leave the room.

"Wait," he shouted, "what about my medicine?"

"Getting out of your clothes is much more important,"

she drawled with distinct mockery. She tossed him the thermometer, then was gone.

"Pau—line," Marcellus bellowed. Instantly, he began to cough and clutch his ribcage. He rolled in a ball on the bed until the coughing stopped. His throat felt raw, and he rubbed his neck. "Damn her," he rasped, more annoyed with himself than her as he turned to lie flat on his back and stare absently up at the ceiling.

He didn't give a damn about that nightshirt. It had been a Christmas present that he intended giving away because it was too small for him.

So why did he have to say something stupid like that?

The intimacy of her wearing something of his unsettled him, he rationalized, recalling she used to wear his pajama tops and shirts. *"To keep you close to me when you're not here,"* she used to say. The suggestive explanation had made him feel ten feet tall.

It would take forever to get her smell out of that nightshirt, this room, his house, he thought. He had gotten this place because it contained no reminders of her, and now she would become a ghost in his new home. A creature to haunt him, taunting him with her sensuality haloing that untouchable, proud carriage of hers, leaving a scent like the color purple to linger everywhere. Making him remember he once overlooked her flaws because he loved her so much. Memories were too costly, he told himself, with a resolute shake of his stuffy head to block out the past. But Pauline was locked in his mind.

Admittedly a spur-of-the-moment man, he was a good judge of character. Usually. He couldn't figure out how he could have been so grossly wrong about her. He pulled the pillow from his back, punched it, then clutched it to his chest.

What was Don thinking about when he hired her?

His expression set in deep thought, his mind drifted, recalling his first introduction to Donald Lewis Wellsing.

A pigskin speared him in the back. He was supposed to catch the damn ball, but Don had thrown it short. To this day, he chortled absently, Don still argued that he had gone out too far.

The stage of the incident was football try-outs in college; both were walk-ons. He only tried out for a receiver position because his mother hated the idea, while Don was hoping to get a scholarship by becoming the team's quarterback. Though both made it, neither suffered delusions of a bright future in professional football. They were average players who played with a lot of heart and spirit. It was that tenacity and competitive drive that sealed their friendship. Consequently, years later, when Don approached him about buying into an aerospace design and research company, he had jumped at the opportunity.

The racial composition of the partnership worked to their advantage. He was able to secure a so-called minority loan, in addition to moneys secured independently. Don, likewise, borrowed from his family and secured a bank loan. In order to assure that the company maintained its SBA loan designation, he owned fifty-one percent, while Don controlled the remaining percentage, less four percent which he gave to Sarah last Christmas. But she had no voice in the company. The old name Spacetronics was changed to CavWell Space Industries, and Don became president and Marcellus, VP, by nothing more than the toss of a coin.

With the disconnected route that thoughts sometimes took, he recalled that Don's gift to his young wife had been partly in appeasement for not being able to give her a honeymoon, and, lately, the company had stolen more of Don's time from Sarah. He wondered how Pauline would have reacted to the amount of time he'd spent working, recalling that she had been more supportive of his new joint venture with Don than his parents had been.

Lingering in that time, unconsciously, a mist of passion

slipped into his resolution. Pauline's belief in him had been immeasurable; still, he had felt something was missing from his life, something that didn't have anything to do with them as a couple. He growled deep in his throat, which retaliated by sending him into a coughing fit.

Telling himself Pauline killed any kind of fond memories he might harbor, he recalled that the breakup had left him plenty of time and anger which he channeled into complete devotion to the success of their enterprise. Though the trust between Don and him was mutual and total, something else drove him. Quite simply, he needed to prove to his family and to himself that he was worthy of the Cavanaugh name and its long ancestry of achievement.

Twisting his head around, Marcellus's gaze strayed to the clock. Where the hell was Pauline? he wondered impatiently, looking toward the opening to the room. Maybe he had made her angry enough to leave without saying so much as a good-bye.

"That would be her style," he said bitterly, flinging the pillow and covers aside to get out of bed. As he placed the thermometer on the table, he noticed his nightshirt. Blue silk with gold stripes: it was a different one. With a curious expression on his face, he wondered when he had changed.

Stomping to the entry, he called, "Pauline!" There was no answer. He walked down the stairs to the kitchen. The smell of homemade biscuits baking filtered past his stuffy nose. He spied the pan of them through the smoked glass oven door and sighed appreciatively. Pauline was an excellent cook, especially when it came to breads and sweets. That alone was probably worth tolerating her presence, he thought.

He retraced his path back up the stairs. Stopping at the guest bedroom, he knocked once on the door, then opened it. The room looked untouched. He wondered where Pauline had slept. Certainly she didn't sit up all night watching over him, he mused curiously as he closed the door.

It shouldn't have taken her that long to run outside, he thought, opening the hall bathroom door.

"I guess you want me to go outside to dress," Pauline said in a testy tone of voice.

"Oops. Sorry."

Pauline was feeling terribly ambivalent. A part of her was urging her to leave, while the other couldn't let go of the late night intimacy she shared with Marcellus's subconscious.

Dressed in a pink and blue velour sweatsuit and white leather Nikes, she walked into the kitchen, carrying her tote bag. She dropped it on the floor next to the breakfast table, then walked to the oven to check the biscuits.

She had been taught to bake by a foster mother who believed a girl who couldn't cook was useless. Though she initially balked at the training, Pauline discovered she enjoyed it. It helped calm her down when her nerves were at full stretch, as they were now. Usually, she thought, recalling her early morning capricious flight, her features bunching into a frown.

More than a minute remained on the timer. She looked around the kitchen to make sure everything had been returned to its proper place. Except for the herbal tea brewing in a teapot on the stove and two cracked eggs in a bowl on the counter next to the stove, it was spit polished and cleaned, as if it hadn't been used.

Normal people would have no reason to complain. Marcellus did not fit that description, she thought, her lips in a reproving twist. Thinking back to his dream state, she wished she had a videotape to show him. That would really tick him off—if she could prove his subconscious differed from his conscious. She chuckled, finding a good deal of humor in the incident.

A shadow of irritation crossed her face. She was in no position to laugh at him, for her subconscious had been even more telling, she reminded herself. She had entered his dream. And wished.

She dropped her hands to the counters and blew out her cheeks. She had done her duty by him and it was time for her to move on for both their sakes.

The clock on the wall over the breakfast table put the time at 8:50. Someone was on duty at the agency, and she decided to update them on her assignment. Then she would call the hospital to check on Donald's condition.

She pulled the phone to the breakfast table, sat down, and dialed the number. Within seconds, the call was answered.

"Morning, Janet, this is Pauline," she said in a deliberately perky tone. "I'm fine, how about yourself? I'm just touching base with you. Yes, I've started with CSI, and, as my luck would have it, the president of the company had a heart attack my first day. Yes, he's a good friend of mine. I'm not sure right now, but I don't see any need to stay on. I'll let you know as soon as I can. Thanks, Janet. Talk to you later."

The second Pauline replaced the receiver in its cradle, the phone rang. Startled, she jumped, then laughed, thinking she needed to get some sleep. "Cavanaugh residence."

It was a woman who spoke in a breathy whisper, and she wanted to speak to Marcellus.

"I'm sorry; he can't come to the phone right now," Pauline replied, matching the woman's haughty tone. "No, this is not his housekeeper," she said with a decided chill in her voice. She fell quiet, as did the woman on the other end, who was awaiting a disclosure. "Yes, Dee Dee, I'll tell him you called."

No sooner than she replaced the receiver, the phone rang again. Pauline debated fleetingly whether to answer.

"Cavanaugh residence."

Another woman was calling for Marcellus and, unlike the first one, her voice rang with assertive intonations. "He's not available at the moment; may I take a message? Dottie West; I'll be sure to tell him," she replied before ending the connection.

Dee Dee and Dottie, she mused with a sarcastic chortle, trying to put faces on the callers. "What kinds of names are those for grown women?" she wondered in a snide whisper. Obviously, *the kind Marcellus wanted,* the gloating inner cynic replied.

Pauline felt a sourness in the pit of her stomach. Inarguably, she had been pining for him in secret, while he hadn't given her a second thought. "Serves you right," she rasped softly as she pushed back the chair to rise. The telephone bell rang before she took a step.

"What am I, an answering service?" she asked herself before reluctantly lifting the receiver. "Cavanaugh residence," she said. Shock flew through her, for the caller was none other than Marcellus's mother, the formidable Barbara Cavanaugh. "Uh," she stammered, "he's not available right now."

Listening to Barbara Cavanaugh dominate the conversation, Pauline felt the niggling return of the self-consciousness that had plagued her off and on during the nine months she and Marcellus were together. She had been uncomfortable with his upper-middle-class upbringing, she recalled, forcing a halt to the menacing uncertainty. She was twenty-nine, she reminded herself sternly, old enough to have outgrown that personality flaw by now.

"Barbara," she interrupted in a tone that put them on an equal footing. "I'll have him call you as soon as he can. No, this is Pauline," she said, unflinchingly. Replying to the surprise on the other end of the phone, she confirmed calmly, "Yes, Pauline Sinclair. I'm fine, thank you. How are you? Yes, it has been a while. Yes, I'll be sure to give him your message."

Replacing the receiver, Pauline cleansed her lungs by exhaling a deep breath. Marcellus's mother was probably having a seizure, believing that her precious son was back with her, she chuckled in amusement. Though Marcellus was by no means the mama's boy Barbara wished him to be, mother and son could have each other as far as she was concerned.

She heard the hacking cough that indicated Marcellus's approach. Breathing a weary sigh, she steeled herself for the sequel to his foul disposition.

Marcellus meandered into the room with his robe hanging open over his nightshirt and his houseslippers grating across the floor. His hair was ruffled, as if he'd combed it with his fingers. His eyes were liquid with fever, and he was sniffing, struggling to breathe through his nose.

Clutching his bottles of medicine against his chest, he looked so pitiful and in need of nursing that she felt ashamed of her disparaging thoughts about him. Compassion was threatening to give way to carnality in her, so she suppressed her rebellious emotions under the appearance of indifference, reminding herself that Marcellus wanted nothing to do with her.

"Who was that on the phone?" he asked.

In spite of his stuffy-nose voice, Pauline noticed that his tone had lost its gruff edge, and his scowling mood had lightened. "Your mother," she replied. "She wants you to call her."

Marcellus nodded, mumbling and set the bottles on the table.

"Dee Dee and Dottie called, too," she said, careful to keep envy of his social life from her voice as she rose with the phone in her hand. "Each wants you to call her."

The timer went off. Relishing having something else to

do, she deactivated it and slipped a cooking glove on her hand to pull out the pan of biscuits. She set it on the counter next to the stove.

"Where did you find these?" Marcellus asked.

Taking the glove off her hand, she replied, "I made them."

"I know that," he replied. "I just didn't think I had anything in here," he said, reaching for a biscuit.

Slapping his hand away, she said, "Wait for the eggs. If you're feeling well enough to do something, set the table."

He didn't seem to be in a great hurry to return his calls, Pauline noticed. She wondered if it was because of her presence. *A hint of sensitivity on his part?* she mused, watching him sidelong as he carted silver and crystal to the table. She turned on the burner under the skillet, then began beating eggs in a bowl. From a sidelong glance, she noticed him looking at her tote bag.

"Don't worry, I'll be out of your place in a few minutes," she said.

"Aw, damn it, Pauline; I didn't know you were in the bathroom. I'm sorry, okay?"

"Forget it," she said, pouring the eggs in the hot skillet.

"What about my medicine?" Marcellus asked from the table.

"You can read," she said, deliberately not looking at him.

"I think I still have a fever."

She couldn't ignore the pathetic tone of his voice and looked across the way to see him touching his forehead with the back of his hand. She wanted to rush right over to him and check for herself; instead, she grunted as if unmoved.

"I don't understand that language, you'll have to break it down into English for me," he said, in an attempt at humor.

"You understood it well enough when you were speaking

it," she retorted. It hurt her to deny him, but she had to consider her own mental health, she told herself.

Pauline scraped the eggs onto a plate, then set it and the pan of biscuits on the table. Removing the phone from the table to attach it to its nook in the wall, she set out a half-empty jar of grape jelly and a pitcher of orange juice.

"Here's your breakfast," she said. Picking up her tote, "Enjoy."

Marcellus said, "Pauline, wait."

The phone rang, and the sound broke the tension filled moment. They exchanged wary stares, then looked to the phone as it began its second ring. Pauline answered.

"Hello. Cavanaugh residence," she said. "Morning, Dr. Hawse. I hope you're calling with good news." Looking across the room at Marcellus with relief in her expression, she repeated for his sake. "Don is holding his own. Brain patterns are normal. Prognosis is promising." Sighing deeply, "Thank God. Now, for the bad news?" she said lamely. Her hand tightened around the receiver. Glancing sidelong at Marcellus with alarm in her eyes, she whispered excitedly, "He was what?"

Marcellus rushed to her side, beseeching her for information with his look.

"Digitalis," she said hesitantly with suspicion pervading her entire countenance. "Yes, yes, I was concerned that it took so long for the lab to finish up that blood work. So, that's why," her face collapsing into a look that was compassionate, troubled and still. "Have you told Sarah? Oh, no," she groaned sympathetically.

Gesturing with his hands for Pauline to give him the phone, Marcellus demanded, insistent and anxious, "What? What?"

Covering the mouthpiece, she whispered to him, "Wait a minute. No, I was talking to Marcellus," she said into the mouthpiece. "He's doing a little better. Hold on, he wants to talk to you." With her mind in a fuzzy haze,

Pauline passed the receiver to Marcellus and walked to the table and dropped into a chair.

Clearing his throat, Marcellus said into the mouthpiece, "Reuben, Marcellus. What was that you were telling Pauline? Yeah, I've heard of it, but . . ." Looking at Pauline's back, her shoulders slumped, he said, resigned, "All right, I will."

Pauline felt Marcellus join her at the table and looked at him. The solemn disbelief of his expression matched hers.

"Reuben said Don had digitalis in his blood. I know it's some kind of heart medication, but I don't understand why Don would be taking it."

Pauline sighed at length—she had been wondering the same thing. "I don't either."

"Reuben said you would explain," Marcellus said. "Suppose you start from the beginning. When did Don ask you to come?"

Pauline replied to his attitude—*Me, Tarzan; you, Jane; and you do what I say*—as well as the question, with mockery in her tone. "Do you mean the day we met to discuss it, or the actual day he wanted me to start?"

He looked at her with an intolerant intensity. "Both."

"He asked me on Wednesday over lunch," she said. "My first reaction was a definite *no.*" Marcellus merely continued to stare at her, and she continued. "He expressed a concern for his scientists, though he denied that anything was wrong. I told him I could start Monday, which would be next week. It would have given me a mini-break, because I'd just completed a grueling assignment with a mean old man the day before."

"But you were there Friday," Marcellus said.

"At his request," she pointed out quickly.

"Doesn't that strike you as a little strange?"

Pauline wasn't sure what he meant by the question, and, mindful that his overall behavior about her presence had not been one of gratitude, sarcasm edged her tone when she spoke. "No more so than your suspicion."

"Damn it, Pauline! Can't you see I'm just trying to get to the truth?"

"And, by truth, do you mean what you want to believe, or what actually happened?"

"I know I don't want to waste time debating the issue while my partner is lying in a coma," he said stingingly. "Stop taking everything so personally and help me out here. What exactly is digitalis?"

"Digitalis is one of the cardiac glycosides . . ."

"Plain English," he interrupted.

"Digitalis is the most commonly effective drug used for treating congestive heart failure. It helps to strengthen heart muscles, which results in lessening the workload of the heart in pumping blood. That's assuming that a malfunctioning heart condition exists. Introduced into a healthy heart, it creates quite different results. I should have realized it then. . . ." she said aloud, absently.

"Realized what?" he asked, impatient and frustrated.

She focused on him before she replied, though a frown lined her forehead. "When Dr. Hawse asked if Donald had suffered any gastrointestinal problems. Small doses of digitalis can result in an upset stomach, vomiting, nausea. Remember?" Marcellus nodded, and she continued. "Those are symptoms which indicate toxicity. If a high enough dosage of it is injected into a healthy heart, it's better than any name brand poison on the market. Judging by Donald's reaction to it, he was overdosed. Poisoned."

"I don't believe it," he said. "Don was poisoned? It doesn't make sense. How could something like this happen?"

"Has Don been holding out on Sarah?" she asked, her lips set in a sign of pique. She didn't know for sure whether or not Donald had reason to use digitalis; she only assumed he didn't. It was quite possible he wanted to conceal a heart condition from his wife. Men often did stupid things in the name of protecting their loved ones.

"What do you mean?"

"I mean," she replied with emphasis, arms folded on the table, "does he have a heart problem or some other illness that he wouldn't want Sarah to know about?"

"I'm sure he doesn't or he would have told me," Marcellus replied with cocky assurance. He averted his head to cough, but he still caught the tail end of Pauline's shrewd look. "Well, if not me, Reuben would have known about it," he amended assertively.

"Not if he went to another doctor," Pauline replied, but soon cast off her own rumination with a wave of her hand. "Oh, forget it. I'm grasping at straws."

"Sarah said he ate from the cafeteria," Marcellus said. "Is it possible that it was an accident?"

"I don't see how," Pauline replied. "Digitalis is not a seasoning."

Altering the question, he said, "I mean, could the delivery people have accidentally sent it to the kitchen rather than the lab?"

"Even though I don't know what chemicals CSI uses in its research, I seriously doubt that you would have uses for that particular drug. Unless you're testing the effects on someone of taking digitalis in space."

"That's not one of the tests we're conducting," Marcellus replied pensively, "but it's a thought. What if the bottle was mislabeled?"

"Now, *you're* grasping at straws," she said.

Marcellus stared at her intently, a curious gleam in his eyes. "Why did Don hire you? We've never needed a nurse before."

Instantly, her eyes flared, then Pauline suppressed her temper. It was a legitimate question and one she had put to Don and herself. "In light of this development, I don't know," she replied, shaking her head, bemused. "I mean, I know what he told me, but . . ."

Interrupting her, Marcellus asked, "What did Don tell you? You didn't come to him for a job, by any chance, did you?"

Bristling, Pauline retorted, "I don't need your company to provide me with employment or anything else. I turned down an assignment in Hawaii to take this position. The only reason I accepted it was because Don seemed to think my services were needed. It was a case of doing him a favor."

"And getting paid for it," Marcellus said.

She didn't have to put up with his insults on top of his piss-poor attitude, Pauline thought, bolting from the chair.

Grabbing her wrist, Marcellus said, "I'm sorry. I'm sorry. I didn't mean that." Overcome by another coughing fit, he released her to dig in his pocket for a tissue. After wiping his nose, he stuffed the used tissue in his robe pocket. "Hell, I don't know what I mean," he said, running his fingers through his hair. "I thought you were in hospital nursing. How could you have time to work for CSI?"

"I got out of hospital nursing after we . . ." She fell silent, but the thought completed itself. *After we broke up.* She drew a breath and continued. "It was a good professional move." Not to mention a healthy salve for her ailing personal life. In response to his pressing gaze, she explained, "The nursing shortage was growing while the money was shrinking. I got tired of administrators who were more concerned with bottom-line management than health care, so I the quit the hospital and joined the agency. I can pick and choose my jobs just about anywhere in the world. I can . . ." She fell silent, noticing the cold, congested expression on his face.

"So Don knew about your career change," Marcellus said, one corner of his mouth twisted upward in a brittle smile.

Pauline merely nodded in reply, wondering why that information seemed to upset him. He certainly wasn't interested in her life, so why should he care?

"He didn't tell me he planned to hire you." His head cocked at an angle, he was looking at her with an indecipherable emotion solidifying in his expression.

Pauline shivered imperceptibly. "It would seem it's not the only thing he didn't tell you. Anyway, you don't have to worry about my presence any longer," she said, picking up her tote. "Consider my contract terminated as of this moment."

"You can't leave now," he said, grabbing her by the hand holding the tote.

Pauline felt a stream of heat so intense it was hot enough to melt her insides. Her heart pounding, she thought she couldn't get away fast enough. "Why not?" she asked in a not-so-steady voice. "It's quite apparent my services are no longer needed."

"And that's why you can't leave," Marcellus replied. "Nothing is apparent yet. If Don wanted you at CSI, then you have no choice but to stay. As you said, it's obvious he didn't tell me everything."

Marcellus dropped her wrist, and Pauline breathed again, only to be assaulted by a terrible sense of uneasiness. When she accepted the position, she recalled, it had been with the belief that she would hardly ever run into Marcellus and a confidence that he would not have sought her out. At least not after the initial shock of seeing her again. But what he was suggesting now was quite a different matter, she thought, wetting her lips nervously.

"I don't think that's a good idea, Marcellus. Donald is in good hands at the hospital. There's nothing more for me to do here."

"Can't you follow just one thing through to completion?" he spat out, staring at her crossly.

Pauline stiffened at the challenge and met his icy gaze

straight on. "I have had about enough of your insults and insinuations," she exclaimed. She readjusted her grip on the tote handles and resumed her departure.

"Certainly you must see that Don felt he needed you for some reason quite different than what he told you," Marcellus said. He stared at her with an intense look that matched his tone, a frustrated plea mixed with logic. "I trust his gut, even if he can't read a balance sheet."

Pauline's steps faltered. Why was she bothering to listen to Marcellus? His reasoning was twisting her up in knots. She didn't know whether his argument made sense because it had validity, or because she was hoping beyond hope that he would change his mind about her and realize she couldn't have done what he thought she did. Her convoluted thinking alone was reason enough for her to get out while she still could, she argued silently, sliding the strap of the tote across her shoulder.

In a quiet voice cracked with weariness, Marcellus said, "I thought Don was your friend."

Chapter Four

He would have denied under oath that he wanted her and faced the penalty for perjury. Yet all he could think of at the moment was that if Pauline walked out that door, he—more than Don—would be the loser.

Marcellus was disconcerted by the thought, and by the measure of relief he felt when Pauline capitulated after seconds of silent debate. She dropped her tote, which landed with a thud, then returned to sit at the table across from him. He wondered—not for the first time, but for the second within hours—how he could have been so wrong about her. He measured her at length—her face, her eyes,—and realized that it was her eyes that had thrown him off balance. Endless depths of brown, they held an enigmatic shimmer that contributed to her angelic features, making her look utterly incapable of deceit.

He blew out his cheeks before he spoke. "Let's go to Friday, when you started. Tell me what happened." He ignored his tempting warm emotions and got right down to business.

"Well," Pauline began hesitantly, "I arrived at Donald's about ten. He escorted me down to where the clinic was to be set up. Mr. Coombs met us there, we signed the contract for my assignment, then he left. Donald and I started putting together a list of needs for the clinic, and after about fifteen or twenty minutes, he got a call from Amy. He told me to get the list to him when I finished, and he went back up to his office."

"Do you know who the call was from?"

"No, I wasn't paying attention. He was on the portable cell phone anyway, so all I could hear was his side of the conversation, which was brief."

"How did he act? I mean, did he seem agitated by the call, or as if he had been expecting it?"

Pauline shrugged. "He seemed normal." She continued without prompting. "I finished my list and went up to his office to drop off the request for inventory supplies the company would need in order to set up the clinic," she replied. "He was on a conference call, so I didn't speak with him. I left the list, and a message with Amy that I was leaving the building for lunch, but I'd get back with him by one. I ran out, bought lunch, and came back to the clinic to eat. I checked in, and Amy told me he was having lunch and had asked not to be disturbed."

"He was probably working on something," Marcellus interjected musingly. He asked Pauline, "Then what?"

"Nothing. I ate lunch and waited. At about twelve-thirty, Amy called back in a panic and told me to hurry and get upstairs."

"So you weren't there when the attack started?"

"No," she said, shaking her head.

"Where is the clinic?"

"It's not a clinic, yet," she replied, talking with her hands. "It's more of a closet space on the third floor across from the gym," she said lightly, with a chuckle in her voice.

If outfitting the clinic was all it took to seal her stay,

then it was a small price to pay, Marcellus thought. "You want a bigger space?"

"No," she said, waving her hand. "I'm not complaining about the size. It'll probably never be used."

"Set it up the way you want," he commanded hastily. "Get whatever you need."

"Marcellus . . ." Pauline said hesitantly, "I know Donald seemed to think your company needed a clinic, but in hindsight, something else must have been on his mind. Maybe he just wanted somebody he trusted nearby in case something happened."

Marcellus was struck by a flippant thought, thinking *Don would trust you over me?* He'd gotten her commitment to stick around and he dared not blow it with his facile tongue. But he could tell Pauline sensed something in his silence, because she was looking at him with a dubious expression.

"What are you thinking?" she asked.

"I'm just trying to figure out what Don was up to," he replied. A suspicion of espionage snipped at his thoughts, prompting a note of urgency when he spoke. "I want to go to the hospital. I need to talk to Don."

"You're still infectious," she reminded him. "You wouldn't be allowed near him, even if he could talk to you, which he is incapable of doing right now."

"Then I'll go to the office. I'm sure the police will find me no matter where I am."

"Police?" she said, dumbfounded.

"It stands to reason that, if a man in Donald's position fell ill under suspicious circumstances, the police would become involved. I think it's safe to assume that this was no suicide attempt." Shaking his head, his mouth in a stubborn set, he said, "My mind won't let me accept that."

Pauline frowned pensively. "Then that only leaves one thing left to consider," she said in a somber whisper.

Nodding his head, Marcellus replied, "Yes."

"Murder," she said, with a visible shudder.

"Attempted murder," he corrected firmly. "And that status will remain if I have anything to do with it."

Pauline drew a deep breath as she got to her feet. She picked up the thermometer, and he noticed that her hand was shaking. He covered it and, unexpectedly, a blast of heat shot up his arm like a torpedo leaving its tube. He smiled to cover the guilt induced by his body's betrayal of him, the warmth catching on and spreading like a wildfire. But he couldn't seem to let her go when she smiled back, and a bolt of yearning landed between his legs. Though it was of no comfort to him whatsoever, the intention of his touch seemed to calm *her* unsteadiness.

She held the thermometer near his mouth. "Open up," she commanded softly.

"Is this nec . . . ?" he started to say before she shut him up by slipping the thermometer into his mouth.

Marcellus growled deep in his throat, then began to cough and had to grab the thermometer before it fell. Muttering a "tsk," Pauline took it from his hand, stuck it in his mouth, then lightly held his wrist. As she silently counted off the seconds on the wall clock, he concentrated on controlling his pulse. Shortly, she slid the thermometer from between his lips and set it on the table, in exchange for a spoon and a bottle of dark liquid.

"Which one is that?" he asked, frowning.

"Benadryl. Dr. Hawse gave you a shot of it yesterday."

He scooted back from her instantly. "Uh-uh," he said, shaking his head. "I'm not taking that stuff again. It knocked me out. I have no memory of last night." That was not exactly true, he thought, for he distinctly recalled a perception of tenderness. He had only to put one and one together for a solution that had nothing to do with arithmetic.

"You haven't been coughing as much since the dose you took before you went to bed," she said, patiently holding the spoonful of medicine.

He didn't remember her ever being so bossy before. Watching her pour liquid into a tablespoon, he wondered if time had simply erased that memory from his mind. "Are you listening to me?" he growled. "I said I . . ."

Pauline shoved the spoon of medicine into the small opening of his mouth in protest. He swallowed it with a gulp. "Yuk," he declared, smacking his lips together, an expression of distaste on his face.

"Now this," she said, extending a glass of water and a large gray and red capsule out to him.

Accepting the capsule, he asked, "What is this for?"

"You're running a low grade fever," she replied. "That means we haven't gotten rid of the infection. It's only an antibiotic."

With his eyes doing a slow slide down to hers in a sheepish look, he asked, "You wouldn't be trying to poison me, would you?"

"I don't poison patients on Saturday," she retorted.

Side-stepping nurses, patients, and doctors in the busy hospital corridor, Pauline glanced up at the numbers posted outside the doors. She was looking for room 802, which had been commandeered for Sarah by Dr. Hawse. She wanted to check on Don's wife before returning to CSI to pick up Marcellus, who was adamant about going in for a meeting with his executives.

Don had become more than a patient: he was now a case, she thought, mulling over the information she had received from Dr. Hawse. Reaching the same conclusion about how the poison got into Don's system as Marcellus had, he notified the police. The doctor was taking no chances, in the event that one failed attempt would lead to another try, she recalled that he had explained.

She located the room, pushed open the door, and walked in. It was dark; the blinds were drawn tight, allowing only a slither of the daylight to come in. Sarah's sleeping form protruded from the white linen on the bed.

As she approached the bed, Pauline heard a click, then noticed light slip between the cracks of the shifting bathroom door; then the light went out. Already disturbed by the news of Don's poisoning, her mind jumped to sinister conclusions as she stared, watchful and still. A female figure stepped from the bathroom and was instantly aware of Pauline's presence. She reached inside the bathroom and immediately, light spilled out.

"Hi, Ms. Sinclair; it's me, Amy."

Pauline sagged with relief, recognizing Amy Bridgewater, Donald's secretary. "Oh, Amy, hi. I didn't know anyone was with Sarah." She had only come in contact with Amy twice, on the morning she reported to Donald's office, then later, when the woman had called her at the clinic, frantic about Donald.

"I had to bring my mother in for her check-up and I thought I'd stop by," Amy said. "I got here just as the nurse was giving her a shot to help calm her down."

Of formidable stature, Amy was an attractive woman who knew how to complement her assets without going overboard. Casually dressed in a bulky gold sweater and pressed jeans, it was obvious she took exceptional care of herself, from her peachy complexion and firm body to her hair, a luminous curly cap of red-gold.

"She probably doesn't even remember I'm here," Amy said with a hint of sorrow in her voice, pointing her chin toward Sarah. "I can't get over what happened to Mr. Wellsing." She shuddered visibly. "It's incredible."

"Yes, it is," Pauline replied soberly.

"I overheard some of the nurses talking," Amy whispered, "and I could have sworn one of them said he was poisoned. How could something like that have happened?"

"Poisoned?" Pauline replied, feigning amazement and

ignorance. Dr. Hawse had asked her not to share his suspicions. "I haven't heard any such thing. Maybe the nurses
were talking about someone else."

"No, I distinctly heard them mention Mr. Wellsing's
name," Amy said, with the conviction of a gossip.

"Well, I don't know," Pauline shrugged nonchalantly,
but she felt as if an ominous cloud was hanging over their
heads. A "no visitors" rule had been imposed for the rest
of Donald's stay, and a hospital security guard had been
stationed near the ICU Ward until the Clear Lake police
arrived. Dr. Hawse informed her that a Detective Collins
had been assigned to the case and would be in touch with
her. It seemed she had become the center of attention
from men with expectations that she didn't know how to
fill. Her life had changed so drastically in a space of twenty-
four hours that she was having a hard time digesting it all.
A low moan slipped past her lips.

"Are you all right, Ms. Sinclair?"

Embarrassed that she had forgotten Amy was present,
Pauline gave a short laugh. "I'm just a little short on sleep,
that's all."

"Me, too," Amy replied. "Well, I better go. My mom
should be ready by now. I guess I'll see you next week,"
she half-asked, half-stated.

Pauline replied noncommittally, "Yeah, I guess so."

Amy left, and Pauline started to leave, as well. Sarah
didn't need her. When she had been informed that Donald
was the victim of a poisoning, Sarah had become hysterical,
she recalled Dr. Hawse telling her. The reaction was normal, she mused, wondering what her own reaction would
be if the tables were turned and it was Marcellus instead of
Donald who'd received a near-fatal dosage of medication.

Unable to stop the flow of her thoughts, she saw Marcellus's face imposed over Donald's in her memory of
working frantically to keep him breathing. The niggling

sense of uncertainty about her performance resurfaced, as well as the fear of death sucking the blood of life from his body.

Shaking her head vigorously, Pauline pushed the frightening image away. It was just the combination of seeing him again and the life-threatening situation that was propelling her thoughts into overdrive. There was nothing to suggest that Marcellus's life was in jeopardy. After all, he had been out of town during the attempt on Don's life. Besides, she reminded herself, halfway to the door, Marcellus was of no concern of hers.

Sarah stirred, mumbling in her sleep. "Don? Don?" she called. She was getting twisted in the bed linen.

Pauline turned and rushed to her bedside to soothe her. "It's all right," she said, taking Sarah's hands in hers. "Donald is all right, he's safe."

Looking up at Pauline in a curious daze, Sarah jerked her hand away and squirmed to the farthermost side of the bed. An odd look of resentment shone in her expression.

"It's me," Pauline said in a calming tone. She straightened the sheets on the bed, tucking in a corner that had come loose. "Donald is resting easy."

Sarah mumbled incoherently, then scooted under the bed sheet and fell back into the drugged sleep.

Restoring the covers, Pauline stared fractionally at Sarah with a bemused look. Sarah's reaction, though a little strange, was the result of nothing more than the disorienting effects of the medication, she rationalized. If she had found out that the person she loved had been the victim of an attempted murder, she would probably act a little strange, herself.

And there, just around the corner of her mind, was the image of Marcellus. Pauline felt an irrational urge to assure herself of his safety.

* * *

Coughing incessantly, Marcellus stepped off the elevator onto the gray carpeted hallway on the ninth floor. With his hand over his mouth, he pressed forward, refusing to give in to his illness. He had spent the past hour talking with Clay Bennington, head of security for CSI. The man had been just as amazed as he when he learned that Don had been poisoned.

Two sets of offices were maintained on the floor, his and Don's, at opposite ends of the hall from each other. Two restrooms directly across from the elevator, a conference room, and storage rooms completed the visible floor plan.

Near the outer room to his office, Marcellus saw Katherine. He had called her from home and requested that she come in for a couple of hours. She was sitting at her desk, talking on the phone, and she handed him a bunch of pink phone messages when he passed. He nodded, then gestured that he wanted to see her when she finished. She acknowledged him with a thumbs-up sign and he walked into his office and flipped on the light switch near the door.

It was a large room, decorated in a blend of browns and greens accented with touches of gold in the carpet, and there were healthy green plants in flower pot stands on each side of the door. The room was exactly as he had left it nearly two weeks ago before leaving for Washington, D.C.

With its back to the floor-length window facing the front of the building, a soft brown leather couch and matching armchairs were placed around an oak coffee table. The table held an eclectic stack of magazines, ranging from *21●C* to *Ebony*. The door to his personal bathroom was closed. Two rolling chairs sat near the shelves which held books on the law, business, and the aerospace industry.

Except for the crystal bowl of round peppermints, the top of the massive oak desk was uncluttered.

There were pictures on either side of his law-school diploma on the wall behind the desk. One was of Ronald McNair, one of the astronauts killed in the Challenger crash that took the lives of its nine passengers. The other was an original Ernie Barnes' print titled *High Inspirations*. It was Marcellus's favorite, his motto.

Opening his briefcase, Marcellus took out several manila folders and spread them across the desk. Just as he dropped into the swivel chair to read through the messages, Katherine walked into the room, carrying a notebook and a fountain pen. She rolled a chair to the front of the desk and sat.

"You're looking a little better," she said.

Barely lifting his head, Marcellus shot her a familiar piercing look, as if he could see right through her, revealing not one iota of emotion. Less secure employees had been known to wither under that look. Katherine was completely undaunted. "I ought to fire you."

"You ought to do a lot of things," she quipped, giving him her wise family-friend look. "They're looking for you everywhere."

Marcellus nodded as he perused the first message. With a snort, he balled it up and flicked it into the wastepaper basket alongside the desk. The second one was from Dee Dee, and it followed the path of the first.

"I don't understand what you see in most of them anyway," Katherine said.

Marcellus raised a sardonic eyebrow at her, though he thought *Sometimes I don't, either*. While the women he dated were fun-loving, undemanding, and helped pass the time, they failed to hold his interest past the date. He didn't know what he was looking for, he mused, though gentle thoughts of Pauline slapped like small waves against the wall of his resolve to view her only as a means to an end.

"Thanks for coming in today, Katherine." He set one message aside as he shuffled through the folders on his desk, deciding he would return the call from Dottie.

"I anticipated it," she said, adopting his businesslike demeanor. "What are you looking for?"

"The notes from my meeting with the senator," he replied, coughing. "I need you to type them up, then fax a copy to Scott as soon as possible. I'll want to talk to him, too."

Scanning the folders, Katherine picked up one with a yellow legal pad inside. "Is this it?"

"That's it," he said.

"I'll get to it right away," Katherine said, setting the folder on her lap beneath the notebook.

He set his briefcase on the side of the desk. "I want to get a copy of Don's schedule for this past week as soon as possible."

"I had a feeling you would ask for it," Katherine said, "so I got it from Amy's desk. She was so upset yesterday, poor thing. It's at my desk. Want me to get it now?"

"Not just yet," Marcellus replied. "Let's just go over a few things first." He passed a hand over his head, his thoughts somewhat distracted. "I'm fairly certain we're going to get a visit from the police. I ran into Clay downstairs and alerted him to be on the lookout for them. I don't know when they'll come, but I'm sure they'll want to search Don's office."

A young company, CSI faced a doubly precarious situation with its president and leading scientist both out of pocket. The thought accounted for Marcellus's silent pensiveness until he was seized by a coughing spasm. Accepting tissues from Katherine, he turned his back until the cold symptom ran its course.

"I think somebody got up before he should have."

"You may be right," Marcellus replied out of breath and pushing himself up to his feet, "but if you tell anybody

I said so, I'll deny it." He tossed the used tissue in the trash and strolled to the window, his hands in his pockets. Opening the blinds, he looked out at the gray, cloudy skies and down below to the deserted parking lot. Impulsively, he angled to look at her sidelong. "Katherine," he said, pensive frown lines on his forehead, "has Wanatabe called?"

"Not to my knowledge. Were you expecting him to?"

Marcellus turned back to the window, replying with an indecisive shrug. Ken Wanatabe worked for the Shishumi Corporation, a Japanese aerospace company. Six months ago, he had approached Don and Marcellus with a request to buy into CSI, promising more capital than they could ever imagine. Neither Don nor he entertained the idea for a second, and then told Wanatabe what he could do with his offer. That didn't mean Wanatabe wouldn't try again. "Bring me up to date, Katherine."

Marcellus listened with two minds, one attuned to Katherine; the other had veered to CSI. The company employed over a hundred scientists and support staff. The scientists were divided into five teams. These teams worked on everything, from studying the effects of weightlessness and exposure to cosmic radiation to recycling air as a side-product of space agriculture and closed-cycle farming techniques in space. Every project was progressing normally, if not as quickly as he wished.

"And that's it," Katherine finished summarily.

Marcellus turned from the window to look absently at Katherine. He had heard nothing that aroused his suspicions. But there was one project of which she had no knowledge. Under the code name *Ba*, Don was working independently of the other research teams. It was hardly a secret in the space community, but a gold mine awaited whoever succeeded in developing the first humanoid equipped with emotions as well as reasoning, and the ability to live in space.

"Thanks, Katherine," he said, striding back to sit in his chair.

"Is there anything else for now?" she asked.

"Were you able to reach everybody?"

"Before I left the house," she said. "Dr. Kent was already here."

"Good. As soon as you get that letter ready to fax, put in a call to Scott. I want him to keep me posted."

Katherine asked, "Is that all?"

"For now," he replied. "You can get me that copy of Don's schedule."

"Okay," Katherine said, rising. She cast a final glance at Marcellus; a disbelieving frown covered her face, for he was coughing again and looked as though he barely had the strength to sit up in the chair. She left the room and she returned with a black folder. "Here it is," she said, placing it in his outstretched hands.

"Thanks," he said.

Katherine left, and Marcellus moved to the couch. Sitting comfortably, a leg crossed over a knee, he began to scan the contents of the folder. He noticed it was thin of entries. But even so, none were out of the ordinary, he thought, with a hint of disgust in his expression.

What did he expect to find, when he didn't know what he was looking for?

Barking a cough, he closed the folder and tossed it onto the coffee table. Settling comfortably on the couch, he closed his eyes and stretched his legs in front of him. He could certainly use some of Pauline's ministrations now, he thought, rubbing a hand across his aching chest.

Thinking of Pauline was like a free association he couldn't control. He was jolted by a thought and sat up quickly, snatching the folder. He remembered something he should have noticed immediately as his eyes flew over the pages. Her name did not appear at all, he noticed, his expression marred by a frown. It was company policy to log in all visitors, both at the lobby desk and again at the intended destination with all executives. The sensitive nature of their work demanded that they take the extra precaution to lessen the risk of being bested—least of all by space spies, he mused. Being first was everything.

Was it an oversight by Amy, or had Don instructed that it be left out?

He made a mental note to ask Clay about it. He closed the folder on his lap, recalling Pauline's meager explanation. She may have been guilty of a lot of things as far as he was concerned, but he really had no reason to suspect her of lying about Don contacting her. Though it was convenient, blaming her was counter-productive. He had to put his personal feelings aside to focus all his energy on a more important matter. She was crucial toward that end, and he intended to use her to get to the truth.

The intercom on his desk buzzed. "Marcellus, Dr. Kent is here and she wants to see you privately," Katherine announced.

Marcellus frowned. Dr. Jacqueline Theresa Kent, who preferred to be called by her initials, J. T. In Don's absence, she would be in charge of the company's research efforts; however, his first choice would have been Dr. James Chin, he mused. Behind her back, some of the employees had nicknamed her the "Mad Scientist." But no one could fault her work.

He returned to stand behind the desk and pressed the speaker bar on the phone. "Send her in."

Dr. Kent marched into the room and stood before the desk like a schoolgirl, clutching a folder in front of her. She still looked quite young at 35, and she could have been an attractive woman if she smiled more often. She had a figure as impressive as her IQ, which was somewhere in the very bright range. Her long, jet black hair was wrapped in a bun at the nape of her neck, and intelligent raisin brown eyes protruded from her heart-shaped face with its high cheekbones and wide, thin-lipped mouth. The knee-length, sterile white lab jacket was part of her usual ensemble. Today slacks, instead of a dress or suit, peeked out from under the white coat.

"What can I do for you, J. T.?" Marcellus asked. The coughing had given him a headache, and he massaged the pain at his temples.

"This is my report on the latest developments. I wanted to deliver it personally," she replied.

Marcellus noted her usual paranoia. He was so familiar with her slew of idiosyncrasies that he was no longer bothered by them. "Thanks," he said, accepting the document.

"I figured you would probably want one, since Don's . . . well, you know, since he's out," she said.

Marcellus was seized by another coughing fit, and began searching about his desk and pockets for a tissue. Dr. Kent quickly stepped away from the desk, covering her nose and mouth.

"I'd take something for that, if I were you," she said, the features of her face screwed up in a distasteful look.

"Thank you, doctor," he replied mockingly, tossing the soiled tissue in the trash.

"Anything new on Don?" she inquired.

"He's holding his own," he said, hoping the answer was still applicable.

"Well . . ." She paused before continuing. "I just wanted to make sure you got this report. I'm going to run back down to the lab until the others get here."

Sensing something else was on her mind, he asked casually, "Is everything okay in the lab?"

Dr. Kent shrugged. "As well as can be expected. If there's anything I can do, you know, regarding Don," she spoke with her hands, "you know where to find me."

A half smile crept over her face, and a crack of friendliness showed in her usual haughty manner. Marcellus's eyebrows arched amazed. Before he could press Dr. Kent with his curiosity, the intercom rang.

"Yes, Katherine?"

"The gang's all here."

Despite the rightness of her decision, Pauline's heart beat with two fears that were as different as any opposites could get. She thought there was something symbolic about the way she felt. The last time she'd raced up to this floor it had been in a mad dash against death. Though the sense of foreboding lingered, it wasn't death she was hurrying to reach this time.

This couldn't be good, she thought of her quivering limbs. But she owed Donald the totality of her friendship: Everything else was secondary.

A second before the elevator doors closed, she hopped off the car; sauntered down the quiet corridor. Valor and dread formed a tacit alliance inside her and accented every step she took. Reaching Marcellus's set of offices, she spotted Katherine standing at the credenza, sorting through some papers.

"Good morning."

Katherine turned and faced Pauline. "Well, hello," she said, beaming. "I see you survived the lion's den in one piece."

"But not without scars," Pauline replied with laughter in her voice. "Where is he?"

"He's in the conference room," Katherine said. "He wants you to go right in. Do you know where it is?"

"I figured the meeting with the executives should have been over by now," Pauline replied. "I know he should be about ready to keel over from all that medication in his system. Is he still coughing?"

"You know him," Katherine said dryly. "The meeting

shouldn't last long, but you better hurry on in. It's right across the hall there."

Pauline looked over her shoulder toward the room, refusal in her expression. She was already in over her head; sitting in on a meeting was beyond her duty. "That's okay; I'll just wait for him right here," she said, eyeing a visitor's chair. "I don't need to sit in on the meeting."

"I don't know," Katherine said skeptically. "He was quite insistent that you attend."

Pauline started to inform Katherine that Marcellus had no idea when she was coming, but noticed a telling gleam in her eyes and knew what the older woman was thinking— which was so far from the truth, she almost chuckled herself. But no one could argue with or deny Katherine anything when she favored you with that flattering smile of hers. Besides, it would be good practice, since the novelty of her renewed acquaintance with Marcellus had worn off. Look at it as an opportunity to prove that the sensations she had felt were sentimental and benign, she told herself.

"Then I guess I better make an appearance."

She returned Katherine's wink with an intrepid smile as she walked across the hallway to the center door. She knocked and walked into the room. Marcellus, who was standing at the head of the large rectangular table, looked up as she entered. His voice broke off in midsentence as his clear, observant eyes moved into hers. Pauline saw nothing else. She felt his gentle appraisal as if he were actually touching her. She stared, muddle-headed, and cleared her throat to speak. But the only word in her head was "yes"—to reclaiming the sensuous flame of life she saw twinkling through the black pearl prism of his gaze.

Chapter Five

"Come in, Ms. Sinclair," Marcellus invited.

The engaging look in his dark eyes, the sweet sensation it produced inside her—both vanished as quickly as a puff of smoke. Pauline felt like the brunt of a joke, and she chided her brief, whimsical flight from reality.

"Do you know everyone present?"

Pasting what she hoped was a friendly smile on her face, Pauline scanned the room before she replied. "I know Mr. Coombs, but I haven't met anyone else." She let the door close behind her and started for the closest chair.

"Then come, let me introduce you," he said, gesturing for her to join him at the head of the table.

Her pulse was tripping as she sauntered to the head of the room, fighting to rid herself of her awful attraction to Marcellus. She focused her attention on the interesting decor—the boomerang-shaped conference table in teak, circled by soft leather armchairs that looked like cockpit seats. One wall was a series of windowpanes, providing a view of high-rise office buildings dotting the overcast sky in the distance. The rest were panels of cherrywood upon which hung scenic photographs of space, and along one of them ran a bar, complete with a cabinet of liquid goodies, a microwave, and a sink.

It seemed the longest walk to Pauline, feeling all eyes on her. She was fractionally relieved when she reached the empty chair to Marcellus's right.

"To my left, here, is Dr. Jacqueline Kent. Dr. Kent is vice-president over research quality control. Thomas Webster is the genius who keeps our computers functioning at high peak, and, of course, you know Leonard Coombs, who's over personnel and accounting."

Pauline nodded politely as Marcellus made the introductions. Opinions sprang to her mind about each of them. Dr. Kent appeared self-contained, competent, and unapproachable. Thomas Webster was a big, florid man who, even in his pink, short-sleeved shirt, was sweating profusely. Leonard Coombs, whom she had met before, was thin-framed, with a receding hairline and big eyes that bulged from his bifocals. A soft-spoken man, he evoked a sense of trust, and he was the only one in the room full of executives that made her feel comfortable. She slid gingerly into the chair.

Marcellus turned his head to sneeze successively into a handkerchief, and Pauline wondered if any of them suspected how ill he was. Though he looked ready for action, dressed in a powder-blue bulky sweater and navy pleated slacks, she knew his body was not up to task. His eyes were glassy with fever, his yard-wide chest ached from so much coughing, and his throat was raw and sore. He was functioning on sheer inner muscle.

"You found Don," Thomas Webster said.

Pauline dragged her gaze from Marcellus before she replied. "No. No, I didn't find him, but I did perform CPR."

"Marcellus told us Don hired you. We've never had a

nurse on staff before," Thomas stated, with a question in his narrowed blue eyes under bushy brows.

"It's a good thing we had her around, don't you think?" Leonard said. "How is the chief doing?"

"He's holding his own," she replied.

Shaking his nearly bald head with disbelief, Thomas said, "Poisoned. I just can't believe it. Are they sure?"

"Yes. They're very sure. Digitalis was found in his blood," Pauline said. Before anyone could ask, she explained, "It's a drug used by people with heart conditions."

As if to show off her scientific knowledge, Dr. Kent interjected, "When injected into a healthy heart, however, it acts like a poison."

"Does that mean we're going to have the police swarming all over the place now?" Thomas asked Marcellus with disgust in his face.

"In all likelihood, yes," Marcellus said, as if it were nothing to be alarmed about.

"Dr. Hawse, with whom you're already familiar, told me before I left that a detective was on his way to the hospital," Pauline said, looking up at Marcellus.

An uncomfortable silence settled over the room. The executives exchanged glances with each other, then made Pauline the focus of their gazes. She tried not to squirm. As if sensing her discomfort, Marcellus spoke, drawing all eyes to him, including hers.

"Well, let's get on with it," he said. "There are a few things we need to cover immediately. Number one is security. I want all of you to double-check the security in your departments. Make sure nothing's missing, that no information has been tampered with in any way."

Thomas asked, "What are you suggesting, Marcellus?"

"I'm not suggesting anything," he replied. "I just think it's a good time to double-check our security. Clay will accompany each of you. I want a full report of your findings."

"What if we don't find anything?" Dr. Kent asked.

"How would we know, if we don't know what we're looking for?" Thomas wanted to know.

"We're not looking for anything in particular, but for anything unusual," Marcellus said. "I want a report whether you find something or not."

The conference door opened and Katherine looked inside the room. "A Detective Collins is here," she said.

"All right," Marcellus said. "Tell him we'll be right out." Katherine disappeared.

"Everyone stay nearby. The police may want to talk to you." Receiving nods from around the table, he asked "Before we adjourn, does anyone have any questions, ideas, what have you?" At the negative nods, he said, "All right. Let's carry on as usual. We'll meet again as the need arises."

Lifting a dark eyebrow in her direction, Marcellus indicated to Pauline not to leave as the others filed from the room. When they were alone, he said, "All right, let's have it. How is Don really doing?"

Pauline took a lengthy breath before she spoke. "The best I can tell you is that the doctors have picked up brain activity, slight, but present. There's no prognosis one way or the other. Don could wake up any minute, or . . ."

"Or he could die any second," Marcellus said.

"Yes."

"Let's go see what this detective has to say," he said.

With his hand on the small of her back, Marcellus led Pauline from the conference room to the outer area of his office. For the entire short walk across the hallway, she held her breath.

From behind her desk, Katherine said, before she was asked, "He's in your office."

Marcellus nodded. He and Pauline walked into the office. A male Caucasian dressed in an all-weather coat was manually flying a brightly colored model airplane made of wood and iron.

"Excuse me," Marcellus said irritably.

"Oh, I'm sorry; I seemed to have gotten carried away." He replaced the airplane on the corner of the bar, then crossed toward Marcellus, flipping open his shield for review. "I'm Detective Collins."

"Detective Collins," Marcellus said. "Marcellus Cavanaugh."

The detective then turned to Pauline, and she sensed a strange reserve come over him. The detective was pale-complexioned, as if he didn't get enough sun. He had a young, serious face with sharp features, barely-blue, inquisitive eyes, and beetle brows. He was a compact man of medium build, and Marcellus towered over him by at least four or five inches, and outweighed him by twenty pounds.

"You must be Pauline Sinclair," he said, eyeing her with intense speculation.

Even though he was a policeman with a creed to protect and serve citizens, Pauline felt wary and was more than a tad curious about his manner toward her. Maybe she was being paranoid, she thought, shaking the proffered hand. "Yes."

"Dr. Reuben Hawse told me I would find you here and save myself a trip, and time looking for you. As I understand it, you performed CPR on Mr. Wellsing, right?"

"Right," Pauline replied.

"How long have you been a nurse, Ms. Sinclair?"

She wanted to reply, *Long enough to know CPR;* instead, she said, "Five years."

"Where did you earn your degree?"

"Prairie View A&M University School of Nursing."

"Never heard of it. I'd like to have a look at Mr. Wellsing's office," the detective announced abruptly, taking them both in his gaze.

"Certainly," Marcellus replied. "This way."

Walking between the two men, Pauline felt her body temperature run hot and cold. For once, she consciously craved the warmth of Marcellus's nearness and concentrated on the clean scent of soap and the woodsy aftershave he wore. She doubted if Detective Collins would understand her anxiety; he would no doubt interpret her need for friendly human contact as some form of guilt.

Detective Collins stopped in front of the elevators and looked in both directions. When he noticed the puzzled looks trained on him, he explained, "I was just wondering if someone could leave without being noticed."

"It's possible," Marcellus said, "if neither of the secretaries is at her desk." Skepticism colored his tone.

"Is there any other way of getting off this floor besides the elevators?" the detective asked.

"The fire escape," Marcellus replied. "It's right over here." He led the detective to the right, and then abruptly left, before reaching the reception area.

The detective examined the iron-handled doors, which opened easily. He looked back to the secretary's vacant desk. "What about rest rooms?"

"Right across the hall across from the elevators," Marcellus said.

"I see," Collins said. Rubbing his chin thoughtfully, he said, more to himself, "I guess getting out by the windows is impossible unless you have a ladder."

Marcellus merely nodded and continued to Don's office. Arriving, he took a set of keys from his pants pocket. He opened the door, and with a gesture, invited Detective Collins and Pauline to precede him into the room.

Standing alongside Marcellus, Pauline watched as Detective Collins scanned the room. She wondered what he was looking for, what his trained eyes saw. The office was a duplicate of Marcellus's in size and set-up; only the color scheme of blues, grays, and white was different.

"I understand Ms. Amy Bridgewater called you," Detective Collins said to Pauline, though he didn't look at her. Before she could reply, he asked, "Where were you at the time?"

"I was down in the office on the third floor," she said, anticipating his next question. "Mr. Wellsing hired me to set up the clinic for the company."

The detective squatted, disappearing from view, to look under the desk. Marcellus and Pauline exchanged looks of curiosity. Detective Collins reappeared, flicking his fingers.

"Find something?" Marcellus inquired.

"Just a particle of dust," the detective replied nonchalantly. Brushing his hands together, he asked, "Do you have any idea who would want to murder Mr. Wellsing?"

"A murder hasn't been committed," Marcellus replied smoothly.

"No," Detective Collins replied, staring head-on at Marcellus, "not yet. Ms. Sinclair, will you show me where you found Mr. Wellsing?"

"Yes," Pauline said, walking toward the desk. She used both hands to indicate a space on the floor behind the desk. "He was on the floor here."

"What was he doing?"

"He wasn't doing anything," Pauline replied in a low voice reserved for dreaded things. Looking directly into the detective's eyes, hers filled with the horrible memory, she said, "He had stopped breathing."

Each was held in a stunned tableau of silence.

With a complex set of wrinkles lining his forehead, Marcellus stared openly at Pauline. He felt as if he were seeing her for the first time, seeing her through Don's eyes, a lifesaver. No one had told him just how close to death Don had been.

Detective Collins jarred the moment free, switching his

body's weight from one foot to the other. "Mr. Cavanaugh, does Mr. Wellsing drink coffee?"

Marcellus was unable to tear his eyes away from Pauline. He noted her rigid posture; her facial features, tight with anxiety as if she were reliving that moment; her gaze still fixed on that spot on the floor. Profoundly touched by her vulnerability, he was assailed suddenly by affection for her.

"Mr. Cavanaugh?" Detective Collins prodded.

The medication must be dulling his brain, Marcellus thought, shaking his head. "Caffeine drives Don up the wall."

Detective Collins plodded onward. "Juice then?"

"Plenty," Marcellus replied. He put a hand over his mouth while he cleared his throat of rumbling phlegm. "Excuse me," he said, pulling a peppermint from his pocket. Unwrapping it, he said, "It's the same, always. Orange for breakfast, grape for lunch." He popped the peppermint into his mouth.

"You and Mr. Wellsing have been friends for a long time," Detective Collins both asked and stated.

"Since college," Marcellus replied.

"And what about you?" he asked Pauline. "How long have you known Mr. Wellsing?"

With a hand at her throat, Pauline backed away from the spot to stand alongside Marcellus before she replied. "I met him through Marcellus."

Marcellus caught the tail end of a suspicious glance Detective Collins shot at Pauline before training that same look on him. Guessing the question behind it, he hoped he wouldn't be required to answer the nature of his relationship to Pauline. Somehow, he would feel like a liar if he had to say she was merely a contract employee.

"I see," Collins said at last.

"I only started my assignment yesterday," Pauline said, returning the detective's hard stare.

"Does the company keep a nurse on staff at all times?" He looked first at Pauline, then at Marcellus.

"Not usually," Marcellus replied.

"So you're telling me that hiring one now is unusual," the detective replied. "Why did Mr. Wellsing hire you, Ms. Sinclair?"

"He told me he wanted health care available in the event of an accident," Pauline replied simply.

Detective Collins spread his arms, feigning puzzlement. "For what reason?" He looked at Marcellus. "Is the work being done here suddenly dangerous?"

Marcellus stared at him scrupulously. Dangerous or not, it was none of the detective's business, he thought, recalling another judicious tidbit of information he'd withheld. There was another way in and out, but no one knew about it except Don and him.

"I also understand Mr. Wellsing didn't consult you before hiring a nurse. Is that true?"

"What . . . consulting me or hiring a nurse?" Marcellus asked.

Detective Collins replied irascibly, "Both."

"Don is the president of the company," Marcellus replied, with a haughty edge in his tone. "He has the power to hire whomever he wants without getting clearance from me."

"And what do you do here?"

"I handle the legal affairs and some of the lobbying."

Detective Collins dropped into the chair behind the desk and began looking through the middle desk drawer.

"I'm also the major owner of CSI, which makes me Mr. Wellsing's partner."

Collins looked up at him sharply. An expression akin to bitter disbelief shot across his face, and he closed the drawer with a slam. Pauline jumped. Marcellus could hazard a guess that the detective was dismayed by the knowledge of his ownership, but he ignored the man's reaction.

He gave Pauline's shoulder an affectionate squeeze, and felt a shiver course through her as she looked at him with a flicker of surprise. The policeman was loving her discomfort, he thought, his brows coming together over the narrowed gaze he turned on Collins.

"Don't you find that curious?" Detective Collins asked. He looked back and forth between them, then settled his gaze on Pauline.

Marcellus wanted to advise Pauline not to say another word, but caution rendered him silent. The detective was up to something that didn't smell of police work, he thought, feeling contentious and curious, himself.

"Mr. Wellsing explained that it was just a precaution," she replied. "I accepted that and agreed. It's not that unusual for companies to have a health-care worker on staff."

Good answer, Marcellus thought with admiration. He did wonder, however, where the cop was going with these questions.

Shifting the conversation as if nothing of relevance had been said, Detective Collins asked, "Is everything in order in here?" He indicated the room with a sweep of his hand.

"I haven't been in this room in two weeks," Marcellus replied, conducting a silent examination of the room. Evidence of Don's love for spacecrafts was everywhere, either in framed pictures or models, like the futuristic spaceship suspended over the bar. His gaze moved back to the desk area where a computer sat on a separate stand adjacent to the desk. A gray phone with multiple lines, a picture of Don and Sarah waving from a boat deck, a decorative container filled with pens and pencils. Everything looked in order to him.

His gaze glossed over the sitting area. Over the couch on the wall was a trio of spacecrafts. Behind the center picture was a safe where Don kept his important notes. He made a mental note to check it later.

Returning his attention to the desk, Marcellus pictured Don sitting at an angle in the chair: his long legs stretched out, and his hands in a praying position under his chin, his blue eyes peering through fashionable glasses perched on the tip of his nose.

Walking behind the desk, Don's image still in his mind's eye, he saw Don leaning over to get a fresh pencil to outline his agenda for the day; running his fingers through his white blond hair; drumming on his desk, making faces at a boring caller on the phone, the receiver held up in the air; reaching into the bottom desk drawer on his left to get the miniature orange basketball to shoot into the small hoop that was usually attached to the gold-coated metal rack near the door.

His gaze shot across the room, looking for the coat rack. Neither it nor the hoop was where it used to be. Was that important? he wondered. Back to the desk, he saw Donald popping vitamins, from a pre-sorted pack, one by one into his mouth and chewing them like candy.

"Mr. Cavanaugh?"

Marcellus opened a bottom drawer; the basketball was accounted for, though not where it was usually kept. He rolled the high-back leather chair from the desk to check the bottom drawer on the other side. A box of vitamins shared the space with pads of sketching paper and boxes of pencils and pens.

"Mr. Cavanaugh," Detective Collins called, more forcefully.

"Yes?" Marcellus replied absently, staring at the box of vitamins, which he now turned over in his hand so he could read the label.

"What are those?"

With an expression steeped in thought, Marcellus replied, "Vitamins. Don never forgets to take them." A dark premonition seized his thoughts. He wondered whether Donald could have taken a heart tablet, believing it to be a vitamin. But that would mean someone had to have switched it.

"Maybe I ought to take those and have them analyzed," Detective Collins said, holding out his hand.

"Maybe you should," Marcellus said. He placed the box in the detective's outstretched hand.

"Excuse me," Katherine said from the door. "Detective Collins, your men are here."

"Send them in, please."

A Saturday-night sitcom blared from the television in the family room, while Pauline stood at the stove in the kitchen, stirring a pot of stew. Another burner was on under a royal blue porcelain kettle.

She looked at the remains of the fresh vegetables and scraps of chicken breasts littering the counter, with thoughts of cleaning up the mess. She decided to leave it for Marcellus to do. She was exhausted.

Following the grueling hours with the police at CSI, she and Marcellus stopped at the grocery store before returning to his home. After giving him his medicines—which surprisingly, he took without an argument—she sent him off upstairs for a hot bath. She would wait until she got home to take hers, she decided, ambling about the kitchen.

She opened the back door and strolled out to the slightly raised step leading to the patio. Except for the old leaves scattered about the wet patio and in the pool, spring waged a losing battle against the wintry weather. Clouds swarmed the muted purple sky and stars fought to shine.

With her thoughts turning to Don, she wondered if he could fight off the winter of his illness. One's will to live was important to the recovery process. Sometimes it was even more crucial than the health care provided. She wished she didn't have to worry about that, but the truth was that she really didn't know. In fact, she felt as if she knew very little right now. She needed rest.

Returning inside, Pauline sat at the breakfast table in a slouch. She folded her arms on the table as a pillow for her head, and closed her eyes, trying to clear her mind. Part of her exhaustion was mental. Trying to anticipate Marcellus's mood was a strain. He had gone from wanting to strangle her, to grudging tolerance, to acceptance, all in the space of twenty-four hours. She had had to catch herself on several occasions, with every kind look and touch he directed her way, from falling victim to wistful longings. Though she knew they didn't mean anything, the looks and touches unnerved her.

She felt herself succumbing to the lethargy that engulfed her whole body as she settled into a tepid sense of peace. Suddenly, a man's slightly roughed hands curled over her shoulders, and she stiffened. The hands remained, and she began to relax as those strong hands kneaded the tension from her tight muscles.

She knew she should put an end to Marcellus's gentle ministrations. His hands were big, warm, and firm, the handling of her flesh caressive. The combination induced a physical and emotional yearning and it was hard to distinguish which, her body or her mind, wanted his touch more. For a shameless length of time, the recently made resolve floated out of her mind. She let herself bask ... in the memory of what it was like to be touched by Marcellus ... in the wondrous assault on her senses.

"Why don't you go up and have a nice, hot bath?" he said softly, as if not to disturb the quiet.

The suggestive tone of his voice, rather than the suggestion, snatched Pauline back to reality. She held herself rigid in spite of his nearness, embarrassed by how easily he seemed to break down the barriers she had worked so hard to erect. The massage stopped, and she pushed herself upright in the chair.

"I'm going to wait until I get home," she replied, masking her inner turmoil with a deceptive calmness. Her voice was the only sign of activity in the chair where she sat so stiffly, with her head lowered and her hands in her lap under the table.

"You're not thinking about driving home tonight, are you?" He stepped from behind the chair to look at her face to face.

She looked up, now, taking him in fully. There was a spark of some indefinable emotion in his eyes, and it increased her level of discomfort because she was drawn by it, even though she couldn't define it. He looked fresh, alert and extremely handsome in a black silk robe with black-and-white striped pajamas under it. She felt about as attractive as a used dish towel.

"I was just waiting for you to come down. The stew should be ready in another fifteen minutes," she said, pushing herself up to her feet. "I put water on for tea. You should be able to manage."

"Pauline, why don't you stay the night? I don't think it's a good idea for you to try and drive home."

His invitation was like a passionate challenge, hard to resist. Pauline shivered inwardly, then crossed to the stove. "No, thank you," she replied. With a spoon in her hand, she stirred the stew as she spoke. "I need a change of clothes. And I want to sleep in my own bed tonight." She replaced the lid on the pot and began flitting from one area of the kitchen to another, cleaning up the mess she had intended to leave for Marcellus.

"I have beds here," he replied.

"Again, no, thank you, Marcellus. I'm going home," she said resolutely.

"Pauline, don't be so mule-headed," he said.

Chuckling tiredly, she replied, "You're a fine one to talk. Did you remember to call your mother?"

"Don't change the subject. Look at you. You're exhausted. You can barely stand up. And will you be still a minute?" he asked, exasperated.

Though her body agreed with his argument, her mind had other thoughts. It wasn't wise to get too comfortable with Marcellus and his languid charm, she reminded herself. Proof of his danger rested in the streamers of sensations unfurling in her.

"I'll be all right, Marcellus," she said, standing at the sink. "Thanks for your concern."

"Damnit, woman," he shouted.

The kettle whistled, and Pauline started for the stove.

"Sit down," he commanded. "I'll get it."

Pauline dropped into a chair, because she felt it was the prudent thing to do. She was running herself ragged and getting no place. Marcellus attended to the tea, then joined her at the table with two steaming cups of the mint-scented brew. He placed a cup in front of her.

Pauline blew over the rim before she took a sip. "Hmm," she said. "Wonderful."

"I bet you haven't eaten all day," he said. "Why don't you go on up and bathe? When you finish, dinner should be ready."

"I don't have another change of clothes," she said, avoiding his gaze deliberately. It was a feeble argument, but the best her brain could do.

With a flicker of a smile rising at the edges of his mouth, he replied, "I have a drawer full of nightshirts you haven't worn yet." His tone was deliberately seductive.

Pauline felt the giveaway heat in her face travel the length of her. She was too startled by Marcellus's offer to counter with one of her own. She wondered what game he was playing.

Either piss on the pot or get off.

In essence, that was the challenge the glaring computer

screen issued. It refused to budge until the request for
PASSWORD had been satisfied.

Don would eschew anything too complicated. But what
simple password would he use?

The company's name was too simple. So were his birth
date, his social security number, and the combination to
his gym locker. Still ... 12131959 ... 460–55–2118 ...
81233.

ACCESS DENIED. ACCESS DENIED. ACCESS DENIED.

What about his wife's name?

SARAH.

ACCESS DENIED.

The company's first day of operation?

January 5, 1996.

ACCESS DENIED.

If entry could be gained to Donald Wellsing's computer,
the date would be a recent one. The thought of having to
go through every last one of them was worth it. A million
dollars for a little bit of time. It was a steal. If only ...

DONNIE.

ACCESS DENIED.

Chapter Six

How was he feeling . . . did he remember to take his medicine . . . what was he doing?

Pauline awakened to the merry-go-round of questions that had haunted her sleep. She sighed, weary of them.

The second hand hit the sixty-second mark on the bed-side-table clock. The bold green numbers flipped in unison to the new time, 7:00 A.M. That it was morning was confirmed by the light peeking through the sheer curtains on the lone high, short window in her bedroom.

She lay in bed, staring absently at the ceiling; a wish that she had spent the night with Marcellus whipped in so quickly that she indulged it in hindsight. Images of what could have been sent a wave of excitement through her drowsy limbs, awakening desire in her loins. The feeling was so powerful that it had to run its course, carrying her away to a memorable time when they were a devoted couple—holding hands, attending a play at the Ensemble Theater, strolling along the streets of the French Quarter in New Orleans where she'd bought a decorative chifforobe from the YaYa's, fishing from his boat, dining by candlelight in the bedroom of his former penthouse.

If only it could be that way again, she thought with a sigh of longing. Instead, she had a fairy tale with a tragic ending, she mused, deliberately souring the memory. She sat up against the headboard and propped a pillow in her lap, as if to conceal the residual evidence of the sweet warming between her legs.

Even had she stayed, she and Marcellus would have danced around each other like cautious competitors, each fearing a slip of the tongue and dodging an accidental touch. Despite his offer to have her spend the night, he wanted nothing more from her than a confession of guilt, she told herself, remembering he once believed the very worst of her. Probably still did.

"Well, he will always wonder, because I'm never going to dignify his suspicion with an explanation," she whispered, a wounded, rather than bitter, expression on her face.

Shaking the ghost of regret from her head, Pauline crawled out of bed and padded to the adjoining bathroom where the lemon-and-white color scheme of the bedroom continued. As she splashed a handful of warm water on her face, the phone rang.

Who would be calling so early Sunday morning?

A longing for any contact from Marcellus seemed to have been waiting for this opportunity to spring forth and imbue her with a moment to marvel. Quickly, she grabbed a towel off the rack to dry her face and hurried to the bedroom, where she snatched up the trimline receiver of the phone on the lamp table next to the bed.

"Hello," she said into the mouthpiece, a hand over her heart as if to hold it in place, for it was beating so hard in her bosom. "Hello," she repeated more insistently, a frown forming across the ridge of her forehead.

She listened to the continued silence with rising dismay,

then finally, the connection was severed by the nameless caller. Her disappointment abated somewhat when she decided that someone had simply dialed the wrong number and had been too embarrassed to speak. Replacing the receiver, she put the call out of her mind and withdrew a set of clothes from the chifforobe. She returned to the bathroom to complete her toilet, first.

The idea to check on Donald didn't come to her until she was standing under the sprays of the shower. While she made a mental note to call the hospital later, she wondered whether the project he had been working on could be motive enough for someone to try to kill him. Since she had no idea of the scientific nature of his work, she was merely stuck with another question.

Marcellus had nearly added to the growing list of questions, she thought, with amusement slipping into her expression. Detective Collins looked as if he would swallow his tongue, she recalled, when Marcellus told him that he was a partner and major owner of CSI. As a black woman, she couldn't help but be proud of him for having his sights set on the stars.

If only . . . she sighed wistfully.

Pauline emerged from the bedroom moments later, fully dressed in an oversized tee-shirt, jeans, and tennis shoes. She passed several rooms before reaching the cozy, mid-size family room, of which a small section doubled as an eating area right off the kitchen. A white overstuffed sofa, two mint-green-and-white-checkered armchairs, and a glass-topped coffee table faced the floor-model television set. Adjacent was a tall wall unit which contained the stereo, albums, cassette tapes, and compact disks.

She popped a disc in the player, then crossed to the back of the room where a square table surrounded by four high-backed, mint-green-cushioned chairs sat atop a sculpted rug in pale tones. She opened the floor length curtains of a sliding glass door that gave a partial view of the backyard, then she headed to the adjacent long, narrow kitchen.

The rich, sultry voice of Gladys Knight filtered through the rooms as she measured ground coffee for two cups into the automatic coffee maker. Retracing her path, she veered to the front door, passing the small, unfurnished living room, and stepped out into the quiet Sunday morning. Shafts of the sun dropped through the clouds, which were gray with the promise of rain.

She walked gingerly across the wet grass to get the newspaper, near the curb. Nothing stirred on the street with its well-tended front yards. It was a predominantly Black middle-class neighborhood, in the southeast section of Houston called South Park. The one-story, brick and wood dwellings were close together, but the three-bedroom, two-bath homes provided ample space for the small families of which the neighborhood was mostly composed. Still a fairly new home-owner of three months, Pauline was proud of her home. It represented a challenge met that helped bolster her self-worth.

She returned inside, dropped the paper on the table, then headed straight to the kitchen. The coffee was ready, so she got a cup from an overhead cabinet, and cream and sugar from the refrigerator, then poured her first cup and took a sip.

Now, she was ready to face the day. Sitting at the table, she set the cup down to open the paper, curious to know if an article about CSI's president appeared in it. As she scanned the stories, the doorbell peeled a two-note chime. Shortly, she opened the door; she was surprised to see who her visitor was.

"May I come in?"

"Of course," Pauline replied, opening the door wider for Sarah to enter. Preceding Sarah to the den, she turned off the music. "Can I get you something? Coffee, juice?"

"Coffee would be fine," Sarah replied.

"Coming right up," Pauline replied, heading to the kitchen. "Make yourself comfortable." As she began preparing a tray, she wondered what to make of the unexpected visit. "How is Donald this morning?"

"The same," Sarah replied with a shrug. Standing at the sliding glass door, she was staring out into the back yard, her face set in deep thought.

"How are you this morning?" Pauline asked with emphasis. With her hair finger combed and her eyes puffy and bloodshot, Sarah looked worn out. She considered offering Sarah use of the shower. Breakfast would also help to restore the woman from her bedraggled state.

"Sarah, how about some breakfast? It won't take long to whip something up."

"Do you mind if I open this?" Sarah asked. She was already halfway out the door.

"Be my guest," Pauline replied, with a curious glance in the direction of Sarah's exit.

When the tray was ready, Pauline carried it to the table. She walked outside onto the cement patio. Sarah was standing near the pear tree deep in the back yard, which was fenced off from homes on three sides.

She knew more about Sarah from Don than from the woman herself, Pauline mused. Before last Friday, the women had never met. When Sarah came into the picture, she was out of it. She'd sent a gift for their wedding, but didn't attend it. Marcellus had been the best man. Time and circumstances had prevented subsequent attempts to form a threesome, but Pauline knew she wouldn't have enjoyed being the third wheel, anyway.

Don had spoken highly of his twenty-seven-year-old wife—twelve years younger than he—Pauline recalled as the silence stretched between them. Though a little shy and quiet, she was mature, responsible, great with money, and an even better cook than he, Don had claimed with unrestrained affection. He had implied Sarah had had a rough childhood, but he never disclosed the details.

As Sarah seemed intent on taking her sweet time before explaining her presence, Pauline filled the strained hush with innocent conversation. "I'm afraid the neighborhood kids have picked the tree dry." She strolled out to stand alongside Sarah. "I got just enough to preserve a few jars."

Facing Pauline headlong, Sarah asked, "Why did Don hire you?"

Caught off guard, Pauline hesitated, alarm rippling, along her spine, before she replied. Sarah's distrustful attitude, very much like the one exhibited by Detective Collins, opened a smelly can of worms, she thought with a slightly raised eyebrow. Yet, aware of the emotional strain Sarah was under, she decided to indulge the distraught young wife.

"In light of what we now know, and despite the fact that we've had this conversation before, I'd say that's still a good question," Pauline replied cautiously, wetting her lips with her tongue.

"If I recall correctly, your answer didn't make sense then, either," Sarah said, a hint of challenge in her voice.

"Like the question, the answer hasn't changed. And you make the third person to ask it, so at least I'm consistent," Pauline reproached subtly with a smile.

Sarah paused for a moment, then spoke in a rush, as if fearing she would forget her point. "Why would my husband decide to hire a nurse all of a sudden?" she asked accusingly.

With anger singeing the edges of her control, Pauline drew a deep calming breath before she replied. "Do you want the reason he gave me . . . again?" she asked, a bright mockery invading her stare.

As if Pauline had not spoken, Sarah asked, "And why you?"

"All right, enough of this," Pauline exclaimed. "Sarah,

just say what's on your mind. Why did you come to see me?"

"Are you having an affair with my husband?" Sarah asked, pinning Pauline fiercely with a look that was equal parts fear and hostility.

Pauline returned her look with open-mouthed amazement. She couldn't believe Sarah suspected her of carrying on an illicit affair with Donald. She wondered if Marcellus shared the same suspicion.

"Do you have so little trust in your husband?" she asked disgustedly, shaking her head from side to side.

"Are you?" Sarah pressed, her demeanor unchanged.

Pauline bristled. False accusations always rubbed her the wrong way. Still, she thought—call it sympathy—she indulged Sarah. "No, I'm not," she replied plainly.

"Why don't I believe you?" Sarah yelled.

Sarah wasn't shy or retiring now; she was as aggressive as any woman bent on keeping her man, Pauline thought sarcastically. The sad truth was that neither she nor Don was in need of a defense, because neither was guilty of anything. She threw up her hands. "Why am I not surprised?" She walked off, returning inside the house.

Sarah followed. "It just doesn't make any sense. The company never had need for a nurse before."

"So?" Pauline said curtly. Picking up her cup, she took a sip of coffee. It was cold, and she frowned.

With torment in her eyes and pleading in her tone, Sarah said, "I'm just trying to figure out what's been going on. Why would someone try to kill Don?"

Snap. The inaudible sound of patience breaking broke in Pauline. Carefully, she set the cup on the table. Her insides were trembling with fury.

"Let me see if I'm following you," she replied, sarcasm dripping in her tone. "Because the company never had a nurse before and, out of the blue, Donald hired me, you believe I tried to kill him."

"No, I didn't say you tried to kill him," Sarah cried.

"Look Sarah, I may not be as smart as Don or Marcellus, but I know an accusation when I hear one," Pauline said, her voice rising with indignation. She flinched inwardly at the betrayal of her own insecurity.

"I didn't mean it like that," Sarah exclaimed, wringing her hands together. Her voice faltered under Pauline's cold stare. "I only meant," she stammered softly, "that it seemed strange that right after Don hired you, something happened to him."

"Sarah, I don't know what you want to hear besides the truth," Pauline said wearily. She slammed the sliding door shut and locked it, then turned to look at Sarah who was staring at her like a lost puppy. But she was all out of sympathy.

"Pauline, please try to understand my position," Sarah said.

"Oh, I understand your position," Pauline replied bitingly. "You believe I was having an affair with Don and you want me to confirm your suspicion. To hell with the truth as long as your peace of mind is satisfied. Now, you understand me, Sarah," she said in a low, taut voice, her eyes brown stones of ire. "I've answered the question that's been burning a hole in your head for heaven knows how long. If you can't take my word, which I'm not going to repeat or beg you to accept, then there's nothing else for us to discuss. Believe whatever you want. Have a good day, Mrs. Wellsing."

Pauline walked off to the front door, leaving Sarah to follow. She opened the door, and Sarah walked out, her eyes cast downward.

Before she closed the door, a car Pauline recognized pulled up in her driveway. It was a 1960-model, dark-blue Corvette Stingray with a black convertible top. Lessons to teach her to master its stick shift had failed, she recalled, as her body vibrated with a new tension when Marcellus got out of the sporty, antique car.

"Now, what does he want?" she whispered harshly.

With her lips set in a disgusted twist, she watched Sarah hurry to Marcellus. Both turned to look in her direction. She could just imagine what Sarah was telling him. He embraced her affectionately, then Sarah got into her car and drove off.

Marcellus leaned inside his car, then reappeared with a grocery bag in one hand and a briefcase in the other. He approached Pauline with his long-legged strides. It was impossible not to notice the rich outlines of his shoulders straining against the fabric of the white Polo, the biker's pants molding his long, brown, powerful thighs; the strength of muscles in his sturdy legs.

Feeling his gaze appraising her, Pauline coached her pulse to a steady rate, determined to fight her reaction to the dynamic vitality he exuded. She erected a barrier of residual anger, standing in a defensive posture, hands on her hips, fire in her eyes.

"Where do you think you're going?" she asked.

Debating whether to continue his approach, Marcellus froze mid-stride, and his eyes widened to collide with his thick brows. The look on his face was comical. Pauline cleared her throat to keep from laughing.

"Uh, I was hoping that if I brought breakfast you would offer me a cup of coffee," he replied.

"You don't drink coffee," she replied.

He glanced at the spot where Sarah had parked in the driveway, then faced Pauline. "I gather you and Sarah had an interesting morning, huh?"

Pauline shot him a withering stare, then spun to walk back into the house.

* * *

Shortly after Marcellus arrived, dirty utensils were scattered on the counter near the sink. The smell of pork dominated the other scents of breakfast that were wafting from the kitchen.

Peering inside the toaster as its grills turned red hot against the bread, Marcellus hummed along with the beat of a melodic, up-tempo instrumental by flutist Hubert Laws which was playing from the CD player. He had brought the tape with him, knowing Pauline wasn't an avid fan and seldom bought any type of African-American Classical Music for her collection.

He rehashed his reason for coming, and he was satisfied with his answer. Accommodating the lunacy of the behavior, he chalked it up to his impulsive nature. He wanted someone across the table from him as he enjoyed breakfast, he told himself, as if needing an extra rationale to justify his rash act.

Tired of his own company and the endless parade of questions about Don, he left his house, heading for the pancake restaurant for breakfast. During the drive, the wheel of the car seemed to steer in the opposite direction. He just happened to have Pauline's new address on him after accessing her personnel file at CSI via his home computer, he recalled with a mocking chuckle.

Two slices of bread popped out of the toaster, and he placed a slice on each of two separate plates, which he carried to the dining table. The plates were filled with eggs, toast, and strips of bacon.

"Breakfast is ready," he announced, pouring juice into the glasses.

Pauline, who was sitting on the couch reading the newspaper, got up and sauntered to the table. Marcellus pulled back the chair in front of the smaller portion of food, and she sat down. He took the chair facing the plate with the sunny-side-up eggs.

"Dig in," he said.

Unfolding his napkin, he watched Pauline close her eyes and bow her head in prayer. Though he wished for a little more enthusiasm than she had shown, he couldn't have asked for a more attractive companion. Then surprisingly, she lifted her head and gave him a look that animated her features brilliantly. His breath caught in his throat. She had no earthly idea of the arresting picture she made, he thought, feeling like a balloon of joy had burst inside him, filling him with pleasant sensations.

"You can have these," Pauline said, removing the bacon from her plate to his. "I've given up red meat."

"Sorry," he said.

"No problem," she replied. "Everything looks good."

"It may look better than it tastes," he said, a chuckle in his voice. "We'll have to see," forking into the eggs on his plate.

She seemed to have gotten over whatever disagreement she had with Sarah, he thought. That was one of the things he had liked about Pauline. When she got angry, as long as she was allowed to vent it on the spot, she was through with it. The problem was, she usually kept it in instead of letting it out.

"You're looking much better," she said casually, spreading jelly on the toasted bread.

"I feel it, too," Marcellus replied. "Thanks to you and your nasty medicines."

"Can't have everything," she quipped, biting into the toast.

"Says who?" he replied.

Pauline looked at him with the cutest expression of marvel on her face. Feeling powerless to wipe away the stupid grin that seemed glued on his own face, Marcellus chuckled softly. She averted her gaze to the neutral territory of her plate, and forked a bite of eggs into her mouth.

"You look well rested," he said, speaking his thoughts out loud. "I guess nothing beats sleeping in your own bed." He could think of a thing or two, he thought, smiling to himself.

"Did you call the hospital this morning?" she asked.

Chewing with extra care as if fearing he might choke, he replied, "There's been no change," with a sudden brooding quality in his voice.

"It's going to work out, Marcellus," Pauline said softly.

She extended a hand across the table to squeeze his. Just as quickly, she retrieved her hand, and it vanished under the table. The action didn't go unnoticed, and certainly not unfelt. The electric imprint of her soft hand lingered on his and spiraled up his arms. He began to feel on treacherous ground and reminded himself again of why he had come.

"It's just going to take time," Pauline said, not looking at him.

Resettled on solid ground, Marcellus said, "I did some checking on my own about digitalis."

"What about it?"

"If a tablet were to have been slipped somehow into Don's vitamin packs, he certainly would have noticed it."

"Oh, sure," she replied, "in tablet form, it's a tiny pill that couldn't be overlooked among some giant-sized vitamins. Of course, that's not to say a pill couldn't have been crushed to a powder and mixed into his food or drink."

"Assuming it was in powder form, wouldn't he have tasted it?"

Pauline shook her head indicating ignorance of the answer. "I can't say. I've never tasted it. I know it has a slight odor, but that's negligible. That may apply to taste, as well. But it also comes in a liquid," she added, "or it can be injected."

"If it had been injected, I'm sure the doctors would have discovered a needle mark, but they didn't." He heaved a winded sigh. "Anyway, I can't picture Don sitting still while someone injects him. He's a big baby when it comes to needles.''

Pauline hid a smile in her glass as she drank a swallow of juice.

"I know what you're thinking," Marcellus said, mirth in his tone, dancing in his dark eyes. "That I'm an even bigger baby than Don when it came to needles."

"Are you going to deny it?"

Her dimples came out, and her eyes sparkled like jewels with her amusement. A jolt of desire bolted through Marcellus, and he bit off a piece of crunchy bacon.

"I'll take the fifth," he replied at last.

"Have it your way," she quipped.

"I usually do." Changing the subject, he casually asked, "Want to tell me about Sarah's visit?"

With her mouth full, Pauline shook her head, replying, "No." Wetting her throat with a sip of juice, she said, "This is really good."

His curiosity piqued, Marcellus stared at Pauline. She was cutting up her food and shoving it around her plate, raising none of it to her mouth. The music chose that moment to stop, and the level of silence intensified, tainting the relaxed atmosphere they had been enjoying.

"As mad as you were when I got here," he said, "I don't think it's going to go away. Do you?"

Pauline sighed, annoyance in her expression. "She accused me of having an affair with Donald," she said, looking straight at him.

Marcellus's chewing rhythm was thrown off for a fraction. He concealed his astonishment by taking a big gulp of orange juice.

"Well?" Pauline prodded.

"Well, what?" he asked, staring at Pauline headlong with a poker face.

"Well?" she replied, dropping her fork on the plate with a clatter. "Is that all you have to say?" Her hands propped on her hips and her head cocked at an angle, she glared at him. "I suppose since CSI never had a nurse before, you reached the same conclusion, too."

With deliberate slowness, Marcellus chewed his food and swallowed it with extra care. Pauline was spoiling for a fight. A wrong word or gesture from him and his plate of eggs could end up in his lap. It was not how he intended breakfast between them to go. Deciding to de-emphasize the seriousness of the charge, he replied nonchalantly, "Is that all she had to say?" He knew within milliseconds that his strategy was a failure.

Springing from her chair, Pauline snapped, "I think it's enough." Stooping to pick up the napkin that fell to the floor, she said, "And I've had all I'm going to take from you two. You can follow the same path Sarah took, as far as I'm concerned," tossing the napkin on the table.

Marcellus was up and across the room before Pauline could vanish into the hallway. Grabbing her by the hand, he pulled her back to the table. With an "aw-shucks" demeanor, he commanded softly, "Sit down, Pauline." She hesitated, tugging gently against his possession. He could smell victory was near. "Come on," he cajoled. "Eat. Your breakfast is getting cold."

Pauline dropped back into the chair, but she didn't touch her food. Looking down at her hands in her lap, she exhaled deeply before continuing. "She went on to imply that I had something to do with poisoning Don," she said in a barely audible tone, gazing into his face with veiled, liquid eyes.

Marcellus gripped the fork in his hand. His handsome face rearranged itself into a tight grimace. He swallowed the food in his mouth with one hard gulp, setting his fork on the plate. Sarah's lack of trust in her husband's fidelity was one thing, he thought, but to suggest a duplicitous relationship with Pauline was quite another. Even he couldn't buy that.

Crushing the napkin in his hand, he said with profound disgust, "Why do women go around looking for trouble?"

"Don't look at me, I didn't start it," Pauline said petulantly.

"And you probably didn't correct the lie, either," he chided. He tossed the napkin on the table, then rose to pace about the room.

"I told her the truth, but she wasn't satisfied with that," Pauline said defensively. "I'm not going to run around trying to defend myself against every little charge, stated or implied, from her or anybody else," she said with a cold edge in her voice.

Reading the message in her eyes, Marcellus knew her warning superseded Sarah's. It was for his benefit, probably more than anything, he thought, his mouth pulled in at the corners. It was one of the few times he felt rendered speechless.

At last, he said quietly, "I'll talk to her."

Pauline snapped contentiously, "I don't need you defending me, Marcellus. I don't want anything from you." She sprang from her seat and stormed over to stand at the back door, looking out into the yard.

Crossing to her, Marcellus said, "Pauline, will you calm down?" He put his hands on her shoulders; they were rigid beneath his touch. He turned her to face him, but she wouldn't return his look. Tilting her face up by the chin, he was stunned by the anguish glittering in her eyes.

His heart shuddered unexpectedly. He felt as if reason were conspiring against him, for he could find none to keep him from doing what he desperately wanted to do. Lowering his head, he touched his mouth to hers, taunted by the thought that this was what he had come for all along. Her cool lips trembled beneath his, but parted invitingly, and he tasted the sun in her mouth.

Like a hidden current, the memories came flooding back. Marcellus lifted his head and studied her silently;

startled brown eyes studied him back. His body tingled with his desire, mingling with a rising fear and disbelief of what he had done and of what he apparently had not done.

This feeling, this uncontrollable sense of losing himself in another person, he remembered, he had never wanted to feel that ever again.

"I'm sorry," he said, stepping away from Pauline. Running his hand across his head, he smiled weakly at her. As if it were too heavy to hold, the smile gave way to a look that was guilt-laden, troubled and still.

"I hope you don't mind if I stick you with the dirty dishes," he said. "I think I had better take your advice and follow Sarah's path." Backing away from her, he retrieved the briefcase from the couch. "I'll see you tomorrow."

Chapter Seven

Why hadn't she seen it before?

A startled gasp frozen on her face, Pauline was standing at the back of her car in the parking lot adjacent to the CSI building, with the trunk raised.

Sarah Wellsing explained Detective Collins's strange behavior toward her, she thought. Even before he met her, he had decided she was somehow responsible for Donald's heart failure.

She didn't know why Sarah believed so strongly that she and Donald were carrying on an illicit romance. Pauline frowned. She did know why she hadn't made the connection before now.

The cross look on her face deepened as one name snuggled against her thoughts. She shuddered anew with embarrassment, just thinking about her brazen response to his kiss yesterday. Raptured by the memory of it, she recalled that Marcellus had been upon her before she realized what he was about to do. His long, strong arms had snaked out to pull her softly against the hard frame of his body. She couldn't have escaped if she wanted to—although fleeing had been the farthest thing from her mind. His firm lips covered hers, and her body betrayed her instantly, accepting him into her mouth, her soul—all over again. With warm shivers of delight coursing through her, she sucked in a deep breath of air.

Marcellus had consumed her entire being, to the exclusion of everything else happening around her, she thought, displeased with herself. The only rationale she could give was her feminine hunger, which hadn't been fed in quite some time. There had been no man in her life since Marcellus, she mused, and quite frankly, none before him that mattered. But he would never catch her off-guard again.

Pauline retrieved her black bag and slammed the trunk shut as if to seal her resolve. She fell in stride with the parade of employees reporting for work Monday morning.

It was a gorgeous day; a white sun stood fixed in the blue sky with a mild wind. But Pauline was too busy wondering what was in store for her today to notice. Butterflies were fluttering in her stomach from the time she entered the smoky glass and smooth red-granite-brick building and during the entire ride up the elevator.

Marcellus was expecting her, she thought, recalling his parting words on Sunday. Though she questioned how her services would benefit the company, she hoped she was sufficiently braced to face him again. The kiss stole into her thoughts, and she felt her heart pound a little harder—seemingly, a little louder—as she strode to his office. Katherine was sitting behind the desk, smiling over a cup of steaming coffee.

"Well, good morning," she said, heartily.

Katherine's cheerful mood was infectious, and Pauline replied similarly. "Morning to you, too. Is he in?"

"Arrived hours ago," Katherine replied, "but he stepped out." She set the cup down and picked up a gray linen folder with *CSI* embossed in blue foil ink across the front. "He wants you to have this."

Accepting the folder, Pauline asked, "What is it?"

"Everything you always wanted to know about CavWell Space Industries but didn't know how to ask," Katherine chortled. "He wants you to read it and, if you have any questions, just beep him. He's somewhere around here. You're also to get a set of keys. Just go down to security on the first floor and Clay should have a set ready for you."

"Keys to what?"

"You're to have carte blanche access to the entire place," Katherine replied.

Stunned speechless, Pauline's eyes widened and her lashes flew up as questions whizzed across her brain like jets colliding into each other. As a nurse, she could be useful, she thought; anything else made her nothing more than window dressing. Was this a sign of trust or a test? she wondered, a wary gaze in her eyes. She bit her bottom lip.

Still, she was as thrilled by the honor Marcellus bestowed on her as she was uneasy with it; wondering what it meant, what he expected of her.

As her gaze focused on Katherine, who was staring back at her with an expectant look, Pauline thought she must have spoken aloud. She couldn't remember what she had said, if anything at all. With her face squinted up apologetically, she said, "I'm sorry. What did you say?"

Chuckling, Katherine replied, "Nothing."

"I guess I'm just surprised," Pauline said lightly. "I didn't expect this. In fact, I didn't know what to expect," she said, a lopsided grin on her face.

Reaching out to pat Pauline on the hand, Katherine said, "Don't worry. You'll be fine. Since the police are finished with Don's office, you might as well use it until the clinic is ready. All calls to Mr. Wellsing are to be routed to this office, so Amy is at your disposal. I don't know if she's arrived yet, but when she does, I'll send her down to you."

Frowning, but with equal parts trepidation and humor in her voice, Pauline said, "You've got to be joking. What am I going to do with a secretary?"

"She'll make setting up the clinic easy; believe me." Then Katherine arched her brow and lowered her chin, adding, "But I can tell you that Mr. Cavanaugh was not in a joking mood when he arrived this morning. No thanks in part to Mr. Jason Ringnald, Jr."

"Who is that?"

"The security chief over at NASA," Katherine replied, hooking a thumb over her shoulder as if the nearby facility were right there. "He wants assurances," she added dryly. Before she could say more, a buzzing din accompanied a lighted button on the phone. "Excuse me," she said, answering the in-house call. "Yes? Oh, morning, Walter, what can I do for you? Yeah, he got them. Changes? All right, fax them up." Replacing the receiver, she smiled apologetically at Pauline. "Sorry, I'll have to send you off on your own."

"That's all right, Katherine. I think I can manage," Pauline replied, though she couldn't hide the smudge of doubt in her expression.

"You'll be fine; don't worry," Katherine reiterated sincerely. "Just call me if you need anything."

Pauline nodded. Out of Katherine's sight and reassuring presence, she drew a deep calming breath. Nothing could beat keys to everything in the way of surprises, she thought. She felt as if she had been given an invaluable gift she didn't know what to do with. It was more than a little daunting.

Just as she walked past the elevators, she heard the conspiratorial din of lowered voices coming from Donald's side of the floor.

"I have to report to her now."

Pauline paused in her stride, wondering why the speaker, a woman, bothered to whisper.

"Why? She's just a nurse."

Identifying the voice as belonging to Dr. Kent, Pauline mused that she really couldn't blame the scientist for her skepticism. She felt similarly stumped by this latest development.

"I don't know."

It was Amy speaking. Good, Pauline thought, now she wouldn't have to worry Katherine. She took one step forward, then heard Amy declare, "I think she used to sleep with him, too."

Shocked, Pauline stumbled. She righted herself awkwardly, clutching the folder to her bosom, the seat of fury rising in her. Not only was Amy helpless in a crisis situation, she was also a gossip and a liar.

"Too? What do you mean?" Dr. Kent asked with dark suspicion in her voice. "Are you saying she and Don were involved?"

Amy's reply was not audible.

"Come on," Dr. Kent replied skeptically. "Believe me, men are not so gracious. Their egos wouldn't permit it. And if there's one thing we know about Marcellus, it's that he has an ego that would fly off the Richter scale."

"I'd say the lady was making the rounds," Amy said. "I heard she told the police that Mr. Wellsing called her, but I bet it was the other way around. If they were supposed to be such good friends, why is it that I never heard of her? I screen all of the calls that come into this office. It's mighty strange that I never spoke to her before."

Dr. Kent asked, "Have you told this to the police?"

"Sure did. Detective Collins came to my house yesterday and interviewed me. He couldn't stay long, you know, because I was taking care of my mother. She just got out of the hospital. She's been in and out of one for the past five months."

Listening as the conversation evolved into mundane matters, Pauline recalled that, as a youngster, she had been the target of other children's cruel speculations about her parents. Knowing how much pain gossip could cause, she avoided the vicious activity, even while working as a hospital nurse among whom the practice was almost as standard as attending patients.

When Dr. Kent mentioned that she needed to hire another scientist and wondering aloud in a sarcastic tone if the request had to go through the new executive, Pauline decided it was show time. Accompanied by performance anxiety, she continued into the outer office of Amy's work station. Both women had their backs to her when she arrived. Dr. Kent was sitting on the corner of the desk; Amy was sitting behind it.

"Good morning," Pauline said. Each woman turned quickly to meet her deceptively composed expression.

Rising, Dr. Kent measured her with eyes as indecipherable as water. "Good morning. It's Ms. Sinclair, isn't it?"

"Yes, it is," Pauline replied, though she knew the scientist knew exactly who she was. Replying in turn, she asked, "It's Dr. Kent, right?"

Dr. Kent lifted her chin haughtily. "Yes," she said in a nearly hissing tone.

"Good morning, Amy," Pauline said, watching the secretary with interest.

"Good morning, Ms. Sinclair," Amy said in a bright, babbling voice. "I didn't know you were here already. Clay—you know, down in security—told me you would be moving in today."

Pauline wondered if Amy was being facetious, or if she simply misunderstood that her stay in Don's office would be temporary. She let the remark pass. "I'm glad you were feeling well enough to come in," she said. "I'm really going to need your help."

Bashfully, Amy nodded her head. "Yeah. I really lost it when . . . well you know," she said with a shrug.

"Well, that's over now and Mr. Wellsing is coming along nicely," she said, though she hadn't the faintest idea how Don was doing. So engrossed in her own personal affairs, she had forgotten to call the hospital this morning.

"Heard you got yourself one helluva promotion," Dr. Kent said snippily. "From nurse to company president."

Pauline cut a sidelong look at Amy, whom she surmised was responsible for the misinformation. She saw no reason to correct either one of them. Instead, she decided to have a little fun. "Is there anything I can help you with, Dr. Kent?"

Dr. Kent met her gaze with a flinty look, her lips twisted sourly. "No. I'll take up my concerns with Marcellus." With a toss of her shoulders, she walked off.

"Would you like me to get you something, Ms. Sinclair?" Amy asked.

"Not just yet," Pauline replied, as she walked into her temporary office. She crossed to the desk and set the folder down, then turned facing Amy. "When I return, we'll have a nice long chat," she said, staring at Amy pointedly. "In the meantime, lock the office behind me. I don't want anyone coming in while I'm not here."

"Does that mean me, too?"

Especially you, Pauline wanted to say. Instead, she replied. "That means you, too." She felt Amy's open-mouthed stare boring a hole in her back as she walked out, heading for the elevators.

The alliance between the two women struck Pauline as odd. The supercilious scientist and the superficial secretary, she thought amused, as she stepped onto the elevator car.

On the ride down, several passengers boarded and debarked before she reached the first floor. She fussed at herself for not having gotten directions as she strolled

uncertainly toward the front of the building, into the lobby.
To her left were two doors, an equal distance from each
other, and she tried to open one. It was locked, so she
looked on the other side of the spacious area. Hidden
from plain view, a door marked *Security* was slightly ajar.
She walked in without knocking.

Taking up an entire wall, an elaborate console served
as host to several TV screens, that displayed the grounds
of CSI, and a communication system. The voices of guards
talking to each other came from the built-in speakers.

Enthralled, Pauline sauntered along the console, looking at the various angles of coverage on the screens.
Though she hadn't known what to expect, she felt as
impressed by the modern equipment as she thought she
would if she were on a spaceship. It was, no doubt, the
top of the line in security hardware.

"Yes, may I help you?"

"Oh," Pauline replied startled, turning to face a man
on the tall side of six feet with a mop of curly red hair
who was staring down at her with peeved green eyes. "I'm
Pauline Sinclair. I believe you're expecting me."

"Oh, right," the man replied, his expression softening
to a friendly shade. "Mr. Cavanaugh told me to expect
you, Ms. Sinclair. I'm Clay Bennington, head of Security,
and I have your keys ready."

Donnie, a silver-suited robot on wheeled legs, followed
one of the dozen or so white-coated scientists around the
massive room. A researcher was perched on a stainless-
steel rolling ladder to attach a piece of equipment to the
side of the large model of the Challenger spaceship suspended from the high vaulted ceiling while several of her
associates looked on from below.

"I don't mean to sound cold and heartless—I really

sympathize with Don—but I don't want you to get caught up in emotion over this and lose sight of what's important.''

Listening to that voice as it came from the speakerphone, Marcellus stared absently from the glass-encased sound-proofed cubicle. Sitting behind the desk, his gaze followed Donnie and the scientist as they disappeared from sight through a cylinder corridor.

"Hold on a sec."

While he was *on hold,* Marcellus scooted his rolling chair from the desk. His expression showed thoughtful frustration, though it was not directed to the silence emanating from the speakerphone or to the activity of the researchers in the pristine white research lab on the other side of the glass.

Jason had called him three times since last night, he recalled, rubbing his temples. Though the security chief for the Johnson Space Center professed concern for Don, he knew instinctively that Jason had more than Don's health in mind. He was worried that a fallout at CSI could affect NASA's reputation and budget.

"I'm back," the voice from the speaker phone declared, seconds before resuming its stentorian oration. "With capitalism on the march around the world, so is government-sponsored espionage. American companies just don't get it, and those that do respond too slowly to protect themselves against it. I'd hate for that to happen to CSI. Don't make the same mistake. The competitive environment has changed."

"Yes, I'm well aware of that, Jason," Marcellus replied, rolling the chair back to the desk. He'd suspected before that something sinister was behind the attempt on Don's life he recalled, but he'd let the thought get away from him. Mired in his conflicting emotions for Pauline, economic espionage had taken a tertiary position in his mind. Until he'd spoken again with Clay.

Jason cut into his thoughts. "The French, the Germans,

and the Japanese view business as a form of warfare. The goal is not just to survive, but to win. You remember Ellery Systems?"

Before Marcellus could reply, Jason continued. "It was a company about the size of CSI that was developing proprietary material and a highly sophisticated software system for us. They were just about to commercialize it when the software mysteriously landed in the hands of a Chinese competitor. Now they're out of business. Even the big boys like Motorola and GM have been victims of espionage."

"Yes, I know," Marcellus replied wearily, massaging the bridge of his nose. Clay had already given him this lecture, he thought—twice within the past twenty-four hours— he remembered, sighing. Just this morning, when he'd requested a set of keys for Pauline, Clay had cautioned him against it. He'd argued his explicit trust in Pauline until Clay's haranguing brought on a sliver of doubt, awakening a taunting memory of the cause of their breakup. But the trilogy of life in him remained steadfast in belief that Pauline was the key—and not merely to solving the crisis CSI faced. He hoped truth, not lust, fired his faith in her.

"It's going to be years before Senator Arlen Specter's legislation becomes law—"

Marcellus's head snapped attentively to Jason's, big voice, which was heavy with frustration.

"And our Trade Secrets Act simply doesn't have the reach or power to deal with foreign-sponsored economic espionage," the security chief continued. "U.S. businesses have lost billions of dollars because of foreign spying, not to mention the betrayals by their own employees who were lured by money. A lot of companies have gone out of business because of it."

"Yes, I realize that, Jason. But . . ." Marcellus said impatiently, before another line buzzed. "Hold on a minute." He punched the hold button, then pressed the lighted one. "Yeah? Katherine, what is it?" he answered. Stiffening, he asked urgently, "What did Reuben say?" What? Damn!" running a hand across his face. "Oh, man," he sighed deeply. "Okay, I've got Jason on the other line, and as soon as I finish, I'll leave for the hospital. Where's Pauline? Page her for me, and tell her to meet me in the lobby"— he looked at his watch—"in ten minutes. I won't come back up."

Leaving the security office, Pauline planned to stop off at her former office before returning upstairs to Amy and the black folder. She caught an empty elevator and rode uninterrupted to the third floor.

As she got off the elevator, the aromas of the day's menu of Italian fare coming from the cafeteria assailed her nostrils. She walked past it until she reached a fork in the corridor. To her left was the gym; the clinic was in the opposite direction.

Recalling how Don had boasted about the fitness facility, she decided to make the gym her first stop. She knew she was stalling her return to the executive suite.

She arrived at the front desk, but no one was present. She recalled Donald telling her that a trainer was on hand three times a week for those willing to pay extra for his services. She peered at the time sheet visible on the counter and spotted Donald Wellsing's name on the top sheet: he had reserved a court for eight last Friday morning. No partner was listed, but he had played on court three.

Walking around the counter, she reached the basketball court. The shine on the parquet floor gave it a wet look. A goal was at each end, and the outline of the court was circled by a running track. According to the sign posted on the wall, eight laps equaled a mile. Across the way was the weight room, for the more rigorous exercises. Racks of silver and black barbells and dumbbells were right inside the door on either side. The room was packed with a variety of machines that helped tone every muscle in the body, from stationary bikes to rowing machines.

She backed out of the room to saunter down a corridor which spilled into a reception area with thin gray carpet on the floors and walls. It contained several gold and mauve miniature backless couches for players to rest on after a grueling game on one of the four glass-encased racquetball courts.

Impressed, Pauline mused that Don had good cause to be boastful. CSI's facilities could compete with commercial fitness centers.

Standing at the door of a court, her hand on the knob, she was filled with memories. Marcellus had introduced her to the game . . . and a whole lot more of what life had to offer those who could afford it, she recalled, sadness scything her expression. Though she had never progressed into a great player she could—in retrospect—give an opponent a respectable game.

Backing from the door, she followed an arrow near the last court into a corridor which veered in two different directions. Black painted forefingers pointed men to the left and women to the right. Here, carpet ended and the conventional dull gray cement floor began. The locker room was composed of a double row of cream-colored lockers, a long sink, and counters with hair dryers protruding from the pink-tiled wall at each end.

Water stains were on the floor in the shower area, which stank with the smell of an astringent cleanser. Just beyond the shower stalls, up a short flight of stairs, was an opening that led to the pool and steam room.

A mist hovered over the long rectangular pool like a country morning fog. Coughing, Pauline squinted her eyes and shielded her nose from the vaporous stench. Why would they use so much chlorine? she wondered.

Whomever the company hired to clean the pool deserved to lose the contract, she thought, suspecting the pH level of chlorine may well have surpassed the non-threatening toxic mark. The mist suggested a hydrochloric acid had been produced as a result of over-chlorination.

Getting evidence to support her recommendation to take action against the company, Pauline kneeled and stuck a finger in the water. It was warmer than normal pool temperatures. With her expression set in a peeved look, she stood, drying the finger on her skirt.

This was something in the realm of her expertise, she thought confidently, mentally outlining some measures to take. Signs needed to be posted around the pool to prevent its use. It was the first order of business, she decided, turning to walk away.

From the corner of her eye, she spotted something bobbing gently in the far end of the third lane. She didn't want to believe her eyes at this distance and guessed the cleaning team had been doubly careless. Counting off the lanes that were separated by blue disks strung to a white rope, she headed in that direction to get a closer look.

When she made out long black hair spread like a fan over the water, Pauline gulped. Her steps faltered as she wiped her stinging eyes, disbelief marring her features. What she had thought was a black rag was a one-piece bicycler's outfit, from which pale limbs protruded, with arms and legs spread apart. With her heart beating like a kettle drum in her chest, she quickly realized what she was observing.

"Oh, my god," she whispered, backing away from the pool. She bumped into the wall, her hands over her mouth. "Oh, my god!"

Suppressing the scream in her throat, she raced from the pool, stumbling along as she retraced her steps to the front counter and raced for the elevators. She pushed the *UP* bottom for each.

"Come on, come on," she pleaded to the elevator, rubbing her hands together and shifting anxiously from one foot to the other. Finally, the elevator doors opened, and she rushed into one of them, bumping into Marcellus.

Catching her by the shoulders before she tripped, Marcellus said, with exhilaration and urgency in his expression and his voice, "I see Katherine reached you."

Pauline nearly collapsed with relief in his arms. "Marcellus," she exclaimed in a whisper. As the elevator doors came together, she frantically lunged for them, screaming, "No."

Marcellus put his weight between the doors, and they sprang open. Alertly, he stared down at her troubled expression. "What is it?" he demanded, gripping her by the shoulders.

"In the pool," she said breathlessly. "There's a dead body in the pool."

Chapter Eight

Pauline paced the floor with her arms wrapped around herself as if she were cold. Fear had chilled her to the bone. Taking a deep, unsteady breath, she wondered how many more shocks she could take before she really became unglued.

Not even the incident with Don had shaken her as much as seeing that dead woman. Though she didn't examine the body closely, she had enough chemistry background to know what a high pH level of chlorine mixed in warm water could do to human flesh. Just the thought made her shiver.

She had been unwilling to return to the pool with Marcellus, so he had set her down before she fainted, and gone off to see for himself what she had barely been able to talk about. With her bottom lip folded in her mouth, she eyed the room that was to become the clinic. The walls had recently been painted a pastel pink, and paint fumes overrode the stale smell of disuse. A wooden desk like the kind school teachers used, two black leather-and-chrome chairs, and a beige, multi-buttoned phone had been commandeered from some other office. A roll of mauve carpet was propped against the wall, waiting to cover the cement floor. A loveseat sat alone under the window.

Pauline returned to the chair behind the desk. With elbows on the desk, she propped her chin on her hands, thinking about the dead woman.

Who was she? Who had she left behind? Had the woman lived her life to the fullest, or had she short-changed herself, surviving on weak excuses?

The questions reverted inward, and Pauline sat up as if shot by a hypodermic needle filled with truth. She had been content to accept what life had to offer—without challenge—she thought. While she had made outward changes to her appearance, the place where change really counted remained the same. She had allowed childhood insecurities, born from her abandonment by the parents she never knew, dictate her life. That history of desertion dovetailed into her fear of being rejected by Marcellus, she thought, making it easy for her to convince herself that she was not worthy of a man of his stature and means.

Simply, she had given up on the things that mattered most.

The rueful acceptance of that terrible knowledge caused her throat to ache with remorse, and a hot joyless tear, trickled down her cheek.

Shortly, Marcellus filled her blurry gaze. Dressed in a French-cut charcoal-gray suit that molded his virile physique with its sterling fit, he looked as if he possessed the confidence of a lion. For the second time in a space of minutes, she had never been so glad to see another person in her life. She realized that not just anybody would do, gazing at him in soft scrutiny.

Pauline couldn't deny that his vitality still captivated her. Delight burst through her melancholy like stardust, filling her with enchantment. She may have kicked Marcellus out of her life once, but her love for him had not ceased to be the sovereign ruler in her head, the sacred compartment in her heart.

With a painful-looking smile trembling on her lips, she sniffed and dabbed at the corners of her eyes—a subconscious gesture for approval—but her gaze never left him. He looked back with his twilight eyes, tremendous compassion blazing in their depths.

A bittersweet sob tore from her throat as he approached, his long strides cutting the already small room down to doll-size. He pulled her up next to him and enveloped her in a protective embrace. She cried softly—tears to mend, tinged by regret—against his chest as he rested his chin on the top of her head and gently rubbed her back.

"I'm so sorry you had to see that," Marcellus murmured. "Shhh. It's going to be okay."

In the circle of his arms, she felt as if she really mattered to him. She didn't even care that his comforting ministration was only temporary: a spontaneous, humanitarian reaction to a suffering soul. As he rocked them under gentle control, even the wretched memories vanished. Pressed against his rock-hard body, thoughts ceased to exist and she reveled in his nearness.

A subtle tension simmered in her. Consolation changed. The more he stroked her and whispered words of compassion, the more the latch holding the dam of too-long suppressed desires began to give way to carnal sensations. She wanted Marcellus to take her right here and now. Hugging him tighter to her, arms wrapped around his waist, a whimper of need slipped past her lips. He misinterpreted it as a sob.

"Shh," he said, tightening his hold of her. "I'm here. Come on, stop crying."

Guilty over the wanton betrayal of her body at a time like this, she tried to put distance between them. He rejected the idea with a tug, not letting her move so much as an inch.

He tilted her chin up to look into her face, and she felt certain he could see her want of him in her tear-stained eyes. The flush of humiliation on her face, she lowered her head and closed her eyes.

"Pauline, look at me," Marcellus commanded in a velvet murmur.

Slowly, Pauline raised her head, as her lids lifted over large, liquid eyes. There were smudges of black eyeliner at their corners but, to Marcellus, the mar of imperfection couldn't detract from their serenely compelling luster. She had never showed him this vulnerable side of her personality before, and he felt suffused with gratification.

As he wiped the last bitter tear from her eyes with caring fingers, he was full of remembering what he had tried in vain to forget. Was it just yesterday, Sunday, that he had kissed her lips?

Every jibe he had made about Pauline, every boast to his ability to treat her as if she didn't exist, returned to taunt him and awaken memories of a time when he often hadn't cared whether he woke up in the morning after spending a night with her. The need to recapture that erotic history pervaded every nerve ending in his body; the impulse to take her was a tangible urge.

Unavoidably, he let his attraction, his emotions for an immensely desirable woman, show in his gaze. A smile quivered on his mouth as he stared into the startled fawn expression on her face. Lowering his head, he pressed his mouth to hers, lightly, as if it were a delicacy to savor. The sweet throbbing of her lips increased the tempo of both his pulse and his appetite for more.

She tasted like sunshine, just the way he remembered, and he entwined his tongue with hers in a languid explora-

tion of her mouth. His body hardened, so much so that
he felt the tremor in him vibrate through her. He deepened the kiss, and it was met with an intensity that made
his senses spin. There was passion in their kiss, but something else, as well. It was a quality he couldn't define and
feared labeling.

With a shuddering sigh, reluctantly, he lifted his head
from hers. As he struggled to bring himself under control,
mixed feelings surged through him. Common sense was
outweighed by the warm imprint of her soft lips on his
and a vitality that was zinging through him along with
the notion that he had wasted precious time nursing an
unfounded hatred.

Marcellus searched for a plausible explanation for the
illogical, even though he felt a sense of surety about his
guess. This time when Pauline pulled away, he let her go.

A strange quiet fell over the room. Pauline was staring
up at him with something very fragile in her eyes. Though
he felt as if he should say something, a lump formed in
his throat, then dropped to his stomach like a lead weight.
The words were jumbled somewhere in between that space.

"Pauline, I . . ."

She cut him off, asking in a faint voice, "Marcellus, who
was she?"

For a fraction, Marcellus looked at Pauline, nonplussed.
As his foggy brain cleared, the side of his forehead bore
the brunt of the reminder. *Damn! Pauline had so filled his
mind that he had forgotten about the latest crisis his company
faced.*

"Her name is Ann-Marie Johns," he replied soberly.
"She was Leonard's secretary." He squeezed the flesh of
his eyelids as if massaging his wits to action. "I need to
alert security and call the police." With the receiver in
his hand, he asked, "Are you going to be all right?" He
examined her with his eyes. "Why don't you sit down?"

The white-hot moment between them was gone; the

room temperature returned to normal. Pauline had figuratively and literally squared her delicate shoulders and crawled back into her protective shell. He longed for the woman who had needed him mere seconds ago, not the paragon of strength, broadcasting regal certainty, who was in her place now.

"I'll be fine," she said. But she took his advice, anyway. "You would think I'd never seen a dead body before," she said, in a tone hinting at self-derision. "I don't know what came over me."

"I'm sure you've never seen a body quite like this one," he said as he punched four numbers on the phone and waited. Shortly, he replied, "Clay? This is Marcellus. We've got a problem on our hands. Ann-Marie Johns. No, she's dead. You need to seal off the gym right away, and don't let anybody in until after the police arrive. I'll call them as soon as I hang up. No, I'm in the clinic. Come up when you finish, and I'll fill you in as best I can."

Expelling a deep breath, Marcellus replaced the receiver. He rapped his knuckles on the desk, then stole a quick glance at Pauline, who was looking down at her hands on the desk. He couldn't get over the fact that she still had the power to make him forget a world existed beyond them.

Walking away from the desk, he stood in the doorway, his back to Pauline and his hands clenched in the bottom of his pockets.

"I got a call from the hospital before this," he said in a voice void of excitement or solace.

"What about the hospital?" she asked, her voice animated by anxiety.

"No, no, Don's fine," he replied hastily, turning to face her. "I was just going to say that when I bumped into you on the elevator, I thought you had gotten my message from Katherine to meet me in the lobby."

"He's going to be all right?" she repeated with dumb-founded relief.

"He's going to be all right," he replied, forcing a smile into his voice. "He came out of the coma."

"Oh, that's great," she cried, her voice choking with emotion.

"Yeah," he replied, his expression at once a pleased and bitter mix. "We needed some good news."

Word of Ann-Marie's death spread through the building like a brush fire, and the third floor became a hotbed of frenzied activity. While Marcellus teamed up with Clay to keep vigil on the gym until the police arrived, Pauline opened the clinic for business. Retrieving her black valise from upstairs, she tended the faint-hearted with smelling salts, took blood pressures, and allayed the fears of the nervous with her calm demeanor.

Patrolmen were the first to arrive. They blocked off the crime scene, manned the exits to prevent anyone from leaving, and waited for the detectives. After giving their statements, Pauline and Marcellus were allowed to leave for the hospital.

Anxious and troubled, Marcellus strode from one end of the room to the other. "I don't understand it," he said, pausing mid-stride. "If Don is awake, why can't we see him?"

Standing in front of the mirror above the dresser, comb-ing her hair, Sarah shrugged. Marcellus resumed pacing the carpeted floor in the VIP room at the hospital, which was bright yellow and adorned by pictures of healthy peo-ple. He stopped to glance at the "get well" cards stacked neatly on the small oak desk in a corner of the room.

"Have you talked to Reuben?" he asked.

"No. Not since I was told Donald had come out of the coma," she replied, setting the comb down. "I thought I was going to be able to see him right away, but the nurse said I had to hold off a while." Eyeing herself critically in the mirror, she added, "At least I look more presentable now. I'm not sure, but I think Detective Collins has something to do with it."

Marcellus nodded and dropped into the chair next to the desk, his legs sprawled in front of him and his head resting against the wall. He wondered what was keeping Pauline, who had gone to see what she could find out. "Are you staying at the hospital tonight again?" he asked, sitting upright.

"Yes, why?"

"I want to get in your place to check Don's computer at home," he replied. He had checked Don's computer at the office early that morning before anyone but Security had arrived, he recalled. In a room hidden between the bathroom's adjoining his and Don's office was a workspace where the scientist sometimes worked in private. Don liked to believe his creativity blossomed there, Marcellus smiled musingly. Albeit small, it also housed a service elevator, which was a holdover from the previous owner, who was a suspicious man with a touch of mischief about him: he liked to drop in on his staff without their knowing. But the latest input on the computer was from two days before Marcellus left for D.C., leaving him to conclude that Don had been working on *Project BA* at home.

Sarah removed a key from a ring holding several of them and gave it to him wordlessly.

"Thank you," he said, slipping the key into his pocket.

"Are you and Pauline getting back together?" Sarah asked casually.

Marcellus didn't respond immediately. He didn't even want to think about the subject of his private turmoil. Finally, he replied, "No."

Sarah faced him headlong, her eyes blazing. "Liar. You think I'm so out of it that I could miss that sick puppy-dog look in your eyes," she accused bitterly.

"Sarah, I don't know what you think you see, but . . ."

"Then why are you defending her?" Sarah demanded, cutting him off.

"I'm not defending her," he said, his voice rising. "Your charge is stupid, plain and simple. Not to mention a little disappointing," he said, scolding. "How could you believe Don guilty of having an affair?"

"He's a man. She's a very attractive woman," Sarah mumbled in a barely audible voice.

Marcellus started to speak, then clamped his mouth shut, his features twisted into a disgusted glower. Though Sarah was right on one count—Pauline was indeed beautiful—there was nothing to substantiate her accusation of a romantic liaison between Don and Pauline.

"You won't consider it because of what it might do to your ego," Sarah said sharply.

"Sarah," Marcellus growled tightly, springing to his feet. "I could strangle you."

"Because you know I'm right," she persisted, her tone and look petulant.

As if I don't have enough to worry about, Marcellus thought, blowing out his cheeks. An employee was apparently murdered at the company, his partner was in the hospital for heaven knows how long, and he had to reason with a wife on a matter that was more nuisance than relevant.

"Come here," Marcellus said gently, waving her to him with his hands. Sarah obeyed, and he held her against him. "Don was not having an affair with Pauline or anybody else. I would stake my life on it. He may be guilty of a lot of things, but infidelity is not one of them."

"How do you know?" she asked stubbornly.

Because, even though Pauline and I had been separated, Don wouldn't do that to me. To Sarah, he replied softly, "Because he's madly in love with you. I should be the last person on earth to have to tell you that."

"I know," Sarah mumbled tearfully against his chest. "It's just that . . ." she paused, then fell silent.

Marcellus lifted her face by the chin. "What?" he prodded patiently.

"He wouldn't talk to me," she said, a tear sliding down her cheek. "He seemed to start depending on her a lot lately."

"What do you mean?"

"Even before you left for Washington, he was talking about her. Pauline this and Pauline that, and what a wonderful addition she would make to the company," she said with bitterness in her voice.

"He said that?" Marcellus asked, a bewildered frown on his face.

"That, and a bunch of other half-phrases that he never really explained," she spat out. "Even . . ." she started, then fell silent.

"Sarah," he said as if talking to a recalcitrant child, "that's proof that he wasn't having an affair with Pauline. A man cheating on his wife is not going to rub her nose it in. He wouldn't take that risk."

"Then why didn't he confide in me, if he was troubled about something?"

Passing a hand across his head, Marcellus replied, "Now, that's something I can't answer. He didn't even confide in me."

The door opened, and Pauline appeared. "Excuse me," she said.

"Pauline," Marcellus said with an eager sigh, relieved to see her. "We were just talking about you."

Staring intently at Sarah, Pauline replied, "I bet you were," and backed out the door instantly, letting it close behind her.

"Damn!" Marcellus drawled out. "You stay here," he

said, bolting from the room. In the hallway, he caught up with Pauline at the elevator, where Detective Collins and Dr. Hawse were standing on either side of her. "What's going on here?"

"Let's find someplace private," Dr. Hawse suggested gravely.

"What's going on, Reuben?" Marcellus asked suspiciously, looking back and forth from the doctor to the detective.

"Let's get to the room," Dr. Hawse said.

Pairing off, with Marcellus and Pauline walking side by side, followed by Dr. Reuben and Detective Collins, the foursome returned to Sarah's room. The detective closed the door behind them.

"Reuben?" Marcellus prompted, with concern etched in the ridges of his forehead.

"Don went back into a coma," Dr. Hawse replied with a lengthy sigh.

"Only it's deeper, and he may not wake up again," Detective Collins said, staring pointedly at Pauline.

Sarah gasped.

"I'm sorry, ma'am."

"But I thought . . ." Marcellus said, flabbergasted.

"I know," Dr. Hawse said. "We did, too. But he only came out for a few minutes."

"But long enough," Detective Collins said cryptically.

Looking back and forth between Pauline, who was standing there with a stolid look on her face, and Detective Collins, wearing the smug look of *"Deputy Do-Right,"* Marcellus frowned, puzzled. "Long enough? What the hell does that mean?"

"Long enough to name his murderer," Detective Collins replied. "Miss Sinclair, I'm going to have to ask you to come with me."

For a long second, the silence of shock roared through

the room. Then it exploded into a cacophony of raging voices. Pauline remained uncannily quiet.

"I told you! I told you! I told you!" Sarah screamed hysterically.

"What?" Marcellus yelled. "Of all the asinine deductions, this beats all. No wonder the criminals are having a field day. Where in the world did you get your badge from, Collins, Toys 'R' Us?!"

"I don't have to take that from you, you . . ." Detective Collins roared.

"You see, Marcellus," Sarah said, shouting to be heard. "I'm not the only one who saw the truth."

" 'You,' what?" Marcellus said challengingly, facing the detective as he stared down into his face with a menacing smile.

Striking the air like a conductor, Dr. Hawse called out over the din. "Please, please, everybody calm down. Come on, Sarah, get a hold of yourself."

With the muscles in his jaw twitching, Detective Collins ground out, "Miss Sinclair," his hand extended toward her.

"She's not going anyplace!" Marcellus shouted. Instinctively, he pulled Pauline behind him.

"Everybody settle down!" Dr. Hawse commanded with ill-tempered impatience. All fell quiet. "Now," he said to Marcellus, "before you came, I was trying to reason with Detective Collins." He paused to flash a disgusted look at the detective. "Before Don went back under, he asked for Pauline."

"Asked for her, or called her by name?" Detective Collins retorted. "There is a difference."

"But we don't know for sure what he meant," Dr. Hawse argued vehemently. "He could simply have remembered that Pauline performed the CPR that saved his life."

"Or he could have remembered she was the last person to see him alive and well," Detective Collins retorted argumentatively. "She's a nurse, so she has the means. The last person to see him alive, she had the opportunity. The only thing missing at this point is a motive. And I'm sure I'll find it, won't I, Miss Sinclair?"

"Unless you're charging her with something, she's staying right here," Marcellus said, his brows drawn together in a contentious scowl.

Ignoring Marcellus, the detective addressed Pauline kindly. "If you cooperate with us, it'll be easier for you, Miss Sinclair," he said in a lowered voice, thoughtfulness in his tone. "I can take you in without a warrant, you know."

"If you're going to take her in, read her her rights, and I'll advise her not to say anything to you," Marcellus said, his fiery eyes narrowed.

Detective Collins arched a brow of warning at Marcellus. "Mr. Cavanaugh, I can take you in for obstruction of justice," he threatened.

"I've prevented you from doing nothing, Detective Collins," Marcellus replied. "I'm advising my client."

Tension was at a breaking point. As though there had been a declaration of war between them, Marcellus's eyes glowed with malevolence as he stared at Detective Collins, and the detective returned the look with one of his own. Sarah whimpered, then threw herself across the bed, crying piteously.

Expressionless, Detective Collins said in a quiet voice, "I understand I have another murder to attend to at your company, Mr. Cavanaugh."

"As far as I know, and I'm sad to have to admit even that, Detective," Marcellus retorted, "there's only been *one* murder."

With a nod, Detective Collins spun around and walked to the door. Opening it, he said over his shoulder, "Don't leave town, Miss Sinclair. I have a feeling I'll be back."

* * *

Standing at the washbowl in the ladies' room, Pauline splashed cold water on her face. Lifting her head, she wiped her face dry with starch-like paper towels, then looked in the mirror. Strangely veiled brown eyes stared back at her.

Strain-tight muscles popped as she rolled her head around her neck. She felt battered, victimized by a cruel irony: accused of trying to murder the man whose life she had tried to save.

With the detective's charge at the forefront of her mind, she reflected that it dovetailed Sarah's conviction of her guilt. But Sarah had to get the idea from some place, she thought, wondering from where, or whom?

Tossing the paper in the trash can, she sauntered into the adjoining sitting area and dropped onto the couch, radiating bleakness. She should have listened to her second mind and stayed in bed this morning. If only Don hadn't muttered her name, or better still, hadn't fallen into a deeper coma before explaining what he meant. If only she had refused his request, she wouldn't be in this predicament.

She also wouldn't have learned a truth that had eluded her about herself, she mused. Letting the back of her head hit the wall, she moaned with frustration. Along with all the thoughts that were running wild in her head, one was frightfully clear. If she didn't find out who had tried to kill Don, she was going to wind up in prison, baking cookies for her sorors in crime.

As for Marcellus, there was no more denying her feelings for him. She hadn't gotten over him where it really counted—in her head.

Taking a deep breath, she pushed herself to her feet wearily. Though she wanted nothing more than to go home, such passivity was not going to change the dilemmas she was facing. Besides, she and Marcellus had come to the hospital in her car, and he expected her to take him back to CSI.

Opening the door to leave, she spotted a policeman coming in her direction. He was the same officer who was stationed at the entrance of the intensive care unit. Quickly, she closed the door slightly, leaving just enough of a crack to see where he was headed. He strode pass the ladies room to the elevators. Within seconds, a car arrived, and he stepped inside and was gone.

A kernel of hope burst in Pauline. This was her chance to see Don, she thought, her gaze sweeping up and down the hallway. But to what avail? He could tell her nothing. And if she were caught in his room, she could kiss her freedom good-bye.

Pauline stepped out into the hallway. She just had to see Don. Maybe it would help her remember something significant that she had overlooked. Maybe he would wake up and tell her what happened.

Maybe . . . maybe . . . maybe. Her head was full of them as she sauntered down the hall, trying to look as inconspicuous as possible. A nurse walked out of a patient's room, carrying a tray of medications. Pauline felt her heart slide up to her throat. All she could evoke was a courteous smile and a friendly nod as she continued as if on remote control.

With fear coiled in her stomach like a snake, she hesitated at the double doors of the intensive care unit. Her hands were sweaty with anxiety, and she wiped them on her skirt. Then, like someone about to plunge into icy water, she took a quick intake of breath and pushed open the doors.

The hum of life-sustaining machines was constant in the quiet. A single path divided the unit in half. Patients hanging onto life by the marvels of technology were sequestered behind see-through plastic partitions on either side of the hallway.

Nearing the last cubicle on the left, Pauline slowed her steps, stopping inches from revealing herself. From Don's room, she heard Marcellus talking in an utterly frustrated, musing tone of voice.

"I feel as if my whole damn world is spinning on a roller-coaster axis and jarring normalcy loose. It's crazy, and, no doubt, it will take a far more intelligent person than I am to figure it out. And to think: problem solving used to be my forte," he chuckled sarcastically. "Right now, I don't think I could figure my way out of a paper bag."

Pauline took another step and peered inside, without being able to be seen through the plastic door. A respirator sat beside the bed, where Don looked as if he were enjoying a peaceful sleep. Only the IV drip, feeding liquid protein into his body, destroyed the illusion. Marcellus's back was to her; he was sitting in a chair inches from the side of the bed.

"I certainly could use your help right about now," Marcellus said, running a hand across his head. He got to his feet sluggishly and sauntered to the foot of the bed. Leaning against the footrail, he said, "In addition to our business coming apart at the seams—I won't bore you with the details—my personal life is tied up in stitches. Pauline is back. But, of course, you already know that." Hitting the rail with the ball of his hand, he returned to the chair. "And I'd have you know I'm feeling a might ambivalent that you made such a drastic decision without consulting me. But I have to figure you must have had a damn good reason. I only wish you would have shared it with me."

Pauline watched as Marcellus picked up Don's hand. She knew the pale, white limb was cold between the warm, affectionate clasp. Her lips quivered, and she had to swallow back the lump that formed in her throat.

"I know I haven't been too social over the past several months," he said, placing Don's hand alongside his body with care. "I'd like to blame it on the mess with Congressman Barrows, but I wouldn't dare give him that much credit. Plain and simple, it's been me. When you get out of here and we put everything back in order, I think I'll take some time off. I need to get my head in order. It's crazy, you know, this whole thing with Pauline," he said ruminatively, then he sighed. "I don't know if it's just because she's changed or if I have, but ..." he lapsed into silence. "Hell, maybe I'm just horny," he chuckled sardonically. "A bachelor's life ain't all what it's cracked up to be. I never told you why we broke up. And now, I'm even more reluctant to tell you because ..."

With the uncomfortable feeling of overstaying one's welcome, Pauline backed away quietly. Hurrying down the hall of the ward, she thought that she really shouldn't make too much of Marcellus's disclosure. When people were confused, they had a tendency to ramble, only to discover later that they didn't mean what they'd said. Still, she felt as if she were pinned between slabs of guilt and gratification for listening to a confession intended only for the ears of a friend.

With the phrase *ears of a friend* echoing in her mind, her steps slowed to a halt. Something about the refrain set the gears churning in her brain. Stereotypical or not, women seemed to be particularly known for telling their friends about their private lives, she thought, pondering whether Sarah had someone in whom she confided. And suppose that friend helped Sarah reach the conclusion that Don was having an affair? She would have been a likely candidate, Pauline mused, because Don must have mentioned that he intended hiring her. Even though farfetched, it was plausible that Sarah would suspect her.

"A friend just might be a good place to start looking for answers," Pauline whispered aloud to herself. Maybe Katherine could help her there, and CSI was the ideal place to start.

In deep thought about her new plan, Pauline headed

straight for the elevators and pressed the button. Within seconds, one arrived, debarking its passenger, the Webster police officer. She had gotten out of ICU just in the nick of time.

A gentleman, he held the door open with his body, for his hands were full with a large plastic cup of coffee and a saucer of donuts.

"Thank you," she said.

"You're welcome, ma'am," he replied, in a hat-tipping tone of voice.

Pressing the button for the lobby, Pauline was already thinking ahead. Her insides were like a jet engine, raring to go.

Chapter Nine

"Hold the elevator!"

Nudged out of her musings by the late passenger, Pauline quickly pressed the *Hold* button just as the doors were closing. She couldn't believe she had forgotten Marcellus, even momentarily. The doors rattled open and he stepped inside the car. In that instant, a cold, lucid thought came to her mind: If she were in jail, she might never again feel his sweet, soothing caresses, or the medley of erotic emotions he sparked in her.

And she very much wanted to experience those sensations again, she realized with utter astonishment.

"I thought you were going to wait for me," Marcellus said. "Where were you going?"

His presence on the heels of her salacious musing arrested Pauline's pulse. "I guess I wasn't thinking," she stammered, talking with her hands. "Well, really, I was, but not about what . . . Oh, never mind."

His voice rumbled with laughter as he replied, "I'm glad you got it off your chest."

Pauline sighed heartily, gathering her wits. "I was thinking about Sarah," she said. "I have an idea I'd like to
follow up on."

"You've got my undivided attention," he said, folding
his arms across his broad chest as he leaned against the
back of the car.

With second-thought twinges, she debated whether to
tell him. Recalling his chauvinistic tendencies, she knew
the likelihood that he would chalk it up as woman's intu-
ition, and ignore its value.

"Well?" he prodded.

Pauline's eyes slid up into his black-eyed gaze, and before
she could put a value on his look or lose her nerves, she
blurted, "I got to thinking that Sarah must have gotten
the notion about this grand affair Don and I are supposed
to be carrying on from somewhere. It dawned on me that
maybe she talked to someone about it, you know, like a
girlfriend. Now, all I have to do is find out who she's close
to, then maybe I can figure out where she got the idea
from."

"Not bad thinking," he replied cautiously, as if not wanting to hurt her feelings, "but first, you have to find this
person."

Despite his less-than-enthusiastic response, she had an
answer for his skepticism. "I thought maybe Katherine
could help me there."

"Okay," he nodded thoughtfully, "say you do find this
person, how do you know she will tell you anything?" He
paused to let the thought sink in. "Assuming it's another
woman, which is a fairly good guess, you have to figure
that she won't tell you anything, because she'll see you as
the other woman who's destroying her friend's marriage."

While he encouraged her to pursue her plan of action,
Pauline mused, it was clear he wanted no part of it, and
that stung. "You're trying to kill my last hope?" she asked
accusingly, fighting her disappointment.

"I'm sorry," he replied contritely. "I didn't say it couldn't work," he added, draping a warm arm across her shoulders. "Or that we shouldn't try. Hell, it's better than what Collins seems to have done so far," he added, with a note of scorn in his voice.

For a moment, Sarah, Detective Collins, and even her idea slipped Pauline's mind. She was trying to breathe without giving away the fact that her rate of respiration had significantly increased. His touch was a courteous one, and she should have been used to it by now, she told herself. If not the actual feel of a part of him physically touching a part of her, then, at least, the reaction it inspired within her. She was embarrassed by the swell of her bosom straining against the silk teddy underneath her suit coat; the nipples tight, begging to be stroked.

"I want you to stay at my house," he commanded in a soft drawl.

Backing out from under his embrace to frown up at him, she replied stunned, "What?"

Though she breathed a little easier, she seemed to have developed an ultra-keen sense of smell. The manly scent of his aftershave stoked the steady flame of her arousal. She felt like a child who had been warned away from a hot fire, but who touched it anyway, knowing the high probability of getting burned.

The elevator doors opened. Pauline exhaled a relieved sigh as they piled off the elevator. A crowd was waiting to get on. Side-by-side, they walked to the automatic doors at the front of the hospital and out into the bright, mid-day breeze, heading for her car in the adjacent parking lot.

"Drop me off at Don and Sarah's," Marcellus said, matching his stride to hers. "It shouldn't take long, but I suspect you won't want to wait around," he added with a knowing nod.

"You got that right," she quipped. "But what is it that you have to do at their house?"

"I want to check into Don's computer," he replied. "See if I can find something that will give us a clue as to what's going on. He started a new project that only the two of us know about. At least, I hope that's still the case."

"Well, I'm going to put my plan in action," Pauline said. "See what I'll be able to find out at CSI."

"Collins will be there," he reminded her.

"Oh, hell!" Pauline exclaimed crankily. She forgot that the detective was heading for CSI to investigate Ann-Marie's murder.

"Should he get a warrant," Marcellus continued, "he'll have to find you to serve it. He can't serve it if he can't find you. Meanwhile, I'll contact an attorney friend of mine who specializes in criminal law."

Pauline felt uncomfortable and realized it was because she didn't want to be beholden to Marcellus. Gratitude had gotten her in trouble before, she mused. "Marcellus, you don't . . ." she began, hesitantly.

Cutting her off, he said, "We probably won't need her services, but just to be on the safe side, I'll give her a call when I get to Don's."

It was good some things hadn't changed, she supposed sarcastically, noting his usual take-charge tendencies. "So, I'm just supposed to sit around your house like a good little woman while you have all the fun?" she said with dry amusement in her voice as they reached her car.

"Yeah, it's time you learn your place," Marcellus replied.

He unfurled an easy smile that was generous, rare, and disarmingly intimate. Even if she had had a retort ready on her tongue, Pauline's heart seemed to have lodged itself in her throat, and she couldn't speak. Staring stupefied and trembling like a sensualist, she didn't realize that he had

taken the car keys from her and was holding open the
passenger's door, waiting for her to get in.

"Let's go, little woman."

There was dead silence. Nothing stirred but his unteth-
ered emotions for Pauline. Marcellus listened and waited
until he no longer heard the motor of her car in the
driveway before proceeding through the dark house.
Though shafts of light shone through various openings,he
needed no lights, for he knew Don and Sarah's home
almost as well as his own.

He stood in the doorway of the study and wondered why
his heart was beating so fast. Residuals of the craving he
felt towards Pauline, or fear about what he might find
housed in Don's computer? He coughed into his fist and
decided it was performance anxiety. He hated to admit it,
but confronting his partner's computer was a little daunting.

But no more so than owning up to those compelling
sensations that booted him with every nudging thought of
Pauline, the silent cynic inside him heckled.

He'd better forget her for the time being and concentrate on providing answers to the horrendous events plagu-
ing his company, lest she be charged with responsibility
for them. Then he'd really have something to worry about.

Marcellus flipped on the light in the room. The walls
were walnut panels; one side contained shelves of books
from the ceiling to the floor. But that was where the token
hints that adults lived here ended, because the rest of the
spacious room looked like a kid's toy room . . . a kid with
a serious fascination with space.

A four-feet-high model rocket sat in one corner on a
porcelain pedestal, while a pair of bootless inline skates
were in the middle of the carpeted floor. Two older ver-
sions of robots stood quietly in another corner under *Star*

Trek posters. He knew that with a flip of a switch, the planets would revolve around the sun over the far corner of the L-shaped bar. They looked heavy like steel, but they were actually made of fiberglass.

Stepping onto the *Aladdin* rug runner, he went straight to the bar, where the telephone sat on the corner. He dialed a Houston number and, after two rings, it was answered.

"Mr. Cavanaugh for Ms. Dottie West, please."

Waiting for her to come to the phone, he recalled meeting Dottie for the first time about five years ago at a lawyer's social. She had drunk him under the table, while making a good argument for changing the Constitution. She was one of those super-assertive women who could scare the pants off an insecure man. The attitude helped in her law practice, since her clients, who were guilty more times than not, quickly learned that it was not advisable to lie to Dottie. He never tried.

She came on the line shortly and, without preamble, he relayed the incidents and a request for her help. Before ringing off, he gave her Pauline's home number . . . just in case. That task completed, he headed for the computer nook far back in the room. He sat before the desk in front of a multiprocessor stacked higher than the screen and keyboard of the computer.

It was an awesome machine, stark white, designed for speed. He didn't fully understand the technology behind it, but he knew the power lay in the chips. Still, he sighed deeply, as if preparing himself for a great challenge, as he booted up the computer.

His partner was a genius; his thirst for learning knew no bounds, and it encompassed more than science, space, and technology, Marcellus mused. He watched the computer come to life. As a hobby, Don studied KMT, which, when translated from the *Medu Netcher,* the language of ancient Egypt, meant *people of the black land.* His lack of

knowledge of his ancient African history had once shamed
Marcellus. But that was no longer true, for he had tackled
the subject with the same zealous drive he had used to
prove his worth to those that mattered. They now made a
game of it. Besides, to access Don's files, he had to be
similarly versed.

In fact, it was he who had come up with the name for
their current project, once Don had explained the details
of the undertaking. In essence, the idea was to create
the sum and substance of man—a thinking, perceptive
humanoid. It was knowledge based on his readings
explaining why the Kemetians mummified their dead that
had allowed him to contribute to their current project.
The ancients believed that the survival of the body was
necessary for survival of the other aspects of their being,
called the *ka,* the *ba,* and the *akh.*

The computer screen settled, and the pointer awaited
Marcellus's command. His eyes scrolled the many files.
There were formula names, as well as those in plain
English: *Project Ba* was one of them. He double-clicked the
representative box, then waited. Rather than plain text, it
opened onto an image of colors and shapes that finally
arranged themselves to compose the *udjat-eye.*

Marcellus chuckled at Don's attempt to best him again.
The image represented the eye of Horus, who was the
son born of an immaculate conception to Osiris and Isis.
According to legend, Osiris's evil brother, Seth, murdered
him, and Horus was raised secretly by Isis to avenge his
father's death. During the battle with Seth, his eye had
been knocked out, only to be restored later by Thoth, the
god of wisdom and magic.

Marcellus wished for a dose of each; he recognized the
symbolic meaning readily. He felt the onslaught of anxiety,
his insides trembling with a bad premonition. The symbol
was a protection against evil, and represented light or truth.
Presently, it raised a more pressing concern in him, as he

stared at the request for the *PASSWORD* that flashed on the screen.

The frown on his face deepened, as did his apprehension. He expected to be allowed directly into text. Apparently, Don had changed the sequence of entry. Reigning in the distress signal buzzing inside him, he popped his knuckles over the keyboard, his expression set in grim determination.

"All right, buddy, let's see what you got."

He typed *Ka*. It was the spiritual copy of the body with all its needs, desires, and expectations. Ghostly in appearance, it was stored in the heart. But it was not the password.

He tried the project name next, typing *Ba*. The *ba* encompassed the total, non-physical aspects of an individual which constitute his character or personality. It wasn't the password, either.

Marcellus sighed at length, typing *Akh*, the entity in which the dead existed in the afterworld. Neither was it the opener into the file.

"Damnit, Don, this is not the time for games," he said, growing frustrated. "All right, let's try this." He typed *Kmt;* he was still denied access into the file.

Wondering if his playful, competitive partner had changed the circle of codes to throw him off, but without introducing a new term—as had been their tacit agreement—he tried them all together. *Bakaakh.*

The eye shifted as if about to change shape, then reformed into its previous design. The demand for the *PASSWORD* returned to taunt him.

Marcellus reared back in his chair, staring at the screen, his face set in a pensive expression. Though he was certainly dismayed that he couldn't access the file, he felt the weight of an even more frightening thought. It seemed certain now that the code changes reflected Don's suspicion or knowledge that someone was trying to steal company secrets.

* * *

His house? Her house?

Pauline had settled the debate hours ago, when she caught herself wondering whether one of the houses could become their home.

The dark secret at her core was out. She needed space from Marcellus to deal with her discovery. It wasn't exactly serendipitous, but it was an amazing revelation, nevertheless. Returning to her home had saved Ms. West a trip, as well, she added to her muse.

"Won't you come in, Ms. West?" Pauline asked in invitation, holding open the door to her home.

Their preliminary introduction had been made over the phone, when the attorney called to confirm the location of their meeting. It lessened the shock of memory Pauline experienced, remembering she had taken a call from Dottie West at Marcellus's. She also recalled the unflattering thoughts she had harbored for the woman.

"I'm Dorothy, but my friends call me Dottie."

Feeling the attorney size her up as—she reciprocated the examination—Pauline was pleased that she had decided to shower and change. Confident and successful-looking, Dottie West was a stunning-looking woman in every way, from a thick mane of shoulder-length auburn hair, down to her narrow feet, encased in expensive high-heeled shoes. This was the kind of woman Marcellus deserved, she thought, insecurity rearing its ugly head.

Dottie West adjusted the alligator briefcase to her left hand and extended her right. Accepting the proffered hand, Pauline replied, "All right . . . Dottie," reconciling herself to the frivolous name. "I'll take that for you." Taking the overcoat Dottie shed, she led the way to her combination den and dining area. "Have a seat; I'll just hang this in the closet."

Pauline returned shortly, to find Dottie standing in front

of the television that was tucked into a corner wall-cabinet unit. The six o'clock news was on, and the camera showed a scene recorded earlier in the day. Weeping employees crowded in front of the CavWell Space Industries building as two uniformed men carried a black body bag to the waiting ambulance. The view switched to a reporter announcing live coverage, as the camera focused on Marcellus leaving the building.

Mourning sat on his handsome face, his eyebrows drawn together and his lips pursed in an expression of agony. It was a look that would bring anyone to tears. Pauline wanted to run to him, to hold him in her arms and soothe the sorrow from his dispirited soul. Unconsciously, she reached for the screen, then quickly, pulled her hand back down to her side.

"We have no comment at this time, thank you," Marcellus replied to the reporter who had shoved a microphone in his face.

With longing a steady beat in her pulse, Pauline's eyes followed the camera as it panned to catch Marcellus rushing to get inside a waiting car. There was a strange symmetry about the events at CSI and her presence there, she mused. She didn't like thinking that what had happened to Donald or Ann-Marie was fate. That left only one thing . . . conspiracy. As for what she felt for Marcellus— although it seemed that fate was playing a game of intrigue with her heart and her mind—she preferred to leave that open.

Dottie clicked off the television, and Pauline felt as if she had been freed from a dramatic episode. "Can I get you something to drink?" she inquired, her voice wavering. "I was about to pour myself a glass of wine."

"That would be fine," Dottie replied, sitting on the couch.

Pauline returned quickly with two crystal wine glasses. Dottie had already laid out a yellow legal pad and a ball-point pen on the coffee table, and she was taking out a pack of cigarettes and a gold lighter from her handbag.

"Do you mind?" Dottie asked, eyeing Pauline through the flame of the lighter.

"I prefer that you don't," Pauline said with hesitation in her voice. She set the glass of white wine on the table near Dottie, whose face, she saw, showed need for a nicotine fix. "If you have to," she relented, "I guess I can tolerate one." She held up a finger for emphasis, although she really felt that she could have used one herself.

"I have to," Dottie replied, lighting the cigarette.

Pauline tried to suppress her distaste as she watched Dottie drag on the cigarette as though sucking in oxygen. The burning tobacco hit the air, and the smoke caused her nose to twitch. She left the room, and returned shortly with a makeshift ashtray. Wordlessly, she set the saucer on the coffee table.

"Just this one," Dottie promised, the cigarette between her fingers. Slipping the lighter and pack back into her handbag, she sniffed the air in delight at the aromas coming from the kitchen. "Smells delicious in here. What's cooking?"

"Cooked already," Pauline replied. "Seared salmon with sweet corn, mushrooms, and spinach, and a lemon pound cake," Pauline replied proudly. "I've had plenty of time to kill." And think. Unfortunately, the only thing she had to show for it was dinner.

"You've used your time most productively," Dottie replied with an appreciative moan.

Pauline didn't know if the sound of Dottie's savoring was for the dinner or the cigarette. "There's more than enough," she offered.

After a second of thought and a glance at the cigarette, Dottie replied, "You're on." She smashed the cigarette out, picked up her drink, and followed Pauline to the kitchen.

"I hope you don't mind eating at the breakfast table," Pauline said, uncomfortable with the intervals of quiet. "I'm not up to pulling down fine china tonight."

Sitting at the table, Dottie replied, "Are you kidding? I'd eat on the floor. My dinner plans had included a microwave TV dinner of the low-calorie variety."

As Pauline set about preparing to feed her unexpected dinner guest, Dottie asked, "How did you happen to start working at CSI? I haven't heard *your* name mentioned in a *looong* time." Stunned, Pauline spun to face Dottie. "Don't look so surprised," the attorney explained laughing. "Marcellus used to talk about you all the time, though he didn't want to share you with anyone else—then he forbade everyone even to mention your name."

She had often wondered why Marcellus had never introduced her to his friends, except for Donald Wellsing and his parents. And, for a while, she had reveled in their cozy dyad, she recalled, only to wonder later whether it was because he was ashamed of her. After all, she was not from his social class, as Dottie was.

"I thought, uh . . ."

"That he and I were lovers?" Dottie supplied. "No way." She laughed, a hearty chuckle. "We're just good friends and, believe me, we could never be anything more to each other except that." She drank a sip of wine, then added, "We're too much alike. And besides, I'm married to my work." She took another sip of wine, then set the glass on the counter. "Now, back to you."

Pauline grimaced at her transparency. "Why did you go out of your way to assure me of that?" she wondered aloud.

Dottie pinned her with quartzlike eyes. They were brownish, piercing, and beneath the intelligence, they glowed with a strange kinship. "I guess because I sensed you needed to hear it," she replied softly.

Dottie West didn't strike her as the kind of person who did or said anything she didn't mean, either to an intimate or a stranger. Pauline nodded her head singularly before she spoke.

"It started when Don asked me to work for the company," she replied, getting two plates down from an overhead cabinet. "It seems like eons ago, now, but it was only last week. Anyway, he knew I worked for a temporary nursing agency, and he told me that he felt the company needed a nurse."

"Did he say why?"

At the start of the interrogation, Pauline believed she could answer the questions in her sleep because she had repeated them so many times. The only difference was that Dottie was a more unbiased listener, she thought, standing at the stove filling plates.

"They must be doing some dangerous work over there," Dottie said. She took a plate from Pauline, then sat at the table. Pauline joined her, then said a silent prayer before she spoke.

"I don't know," she said, shaking open a napkin to spread across her lap. "I had a folder of materials to read about the company and its research, but I left it at the office, so I'm not really sure what kind of research they do over there."

"If it's needed, I can get that later," Dottie said, putting a bite into her mouth. "Mm, this is delicious," she declared. "Then what?"

Pauline never got a chance to express her gratitude to Dottie's appreciation of the meal, for the attorney kept a steady barrage of questions going. "What about this woman you found in the pool? What was her name again?" Dottie asked as she chewed.

"Ann-Marie," Pauline replied. "Ann-Marie Johns. I never heard of her before today."

"How did you happen to find the body?"

Snorting sarcastically, Pauline said, "Just my dumb luck." She picked up her fork, then set it back on her plate. "I was really on my way to the clinic. I didn't have a good reason for going to the gym. I just did," she said, shrugging. "See . . . I had no idea what I was supposed to do at CSI when I got there this morning and discovered that Marcellus wanted me to have keys to the building."

"You were feeling overwhelmed," Dottie said. "That's understandable. Then what?"

"Well, I hadn't had a chance to check out the gym," Pauline said. "So I went to have a look. Everything seemed fine until I walked into the ladies' locker room."

"What was wrong in the locker room?"

"I could smell the chlorine from the pool," Pauline said.

"Isn't that normal?" Dottie said. "It seems that every time I go to the gym, it takes forever to get that Clorox smell out of my nose, even if I don't get in the pool."

"Yeah, but this was different," she replied somberly, her thoughts filtering back to that time. Though she relayed her story from rote memory, her appetite had waned by the time she finished. She pushed aside her plate and reached for her glass of wine.

"Did you touch it?"

Shaking her head, Pauline replied, "No way. I ran out of there like I was being chased by the boogie man. Oh, but I did put my hand in the water."

Chuckling, Dottie said, "Don't worry. It's not traceable."

"No, you don't understand," Pauline said with a sense of urgency. "Compared to normal pool temperature, the water was hot. That's what caused the chlorine to mist up like that."

Setting her fork on the side of her plate, Dottie picked up her glass of wine, her actions as quiet as her expression. "Okay," she said, nodding her head thoughtfully.

"Okay, what?" Pauline asked.

"Okay, somebody tried to mask the smell of a dead body," she replied, as if talking to herself, tapping the glass with a long manicured rose-frost nail.

Pauline felt little relief that Dottie shared her conclusion. "Now I wished I would have checked thoroughly. At least then I would have been able to hazard a guess about the killer's intention, after I'd seen the condition of the body and tried to determine how long it had been in the water."

"Oh?"

"When you add warm water to a high-enough concentration of chlorine to cause a mist, after several days decomposition is inevitable," Pauline replied. "Had the water been cold, the chlorine wouldn't have vaporized, and decomposition would have been retarded."

"You know this stuff, don't you?" Dottie asked, staring at Pauline, lips pressed together.

As if in slow motion, Pauline straightened to sit stiffly in her chair. "I'm a nurse," she replied warily. "I studied chemistry." She wrapped her hands around the stem of the glass.

Reaching across the table to cover Pauline's hand with her own, Dottie replied, "No, don't get me wrong. I didn't mean anything by that except to point out what the detective will look at in terms of means. You have the knowledge."

With nervous fluttering pricking her chest, Pauline asked, incredulously, "Do you think the police are going to suspect me of killing Ann-Marie?"

"I don't know," Dottie replied. "But don't worry. Too much," she amended, a hint of a smile on her thin lips. "That's why Marcellus called me," she said, putting more food into her mouth. "I don't believe they have a leg to stand on."

"What about Sarah's claims?"

"Sarah sounds guilty of something," Dottie said, taking a sip of wine. "Pay her no mind."

"Tell that to Detective Collins," Pauline said, forking a bite of salmon.

"You have to understand that you're the most convenient suspect right now," Dottie said. "The finger is being pointed at you, and probably by more people than Sarah. He can't overlook that fact; he has to start with what he can prove, the known. But since he hasn't taken you in . . ." she fell silent, shaking her head with a musing smile, "when Marcellus told me about his grandstanding at the hospital today, I cringed. Anyway, he hasn't taken you in. That means he still has too many holes he can't fill. Right now, all the evidence he has against you is barely circumstantial."

"Can he take me in?"

"Oh, most definitely," Dottie replied. "And if that happens, go along quietly, and stay that way until I get there," she said, with emphasis in her voice. "I want you to be very clear about that, Pauline. Say absolutely nothing until I arrive. Got that?"

A single low beam of light followed the soft click of a closing door. Guided by a steady hand, it made a slow sweep of the room, landing on the desk.

Reacquainted with the surroundings in the dark, the holder of the light walked to the desk. With purpose and efficiency, the desk received a thorough search; each drawer was opened, examined, then closed, before similar care was inflicted on the next.

Simple. That was the operative word. Though there was no disputing his genius, Don liked simple things.

The light moved, beaming onto the wall over the couch to encompass a trio of photographs depicting NASA's first age of interplanetary exploration. The *Luna* and the *Lunar Orbiter* were on either side of the *Ranger*. All were spacecraft of the 60's that had explored outer space for the first time in the history of mankind.

Don was also sentimental.

The light shook slightly with the movement of sardonic mirth of the holder, before changing direction to scan more of the room. *Simple,* the light holder thought, while absently musing the reminders of space exploration.

NASA was in its fourth age of exploration. Hopes were pinned on a new miniaturized, high-tech craft exemplified by the New Millennium spacecraft. A photo of it hung in a frame on the side wall over the bar. It looked like a butterfly with blue-paneled wings spread from its metallic-gray, socket-like body.

The New Millennium was scheduled for a 1998 launch. It featured a solar-electric propulsion system, which CSI—or, more specifically, Don Wellsing—had had a hand in developing. It was simple in comparison to the *Pluto Express,* which had been launched in '95, but more important, plans called for it to be an autonomous space-craft.

The country wanted down-to-earth prices for its out-of-space program, the holder thought snidely. At one point, NASA was given whatever it wanted to beat the Russians to the moon. Since the 80's, the agency had been scraping for money. Each *Discovery* mission had to come in under $150 million, with less than $35 million for operating costs, and a maximum development time of three years.

Currently, about a third of a mission's budget was spent on personnel who were responsible for monitoring the spacecraft's systems, making decisions, and ordering ma-neuvers. The goal was to reduce the operating staff to twelve. But a humanoid—a robot who could perform most, if not all, of those duties—would cut that number to less than half. Such savings would be astronomical, and the owner of the invention could rule the world or, better yet, space.

The light was held on a charcoal sketch of Sarah Wellsing. *Simple. Sentimental.*

Chapter Ten

Only the cleaning crew and the security guards were present when Pauline arrived at CavWell Space Industries the following morning. It was another one of those weather-record-breaking March days, the temperature around fifty, with a chilly wind blowing across the white face of the sun that was yawning in a cloudless sky.

A beat-up looking black van with WILSON INDUSTRIAL MAINTENANCE & CLEANING etched in bold white letters on the side was the lone vehicle in the parking lot. A CSI security guard, padded against the cold, drove across the front of the building in a motor cart. He peered at Pauline as she got out of her car, spoke into his walkie-talkie, then flashed her a salute and drove on.

She pulled her long, all-weather coat around her tightly and walked briskly across the parking lot, heading for the front door.

It was only upon waking this morning after a fitful sleep that she had decided to return. She really had no choice, she reminded herself. Implicated in deadly developments beyond her control, she had to find out who was manipulating her life, whether it was deliberate or she had become a handy pawn in someone's sinister games. She also planned to implement her idea. Although Marcellus had no belief in it, she intended to start by talking with Katherine, whom she assumed would also arrive early.

Entering the warm building, she headed for the elevators, unbuttoning her coat. She pressed the elevator buttons, and both cars arrived simultaneously. As she was about to step onto one, she gleamed the impression from the corner of her eye of a tall, stout woman in uniform dress getting off the other car. It made her remember having felt a sense of purpose upon being granted carte blanche by Marcellus yesterday. Until she realized differently, she thought, shuddering, knowing that a killer had been responsible for the carnage in the pool.

During the quiet ride on the elevator, Pauline thought about the risk she was taking and sighed heavily. That she would see Marcellus again was a foregone conclusion. She didn't know what to expect from him and didn't want to guess; if she did she would tire herself out before the day got started. She could only hope that, by then, some flash of genius would come to her and help ease the moment.

She hadn't resolved her other dilemma, either. And loving Marcellus was certainly that. But she wasn't the first, nor would she be the last, woman who had loved wrongly, she reminded herself. The admission was of little comfort.

The elevator stopped, the doors opened, and Pauline stepped off. She looked both ways up and down the corridor. Hearing nothing but the roar of silence in her head, she headed for Donald's office, walking lightly as if not to disturb the quiet.

It was too soon to call in the FBI.

Shaving cream smoothed over his cheeks and jaw, a

towel draped around the back of his neck, Marcellus looked down at the file opened on his desk. It was labeled VACATIONS.

Angry disapproval showed in the wrinkles lining his forehead, though his eyes showed the tortured dullness of disbelief. He pulled at the ends of the towel, tightening the pressure and sighed as if exhausted.

When he and Don started the company, even though they discussed it, never in their wildest imagination did they actually believe that spies would pose a problem: the elaborate security they employed was to keep potential thieves of their inventions out. They had banked on thorough interviews and background searches to cull the duds from the launchers and hire the kind of people who were not only qualified, but loyal. They certainly paid for those qualities in their salaries but, apparently, someone wanted more.

Albeit disheartened, he started his guesswork with the executives of CSI: and topping the short list was Dr. Jacqueline Trent. Seeing her vacation request, he was ready to convict her. It was dated the day after he left for D.C., to start two weeks after his return. One week remained before the 'Mad Scientist' would embark on a three-week absence. However, his excitement was deflated like a punctured hot air balloon. Don had also filed a vacation request that would have began upon his scheduled return from D.C.

J.T. had her quirks, he conceded with an exhausted sigh. Still, if it was *Project Ba* that someone was after, she had both the contacts and wherewithal to explain Don's genius. If he had completed the humanoid, she would know how to make it work.

Then there was Thomas Webster who kept their computers running at high-peak performance. He was capable, but not personable—except to his computers. He could also break into any computer, Marcellus reminded himself, his face squinting as if he were in pain.

Last, but not least, was Leonard Coombs, whose genius lay in personnel administration and development. Ask him about the best insurance, and he need only be told how much you wanted to spend. Beyond that, he was out of his depth.

Which one?

With the executives' names rolling round like loose marbles in his head, Marcellus wondered if his list was too short. If only he knew whether his partner had struck pay dirt.

Exhaling a frustrated sigh of finality, he closed the folder and began thinking about hiring a private investigator. If he were wrong, then no one of significance would be the wiser, he told himself, strolling to the small bathroom adjoining his office. He stood over the sink in front of the mirror, picked up a throw-away razor from the counter and begin shaving.

He'd been at the office since five-thirty. But he could have spent the night for all the sleep he'd gotten. Mostly, he napped through the slow passage of time and awakened early with his heart beating wildly in his chest while blindly groping for Pauline. Within seconds, he realized she had been but a ghost in his sensual dreams. He shuddered; the movement jarred his steady hand, and he nicked the underside of his jaw.

"Another illusion," he growled under his breath, dabbing the cut with a piece of tissue.

But he didn't believe it for a moment. Just thinking about the power she seemed to hold over him made him moan, a purr of sweet ebullience in his throat. He pondered how he had lost that feeling, even temporarily. He scraped the smooth white foam from his face with the razor.

Ribbed forehead and hooded eyes gazed back at him as he consciously thought back to the night she chose to tell him about their pending parenthood. Though he wasn't angered by her announcement, he was surprised: Pauline was a nurse, and he had assumed she was taking care of such matters. Of course, in his defense, he thought, with self-righteous chivalry, he was prepared to do the right thing.

Marcellus felt his heart skip a beat and he stilled, staring into the mirror. Guilt stared back in his reflection as he recalled his less-than-enthusiastic suggestion that they get married. His plate had been full at the time, working days for his family's Savings & Loan, while in-between hours and nights were spent formalizing the plans for CSI. His weak response to Pauline had nothing to do with his feelings for her. However, he was forced to admit that he had been frightened by the prospect of adding a family to his life. Pauline declined his offer, and less than twenty-four hours later, it ceased to matter.

He frowned wistfully and resumed shaving. He couldn't change the past. Or could he?

Hearing a creak, he quelled his thoughts to listen. A sound was coming from Don's office. He wiped the smudges of shaving cream from his face with a towel, then slid the closet door closed and tiptoed to the one adjoining the area at the opposite end of the narrow walkway. With one hand on the doorknob, and another against the frame, he opened the door to peek into the room.

The curious frown on his face melted like butter in a hot skillet when he saw Pauline standing at the bar. Her back to him, she was examining the model spacecraft. He stared with beautiful candor in his eyes, revealing emotions he was past the point of denying.

The brownish-red color of her dress complemented her roasted-peanut complexion, picking up the reddish hue in her smooth skin, he noted secondly. He remembered she preferred wearing earth-tone colors because she mistakenly believed they hid the ardor he knew was in her. With an unexpected flash of jealousy, he felt protective of his intimate knowledge of her, wondering if another man had discovered the secret of her passionate nature.

"Uh-hum." He cleared his throat softly.

Pauline spun, startled, juggling the aircraft in her hands. Marcellus rushed across the way, reaching for it as she did, and their heads bumped as he grabbed the pewter model before it hit the floor.

"Ouch," she cried out, straightening as she rubbed her forehead.

"Sorry," he apologized. He set the spacecraft on the counter and turned back to her. "Are you all right? Let me see," he said, brushing her hand aside to inspect the spot above her left eyebrow.

He knew there was no bruise but, unconsciously and quite simply, he couldn't pass up a chance to touch her. It was his undoing, for his hand lingered—an embarrassingly familiar habit, he mused—unwilling to sever contact with the swanskin feel of her brown-velvet flesh. As if self-willed, his hand palmed the side of her face, then an index finger trailed the soft contour of her jaw.

His eyes riveted on her face, he was enthralled by the metamorphosis of emotions, from wariness to wanting in her eyes, the movement of her throat as she swallowed, and the barely noticeable heaving of her shoulders with her altered breathing. His pulse continued its ascent as his eyes made a slow inspection of her body—hidden from sight, but not from his memory—beneath the appealingly simple dress. It was cinched at her waist, with wide, deep pockets running the length of her thighs to stop at a hem just below her knees. It hugged her figure, accentuating the protrusion of her firm breasts, tiny waistline, and flared hips—as his hands itched to do.

He gulped thickly—it felt as if he swallowed his heart—before he spoke. "I thought you were going back to my place."

There had been a time when she would have acquiesced

to his every wish. That she hadn't was a clue he should take to heart, he thought, suddenly unsure of himself. Only, his *ka* seemed filled with a need to reclaim her in every aspect of her existence.

Pauline's tongue snaked out from her mouth to dampen her lips. He watched like a mendicant, filled with sensations that could only be satisfied in one way. Frustration born of insatiable desires mounted in him. He dropped his hand and stepped away from her discreetly. The scent of her perfume followed and kept his senses simmering with his want.

"I decided to go home," she replied at last, a hand at her neck. Hastily, as if nervous, she added, "I saw you on the news."

"I waited up for you," he said, staring at her intently, as if looking for an opening.

"Why didn't you call?"

Her eyes stirred slightly with the hint of challenge in her voice. His level of frustration inched up a notch with his restraint as he stared at her from under a crescent-arched eyebrow.

"Would you have come if I had?" he asked, imperceptibly cringing at the eagerness in his voice for her answer.

"I . . . I don't . . . no, probably not."

When she spoke, the words didn't match the message in her eyes. Somewhat indecisive, they bordered on assent before the delayed reaction of certainty settled in her gaze. Not so calm and unaffected, he amended silently, wondering if thoughts of him had tormented her sleep as his of her had tormented him. The possibility spurred the wanting wish to take her right here in Don's office. But he knew better than to push the issue, remembering his pit-bull tenacity had sent her running from him before.

"That's what I figured," he replied, measuring her with a sidelong glance.

"What did you figure ... that I was tired, or that I wouldn't come?" she asked lightly.

Pauline was toying with him, Marcellus thought, amazed, watching the sweet musing look in her expression. Not the shy, fastidious Pauline he remembered, confirming his notion that she had changed more than her outward appearance showed. He preferred not to answer, except with a cryptic smile on his face.

"I was exhausted," she added feebly.

Facing her headlong, wordlessly, he tugged the ends of the towels at his chest where her gaze dipped. Her obvious interest, the sudden nervousness she displayed, inspired him with hope. His heart pounded with it, as if his *ka* had already made up his mind. *Take it slow, make it last,* he cautioned himself.

"Did Dottie catch up with you?" he inquired casually. He already knew the two women had spoken.

"Yes. We talked. She seems quite capable. Thanks for the recommendation."

"The company's going to pick up the tab." He spoke rapidly, in a tone that brooked no argument, to show that he had already decided.

"No, thanks," she replied with equal firmness.

"Legal fees in a criminal matter are costly." No more so than matters of the heart, he reminded himself.

"I can handle it," she replied, her chin lifted as she gazed at him with a hint of defiance flashing in her clear brown eyes.

He was surprised by her rejection; but then, he shouldn't be, he told himself, with a quiet smile of admiration spreading across his face. "Can you?" he bantered.

Pauline felt riveted to the spot under his compelling gaze. Unable to turn away, she was forced to make an involuntary appraisal of his splendid body. Freshly shaven, the smooth strong line of his cheekbones seemed more pronounced somehow, the hawkish features of his face appealing. The powerful set of his shoulders strained against the fabric of the white undershirt molding his bronze chest and tucked in at the slim waistline of the smoke-gray slacks that fell cleanly down his stalwart lean length atop tasseled black loafers.

With his masculine challenge ringing in her head, she recalled reconciling her warm emotions for him with cool reasoning and reminders of the trouble she faced with the law. That had been on the ride up in ignorance of his presence. But all that logic was ducking into the shadows of the bright room, breathing molecules scented by his woodsy aftershave—and desires. Whether mostly his or hers, she couldn't swear, for her heart was beating as if rocket-launched, no landing in sight.

"Several ideas occurred to me last night," she said falteringly, "so I thought I'd come in early to catch up on my reading about the kind of research your company does."

"What it is that you hope to find?"

"Something that would point to a saboteur." After excluding Marcellus and even Sarah Wellsing, who deserved suspicion, she had wondered who would benefit by their absence. The answer partly explained her early-morning presence. Trying to read his closed expression, she wet her lips and continued, "Even though there doesn't appear to be a tie-in between what happened to Donald and what happened to Ann-Marie, I couldn't help thinking . . . what better way to sabotage a company than to take away its star . . . which Donald certainly is." She waited for Marcellus to laugh.

"That's fairly close to what I've been thinking," he replied, his voice shaded with a tad of amazement. "It would seem that great minds think alike."

The look he gave her was purely sensual. Molten eyes embraced her from head to toe, undeniable hunger flowed like lava in the hot hue of their gaze. The pit of her stomach churned and she felt marked as his next meal. Ironically, she would have gladly laid on his plate for the devouring.

With her knees threatening to collapse, she looked for the nearest comfortable place in which to sit. It was a cushiony armchair in front of Don's desk, and it also afforded her a flagrant view of Marcellus. She didn't want to give the impression that he could scare her off, but she had to admit that her feelings were frightening in their constantly growing intensity.

"I forgot to take the packet of information about the company that Katherine gave me yesterday," she said feebly, to cover the disquieting silence.

"Well." He sighed heavily before continuing, "I can save you some reading and tell you what everybody in the aerospace industry would like to get his or her hands on. And that's a human-functioning robot that could do the work of astronauts aboard a spaceship."

He walked around, tugging the ends of the towel around his neck, as he elaborated on the duties that were performed on a space flight. His arms were bare and silky with hairs, and her eyes glazed with temptation as she daydreamed of being crushed within his embrace. Marcellus stopped talking, and Pauline noted the expectant look on his face. Caught staring at him, a flush of embarrassment warmed her. She swallowed hard before she spoke.

"Aren't there computers that can do that already: think? I mean, a robot is based on computer chips, isn't it? I vaguely remember reading an article about testing a computer's ability in a chess match."

"Ah," he nodded grandly, a twinkle in his eyes, "you're talking about the match between chess champion Garry Kasparov and Deep Blue in February, '96. I don't think Don breathed during the entire game," he chuckled. "Kasparov won, by the way, and it only made Don more determined to design a computer with common sense. That's how Deep Blue lost; it didn't have the common sense to adjust its strategy, and that's what we and everyone else—from computer scientists to aerospace engineers—are trying to come up with: an artificial intelligence that can perceive and make common-sense decisions as spontaneously as a man."

"I presume Donald was working on such an invention."

Bobbing his head up and down, Marcellus sat down on the edge of a barstool before he spoke. "Yes. It would save NASA millions of dollars in personnel, money that they could spend elsewhere."

"Had he perfected it?" she inquired.

"That, I don't know," Marcellus replied bemusedly. "I checked his computer here and at home, and found nothing. Well, that's not exactly true. But what I found only increased my suspicion that he felt something was not kosher. He changed the access codes, and I haven't cracked them yet." He sighed exhaustively, then bit on his bottom lip in a thoughtful and frustrated expression.

"Well, I can't help you there," Pauline said regretfully. "I don't know much about computers, particularly those with codes to crack."

"I could give you a list of codes we've used in the past," he said. "Maybe another vision might help," he shrugged.

Duly amazed, she asked, "You'd be willing to trust me with that information?"

"Sure, why not?" he replied, shrugging. "I've given you keys to everything else. Well," he amended, "except for one floor. I'll take you there myself when I get a break. It's going to be a long day." He pressed the inner corners of his eyes over his nose, then passed a hand over his mouth. When he spoke again, his voice was uncharacteristically docile. "I talked to Mrs. Johns last night. She's coming in from Little Rock on the first flight she can get. I'd like for you to accompany me when I meet with her."

Pauline nodded. She recalled thinking about the murdered woman with her own inadequacies in mind. Recognizing her weaknesses was one thing, but doing something to change them was quite another, she mused.

"I want you to plan a memorial service for Ann-Marie here at the company," Marcellus said, breaking into her thoughts.

Before Pauline could reply, the phone on the desk rang. She looked at Marcellus with questions in her expression, but he seemed to be expecting the early call, and he strode to the desk to answer.

"Yeah?" he replied casually. "All right, let them in." Ending the call, Marcellus smiled at her as if possessing a secret.

"What was that all about?" she asked.

"The accountants are here," he replied, obviously pleased with himself. "Like you, I spent the night trying to look at all the angles that would explain what's been happening. Money is a helluva motivation. I couldn't overlook the possibility of embezzlement, so I arranged for an independent accounting firm to come in and check the books. I better finish dressing. We'll talk later."

"But . . . ?"

"Later," he reiterated, with promise in his eyes.

Pauline merely nodded, for it was impossible to speak around the lump lodged in her throat. The undeniable magnetism between them just kept on growing. She wondered how much longer it would be before they completely ran out of diversions.

A premier showcase of space achievements, Space Center-Houston was the official visitors' center for NASA's Johnson Space Center. This mid-morning, it certainly lived up to its reputation for creating interest, as the Plaza, the central hub of activity at the museum, was packed. Children from yellow school buses packed every space—from the theater to one of a handful of simulators—scampering from teachers who were trying to subdue their eagerness to touch.

The visitor handed over the ticket to the woman manning the entry. A glance showed a massive structure with high ceilings, several points of entry and exit, and curving corridors filled with pictures, gadgets, and even a shuttle mock-up with its rocket head protruding from one of the walls.

The contact was spotted, a Japanese man in his mid-thirties, maybe even younger. He stood in front of one of the photos exhibited on a standing flat, eating from a small cup of space ice cream, the only food permitted in the Plaza. The picture was of Ed White's first space walk on the Gemini 4 flight, dated June 3 to 7, 1965.

"Did you get it?" he asked.

"No. Ever since DW's prognosis pointed to poison, security has been tightened immeasurably. One can't even go to the restroom without having a camera spying on them."

A hint of a smile flashed across the Japanese man's face as he moved to stand in front of the next photograph, depicting the Skylab crew's return from fifty-nine days in orbit in 1973.

"You disappoint me," he said, scooping a spoonful of the beady ice cream into his mouth. "I was led to believe you were resourceful."

"Resourceful, yes; stupid, no. Cavanaugh is suspicious. He's brought in a battalion of accountants, and he's called for a meeting—in a couple of hours, as a matter of fact."

"I see," he said, without emotion in his expression or his voice.

"Another time . . . when the smoke clears. Besides, we're not even sure he's developed it yet."

"This ice cream is really tasty: light; not so filling as to ruin lunch," the Japanese man said smilingly as he held up the empty cup. "I think I'll have another." He walked off, ending the conversation.

"Do you prefer artificial flowers or plants? Or I can make sure you get fresh flowers delivered everyday, if you want," Amy said cheerfully as she took notes on a small pad.

"A couple of plants would be fine," Pauline replied absently as she inspected the clinic with pleased surprise. It had been turned into a pleasant, functional area. After installing supplies in the glass-encased cabinets lining the back wall near the examination bed made of black imitation leather, it would be wholly functional.

She couldn't get over the changes, or the fact that Amy had overseen the set-up of the clinic without instruction. The carpet had been laid and the beat-up old desk had been replaced. A new computer-desk ensemble sat in its place with a metal file cabinet tucked underneath and a matching rolling chair. A glass and chrome coffee table provided companionship for the loveseat.

Despite the woman's penchant for gossip, Pauline thought, walking around the room, she was a capable and competent worker.

"I tried to get you another phone besides that ugly black one on the desk," Amy said, twisting her face in a grimace, "but the request has to go through Clay now. He wasn't in, so I left the paper work. He should let me know within a day or two."

"That will be fine, Amy," Pauline replied with a shrug. The color or style of the telephone ranked low on her list of concerns. Besides, she didn't know how much longer she would be an employee of the company. The answer didn't solely depend on finding a murderer.

"I'll get your paper supplies tomorrow," Amy offered. "You know, stuff like folders, paper clips, pads."

"Amy, I'm truly speechless," Pauline said sincerely. "And grateful. You've done a bang-up job, and I appreciate it." She started to tell Amy that she might have gone through all this trouble for nothing, but held her tongue.

"I aim to please," Amy said cheerfully.

"And you have," Pauline said, looking at her wristwatch. "Lunchtime is almost over. You better hurry; I don't want to keep you any longer."

"Oh, I'm just going to grab something from the cafeteria and eat at my desk. I report to Mr. Coombs now, but basically, I'm a floating secretary. So if you need anything else, just call Personnel and someone there will know how to reach me."

Pauline thought it was a good time to ask about Ann-Marie Johns, but again, something held her back. With a closed-lipped smile, she said, "Well, I can't think of a thing at the moment. Enjoy your lunch."

Marcellus wondered which of them was out to destroy CSI as he studied the executives filing into the conference room one by one. The question had plagued him all morning long, and his suspects kept changing like a volleyball sailing back and forth over the net of his mind.

There was little similarity in their expressions. J.T. looked annoyed and impatient, while Leonard wore melancholy like a kabuki mask, and he wondered if the look was real. Thomas, with his unlit cigar stuck between his teeth, looked as if he didn't have a care in the world.

Marcellus rose from his chair when all of them were seated. It was only eleven-thirty, he mused tiredly; the day wasn't nearly over. Mrs. Johns was scheduled to arrive at seven tonight.

With his fingers arched on the manila folder before him as if it were a keyboard, he opened the meeting. "I know everything is up in a state of madness around here now," he said. That was an understatement. "The best advice I can give you is to grin and bear it, because we don't have a choice in the matter."

As if too drained to continue, his voiced trailed off, hands resting on the table, motionless, like empty gloves. In addition to the police officers who were still searching for clues in the gym, the accountants from Belle & Freddie had arrived; they had stormed into the building like a paratrooper unit—exactly as Marcellus had wanted. Immensely displeased by their presence, however, some employees had attempted to stonewall them, while a few others had used their presence to spread gossip, questioning the solvency of the company. The paranoia was frightening, and he was hoping to get the executives to quell it.

"Some of our staff are having a hard time dealing with the accountants' presence; I know it's an imposition, but it's up to each of you to make sure that everyone in your department cooperates," he said, looking at each of them pointedly. "Assure them that we are not going bankrupt, and that next week's paychecks will go out as scheduled."

"What *was* the reason for calling in the accountants?" Dr. Kent asked.

"The same reason we have for conducting an intensive security check," he replied. "And if outside accountants do it, we can't be accused of bias."

"Does that mean you're going to bring in an outside security company, as well?" she asked. "All these interruptions," she mumbled, annoyed. "People can't get any work done."

"It's possible," Marcellus replied noncommittally. That information would not be shared. He wanted the guilty party guessing, in the hopes that he or she would slip up. "Speaking of security checks," he said, "Leonard . . ."

Cutting him off, Leonard said, "I know, I know. You haven't received one from Personnel. But with Ann-Marie gone, it's . . ." he fell silent. Swallowing the tears in his throat, he said in a weepy voice, "She was a good person. I don't understand how anyone could do such a thing. I'm going to miss her terribly."

"I know, Leonard," Marcellus said with sympathy. "But now, more than ever, you've got to get with Clay and conduct that security check. Have that report on my desk by the end of the day."

Looking around the table, he felt Pauline's absence poignantly. He wondered where she was. Though he hadn't seen her since their unexpected rendezvous in Don's office, she was never far from his thoughts. He recalled the dual conversations that occurred simultaneously between them. One spoken with protective tongues, questions and answers that belied the scorching tension that had filled the room, the residue of its warmth which filled him even now. The day of reckoning was fast approaching, he thought, his blood throttling with his mounting want of her.

He had heard that Pauline had been talking to employees, asking questions about Ann-Marie Johns. She was following up on her idea, as well. A staff member had asked him if it was true that she was putting together the company's memorial service for the late secretary. Paranoia was rampant and rabid, he mused, amazed.

"Well," he said, summarily, "that's about all I have to say. Let's keep our projects on schedule. Ms. Sinclair will let you know about the memorial service. That's it; meeting adjourned."

Thomas was the first to leave the room. While Leonard and Dr. Kent chatted in hushed tones, Marcellus feigned busywork, shoving loose papers into a folder. When they headed for the door, he called, "Dr. Kent, may I have a word with you?"

Dr. Kent looked at him over her shoulder with irritation

in her expression. She checked the time on her wristwatch, then nodded with a grudging frown.

"What's this about, Marcellus?" she asked, slapping her file folder onto the table as she rested an arm across the top of the chair nearest the door. "I have to get back to the lab." Miffed, she added, "You know about the problem we had with Gunter Manufacturing sending us the wrong specs on those ballbearings."

"I know you're eager to get back to the lab," he replied with forced patience. He would not be hurried along to suit her schedule. "How's the research going?" he asked conversationally, for he had in his possession a report from her that more than adequately detailed the progress of her department.

"You already know about the ballbearings we got," she said in a snappy tone. "Those stupid people only sent the 51200s and not the 440C steels for the tests we're running to implant the ballbearings with titanium at 120Kv. You're familiar with the present problems. The bearings need to be changed after every space shuttle flight because of the corrosive environment of the shuttle's liquid oxygen turbopumps."

Marcellus held up his hand like a traffic cop to stop the flow of scientific jargon. "Okay, Doctor, but I understand Thomas found another company who can supply your ballbearing needs," he said with a hint of laughter in his voice. The laughter faded with a new question: Could such an unlikely pair as Dr. Kent and Thomas be working together to sabotage the company?

"I fail to find humor in the situation," she said in a haughty manner. "If these tests with the titanium and chromium implants are successful, then the life expectancy of the ballbearings will be about sixteen flights. That means that *CavWell's ballbearings,*" she emphasized the last two words sarcastically, "will be in space, and so will our profits."

Marcellus was not impressed by indignant concern over ballbearings, even though she spoke the truth. "All right, J. T.," he said gruffly. "This incident with the ballbearings from Gunther: is it the first time they've screwed up an order?"

Dr. Kent hesitated, her face squinted in a frown. He studied her intently, wondering why she was so slow to answer. He knew she possessed a steel trap for a mind, with total recall.

"No, it's not," she said at last. "As a matter of fact, this past January, they cut our order significantly. And we did what we usually do, found someone else to make up the difference." She returned his stare unflinchingly. "So it really didn't affect our research one way or the other. Though some of our research has been slowed because Don has been consumed with his pet project."

"What pet project?" Marcellus asked, pretending ignorance.

Shrugging her shoulders, she replied saucily, "I don't know. I just know we've been falling behind schedule because he apparently had been spending a lot of time on something he's not telling the rest of us about."

"When was the last time you saw or heard from Jason Ringnald?" he asked casually. The idea had been another one of those niggling resonances of suspicion he had— that she could have been the one feeding information to the NASA security chief who seemed to know more about the inside of CSI than would be expected. Though he had no proof, he didn't have anything to lose.

Stunned, Dr. Kent froze. Wetting her lips nervously, she replied hesitantly, "I talked to him after news about Don got out."

A measure of truth within a lie? Marcellus wondered. "Yeah? And what are his feelings about what's going on?"

"I think you already know that," she replied, displeased by the line of questioning. "Now, if there's nothing else."

His hands splayed out on the table, he stared straight at her with a caustic look on his face. Words threatening bodily harm were on the tip of his tongue, but he clamped his mouth shut tight. "No, there's nothing else."

Dr. Kent examined him with a hard-eyed stare, then spun sharply and left the room.

With his lips pressed together pessimistically, Marcellus stared vacantly at the door. Maybe he needed to add Jason Ringnald to his list of suspects.

Chapter Eleven

The workday was drawing to an end. Though Pauline had not seen Marcellus during the day, the morning fire he had stoked inside her was still smoldering at four-thirty in the afternoon. As he had declared, it had been a long day, made longer by the dual assault of dread and anticipation she felt about seeing him again.

Arriving at the top floor, she stepped off and strolled purposefully toward his set of offices. She was just getting around to speaking with Katherine, who'd been busy all day long, carrying out his orders. The reception area came into view, and she began tip-toeing on the carpeted floor. Her heart was thumping in her chest; her gaze was wide, watchful and wary, as if on the lookout. Realizing how foolishly she was behaving, she shook her head, though her heartbeat did not return to normal.

Quiet greeted her, and she wondered where Katherine was. Listening, she followed the sound of the low hum of a machine nearby and found the secretary at the copier in a side room adjacent to the reception area.

"I'll be glad when this day is over," Katherine declared, sounding winded and tired.

"I think everybody in the building feels the same way," Pauline replied. Though the day hadn't been a total waste, she certainly felt uninspired by her accomplishments, she mused. "Need some help?"

"No, this is the last of it," Katherine said, then tagged on, "for now, anyway." She removed the copies from the machine, laid them out in stacks on the wooden table nearby, and began stapling.

Pauline leaned with her back against the doorway, her arms folded across her bosom. The position afforded her a view of the corridor leading into the reception area, and the advantage of seeing Marcellus before he saw her. As if she could prepare herself, she scolded herself silently. She turned her head to watch the secretary busy with her work, and reviewed the shortcomings of her own efforts today.

Under the guise of soliciting feedback to plan the memorial service and program for Ann-Marie Johns, she had been forced to listen to some of the gossip employees had been willing to divulge. It was whispered that Leonard Coombs was carrying on a secret affair. The woman was unknown, but the names of several employees were speculated upon, including Ann-Marie's. A Dr. Chin, whom she had never met, was filing for a divorce from his American wife, allegedly to marry the 'Mad Scientist,' whom she now knew was Dr. Jacqueline Kent. The last bit of rumor featured Amy Bridgewater. According to gossip sources, she had her romantic sights set on Clay Bennington, CSI security chief. General run-of-the-mill office talk that yielded no information about who had tried to kill Donald or succeeded in murdering Ann-Marie Johns. Disgusted, she decided not to mention any of it to Katherine.

"Katherine," she began hesitantly, "how well do you know Sarah?"

"Not very," Katherine replied after a brief pause. "She didn't work here very long, but she used to come . . ."

"Sarah used to work here?" Pauline broke in.

Katherine bobbed her head affirmatively. "It was during the early months of operation. Mr. Wellsing's first two secretaries turned out to be bummers. The first one got married and her husband was transferred out of the state, and the second one was a nincompoop," she said with laughter in her voice. "Plus, she was making goo-goo eyes at him all the time. Leonard had just hired Sarah for Thomas's department, but she was quickly assigned to Mr. Wellsing instead. She stayed maybe a month, I'm not sure. But it wasn't long."

"When did they start dating?" she asked, purely out of curiosity.

"Oh, my gosh!" Katherine exclaimed. "It wasn't for a long time after she left. At least I never heard about them as a couple until maybe a month before they got married. It seemed like one of those whirlwind things."

That was about right, Pauline mused, remembering that Don had first mentioned Sarah's name at the same time he had told her he was getting married.

"Do you know if she ever favored the company of anybody here at CSI?"

With a pondering mutter, Katherine replied, "I would have to say she's probably closer to Amy than anybody else, as far as I know. But, then again, that's a natural link, because Amy is her husband's secretary. I don't know if that makes them close friends, if that's what you mean."

Sighing heavily, Pauline replied, "I was just curious." She readjusted her position against the door frame and crossed her legs at the ankles. "Do you know if Don had had a run-in with one of the executives?"

Chuckling, Katherine replied, "You sound like that Detective Collins."

Pauline joined her in mirth, though she felt that none of

her suspicions was getting her anywhere. "That's probably because I've spent so much time in his company."

Katherine intoned a sound of revulsion. "I could tell from the beginning he was going to be as annoying as cockroaches in a dark kitchen. But I never believed he would turn out to be as stupid as one that couldn't find a hole to crawl into."

"Oh, he's not stupid," Pauline muttered, with disdain edging her voice.

"You know, he asked the same thing," Katherine said, lifting the stapled papers to carry them to her desk.

"And?" Pauline prodded, following alertly Katherine's heels.

"Well, Dr. Kent and Mr. Wellsing were always arguing over something. Just last week—the day you first arrived, as a matter of fact—she marched into the office demanding to speak with him. But, of course, he wasn't in. I don't know how he sneaked out past Amy," she added. She shrugged, then began shoving the stapled pages into file folders and stacking them on her desk. "All I know is that she left a message about needing another researcher in the lab. I understand they had been battling over that same thing for a couple of weeks."

Rapping her fingers on the desk, Pauline wondered if the running argument was significant. "What about Ann-Marie?" she asked, impulsively. Desperate, she felt as if she were grasping at the wind.

"What about her?"

"Did she ever work with Mr. Wellsing?" she asked, adopting Katherine's formal recognition of CSI's president.

"Hm." Katherine thought a moment. "Yes, yes, she did," she said, obviously still collecting her memory. "She had to cover for Amy as recently as a couple of weeks ago. I remember because he asked me about spearheading the committee to plan for the company picnic this summer. I was swamped, with Marcellus getting ready to leave town, so he said he'd ask Ann-Marie." Adding a note of caution, she said, "But don't quote me, because I'm not positive that he got around to asking her."

"What kind of person was she?"

"Quiet, but friendly," Katherine replied. "She and Amy played racquetball together, but I don't think she was very good at it. Amy used to beat her all the time. Or at least, Amy claimed she did," she added with a cocked brow of suspicion. "I don't know. I never use the gym . . . as you can tell," she chuckled, patting her ample hips. "But ever since Mr. Wellsing had the gym installed, all the little career-climbers have come out of the woodwork. And if they hadn't known how before, they learned to play racquetball, because they knew he and Marcellus loved the game."

"Amy wants to advance her career?" Pauline asked impetuously, with disbelief. Though, in hindsight, she thought, Amy's independent actions today would make her a candidate for promotion, if that was what she sought.

"Oh, I don't think you could melt Amy and pour her into any place other than his office," Katherine replied. "She is very proud of her position. Not that I'm dissatisfied, mind you, but I'll insist that Marcellus get up and go down to the cafeteria if he wants his lunch, just to make sure he stretches his legs. Unless he's extremely busy with paperwork and simply can't get away, he prefers it that way. But Amy and Mr. Wellsing had a different kind of relationship. She waited on him hand and foot."

"Does she have a crush on him?"

"I don't know if you could call it that," Katherine replied. "To a degree, we are all a little protective when it comes to our bosses—if they're good people. And ours are."

Sighing dejectedly, Pauline propped her hands on her hips. "So much for that," she said, flashing Katherine a pitiful smile.

"Well, how about you? How was your day?" Katherine asked, a look of satisfaction and relief in her expression.

"Yes, how was it?"

Pauline spun sharply around toward the fetching masculine voice and the man who controlled it. Marcellus stood in the doorway of his office, practically filling the space with his commanding presence. She was conscious that a reply was expected from her, but her senses were engaged in rapture, and her heart was pounding. She could only manage to mirror his look, with sensual wonder reflecting in her gaze.

An odd silence washed across the room, and Marcellus experienced an extraordinary sense of continuity, a kind of esoteric feeling as he stared into Pauline's gaze. Something inside her crossed the chasm between them, closing the distance to strike him with a positive electrical charge. His entire body seemed to swell and the slow beginning of something warning echoed in his head.

"It was all right." She spoke at last, her voice reduced to a whispering vibrato.

"Good," he replied. That was all he could manage. Her bright almond eyes were examining him with such sweltering intensity that the blood rushed to his head.

He strode over to stand alongside her near the desk. He was aware of Katherine eyeing them; she was trying to suppress a smile, but her lips kept twitching. He glanced down at her with a look permitting her to comment. She remained wordless, though her eyes were lively with a gratifying glow. "I guess you're about finished for the day," he said.

"If that's an invitation to leave, I'll take it," Katherine replied, her tone amused. With her hands pressed on the stack of file folders atop the desk, she said, "Here are the security reports you requested from each department, including one from Clay. He said that the tapes will be ready by five," she looked at her wristwatch, "which means he should be walking up here in about ten minutes."

"Thanks, Katherine, now get on out of here, and I'll see you first thing in the morning."

"Oh, one more thing," she said, bending to retrieve her purse from the desk drawer, "don't forget to call your mother. She phoned several times and I had to give excuses for your neglect," she added with a hint of scolding in her tone.

"Will do," he replied. "After I get a bite to eat. I haven't eaten all day. How 'bout you?" he asked, looking down at Pauline. "Hungry? My treat."

"I accept," Pauline replied.

"Then let's get out of here," he said. "I need to get my briefcase, then I'll meet you at the elevator."

The peal of the phone bell halted all movements toward leaving. Katherine answered, after she had determined which line was ringing. "Hello. She is?" She flicked a surprised look toward Marcellus. She covered the mouthpiece. "Ann-Marie's mother is downstairs. She wants to know if she should send the cab away."

With his plans shot to hell, Marcellus emitted a tsk, disappointment in his expression. He had hoped to have had a couple of hours, and a full stomach, before meeting Mrs. Johns. Both were solely needed to give him time to process what he'd learned about Ann-Marie's death from Clay. According to the autopsy report, she was dead before she hit the water. The choice of weapons had been a barbell from the weight room.

"Have someone pay the cabby and tell them I'll be right down to collect Mrs. Johns, then call the hotel to make sure she can check in early."

Katherine nodded as she spoke into the mouthpiece.

"Sorry," he said to Pauline. "Dinner will have to wait."

* * *

"Can I have a pink casket? My Ann-Marie likes pink, you know."

"You can have anything you'd like, Mrs. Johns," Pauline replied. She looked sidelong at Marcellus whose hand was in hers as he seconded her declaration with a nod.

Upon leaving CSI in Marcellus's Toyota Landcruiser, the threesome—Mrs. Johns, Marcellus, and Pauline—arrived at the NASA Road Holiday Inn. They sat huddled in the sitting area of the suite, which overlooked the Clear Lake Bay thirteen floors below. A serving tray sat within their reach on the coffee table, where three cups of tea had grown cold and a basket of breads remained untouched.

Mrs. Johns fell silent, as she had often done since arriving: fading in and out of the conversation, forgetting for brief periods of time that she was not alone. Despite the warmth in the room, she was still wearing her long wool coat, refusing to relinquish it.

From the photos she'd seen, Pauline noted the resemblance to her mother in Ann-Marie visible in their tall, fragile builds and their eyes, soft brown and slightly protruding like those of a frightened doe. Claire Johns looked to be in her fifties; a life of hard work showed in her pale, narrow face and thin, gray-streaked dark hair hanging limply around her shoulders.

"Are you sure you wouldn't like to have dinner with us?"

Pauline knew what it cost Marcellus to make the offer. For as long as she'd known him, she had never seen him so uncomfortable. He'd latched onto her hand—his was damp with nervous perspiration—as soon as they arrived at the hotel, and he was still holding on to her. Even as she told herself not to make a big deal of it, she felt needed: she had never believed that she could give him anything of value, or that something as simple as quiet support could represent a meaningful contribution. She held the knowledge, and the sensation it wrought, close to her heart.

Shaking her head in the negative as she attempted a smile, Mrs. Johns replied, "No, thank you, Mr. Cavanaugh. I better let you busy people get on with your work," she added bravely, albeit reluctantly.

"You're not keeping us from anything," Marcellus replied.

Pauline knew he was lying. It was almost seven now, and his workday was far from over: Clay was waiting for him at CSI to review the security tapes.

"Mrs. Johns," Marcellus said, "I can't tell you how sorry I am to meet under these conditions. If there's anything, anything you need at all, don't hesitate to call me or Pauline."

"I really appreciate everything you've done . . . you know . . . putting me up in this place," Mrs. Johns replied, splaying her hands to indicate the luxurious suite. "Not knowing anybody here," clutching her handbag close to her, "I admit I was a little reluctant about going to Ann-Marie's apartment alone. I know I have to, it's just—"

At the threat of tears in the brief silence, Pauline piped up to her rescue. "That's all right, Mrs. Johns. We understand, and we really didn't want you to be alone. A couple of Ann-Marie's friends from the company will go with you tomorrow to help you through the process."

"Thank you," Mrs. Johns replied. "She was so proud, working for your company. When can I see her?"

"Tomorrow," Marcellus replied, barely audible. He sighed wearily before adding, "But I'm not sure if she will be released then."

Pauline noted his choice of words, his reluctance to refer to the woman's dead daughter as anything less than a person. His sensitivity endeared him to her even more.

"You know, when Ann-Marie was little, she wanted to

be a baseball player," Mrs. Johns said with a fond chuckle
in her voice. "She was a good athlete, my Ann-Marie," the
mother rambled on. "Tell Mrs. Wellsing that I'm praying
for them. It's such a horrible thing that happened to her
husband. So young—," she shook her head, tiny puddles
of tears forming in her eyes. "So young," she sniffed, her
sad face lowered. "You and your lovely wife have been so
kind," she said, including both of them in her gaze.
"Thank you both so much."

Neither bothered to correct her. Instead, Pauline
replied, "You're more than welcome, Mrs. Johns."

"Don't forget, if you need anything, just pick up the
phone and call us," Marcellus said. "You have my number
at home, right?"

"Got your numbers right here," Mrs. Johns replied,
patting the side of her big handbag. "Ann-Marie gave me
this purse," she said fondly. "A Gucci." She chuckled
reminiscently. "Cost more than anything I got in it."

"Oh, I forgot," Marcellus said, reaching inside his suit
coat. He pulled out a bulky white envelope and passed it
to the grieving mother. "Just a little something while you're
here," he said. "I'll have Ann-Marie's pay and personal
effects ready before you leave."

Then the tears began to fall, streaming down Mrs. Johns'
face as she fingered the envelope. "My baby's gone," she
sobbed quietly.

Pauline felt helpless in the face of this mother's grief.
She crossed to Mrs. John and embraced the woman as she
cried. It was always hard, reconciling with the death of a
loved one.

"I'll get some water," Marcellus said, springing from his
seat, heading for the adjoining room.

"I know God had a reason for taking my baby," Mrs.
Johns said, sniffing, struggling to recover her composure.
"I know Ann-Marie is in good hands." She looked up at
Pauline with the most animate expression Pauline had

seen on her face since they arrived; a sincere smile showed through her bereavement. "It's the living that better take care. You two take care of each other now."

The Sky's The Limit blazed across the blue tee-shirt Donald Wellsing was wearing over a white dress shirt with the sleeves rolled up to his elbows. Navy dress slacks and soft-soled white tennis shoes completed the casual attire he always wore.

Clay Bennington, CSI's head of security, was sitting at the console, viewing a video that showed CSI's lab. Unbeknownst to him, someone else watched stealthily from the doorway.

The picture showed Don conferring with Dr. Chin in the D & A Division, which worked on perfecting old and designing new and smaller technologies for use in space. He held up a clipboard for Don to examine.

Don searched his person, then located reading glasses that were tucked into the front of his tee-shirt. He slid them in place to review the information from Dr. Chin.

The pair of eyes watching the video exchange squinted, trying to make out the scribbling. But the attempt was as futile as the previous one to try to find evidence of Don's project. Except for tiny scraps of paper that someone had obviously failed to destroy completely, Don had left no clues in his office. It was as if the talk about his pet project was just a rumor. However, there was one place left to check.

Unexpectedly, Clay shifted to look toward the door. He was slightly startled.

"Oh," Clay said, "I didn't realize you were there."

"I'm certainly happy that you're here, because I'm locked in. I feared I was going to have to spend the night in this place. What are you doing?"

Clay diverted his attention to the console and pressed

a button. The screen went black before he explained, "I'm waiting for Mr. C. to get back," he replied.

Mr. C. was Marcellus, who was making the task more difficult. He seemed to be covering his back with these new security measures. Pauline Sinclair had not been the blinding light of Marcellus's life, as had been hoped. "Anything new on Don?"

"Nothing's changed as far as I know," Clay replied.

"How's his wife holding up?"

"About as well as can be expected," Clay said, shrugging his shoulders.

"At least she's at the hospital where someone can keep an eye on her."

"She's safe there," Clay agreed, nodding. "Are you done for the night?"

"At last," a chuckling voice replied. "It's a wonder anybody got anything done today. I'm not so sure I like these new security measures, if you don't mind my saying so."

"If we worked in a kinder, gentler place, there would be no need," Clay replied, before laughing quietly. "Then, of course, I'd be out of a job. If you're ready, I'll buzz you out," he said, rolling the chair to another section of the console.

"Yeah, well, goodnight."

"G'night," Clay replied.

An upbeat Jazz Crusaders' composition played throughout the house from an unseen source, but it could have been Duke Ellington's melancholy "In My Solitude" for all the effect it had on lifting Marcellus's mood. He was pacing a circular trail from his front door to his dining room, occupying himself with a solitaire variation of "She loves me; she loves me not," wondering whether Pauline would come.

A long-stemmed glass of wine in his hand, he opened

his front door to look out into the black night. It was chilly, starless, and nothing stirred on his block. Returning inside, his anxiety climbed another notch.

It was a quarter after nine, according to every clock in his home and the black leather-band Seiko on his wrist. Fifteen minutes past the hour at which they had agreed to meet after separating at CSI, where he had returned to review the security tapes.

Clay had been waiting, Marcellus recalled absently, but his mind had refused to focus on the videos so he'd packed them in his car and hurried home to prepare for Pauline's arrival.

He took a sip of his drink and ducked to his left, off the foyer, to resume his aimless pacing. As he passed the closed door of his study, he paused there briefly, with a fleeting mind to look at those tapes. But it left him soon, and he sauntered on into the dining room, a formal yet cozy square schemed around burgundy and royal blue, with polished cherry furniture.

A chandelier hung over the oval dining table for six, set for two with his finest china and best silver. Twin candles in bronze holders sandwiched a petal-shaped vase of colorful flowers. Dinner—take-out which he had contrived to have delivered from a seafood restaurant—was warming in the oven.

Marcellus hoped it wouldn't be ruined before she arrived.

He dropped onto a side chair and held his drink on the table. He spun the base of the glass with his thoughts bouncing around in his head. He was unable to hold onto a single matter other than Pauline.

This time when he had asked—"Will you wait for me at my place?"—Pauline had accepted with compromise, but without equivocation, he recalled, mirth turning up a corner of his mouth.

"Are you still treating me to dinner?" she had quipped, smiling resplendently.

That, and a whole lot more.

He chuckled with the memory of the reply he hadn't voiced, though he had been stunned by her easy acceptance. Instead, he promptly proceeded to hedge his bets. "Will you stay the night?" Before she could reply, he added, "You can borrow one of my nightshirts to sleep in . . . if you want to."

Marcellus stopped the restive movements of his glass. Just remembering, anticipating, caused a reflex of warm emotions to rush through him. As the sensation settled into a quiescent yet hard knot in his limbs, it recurred to him to analyze the implication behind his invitation. It made him wonder . . . fear, almost . . . that she had gotten cold feet and wouldn't come.

Even though he didn't know what to expect of the evening, he thought to prepare himself for anything.

He blew out his cheeks, then absently lifted the glass to his lips. A contemplative frown shaded his expression. He set the glass down to slouch in the chair, absently fingering the gold symbol of life, an *akh* hanging from the chain around his neck.

While he still wondered why Don had chosen to engage Pauline's services, he no longer rued his partner's autocratic decision. It occurred to him that, in addition to suspecting espionage within the company, Don might have known something else . . . something that he had been too blind to see.

Had Don guessed that he, Marcellus, had been going through the motions of living, while all the time he was nothing but a body searching for its *ka?*

The music stopped and, filling the sudden silence, the telephone rang and the doorbell chimed. There was no debate as to which took precedence.

Marcellus was on his feet in a flash, heading for the front door at the same momentum, ignoring the telephone.

He reached the door and pulled up. His heart was pounding so hard and fast, he mused, that it might jump right out of his body. He breathed a restorative sigh, his eyes closed as if in prayer. Then, with a look of welcome on his face, he opened the door.

Chapter Twelve

Standing under the light over the porch, Pauline faced the heavy door with her eyes closed, performing a ritual to gain the upper hand over her elation. Irrepressible, the sensation flaunted itself like a brazen entity, teasing her mind with endless possibilities about the outcome of this evening.

Finally, she drew a deep breath and pressed the white buzzer. Within seconds, she heard the click of the lock and sensed the knob turning. Her breath slid up to her throat. The door opened ... revealing Marcellus. Speechless, her heart reacted instantly, tumbling in her bosom.

Framed by the door to the lighted foyer, he appeared the picture of majesty. Topping silk-like black slacks, the contrast of the white Tuxedo shirt—opened at the collar, French cuffs at his wrists—against his gold-brown flesh was striking, perfect even. The symbol of life—a gold *akh*—hung from the gold chain around his neck to rest in the bed of hairs on his chest.

Pauline's gaze rose to Marcellus's, and she felt a shock run through her. He was looking at her with something deeper than mere masculine interest, and he was, indisputably, as masculine as any man she had ever known. He could have any woman he wanted. Her mouth went dry.

Startled at her own voice, her coy tone, she asked, "Have you enjoyed your wait?"

Marcellus's mouth dropped open, then instantly, formed an irresistibly devastating grin with featherlike laugh lines crinkling around his eyes.

"Apparently, not as much as you have," he replied. "But, you know what they say about it . . . good things come to those who do," his voice vibrating with sexual innuendo. "Won't you come in?"

Pauline shivered imperceptibly before she crossed the threshold. As he secured the door, she wondered if he were as nervous as she. If she didn't get control of her pulse, she told herself, she would have a heart attack.

"May I take that for you?"

He indicated the department store shopping bag in her clutches. It represented time spent questioning her decision to come. She had known what accepting his invitation could mean—disappointment, as easily as fulfillment—but she wasn't even sure what she *wanted* to have happen.

Marcellus took the bag, then helped her remove her coat. The nearness of him at her back induced erotic notions in her mind. She pressed her lips together tightly to suppress a soft gasp.

Putting the coat on a hanger in the hall closet, he said, "We should probably eat now, if that's okay with you."

"That's fine."

He faced her to stare with glad musing in his face. "Why don't you go on to the dining room, while I put this away," he said, referring to the bag. "I'll be right there."

* * *

"Hubert Laws," Marcellus replied to Pauline's query as to the musician covering "Moonlight Sonata," which was playing from a hidden source.

"It's very nice."

Dimmed lights, mellow jazz, and burning candles secured the delicate thread of tension in the room. Pauline felt herself being swayed by the intimate aura Marcellus had conjured. She looked at him through the steady blaze of the flames, thinking she should be on guard. But she could taste her awareness of him as certainly as she did the seasonings in the scrumptious meal of grilled orange roughy with asparagus in a Marsala wine sauce.

As promised, they were eating mere minutes after she arrived. She was impressed by the painstaking care taken to create this moment, this provocative setting. She hadn't been on a date in such a long time, she thought, that anything could have amazed her. But she didn't believe that, for the Marcellus in her memory would have sooner hired someone to stage the occasion than do it himself.

A number of other things pointed to changes in him, she mused, recalling his discomfort with Mrs. Johns, as well as the times he had acquiesced to her decisions. Even now, with everything that was happening at CSI, he seemed uncannily relaxed, she thought, stealing a glance at him. An energy radiated from him, for sure—but it wasn't that frenzied, hurry-hurry kind, as if time was running out on him—that he used to project.

"Was that outfit among your purchases?" he inquired lightly.

"Uh, yes," she said, unconsciously looking down at herself. As if she could forget what the dress cost, she thought. Not just a dress, but a tangerine knit, with a soft, round neckline and long sleeves, by some famous designer. The sales women who gathered to gawk while she modeled it had convinced her it was worth every penny because of the way it hugged her figure and complemented her complexion most flatteringly. The look in Marcellus's eyes confirmed it.

"It's most becoming," he declared in a sotto voice.

"Thank you," she replied shyly.

"What else did you buy?"

"Huh?" Feeling the heat of shame steal into her face, Pauline swallowed the food in her mouth before she answered. Of all her purchases, a very expensive silk and lace negligee in black was most keen in her memory. "Oh, stuff," she said, trying to make it sound insignificant.

"Uh-huh," he replied. His eyes held a mischievous glint as he lifted his glass to drink a sip of wine.

She treated him to a suspicious sidelong glance. "Did you peek?"

Amused chagrin stole into his expression. "Well," he hedged, talking with his hands, "not exactly. I kind of . . . squeezed . . . the bag."

"Patience at play?" she quipped, looking sidelong at him from under an arched brow, mirth on her mouth.

"Yeah, I guess you could call it that," he replied, reaching for the bottle of wine. Tilting it over her glass, he asked, "Would you like more?"

She nodded in reply, and he refilled her glass to the brim. As she watched him return the bottle to its cooler, she couldn't help thinking that Marcellus was charming, successful, and good-looking, by any standards. What more could a woman want? she thought, sipping her wine.

He surpassed what a woman like her could ever hope to expect—the thought launched a major attack on her self-confidence. Under the sudden attack of apprehension, butterflies joined the food in her stomach. She wondered what Marcellus expected from her . . . what she could give him in return. Quiet support was nothing to a man who *already* possessed the lionlike qualities of leadership.

Marcellus looked up and caught her staring. She smiled a dumb smile. For a minute, actually no longer than a few seconds, he stopped chewing, seeming mesmerized. Then a smile curled around his lips like contentment, and his eyes glowed. The look was enough to douse her anxiety and ignite wanton desires. With a sigh, she released the breath she had been holding.

"What?" he asked softly.

She lowered her eyes to her plate. "Nothing," she replied, shaking her head.

"Will you please relax?" Marcellus asked.

Startled by his sensitivity, Pauline blinked, feeling lightheaded. She flashed him a weak, embarrassed smile and forked a bite of food to put into her mouth. She ate by rote, for she was feeling suspended somewhere between the alpha and omega of enchantment.

Marcellus put his fork down and folded his hands together over his plate. He was looking at her uncertainly, his brow wrinkled in contemplation. Then, quite unexpectedly, he reached across the distance with his hand, palm up in implied invitation. Setting her fork alongside her plate, Pauline accepted the wordless offer. Gently, he squeezed her hand, his eyes boring into hers warmly, friendly, as if requesting a truce.

"I know we each have ghosts, but let's not worry about them now. What happens happens. I just want us to enjoy the moment. Okay?"

Pauline nodded agreeably; it was what she wanted, as well: to enjoy. They both resumed eating, she with more gusto. She was still musing with surprise that the olive branch seemed to have reduced the pressure she felt, when Marcellus interrupted her thoughts.

"Did you have any luck today?"

However, she wasn't amazed by the hunger of a different nature that remained in her. "Luck with what?" she replied.

"Trying to find someone who's close to Sarah," he supplied.

Shaking her head, she said, "Not really. I picked up more gossip than useful information. I was surprised to learn she used to work at CSI."

"She didn't work there long." He swallowed his food, then drank a sip of wine before continuing. "Hell, I had even forgotten she worked there until Don announced he was marrying her."

"Why did she leave?"

"Her father had a stroke, and she decided to go back to Dallas to take care of him. Her mother committed suicide when she was a little girl, so it was understandable that she wanted to be near him."

Pauline nodded her head woodenly in agreement before she spoke. "Everybody claimed she was well liked by everybody. But, of course, I was told the same thing about Ann-Marie, when obviously somebody didn't. I don't know whether to attribute their answers to the fact that I'm an outsider, or whether I'm on the wrong track altogether."

"Okay," he said thoughtfully. "What's your next move?"

"I plan to go through the gym logs to see who's been playing racquetball with whom," she responded quickly.

"That's an unusual place to check."

"No so, when you consider what I learned from Katherine today. I guess you're not aware of it, but there are employees who want to advance their careers. And since it's common knowledge that the owners enjoy playing racquetball, a lot of people have been learning. By the way, who have you played with lately?"

Marcellus angled his head, his expression one of quiet introspection. "Usually, I only play with Clay or Don. And occasionally, Reuben, when he can get away from the hospital," he added.

"Are you such a hard competitor that you've scared other people off from even challenging you to a game?"

she teased, holding the glass of wine as if about to drink. "I know you," she said, before he could respond, "you have very little patience for beginners."

Marcellus laughed. "I didn't think I was that bad," he said mildly, with disbelief, then he paused in consideration. "Was I?" he asked, looking at her from a pained mask.

She stared at him with her gaze narrowed, but she couldn't hold the chiding look, and she burst out in giggles. "Except when it came to your precious Vet."

"Aw, you can't hold that against me," he exclaimed laughingly.

She joined him in laughter. "No, you weren't *that* bad," she said, letting him off the hook. "But you *could* have been a lot better."

"I'll make it up to you."

Pauline reacted not to the words, but to the lowered register of his voice and the covetous look filling his gaze. Longing knotted in her loins, creating an ache so intense she wondered how she'd get through the rest of dinner.

Marcellus unbuttoned his shirt another notch lower as if the temperature in the room had changed. His certainly had. Pauline, sitting *right* there, was transmitting an aura of beguiling innocence that made him want her even more. Though dinner was over, and he'd eaten more ice cream than he cared to, the craving inside him was insatiable.

"You've changed," she said.

So have you, he thought, but Marcellus squashed the facile retort on his tongue: more than anything, he wanted to talk, to really communicate with Pauline—not entertain her with irrelevant banter. It dawned on him that during the eight or so months they had been together, he'd spent much more time trying to impress her than getting to know her. Or allow her to know him.

"Good or bad?" he asked.

Pauline flicked a wavering hand in the air, as if debating her reply.

They had retired to the family room. Each was nursing a brandy, Pauline at the far corner of the couch with her legs curled under her, less than an arm's length away within his reach. He quelled the urge to do so, from the middle of the couch, where he sat in front of the coffee table.

"Good," she decided at last, the smile on her face also in her tone. "Unless—" the teasing light returning to her gaze—"old age is what's slowing you down."

The music had stopped, but neither seemed to notice or care. Their presence created its own pleasant sounds.

"No doubt some of that, too," he chuckled in reply. "I suspect Don's being in the hospital has something to do with it, as well."

"Ah," she guessed, "an issue of mortality."

"Yeah, I guess you could say I'm coming closer to accepting mine," he replied softly. *That wasn't the only thing he was beginning to accept,* a silent taunt reminded him. He had never realized the intoxicating value of jasmine, for he could smell the fragrant scent on her skin. Her essence was part of what was conspiring against him. "Mostly, however," he said, sliding the brandy glass onto the table, "I don't feel that constant sense of urgency, the need to prove myself."

"I beg your pardon?" she asked with amazed skepticism.

"You know," he said, casually crossing his right leg over his left knee, with his arm across the back of the couch, "the youngest sibling has a tendency to benefit more than the older children. He gets more attention from his parents, particularly if they have reached that comfort zone where they don't have to work 24 hours a day, seven days a week, to make sure they have a worthwhile inheritance to leave their children. The youngest can start taking things for granted and slouch off . . . if he's not careful."

"You were never lazy," she declared succinctly.

"No, I went in the opposite direction for fear that I would get lazy," he laughed at himself. "Only, I may have gone overboard." He was aware that the color had been eaten from her lips, leaving them in their natural gloss. She had no need for mascara, and he tried to remember if he had ever told her that before. But he knew the answer was no, for he had been too busy to appreciate the simple pleasures of life, including the exquisite woman he'd had in his for a short time.

"I never knew you felt that way," she said softly, intrigued.

"What did you think?"

Pauline stared at him intensely as if analyzing his admission. He wondered what she would do if he reached over to stroke the black eyebrows that were bunched over her brown eyes until they relaxed.

"I thought you were comfortable with yourself and everything about your life. It never dawned on me to suspect you feared not living up to the standards set by your parents. I guess that, not having parents, I wouldn't know what that's like," she added in a rueful tone. As if casting off the melancholy moment, she said lightly, "Probably just as well."

"What's just as well . . . not having parents?"

"Yes; they were probably poor and uneducated," she added flippantly.

Though he had once believed the same and that Pauline was better off without them, he didn't realize the extent to which it apparently bothered her. "Well, I won't go that far," he said judiciously, "but I believe you have to be proud of all that you've achieved. You've done quite well for yourself, lady," he said with admiration. "Consider it their loss."

She looked at him as if surprised by the compliment . . . and pleased by it. A transitory look of satisfaction flashed across her face before she looked embarrassed and cast her head downward. He felt humbled, maybe even honored, by the simple, unconscious gesture.

His eyes roamed her face, caressing the features framed by the haircut he liked more and more each day. He wondered if its shorter length, skimming the collar line, meant shorter time with her toiletries. He wanted to know the answer, to see for himself. Desperately.

"Pauline, I've made up my mind." Too much stock had been placed on patience, he decided.

"Oh?" she asked, arching a curious brow at him. "About what?"

"About what I want," he said, knowing the message shone as clear as day in his gaze.

He saw the breath tremble in her bosom; he shivered, himself, watching her soft bright tongue emerge from her mouth to slide across her lips. He growled in his throat, and before he even knew what he was doing, he had invaded her warm space, as she had his want-filled thoughts. She emitted a startled sigh, and he could smell the brandy on her breath.

"I want you," he announced unabashedly, with a list in his mind . . . *to touch you, to brush the stray hair back in place, to outline your soft lips* . . . but he dare not touch until . . . "If you don't want this between us, tell me now," he demanded in an aroused whisper, holding himself tightly in check.

"Run all out of patience, have we?" she joked in a barely audible voice.

"Tell me what I want to hear," he insisted, determined urgency in his voice.

"I don't know . . . I can't seem to think when you're so near," Pauline stammered in reply.

Marcellus observed the wanting hue glaze over her eyes, creating a dreamy look on her face. Slowly, he shook his head from side to side. "That's not good enough. Tell me what I need to hear, Pauline. I know you want me, but

have you forgiven me? *Can* you forgive me? If you can't . . ."
He swallowed thickly before he spoke again. "I can handle
whatever you decide," he lied.

"I thought you didn't want any part of me. I have nothing to offer you."

Marcellus rasped a curse.

"We're so different," she pressed, as if arguing against
herself.

Marcellus took her hand and held it on his chest where
his heart was beating like a kettledrum. "Hear that? Sounds
like it's launching for a moon flight. You're the only woman
who can do that to me. You're the only woman who can
make me mad. The only one who can bring me joy."

"I'm not good enough for you," she cried.

"At last we get to the truth," he said ruefully, his expression pained. He sighed exhaustively and shook his head
before he spoke again. "And it shows I failed you misera-
bly." Pauline's lips parted as if to deny the truth of his
words, but he placed a finger on her mouth to shush her.
"Give me another chance, Pauline. Another chance to
prove that you're better than I deserve."

"Oh, Marcellus."

"Is that a yes?"

"That's a definite yes," she said, pulling his head to her
face for a kiss not unlike the soldering heat that joins
metals.

His kiss was like magic, bursting bubbles of doubt and
fear. Pauline gave herself over to him: his lips were firm
and moist on hers as he kissed her sweetly, with greed on his
tongue. And she took from him: his kisses and conviction in
the rightness of her decision mixing right in with desire.

Not missing a beat of rising rapture, Marcellus peeled
away layers of knit and silky garments meticulously. Each
piece followed the path of the preceding one, tossed care-

lessly aside. Left robed in ardent sensations and delicate panties that revealed more than they covered, Pauline sat in silent splendor, free to bask in the wake of his compelling gaze, his eyes smoky-black with scorching intent. He trailed a finger down the center of her slender build of wheat-brown flesh. She trembled, watching him watch her body come to life. Her breasts rose and swelled, and her stomach muscles contracted under his light touch. He saw it all, with a mouth-watering look etched on his face to taste her arousal on his lips. His restraint was surprising.

"I could be content with just looking at you," he said, fine beads of perspiration dotting his forehead. "Did you know that?"

Too thrilled to speak, Pauline merely nodded in agreement, at which Marcellus threw back his head and laughed. "Liar," he declared, capturing her mouth in a quick, hard kiss.

As he lifted his head, she watched transfixed, as the mirth faded from his expression, and in its place, a bittersweet look imposed its sad mark. Guessing at the thought stealing him from her, she said softly, "Marcellus, it was yesterday. And yesterday is gone."

With his face cradled between her hands, she watched as he interpreted the metaphorical message and a sanguine look molded his expression. Tracing the sexy formation of his mouth, she said, "I missed you."

A scrumptious sigh left his throat, and as if she were weightless, Marcellus swept her up into his arms. Cradled against his chest, as if she were a baby, he carried her up the stairs. "I shall hold you to your word," he said in a voice husky with anticipation.

"As long as you hold me," she replied, her face buried against his throat, arms around his neck. Crossing the threshold of the bedroom, she said, "The lights," reaching out for the switch as they passed it.

"The better to see you, my dear," he replied in a low,

purposefully seductive voice. He lay her in the center of
the bed and was about to join her when she scampered to
her knees. His eyebrows shot up in surprise. "Changing
your mind already?"

"Just getting the minor details out the way," she replied
laughingly, reaching for the top button on his shirt. Dally-
ing as she removed his clothes with her hands and teased
his exposed peanut-butter flesh, she stripped him. With
each glimpse of his body, she felt a delightful shiver of
wanting shoot through her. When the last barrier landed
somewhere on the floor, she ran a finger up the inside of
a muscular thigh, eliciting a tight groan from his throat.

"I'll get you for that," he promised.

"I'm looking forward to it," she replied, pushing him
back onto the bed and straddling the powerful and naked
man beneath her. Her hands skimmed the fine, silky black
hairs on his chest, and the planes and hard-muscled ridges.
He was more stunningly virile than she remembered, she
thought, feeling drugged by the clean, manly scent and
omnipotence of him.

She felt him tremble as she worshipped his body and
rejoiced in her power. Alternately, she kissed and stroked
his satin skin, excluding no part of him from her hands
and lips of fire. Each fervent murmur she elicited from
him affected her equally, drawing her closer to the heat.

Marcellus clasped his big hands around her buttocks
and pulled her into him harder, to let her feel the result
of her stimulation. "Pauline," he groaned impatiently. She
smiled with wicked delight against his flesh.

With the speed and agility not expected from a man his
size, he flipped her over, pinning her beneath him. "Two
can play this game," he mumbled piquantly, fastening his
mouth on hers, his tongue foraging past her lips.

While he explored her mouth, she felt a warming surge
spread from her fingertips to her toes. Marcellus seemed
to find glory in the feel of her skin. His hands moved

marvelously over her smooth breasts, then roved down her back to her buttocks and up again. How could she have ever feared this fire he set in her, or even think she didn't deserve it?

"I love the way you feel," he said. He grazed a dark-tipped nipple, tautly attentive, with his palm, and she groaned through the cry in her throat. "Do you taste as good as you feel?" he asked with rhetorical passion. She couldn't have answered if she wanted to. He nibbled at the underside of a breast, laden with sensitivity, then bathed the mound with his tongue, causing her to writhe under him.

The touch of his hand was almost unbearable in its tenderness. Nothing in her memory came even comparably close to what she was feeling. It was as though a million pieces from a shooting star attached exquisite particles of want to every fiber of her being.

"Marcellus," she exclaimed breathlessly, frantic hands skimming his back and sides, trying to touch the breadth of him. She arched her hips into his, taunting his manhood with promising delight as her tongue dipped in and out of his ear. Just when she began to entertain thoughts of begging him to take her, his mouth covered hers in a most amazing, gentle kiss.

The graze of a hand, a warm breath, a kiss as light as a feather, on enflamed flesh. These were the instruments of sweet torture he inflicted, and she returned them. In the light, the mirror reflected the foreplay ritual occurring on the bed, a haven that they were using maximally to create new memories. They explored each other's bodies like virgin teens, first-timers to a wondrous experience.

A duet of wanting filled the room; reality was a harmony of sensations. As one, they reached the point of no return, each primed for complete possession of the other.

He pulled her head to his face, then her mouth was on his. Her lips were soft, yet demanding, as they parted his, and her hot tongue slid into his mouth in a sensuous journey. He moaned like a savage animal, dominated by a single thought, to be one with her.

Tearing his mouth from hers reluctantly, he looked down into her face, her eyes. The sparkle in their brown depths created a deep emotional commitment in him.

"Pauline," he half asked, half stated in a tremulous voice.

Reading the mutual message in his eyes, she wordlessly captured his hardness in a gentle clasp and guided it into the soft warm treasure between her thighs. The slow intrusion brought a single cry from them both. With his forehead resting against hers, Marcellus paused, allowing her to adjust to his size before he retreated, then entered her again.

Gasping in sweet agony, she met his strokes measure for measure, arching her hips to meet the steady thrusts of possession. Holding him tighter, she wished this divine ecstasy never had to end.

The tempo increased. The golden wave of rapture widened to capture the love flowing between them. Clutching his muscular shoulders, legs wrapped around his waist, his name became a song on her lips.

"Marcellus. Marcellus. Marcellus," she moaned in surrender as her body began to vibrate with liquid fire.

He freed her in a dizzying, uncontrollable burst of joy, as he, too, yielded to the searing need, and he joined her in that place past naked desire in fulfillment.

An exhausted grunt followed out-of-breath gasps of air as he dropped his face next to hers. "Wow," he breathed softly, wrapping his arms under her.

Pauline looped her arms around his neck and nuzzled his face with her nose, sighing, "Uh-huh." A Cheshire cat's smile was in her voice.

"Now what do you want to do?" he asked in a humor-laced voice.

Pauline chuckled and returned in kind, "Want to try it again, see if you can get it right, this time?"

"If it gets any righter than that, then I'm a dead man," he said laughingly. Then he whispered against her mouth, "Goodness, woman, you're lethal."

Feeling more than satisfaction from physical release, confident and invigorated, she replied with coy courage, "What do you plan to do about it?"

"As an officer of the court," Marcellus replied in an attorney's summational voice, smiling down at her, "it's my duty to put you under house arrest."

As if contemplating the punishment, Pauline said, "Hmm, sounds like a wonderful sentence," a salacious gleam in her eyes.

His mouth hovering above hers, he retorted pleased, "You greedy witch." He pressed his lips to hers; the doorbell chime rang, and he froze.

"Saved by the bell," she said laughingly.

Growling in the back of his throat, he said, "Don't move." He sat up grudgingly, grabbed his slacks from the foot of the bed, and slid them on. Leaning over the bed to steal a quick kiss from her mouth, he promised, "I'll be right back."

Chapter Thirteen

Marcellus bit back the profanity in his thoughts out of respect to his parents who stood in the doorway. "You've picked a most unfitting time to visit," he said annoyed.

"Well, you never answered any of my phone calls," Barbara Cavanaugh chastised as she walked inside, Malaby Cavanaugh following.

"Hi, Dad," Marcellus said.

"Hello, son," Malaby replied, looking at Marcellus sympathetically behind his wife's back.

Chuckling wryly, Marcellus closed the door and followed his parents into the family room. He wondered how Pauline would feel about this development.

Standing over the couch, Barbara said, "I see why you couldn't answer my calls." She had her arms folded across her hefty bosom, and a dubious look on her face.

"I was busy," Marcellus replied unapologetically.

"Yes, I see," she replied, picking up the bra.

"It would seem you were right, son," Malaby said, a smirking grin on his face, "we caught you at a bad time."

Rolling his eyes, Marcellus snatched the bra from his mother's hand. "You should have called first," he said grumpily as he picked up the remaining discarded garments.

"We did, dear," Barbara replied in a sweet, significant tone. "Since we've made this long drive, you might as well tell Pauline to come down. I assume it *is* Pauline you're entertaining," treating him to a narrow-eyed gaze. Marcellus grumbled unintelligibly under his breath. "I don't like finding out from the television what's going on at my son's company," she said contentiously, in defense of her actions.

"There were some conflicting reports about Don's condition," Malaby said, sitting on the couch next to Barbara. "One time, we heard he had come out of the coma; then, on the ten o'clock news tonight, there was a report of uncertainty about his condition. What's the truth?"

"He did come out for a brief time," Marcellus said. "Long enough to call for Pauline."

"Why would he call for Pauline?"

"Mother, I don't know," Marcellus replied, shaking his head bemused. "The detective on the case believes he was implicating Pauline for giving him the poison that caused the heart attack."

"Oh, how utterly ridiculous," Barbara snapped, smacking her lips with disdain.

Marcellus chuckled to himself and smiled at Barbara with a fond expression. "Thank you for that, Mother. We appreciate your support, but I do wish you would have picked another time to drop in."

"You know," Barbara said hesitantly, looking up at Marcellus from a keen sidelong gaze, "I was surprised when I called last week and Pauline answered the phone. You haven't mentioned her in quite a while. Is there something else you want to tell us, Marcellus?"

"I respectfully refuse to answer on the grounds that I

might incriminate myself," Marcellus replied laughingly. He was not about to subject himself to his mother's interrogation. "I'll go get her." As he started for the stairs, the doorbell rang.

"Expecting company?" Malaby asked with a chortle of amusement.

"I wasn't expecting you," Marcellus retorted as he changed directions to walk to the front door. "Who is it?"

"Detective Collins. Open the door, Mr. Cavanaugh."

What the hell was going on? Marcellus wondered as he opened the door. "Yes, may I help you, Detective Collins?"

"We're here for Ms. Sinclair," Detective Collins replied. He walked in, his audacity bolstered by a uniformed policeman at his heels.

"Couldn't this wait until the morning?" Marcellus asked, slamming the door shut.

"No, it couldn't, Mr. Cavanaugh," Detective Collins replied. Staring at the garments bunched in Marcellus's arms, he arched a brow in a suggestive look. "I had a feeling we'd find her here," he said as if to himself.

Marcellus felt as if he would blow his top from suppressing the urge to strike the annoying detective. He also felt a wad of self-directed disgust for not anticipating this move by the detective. "What do you need to talk to her about this late?" he asked sharply.

"I understand she found the body of Ann-Marie Johns," Detective Collins replied. "She shouldn't have been allowed to leave the premises in the first place. Now I'll have to take her in for questioning."

"There's no reason to do that tonight," Marcellus snapped. "She's not going anyplace." He remembered the tapes he'd put off reviewing, and he wished he hadn't.

"Someone attempted to assault Mrs. Wellsing as she was returning home from the hospital earlier this evening," the detective volunteered with pleasure.

The news wiped the hostility from Marcellus's expression, and in its place, shock came in a quick uttering, as if he'd been kicked in the gut. "Who? . . . Is she all right? . . . Where is she now?"

"She's back at the hospital, and, yes, she's all right," Detective Collins replied matter-of-factly.

"Did you catch the guy?" Marcellus asked, his mind racing with plans not only to go over those tapes, but to return to Don's computer.

"It wasn't a guy, Mr. Cavanaugh. It was a woman," he delivered with a deadpan expression. "Now, will you get Ms. Sinclair?"

"You can't believe Pauline assaulted Sarah!" Marcellus rasped bitterly. Though he shouldn't be surprised, he thought: Only Collins could get five from adding one and one. "Hell, she was here with me all evening anyway."

Muttering a cocksure sigh, Detective Collins replied, "That's exactly what I'd expect you to say. Get Ms. Sinclair, will you please," he added impatiently.

Marcellus gritted his teeth as he stared stonily at the detective for a second before storming off. The uniform proceeded to follow, and Marcellus stopped in his tracks to glare at Collins over the officer's head.

"It's all right, Officer Shelton," Detective Collins said, returning Marcellus's stare with a smirk of a smile. "I don't believe an upstanding citizen like Mr. Cavanaugh will try to obstruct justice."

"Marcellus, what's going on?" Barbara asked.

"Not now, Mother," Marcellus replied impatiently.

As Marcellus started up, Pauline was coming down the stairs. She had dressed in his black silk robe that dragged the floor, because she had known he would not have been able to get rid of a late night visitor quickly. With love brimming in her eyes, she smiled down at her bronze prince. From midway up the stairs, he paused to look at her in a frozen stare, the bra strap hanging from the bunch of her clothes in his arms. It was a hilarious sight, she amused herself, sauntering down to meet him.

"Cute, but I don't think it will fit you," she said for his ears, a teasing smile brightening her features. Kissing him on the cheek, she said, "We'll just have to finish what we started another time."

"Pauline . . ."

His tone of voice, the expression that came over his face, caused her to tense. She looked down into the family room and saw what had caused the pained look on his face. Her pulse skipped a beat.

"Ms. Sinclair."

"Pauline."

Barbara and Detective Collins called her simultaneously.

"Don't worry about a thing," Marcellus assured her softly.

Pauline nodded. She felt an odd, serene feeling, in spite of the awkward situation, as she proceeded into the room.

"Ms. Sinclair, I'm going to have to ask you to come in for questioning," Detective Collins said in a terse, vigorous voice.

Ignoring him, she calmly gazed at the elder Cavanaughs, who were looking at her with concerned expressions. Marcellus took his physical stature from his father, she thought, looking at the older man. Though a powerful and shrewd businessman, next to his delicate-looking but aggressive, outgoing wife, he was quiet and unassuming. Together, they proved that opposites attract.

"Hello, Barbara. Mr. Cavanaugh. How are you?" Pauline asked as she approached them.

Malaby rose from the couch to squeeze her hands affectionately. "I don't want you to worry about a thing," he said softly, in his usual paternal voice.

Showing her appreciation with a nod, Pauline moved to take Barbara's outstretched hands. Looking into the older woman's sensitive gaze, she felt a connection, a psychic link. She was somewhat surprised, for she had always believed that Barbara had never thought she was good enough for Marcellus. She now knew that it had been her own insecurity that had marred their relationship. She hoped she had a second chance at this one, as well, she thought, looking over her shoulder at Marcellus.

"You listen to Malaby," Barbara said, patting her hand gently. Over Pauline's shoulder, she spoke to Marcellus. "Don't just stand there. Call Dottie."

"Ms. Sinclair," Detective Collins said, prodding her.

Pauline looked down at her bare feet and wiggled her toes. "Is it all right if I get dressed?"

Like in a movie theater, it was dark inside the room except for the bright glare of the monitor. Scowling, Marcellus stared at the *Eye of Horus*. In addition to the "eye", a request for the PASSWORD glowered back at him.

But he was all out of ideas. It was late, and the clock was ticking. Pauline must still be at the police station since she hadn't called to inform him otherwise. He hadn't wanted to leave her, even though Dottie was present. The attorney had arrived, fire-breathing mad, he snickered in memory.

At her encouragement, for he knew he was of no help to Pauline there, he left to drop by the hospital to check on Sarah. Reuben wasn't there, and the head nurse wouldn't let him visit her. Instead, he had to accept the nurse's assurance that Sarah was resting peacefully.

He started for home, intending to review the tapes, then veered to the Wellsings'. The answer was here . . . in Don's computer, he thought, strongly suspecting that whoever had assaulted Sarah must have come to the same conclusion. Sarah had claimed that her assailant had been a woman, but he didn't know whether or not she was a reliable witness. Implicating Pauline could be just another of Sarah's warped suspicions of her.

Unexpectedly, he was flooded by memories of their love-making. The image was vivid and clear, the sensations almost tangible. Heat rippling under his skin in remembrance of her touches, Marcellus shuddered, stirring from his stillness. Though he had no idea what he was doing, his hands reached for the keyboard. As if on a whim, he typed "PAULINE."

Miraculously, the shape changed from the *Eye of Horus* to a picture of Cupid pointing a bow toward a red heart on the screen.

"Ha-ha," he chortled sarcastically. "You cheated," he exclaimed accusingly, but triumph shone in his expression.

But as he scrolled down the screen, his expression underwent a metamorphosis. "That's it?" he asked perplexed, his lips pressed together and his eyes narrowed in a pensive frown. He scrolled frantically for more information, but there was no more.

Arms folded across his chest, he stared crossly at the screen as if he could make it fill up miraculously with information. He wasn't sure how to interpret this message of nondisclosure. And there was something else he hadn't considered before now.

Why would Don leave any message at all unless he didn't expect to be able to deliver it in person?

Standing at the counter in the kitchen, Pauline absently stirred the spoon in the cup of hot coffee. She wore Marcellus's pajama shirt that fell to her knees with a white towel wrapped around her head. Despite her shower, she was nearly wiped out.

She had been released an hour ago; it was now half past the hour of seven. Yet she was still too wound up to stay in bed. If there was any consolation to be found in her ordeal, she thought, it was knowing that Collins had to be as exhausted as she was.

He had implied over and over again that she was a gold-digger who, without compunction, murdered anyone who got in her way. Despite the lack of evidence, he promised to tie her into Ann-Marie's murder, as well as the attempt on Don's life. Though Dottie had been a field marshall during the interrogation, it had been holding on to the memory of what she stood to lose if Collins acted out his promise to lock her up that made the ordeal tolerable.

A bounty of indescribable sensations was impressed in her thoughts, teasing her senses with what the future held for Marcellus and her. She blushed unconsciously, remembering the feel of him on her . . . in her . . . surrounding her with his awesome essence. Her flesh tingling from the memory of him, she felt like an addict who was suffering a relapse from recovery—needing and wanting him even more than before.

But, she cautioned herself, the "chance" he had spoken of was a trial of, not a commitment to, permanence. In the skip of a heartbeat, she remembered the idyllic times when passion had flowed unending between them and nothing else seemed to matter. Was she in danger of traveling that rollercoaster ride again?

Her musings were interrupted when Dottie strolled into the room, a cigarette hanging out of the side of her mouth. She was shoeless, and the silk blouse she had worn with a pants suit to the police station hung wrinkled at her waistline.

Heading straight for the coffee pot on the counter, Dottie said, "I expected you to be counting sheep."

"I wish," Pauline replied with a sardonic snort. Setting the spoon on the side of the cup, she massaged the inside corners of her eyes just above her nose. "Every time I close my eyes, I see a bunch of Detective Collinses running after me." She strolled to the breakfast table, cup in hand.

"I guess that's understandable," Dottie replied, pouring coffee in a cup.

"You handled him rather nicely," Pauline replied, blowing at the steam rising from the cup. "He seemed to be quite taken with you."

"The little beady-eyed bastard," Dottie said. "I don't know what he thought he was doing. I could have puked on him ... making all those stupid, unsubstantiated remarks. He knows he doesn't have a case."

Pauline smiled as she sipped her coffee. "I got the distinct impression that, if it weren't for you, I would still be in that grubby little room, listening to him drone on and on about how I could have committed the crimes. If I had to stay there much longer, I think I would have confessed to anything."

"That's what they usually hope for," Dottie replied, drinking a swallow of coffee. "Where's Marcellus?"

"He had to go in early," Pauline replied. Marcellus had left a note explaining that he wanted to return those tapes to CSI before the employees started to arrive. He promised to fill her in later on what he had uncovered. And it was that partial revelation that explained part of her excitation: she wondered what he had found in those tapes. "He suggested that I get some rest, and ordered me to stay away from CSI."

"Can't blame him," Dottie replied, sitting at the table. "That place has turned into a grief factory."

"I'm going in anyway," Pauline said, spreading her elbows on the table, cup in her hands. "I need to finish up the program and plans for the memorial service." Taking a sip of coffee, she said, "I don't think I can sit home all day, wondering what's going on." Besides, she thought, she still wanted to check those logs. "Oh, damn," she swore.

"What?"

"I was supposed to organize some employees to pick up

Mrs. Johns from the hotel and take her to Ann-Marie's place. I completely forgot."

"Certainly anyone with keys to CSI can call over there and instruct a secretary to do that," Dottie said. "You need to get some rest before you fall on your face."

"I know," Pauline agreed reluctantly, "but I'd end up feeling like I'd abandoned her."

"Well, suit yourself," Dottie replied. "After this," she said, holding up her cup, "I'm going to head back to the city. I need to stop off at the house and change. I have a couple of court cases this afternoon. If that little gnat of a detective tries something else, my secretary can always find me if you need me." Downing the coffee and pinning Pauline with a hard stare, she said, "Don't forget."

Bobbing her head, Pauline replied, "Hear no evil, see no evil, and speak no evil, until my attorney gets there."

"You got it," Dottie said. She got up to set the empty cup in the sink and hold the burning cigarette under a flow of water. Dumping the wet butt in the trash, she said, "I'm out of here."

He couldn't help it, Marcellus smiled to himself with amused memory. He had looked into Pauline's shopping bag, he recalled, and seen what had brought the blush to her face during dinner. Too bad he hadn't given her a chance to wear it, or himself the opportunity to take it off her body. But there would be another time.

With a flicker of desire burning inside him, he wished he were home instead of here. He made a play for the telephone, picked up the receiver, then changed his mind. Instead, he picked up the mug of steaming liquid on the corner of the desk. "Let her get some sleep," Marcellus said softly.

He recalled that, before he left the house, Dottie had called from the police station to let him know they were heading home. Unfortunately, he wasn't in a position to wait for them. He glanced toward the serving tray of tea that had been set up between the two chairs in front of his desk. His first visitor of the day should be arriving soon.

As long as Pauline was out . . . that was all that mattered. There would be another opportunity to see her in that negligee, he smiled into his mug of hot chocolate.

Drink in hand, he sauntered over to stand at the picture window. A gray overcast complemented the chilly morning. It was almost eight. From his vantage point, he could see the parking lot below fill up as employees paraded into the building. Most of the researchers had arrived a good fifteen minutes ago.

While reviewing the tapes, he recalled, he had noticed that, on several different occasions within a three-day span, Don had talked with Dr. James Chin. Though he supposed it wasn't unusual, his curiosity had gotten the best of him. It was what explained his hurry to the office this morning. After returning the tapes, he had instructed Clay to have Dr. Chin contact him as soon as the scientist arrived.

At the tepid knock on the door, he turned slightly, waiting. The door opened, and Katherine peeked in. "Dr. Chin is here to see you," she announced.

"Send him in, please."

Marcellus returned to the desk and set his mug down before sauntering across the room to greet the Chinese-American scientist whose mixed Caucasian and Oriental ancestry was evident. A big man, Dr. Chin reminded him of a Western-Asian version of Tom Sellick.

"Good morning, Doctor; I'm glad you were able to come right up," Marcellus said, his hand extended.

"When the man who signs my check calls, I answer," Dr. Chin replied, chuckling, as he accepted the outstretched hand. "I see you're over that nasty cold."

"Yes," Marcellus replied. "I had an excellent nurse. Tea?"

"Aw, you know my weakness," Dr. Chin said. He helped himself without waiting for a formal invitation.

Marcellus returned to sit behind his desk and resumed nursing his chocolate. When Dr. Chin took one of the chairs in front of the desk, he spoke. "I don't want to take up too much of your time, Dr. Chin, so I'll get right to the point." His chair angled to the side, he asked casually, "Did you notice any friction between Don and any of the other scientists?"

"Friction? What kind of friction?" Dr. Chin asked, the cup of tea hovering at his lips.

"Any kind," Marcellus replied and then he clarified, "personal or professional. Maybe you noticed something between Don and Dr. Kent."

"Hm . . . friction between the Mata Hari and Einstein," Dr. Chin said thoughtfully, his head angled.

Marcellus hid a smile behind his hand; he hadn't heard Don and J.T. referred to by those names before, but he supposed they fit.

"What you might call professional jealousy," Dr. Chin said carefully, "does not exactly apply." He drank a sip of tea before continuing. "I guess you could say one falls on the wet side of nanoscience, and the other on the dry side."

He had asked a simple question, and he was getting a scientific lecture, Marcellus mused sarcastically. But he knew not to rush Dr. Chin who had a propensity for reducing everything to its nanometric size: nanoscience was his specialty. CSI had gotten into a bidding war with Rice University which wanted the engineer for its Center for Nanoscale Science & Technology, he recalled. At Don's insistence that nanoscience was the wave of the future, Marcellus had agreed to the six-figure salary and expensive lab equipment Dr. Chin needed to advance his research in miniaturization.

"As you know," Dr. Chin was saying, "some of the most

intriguing new developments in biomedicine and pharma-ceuticals will come from interfacing wet and dry nanoscale science.''

"What does that mean in terms of Don and J.T., Dr. Chin?" Marcellus asked, suppressing his impatience.

Dr. Chin readjusted himself in the chair, the corners of his mouth in a sheepish smile as he sipped his tea. "I guess you could say they have not reached the coherent phase of interfacing. Naturally, she wants to advance her physics research to strengthen and increase the longevity of rock-ets, while Don, the engineer, wants to reduce the size of the mechanism that guides the spaceship."

For a second, Marcellus's heart skipped a beat, fearing Don had disclosed *Project Ba* to Dr. Chin.

"But he said he was going to take off a few days," Dr. Chin picked up, his expression and tone wistfully absorbed, "spend some time with his lovely wife, whom he'd been neglecting, and make a decision when he returned."

Apparently Dr. Chin did not know about the project, Marcellus thought relieved. "What was he was going to make a decision about?"

"Whether or not to hire a physicist, as J.T. has been insisting we need," Dr. Chin replied as if the answer was obvious.

"Okay, Doc," Marcellus said, forcing a smile to his face, "thanks a lot. You've been a big help," he lied. "Do you play racquetball, by any chance, Dr. Chin?"

The only set of clean clothes Pauline had left was a green, white, and navy nylon sweatsuit, which she wore with white Nikes. She had toyed with the idea of going home first, but decided she was presentable enough. She knocked on the hotel door.

"Who's there?" Mrs. Johns asked from inside the suite.

"It's Pauline from CSI, Mrs. Johns." She elected not to

confuse the woman, recalling that Mrs. Johns had believed she and Marcellus were married.

"What do you want?"

Pauline's head snapped at the vestige of hostility in Mrs. Johns's voice. A frown rolled across her forehead, and confusion knotted her insides.

"Don't you remember? Someone from the company was coming to accompany you to Ann-Marie's," Pauline replied somewhat anxiously. "That someone turned out to be me," she added, forcing levity to her voice.

"Well, I already talked to one of Ann-Marie's friends, and she's coming to get me on her lunch break."

With her mouth gaping open, Pauline stared silently, with a frown on her face. She was trying to think what to do, but a question dominated her thoughts: who from CSI had called? Before she could fathom a guess, Mrs. Johns's voice penetrated the barrier again.

"How dare you show up here, knowing you killed my daughter?"

The question was rhetorical, the harsh accusation very real. Pauline gasped, thoroughly dumbfounded. "Mrs. Johns . . ." she sputtered. Her disbelief was so great that she couldn't get her thoughts in order.

She heard the lock turn, then the door opened with a jerk. Mrs. Johns stood there, a statue of rage. Pauline could feel the mother's hatred between them like a brick wall. She quivered inwardly.

"And to think that I believed you were such a nice person," Mrs. Johns said. Her voice was as stern and mocking as her expression.

"Mrs. Johns, where did you hear that lie . . . that I killed Ann-Marie?" Pauline asked, her astonishment pronounced in both her expression and her tone.

"Well, if you didn't actually kill her"—Mrs. Johns vacillated somewhat—"then you know who did. Otherwise, the police wouldn't have taken you in for questioning."

Pauline swallowed thickly. She tried guessing the identity of the informant, but she couldn't get over the indictment. "Yes," she admitted softly, with regret, then strength injected into her voice, "the police did ask me some questions, but that was because I found Ann-Marie's body. But I swear to you, I didn't have anything to do with her death. Who told you that?" she repeated in desperation.

"Never mind who told me," Mrs. Johns replied stubbornly. "The point is," she added insultingly, "I don't want you anywhere near me or my daughter."

On the verge of tears, Pauline gulped before she finally found her voice. "But, Mrs. Johns . . . !"

"I wonder if that nice Mr. Cavanaugh, *who is not your husband,*" she emphasized bitterly, "knows what kind of woman he's gotten himself involved with."

With that, she slammed the door in Pauline's face, leaving her to contend with her shock and hurt.

Chapter Fourteen

Since leaving the office yesterday, he had felt an odd sense of foreboding, Marcellus mused during the elevator ride up. But knowing he was going home to Pauline, he had discounted the disturbing sensation. When he arrived at an empty house, it had returned full-blown.

He felt it now—even stronger, he thought, as the elevators doors opened to let him off. He started for his office, then impulsively, changed his direction. As he headed for Don's office, recalling that he'd spoken to Pauline on the phone last night, he wondered if she would keep her word.

It was soon obvious that no one, neither Pauline nor Amy, had arrived. Noticing the slice of light under the door of Don's inner office, he tsked that someone had left it on all night. He opened the door, scanned the room quickly, then flipped off the light.

Closing the door, he headed for his original destination, Pauline still on his mind. He couldn't rid himself of a nagging idea that something must have happened that would explain her absence. Or maybe being taken in by the police had affected her more than he had realized. That was why he had let her off the hook with a claim of exhaustion last night. But he was not going to suffer another one without her, he decided, determined. Either she was going to stay at his place, or he was going to hers. One way or the other, they would be together.

Before entering the area proper, he heard, "No. Ms. Bridgewater, today?"

Marcellus stopped in his tracks to exhale a weary breath. "Collins," he rasped in a whisper. He wondered what the detective wanted this time.

"I haven't heard from Amy this morning," Katherine replied, "but it's early yet; I'm sure she'll be here shortly."

"What about Mr. Cavanaugh?"

"He'll be here, too," said Katherine.

"What time does he usually arrive?"

"Usually very early, around seven. He's just running a little behind schedule this morning."

"Have there been any arguments or misunderstandings between Mr. Cavanaugh and Mr. Wellsing lately?"

"Not to my knowledge."

"Aw, come, Mrs. Lacey," he cajoled. "You're an executive secretary. Certainly if anyone would know, you would."

"Detective Collins, you've already asked me these questions before," Katherine said with bored irritation in her voice. "My answers haven't changed. No arguments, Amy is a good secretary, and I have no idea whether or not Mr. Wellsing had a woman on the side."

Deciding it was time to save Katherine, Marcellus advanced to his section of the floor. He arrived unnoticed. Detective Collins was making himself at home in the cushy arm chair adjacent to Katherine's desk. She was behind it, typing a document on the computer. Collins looked up squarely into his face.

"Uh, Mr. Cavanaugh, I'm glad you decided to come in," he said, springing to his feet.

"I didn't realize I was on your clock, detective," Marcellus replied, eyeing the detective coolly down the length of his nose. "Morning, Katherine," he said in a tone reserved for friends and respected associates.

"Morning, boss," she replied.

"We have a lot to do this morning, Katherine," Marcellus announced, continuing to his office.

"I'm right behind you." Getting a pad and pen, Katherine followed Marcellus into his office.

"Mr. Cavanaugh," Detective Collins said from Katherine's heels, "I was hoping to get a little time with you this morning. I have a few questions to ask you."

Marcellus set his briefcase on his desk, replying, "Not now. Katherine, schedule Detective Collins for an appointment sometime after two this afternoon."

Katherine had turned to usher the detective out the door when Collins blurted out, "Mr. Cavanaugh, as I understand it, Mrs. Wellsing owns four percent of the company."

Marcellus didn't stop to reply. He set his briefcase on the side of the desk, then faced Collins with a "so what?" expression.

"But she's never taken an active role in running the company," Collins continued.

Speaking of Sarah, Marcellus mused distracted, he needed to speak with her, to see her face as she described the assault and the person who had attacked her. Collins was still running off at the mouth, he heard, drawing his attention back to the detective.

"Which means you're the partner who stands to gain the most in the event of Mr. Wellsing's death," Collins concluded.

Marcellus froze fractionally in the act of removing his suit coat. He looked across the room at Collins with knitted eyebrows and a clenched jaw. He knew Collins was baiting him, but the way he was feeling this morning . . . Holding onto his temper, he bit the inside of his jaw, but rage exuded from his expression.

"I think you had better leave, Detective," Katherine suggested anxiously.

"Aerospace and technology are expensive fields. Where did you get the money to start this business . . . your family's S&L?"

It wasn't a question—it was an insult. Instinctively, Marcellus's shoulders rolled and flexed as he leaned over the desk, looking every bit like a lion about to prey. The detective took a quick look behind him, as if assuring himself that no obstacle blocked a hasty exit should he need to make one.

"Detective, you can't believe I'm as stupid as you imply by your insulting questions and comments," Marcellus replied with measured menace in his tone. "Since you know of my partnership in CSI, you have the wherewithal to locate any other piece of information you need. Now, don't waste any more of my time."

"If I have any more questions, I'll be back," Collins said, backing out from the room.

"What a stupid little man," Katherine declared.

"No, he's not stupid," Marcellus replied, running a weary hand down his face. "He's jealous and afraid." Quickly discarding the detective from his thoughts, he asked, "Is Pauline here?"

"Not yet," Katherine replied hesitantly.

Marcellus paused thoughtfully for a second. He had to consider that Pauline wasn't coming. He had learned to distance himself from the humiliation and pain he had felt after their initial breakup. He knew he could do it again if he had to, but he prayed it wouldn't come to that. "Give me a minute alone, will you, Katherine?"

* * *

A soft musing look in her eyes, Pauline stared absently out the window. Mid-morning, the sun was threatening to break through. But the weather was not what was on her mind.

Curled on the loveseat in the clinic with a pen between her teeth, temptation nudged her senses. Marcellus was on the premises, a mere phone call away. She knew from what Katherine had told her when she arrived that he was anxious to see her. But not as anxious as she, she thought, the past twenty-four hours darting across her mind in spurts.

Leaving the hotel yesterday, she had decided not to tell Marcellus about her encounter with Mrs. Johns. The woman's hostile histrionics had affected her badly, and she didn't want him to know. He might not think too highly of his queen.

She had also decided not to return to CSI, in spite of the mounds of work she had promised to do. Certain that everyone at CSI knew that the police had picked her up from Marcellus's home for questioning, she had felt that he didn't need his employees looking at him suspiciously because of her. Even though he knew she had nothing to do with the incidents at CSI, she didn't want him to endure any more embarrassment because of her.

But the night had been pure torture . . . wanting to go to him, yet fearful. The barrier, she knew, had been of her own making, but she'd been unable to shake it off. It was best all around to stay away—from CSI and from him.

Or so she had told herself, until he called last night.

"Where the hell are you?" he had demanded.

"Where did you call?" she quipped, thrilled by the mere sound of his voice.

"You're supposed to be here . . . with me," he had shot back gruffly. "Why aren't you?"

"I guess I was more tired than I thought." She lied

glibly, her fingers crossed in her mind. "I slept the day away, and when I woke up, I ate and fell back in the bed."

"All right; that'll get you off the hook this time. See you tomorrow."

She had done none of the work she had planned last night, she chuckled lightly, her mind returning fully to the present. And she was getting no work done now, she told herself.

As she was about to rise, there was a knock on the door. A cheerful thrill coursed down her spine: Marcellus's impatience to see her had gotten the best of him, she thought, pleased.

Amy peeked her head through the opening.

"Good morning, Ms. Sinclair," she said cheerfully. "I'd heard you had arrived. I've been helping Leonard pack Ann-Marie's things for her mother."

Disappointed, Pauline had to force a warm greeting for Don's secretary. "Good morning, Amy."

The mention of Ann-Marie and her mother stirred contradictory emotions in her. She recalled that Mrs. Johns had said a friend of Ann-Marie's had phoned her—which naturally led to Amy. But she was hesitant to eliminate Dr. Kent as a possible culprit. She hoped an inherent distrust of her wasn't making her suspicious of the scientist.

"Just checking to see if there was something I could do for you," Amy said.

Is it you? Pauline asked silently of Amy, recalling Mrs. Johns's vicious accusation. "No, thank you," she replied.

"Dr. Kent asked for you," Amy added with sudden recollection.

The surprise was too great for Pauline to school from showing. "She specifically asked for me? What does she want?"

"She didn't say. Only that she'd get back to you," Amy replied. "Well, since you don't need anything, I'm going to run back down to two to help finish the job."

"Okay. Thanks."

The instant Amy closed the door, the expression on Pauline's face metamorphosed to match her furtive thoughts. The puzzle pieces were piling up, but not falling into place, she thought.

Tapping the pen in her hand, she remembered she hadn't gotten around to checking the logs in the gym. After a moment of silent debate, she decided to finish arrangements for the memorial service first.

She crossed to the desk and began searching the drawers for a fresh notepad. Finding one, she pulled it out. As she flipped it open, she noticed that the top page was nearly filled with pencil doodles. She tore off the sheet and tossed it in the trash.

Returning to her seat with the stenopad, she settled down to work on the program. Engrossed, she wasn't aware of how much time had elapsed until a knock on the door aroused her. She looked up, replying, "Come in."

The door opened and Marcellus stepped in. Pauline felt her insides turn to mush, her gaze feasting on the sight of him. "Hi," she said in a gentle-toned voice, with an expression that matched.

"Hi, yourself," he replied.

He closed the door at his back and leaned against it. Recalling his displeasure during their conversation, he seemed cautious, uncharacteristically docile, she thought, regretfully. She understood his attitude and was ashamed of herself for causing it.

"How are you feeling this morning?" he asked. "Did you get enough sleep last night?"

Pauline noted the impish gleam in his dark eyes, the half grin on his mouth. The look was almost a challenge, daring her to lie. "I suppose," she replied diplomatically, smiling back at him.

The smile fell from his face, and a different kind of emotion unmasked his private thoughts. No longer uncertain, his piercing black eyes raked her with a fiercely posses-sive look. She wet her lips with her tongue, and a sensation streaked with longing began to swell in her. He crossed the room to sit on the small couch next to her in a snug fit.

"I thought you could use a break," he said. "I have to go up to the lab and wondered if you'd like to accompany me."

"Yes, I'd like that."

"Good," he replied, nodding his head, his eyes never leaving her face.

The atmosphere hummed with rhapsody, and, for a long time, neither of them stirred. Her eyes were level with his mouth. Firm, succulent lips beckoned her. Her heart beat erratically as she tried to shake the notion of silent, luring lips calling to her. Her gaze slid slowly up to scan his face: he was more enticing than a bit-o'-honey treat. And from the way he was looking at her with his black bedroom eyes, she nearly moaned from the heat that ripped across her flesh. As if on impulse, he pulled her foot to his lap and casually, began to stroke its bottom.

"Did you miss me last night?"

Pauline bit down on her bottom lip as if the gesture could control the aroused sensations building inside her. "Marcellus," she said in a tone that contained equal sounds of wanting and warning. "We have to maintain a sense of propriety," she added in a tremulous voice. "Somebody could walk in on us. Amy was just here."

"Not that I care, but Amy is nowhere near now," he replied, his voice low and husky, reflecting the desire in his expression. As if to prove his point, his hand stole up her leg, his finger drawing a circle over the spot at the back of her knee. She sucked in a deep breath and held it. "As for propriety, I don't know what that is where you're concerned," he declared, his hand behind her head, pull-ing her face to his.

Pauline had a millisecond to draw a quick, unsteady breath before her mouth was smothered by his warm lips. Her hands curled behind his neck, her fingers in his hair, and she gave herself up to the pleasure of his kiss. Tremors shook her body as his tongue swept inside to caress the walls of her mouth and kiss her with provocative insistence. She returned his kiss fiercely, shifting closer into him, wanting the kiss to go on forever.

Finally, he lifted his head and a meow of disappointment seeped past her lips. Their foreheads locked together, his heavy, hot breath mingled with hers.

"We better go," he said, a hint of regret in his voice.

Reluctantly, they parted, staring into each other's dreamy gaze. With the unfulfilled ache in her loins like a dead weight, Pauline nodded.

Suffer ye, man, of wants, from acts of indiscretion, Marcellus chided himself moments later as he led Pauline from the clinic. It was a struggle trying to ignore the wanton sensations that clung to his limbs and every nerve ending in his body. He'd meant to be cool, but Pauline had looked so incredibly enticing that his brain had catapulted from its usual residence in his body.

They proceeded to the elevator, where a car arrived in a flash. Once the doors closed, Marcellus inserted a flat key into the box, then the elevator took off like a jet.

"Access to the lab," he explained, holding up the key before putting it in his pocket.

"I had wondered. What's going on in the lab?"

"I need to talk to Dr. Chin. He's one of the engineers who works closely with Don." Following his initial meeting with Dr. Chin, he recalled, he had instructed Clay to double-check the engineer. It was only within the past hour that both Clay and he were satisfied that Dr. Chin was clean. It had become painfully clear that he had no choice but to return to the scientist to ask him directly what he knew of *Project Ba*.

"You implied that you found something in Don's computer," she said. "We never got around to discussing it."

"Yeah," he said, running a hand across his head. "Clay and I are ninety-nine percent certain that Don was worried about something, though we haven't figured *that* out . . . yet."

"That means you remembered the password, then."

"Not remembered; guessed," he replied chuckling. "I lucked upon it."

"What was it?"

"You."

"Me?"

"Yes," he smiled broadly down at her. "It was Pauline."

The doors opened into a silent hallway. With his hand on the small of her back, Marcellus guided Pauline down a concrete floor corridor.

"We're going to the Special Projects lab," he said. "The other way would have taken us to the bread-and-butter research department."

Stepping into a room as large as a gymnasium, Pauline whistled in awe. "I feel as if I just entered a space museum," she said.

Men and women in white lab coats, some even in space suits, were in huddles of threes and fours before the many electronic work stations set up about the room. A spaceship hung suspended from the ceiling nearby. A person in a spacesuit was walking around, his or her sex indeterminable.

"Excuse me, Dr. Timmons," Marcellus said, stopping a white-coated researcher who passed before them carrying a large steel triangular object.

"Oh," Dr. Timmons replied absently. "What can I do for you?"

"I'm looking for Dr. Chin," Marcellus replied.

Straining his neck to look around the room, Dr. Timmons replied, "Well, he was here a little while ago, that's all I can tell you."

"Thank you," Marcellus replied dryly, and the researcher continued purposefully on his way.

"He seemed to be preoccupied," Pauline said with mirth in her voice.

"Most of them seem to be in space all the time, if you ask me," he replied. "But they produce."

He heard Pauline gasp and looked to see what had caused her sudden alarm.

"What's that coming this way?" she asked with anxious intrigue in her voice.

Marcellus chuckled. "That's Donnie," he explained of the three-foot midget of shiny stainless steel rolling toward them. "I thought you'd get a kick out of meeting him." The robot neared. "Hello, Donnie," he said.

"Marcellus," the robot replied, with excitement in his high-pitched mechanical voice. "What's happening, dude?"

Donnie had a half-moon clear plastic head from which red lights flashed when he spoke. A silver pole with blue hydraulic cylinders ran the center of his square circuitry-board chest. His legs looked as if they were sealed together, with rollers attached for feet. His arms were the closest things to human limbs, long and ribbed-like accordions, with three-prong pliers for fingers.

"You got it, dude," Marcellus replied laughingly. "I have somebody I want you to meet."

In jerky movements, Donnie twisted his metal body toward Pauline. Suddenly, the blinking lights of his eyes twirled around his clear plastic head. "Pauline. Pauline. Pauline," he exclaimed.

Stunned, Marcellus said aloud to himself, "Why, that sneaky rascal. He didn't tell me he had programmed Donnie to recognize you."

Donnie extended a silver hand to Pauline. She looked at Marcellus stupidly, then shook the non-human limb.

"Hey, Donnie, get over here!" a researcher called from across the room.

"Slave driver," Donnie muttered in his stilted voice, then spun on his wheels and rolled off.

With an astonished chuckle, Pauline said, "I'm impressed."

"Just another of Don's little expensive toys," Marcellus said. "Come on, I need to find Dr. Chin." Before he took a step, the portable phone in his pocket rang. He pulled it out and flipped it open to answer.

"Hey! You can't use that thing in here!"

Marcellus looked across the way, where a group of researchers were staring at him with ire and disgust in their expressions. "Sorry," he said, with a sheepish smile. To Pauline: "Excuse me. I'd better go find a room. Satisfy your curiosity," he invited, pointing toward the researchers. "They don't bite."

A deep frown etched Pauline's expression. She was standing behind the high reception counter of the gym area, a black binder filled with log sheets under her hand. She rapped her fingers on the page, wondering if she were mistaken.

She was positive she'd seen the log sheet with Don's name listed to play racquetball on the day before he'd fallen seriously ill, she thought. It was no longer here.

Thinking the logbook could be out of order, she examined the day of each page, then it dawned on her that maybe the police had taken the sheet as evidence when they came to claim Ann-Marie's body. With a sigh of disappointment, she glanced at her watch: it was nearly five. As far as she knew, Marcellus had yet to return from leaving to take his call earlier while they were in the lab. Though

he hadn't had time to give her an explanation, the call
was urgent, and it had taken him from the building. She
knew he'd stopped at his office on his way out to grab his
coat and leave his house key with Katherine to give to her.
There was no debate that she would use it, Pauline smiled
unconsciously. She might even cook dinner for him.

She rapped the desk counter a final time and was about
to step away when she saw Dr. Kent heading toward the
gym. She was walking alongside a man who dwarfed her,
and Pauline's curiosity was piqued as to the identity of the
man. She couldn't forget that she and Marcellus believed
there was a spy in their midst.

Both were dressed to play racquetball. Dr. Kent's steps
faltered upon seeing her, then the scientist seemed to lift
her chin a little higher as she and her partner neared. He
wore his mixed ancestry more in his physical stature—tall
and broad-shouldered—than in his round face, with its
slanted shape of slightly protruding eyes.

"What's this . . . a new position?" Dr. Kent asked, with
snippiness in her tone and a snake-like smile on her lips
that was anything but friendly. Before Pauline could
answer, Dr. Kent turned to her partner. "Jimmy, have you
met Pauline yet?"

"No, I haven't had the pleasure," he replied, extending
his hand. "I'm James Chin."

"Pauline Sinclair," she replied. "How do you do,
Mr. . . ?"

"It's Dr. Chin," Dr. Kent corrected arrogantly.

She was finally getting to meet Dr. Chin, the subject of
idle gossip, Pauline mused, smiling politely at him. "I see
you're all set for a game of racquetball," she said. "Do
you play often?" She wondered if he ever played with Don.

"J.T., here," he replied as if amused, "has promised to
teach me. I prefer golf, but it's hard finding a partner
around this place. Everybody seems to be into racquetball."

Pauline turned her attention to Dr. Kent. "I understand you were looking for me."

"Me? I don't think so," Dr. Kent replied as if taken aback by the suggestion.

"That was my understanding," Pauline replied.

"It wasn't me."

"Well, enjoy your game," Pauline said, wondering what game Dr. Kent was playing. No, she didn't like the woman, and her distrust of her simply grew each time they met. And it was hard imagining the woman befriending anyone—least of all Ann-Marie's mother, Mrs. Johns.

"He was stone drunk, babbling like an idiot, and bawling in his gin and tonic," Marcellus replied, profoundly annoyed. He took it out on his burger, tossing the half-eaten sandwich on the coffee table, where he was sitting on the floor with the couch at his back. Pauline had offered to cook, he recalled, but he'd disallowed it. He had had other plans for them tonight.

"What was he babbling about?" Pauline asked.

He really didn't want to talk about CSI or its problems, he mused absently. Pauline looked like a gorgeous lady of leisure stretched on the couch, sipping a chocolate malt through a straw. He wanted to talk about them, for it was their mercurial relationship that he wanted to define. Once that had happened, he could devote his full attention to the problems affecting CSI. But Pauline insisted on having her curiosity satisfied.

"It seems our mild-mannered and very married Leonard was in love with Ann-Marie Johns," he replied. The call he'd taken earlier in the day had come from Clay. The head of CSI security had gone to Brewsky's, a restaurant and bar in the Holiday Inn nearby, for lunch. He ran into Leonard Coombs, who had already downed more than a few drinks.

"Wow!" Pauline exclaimed. "I'd heard that on the gossip circuit, but I didn't put any stock in it. His poor wife."

Marcellus smiled to himself at her reaction, thinking that he was the one who was suffering. He'd returned to CSI just in time to catch her as she was leaving, he recalled, picking up his drink to take a sip. He smiled unconsciously, remembering the way Pauline had dangled the house key in his face, answering the anxious question inside him.

Setting the drink on the table, he said with bemusement, "He did say something I'm not sure how to interpret. It could have been the liquor talking."

"Since you've given it a second thought, maybe there is something to it. What was it?"

"Lightning strikes twice," he replied, looking up at her with an expectant gaze.

"Lightning strikes twice?" she repeated, pondering. "Hm. That is curious. What could it mean?"

"He could have been referring to the fact that two people from CSI have met with foul play," he said with sarcasm in his tone. "Hell, I don't know," he erupted with frustration. He set the plastic cup containing his soda on the table, lay his head back on the couch, and closed his eyes.

He felt Pauline stir, moving near him, her leg brushing against him. "Where are you going?" he asked.

"Come right here." She instructed him to sit between her legs.

"Kinky, but I like it," he said amused, as he obeyed and was soon rewarded for his compliance. He groaned appreciatively at her first touch, magical fingers in his silky hair, rubbing his scalp. Light, then firm pressure moved down the back of his neck and shoulders. With his eyes closed, his body relaxed under the ministrations of her balmy touch. The entire time Clay and he were wrestling with a drunk Leonard, he was wondering whether Pauline would remain when they were no longer bound by the unfortunate events that had brought them back together.

"You're not going to sleep on me, are you?" she asked in a soft-colored voice.

"If I am, it's your fault," he replied dreamily. "That feels wonderful. Where were you earlier today when I needed this?"

"All you had to do was call," she replied.

"Really?" he asked.

Her hands stilled on his shoulders. "How do you want me to answer that?"

Marcellus faced her from his kneeling position between her thighs to stare into her face with a searching gaze. He had promised he wouldn't do this to himself again, but his expectations wouldn't be grounded by reason. It was good between them. He couldn't, or wouldn't, allow himself to believe that even Pauline would deny it, even though she had let him down before.

"I want you to move in. We don't need to maintain two residences." His heart was beating fast, out-racing his tongue, as quick-on-his-feet words spewed from his mouth. "I know what I said about taking time to get to know one another, and that this seems fast . . . We can still do that, but this way . . ."

Pauline cut him off succinctly. "Let's just take it one day at a time." A beat of silence passed before Marcellus turned to look at her. "All right?"

"No, it's not all right," he replied contentiously. She seemed unmoved by his angry disappointment.

"Tell me what you're thinking. I don't want to guess," she said.

"I've never made any secrets about what I wanted," he replied.

"We've been separated a long time. Are you sure you aren't superimposing something over what's not really there?"

"Suppose you tell me," he quipped. "Are you masquerading as the woman I fell in love with a year and a half ago?''

"I'm not that same woman."

Marcellus fell silent, entranced by the pensive sadness in her expression. "Are you sure you ever knew that woman at all?" he said after moments of considering the declaration she uttered so guilelessly.

She licked her lips with her tongue, unaware of the effect the innocent gesture had on him. "I don't want to be unfair to you," she said, stroking his jaw tenderly. With a self-deprecating chuckle, she added, "And I don't want to be unfair to myself, either."

"It seems that, rather than make any decision, you've decided not to make one at all," he said harshly.

"Marcellus, don't be that way."

"What way? Indecisive? No, I can't. I want you. And if you're saying all I can have is sex, then . . . well, that's not true, either," he amended, speaking to himself. "If I thought I could be satisfied just sleeping with you, then I would. But I can't. I won't settle for that, Pauline."

The doorbell rang, and Marcellus bit off a curse.

"Detective Collins again?" she asked, her lips twisted sourly.

"For his sake, I hope not," he replied, pushing himself up to his feet.

"I need to run upstairs."

Marcellus stared after Pauline as she skipped up the stairs. He wondered what the hell it was going to take to nudge her from her fear. The doorbell rang again. "Coming," he shouted irascibly, loping toward the front door. He opened it, surprise making him blink his eyes. "Sarah?"

"May I come in?"

"Sure," he replied. He stepped back to allow Sarah to come in with a pad clutched to her chest. Closing the door behind her, he asked, "What brings you this way?"

"You seemed to need proof that Don and Pauline were having an affair," she said. Shoving a sketch pad at him, she said, "Here it is."

Frowning as if in pain, Marcellus looked at the pad, then back at Sarah. Noticing the tear stains on her cheeks, and her red rimmed eyes, he felt utterly defenseless. "Sarah, let me get you a drink," he said, looping an arm across her shoulder to guide her toward the family room.

"I don't need a drink, Marcellus," she snapped. "Why is it people always offer you alcohol as if it would anesthetize the pain?"

"Well, come sit down, anyway," he said. Helping Sarah out of her short jacket, he gestured for her to sit on the couch. Sitting next to her, the pad held loosely in his hands, he asked, "What's this, Sarah?"

"Open it," she said, her voice rising as if on the verge of hysteria. "See for yourself."

"Okay," he replied with a weary sigh. He scooted back against the couch, the pad resting on his thighs. It was a typical wire-rimmed artist's sketchbook, with a dark-green cover. He flipped the top; the first sketch was a pencil profile of Pauline. Shooting Sarah an unimpressed look, he said, "So what?"

She returned his look with challenge brimming in her eyes. Though his curiosity was aroused, he flipped the next page as if reluctant to do so, knowing he could no more stop looking if his life depended on it. With each page he turned, he kept telling himself, *'None of it means anything,'* like a man in denial. Chuckling to himself, he thought that maybe if he said it enough he wouldn't feel so culpable for the jealousy threatening to overrule reason. But logic held out.

"Sarah, I don't see any signs of an affair here. I mean, we both know that Don likes to draw. I'm sure he has a sketch pad full of drawings of you, me, and heaven knows who else."

"Keep going," she said with entreaty in her voice. "And pay careful attention to the dates. Go back to the beginning," she said, flipping the pages back herself.

Noting that the first sketch was dated *1–15–97*, he turned the page. Several more renditions of that same sketch bore the same date. He kept turning the pages on the series of Pauline pictures: a different date for each set. The last group was a kaleidoscope, faces of Pauline all over the page, depicting her various moods and expressions.

Flipping to the last page, he froze, suspended in a deep private place. Deeply touched by the drawing, his mind imposed color to the black and white full facial picture. A pair of beguiling brown eyes stared straight at him, the hint of a smile turned up the corners of a soft mouth in a look of a woman in love. He felt a softening in his chest, as if his heart was melting; then he gripped the edges of the book. Looking at these drawings on the heels of Pauline's reticence to make a commitment to him only fueled his anger. How could she deny with words what had been so clearly captured by Don—or anyone else with eyes?

"I know what you're thinking," Sarah said, cutting into his thoughts. "That Don is your friend, and that friends never betray each other. But it happens all the time."

Closing the pad with finality, his face set in a stubborn mold, he said, "Sarah, this doesn't mean anything." He attempted to return the sketchbook to her, but she refused to take it.

"I had a feeling you would stick to that," Sarah said, shaking her head, disgusted. "You're so loyal. But I've got something else." She dug inside the pocket of her jacket. "Here," holding out a white card with a pink rose in raised ink.

"Aw, Sarah," he moaned.

"Take it," she said, shoving it at him.

Resignedly, he took the card and unfolded it. " 'I know what I feel for you is taboo, but I just can't help myself,' " he read aloud. Dated a month ago, the note was not signed by name, but with an odd arty scribbling. Slowly, Marcellus uncrossed his legs, folded the note in its natural crease, then rubbed his forehead. He didn't know how to handle Sarah.

"Finally," Sarah said, exhaling a relieved sigh.

Making her presence known at the bottom landing on the stairs, Pauline cleared her throat loudly. For several tense seconds of lingering silence, she felt as if life died in the room as Sarah and Marcellus looked up at her. Then animation came to their expressions. She was unaffected by the joyful hatred blazing in Sarah's eyes. Rather, it was the grim mask of Marcellus's face that was tearing her insides apart. She felt a wretchedness of mind she'd never known before. Holding her tears in check rigidly, she hid her pain under the appearance of indifference, completing her descent into the room. Calmly, she picked up her purse from the couch table, then proceeded to the front door, her head held high.

Galvanized into action, Marcellus raced to reach her, yelling, "Pauline! Pauline, come back here. It's not what you think," he argued.

"Isn't it?" she replied, glaring at him with burning, reproachful eyes. "I know what I saw. She finally got to you," she said, twisting the knob. "You and Sarah enjoy your evening, comparing notes."

Chapter Fifteen

Move in with me. We don't need two residences. Ha! What a laugh, Pauline chided herself bitterly.

No sooner than she wiped the tears from her cheeks, more fell to take their place. And she continued to wipe them roughly from her face as she maneuvered her car across the lanes on the freeway in moderate night traffic.

Not even a good hour ago, Marcellus was insisting on a commitment from her, causing her to wonder whether cold feet alone explained her hesitation. She now realized the value of her uncertainty. It had nothing to do with what Mrs. Johns said, but rather, was her own honest emotion. Just like the first time, she recalled: only then, she'd had the sense to listen to the warning.

Inexorably, she replayed the gloating smile on Sarah Wellsing's face and the look of condemnation that was on Marcellus's. She'd seen that look before, she thought, her mind skipping back to the past, a hot September in '95.

Even though she had believed he loved her as much as she loved him, she hadn't intended getting pregnant, she remembered. Naturally, Marcellus proposed, but she refused. It opened a source of contention between them— until destiny stepped in.

The morning after his proposal, followed by a particularly heated argument and his subsequent departure, she lost the baby. Don, who had dropped by the apartment to meet with Marcellus, found her, instead doubled over with premature contractions. He drove her to the hospital, where a D&C was performed after her miscarriage. Swearing Don to secrecy, she was back home that night when Marcellus returned, armed with a dozen roses, an engagement ring, and the determination to change her mind. She told him then about the miscarriage. He didn't believe her.

Though he didn't voice the accusation, she saw it in his eyes, she recalled with the old grief ripping through her anew. Mistrusting her was a habit with him, she thought, wrapped in a cocoon of anguish. And the tears began all over again.

Why, Marcellus? Why? she groaned silently, her hands twisting tightly around the steering wheel. Wiping her eyes with the backs of her hands, she caught a glimpse of the speedometer, noticing how fast she was driving. Rather than slowing, she maintained the over-the-limit speed, eager to get home.

Several other cars followed her exit off the freeway. After a series of turns and stops at red lights, a pair of headlights glared in her rear-view mirror. It was a vehicle similar to the CSI car Marcellus drove, and her heart began to beat crazily in her bosom.

The instant the light turned green, she sped off. The vehicle behind her made a left turn, and the headlights of a small car appeared in her mirror. A strange mixture of relief and disappointment trickled through her. Still, she kept vigil on the cars behind until she pulled into her driveway—just in case.

Minutes later, she was getting out of her car when another one turned onto her street. A small, black, sporty car; it wasn't the Vet, either. Her spirits dropped like an anchor, and a disappointed breath left her lips.

Slowly, the car cruised by, the driver barely gassing the engine. With a nervous flutter in her chest, she made sure she had the right key and hurried to her front door. She peered repeatedly over her shoulder, and her hand shook as she inserted the key in the lock. The car breezed along, disappearing from view.

Sighing relieved, she retrieved the mail from the mailbox, walked inside, and bolted the locks. She made a light path on the way to her bedroom, dropped her purse on the bed, and headed straight for the bathroom. Flipping the light switch, she stared at her reflection. As was expected, her eyes were tear-swollen and red.

She looked horrible, she thought, muttering an expletive. Determined that she had cried her last tear over Marcellus, she turned on the shower and began to undress. The phone rang. She froze, then drew a deep gulping breath.

It was probably him, she thought, her lips folded. Deciding to let it ring, she disappeared behind the shower curtains.

If it was revenge he was after, he certainly got it, she thought, feeling sick with pain, a fiery gnawing in her bosom. She had only herself to blame, for she had walked into the trap with her heart wide open. With her head bowed and her body slumped in despair against the tile wall, she vented her agony, the water pouring over her, mingling with fresh tears. She was not going back to CSI ever again.

Slapping herself on the forehead with the ball of her hand in dismay, she remembered the unfinished preparations for the memorial service. Cursed by a sense of obligation, she delayed making a decision. She was a survivor, she reminded herself. Maybe she would feel different in the morning after a glass of wine and a good night's sleep.

Taking a final rinse, she dried, then pampered her body with lotion. Standing in front of the sink, she attended her hair, blow-drying, shaping, and combing it to perfection. As she was setting the dryer aside, the corner of her eye caught the markings on the wall calendar: an entire week had been blocked off with a black marker, but not X'ed in red.

Pauline emitted a groan of dread. Lowering her head in disgust, she remembered that she hadn't protected herself from getting pregnant. Though she and Marcellus had only slept together that one time, once was all it took. She of all people should have known better, she railed at herself.

She walked into the bedroom, and the phone began to ring again. Forcing her thoughts to block out the sound, she searched the dresser drawer for her prettiest gown. A see-through lacy midriff with thin straps and a long, flowing silk bodice in azalea. She pulled it over her head, then posed for the mirror, as if taking inventory.

She didn't need Marcellus to make her feel like a woman. There were plenty of men out there who would want her. Just because he made her heart sing didn't mean no one else could, although no one had so far.

The phone stopped ringing. Wondering who she was trying to fool, the features of her face contorted into a woebegone frown. Her mind languid, without hope, she turned from the mirror and meandered to the kitchen to pour a generous portion of wine in a water glass. While taking a sip of wine on her return to the bedroom, she was halted by the peal of the doorbell. Startled, she spilled drops on her gown.

"Who is it?" she asked, her stomach churning anxiously.

"Pauline, open the door."

Suddenly, a candle of hope lit up in her heart. Before its fiery brightness could spread, she doused it with embittered emotions. "Go away," she shouted. "We don't have anything to say to each other."

"You better open this door right now or I'll wake up the entire neighborhood," he threatened.

Rasping disbelief, she replied, "Be my guest," as she walked away.

Outside, on the other side of the door, Marcellus was leaning against the frame, straining to hear signs of life inside. With a film of sweat on his face, he recalled that it had been a long time since he had driven himself at night: a boring process, it made him sleepy, thus accident-prone. But he couldn't let Pauline sleep on the damning scene with Sarah.

After getting rid of Sarah, he suffered through a silent debate that taunted him with the possibility of losing Pauline again. The growth of a deep, unaccustomed pain in his chest warned him that it was a risk he didn't want to take. Without further thought, he jumped in his car and drove off into the night like Paul Revere.

It hadn't bothered him at first, night driving, because he was preoccupied with damage control—convincing Pauline that he didn't buy a word of Sarah's rambling. Coupled with his firsthand knowledge of the powerful combination of pride and ego, making her realize he loved her was the most important thing in his life. It was the only solid reality in his shifting world, he thought, tugging at his sweaty shirt.

Hearing nothing inside, he mashed the buzzer repeatedly with his thumb. Getting no response, he started banging on the wooden barrier with his fist, yelling at the top of his lungs, "Pauline, open this door."

Finally, persistence paid off and the door was opened. Marcellus walked into the lit entrance hall where Pauline was standing guard as if to prevent further invasion. A supercharged tension loomed in the psy-war between them. His black eyes impaled her and unflinchingly, she returned his look.

"I see you were expecting me," he said at last, a triumphant gleam in his eyes.

"What?"

Eyeing a dark-tipped nipple of her brown bosom peeking through the lacy bodice, a corner of his mouth turned up in a half-smile. He reached out to touch the object of his desire-intense gaze. "You dressed for me," he replied, skimming flesh and fabric with his hand.

In a flash of time, he watched Pauline undergo an expected metamorphosis, from want to struggle, in an attempt to hide the betrayal of her body. Filled with masculine pleasure, a wide grin almost split his face in half.

"You arrogant son of a bitch," she replied, slapping his hand away. She spun on her heels and marched off.

Bringing his hands together in a thunderous clap, Marcellus laughed, but the sound was diluted by a hint of nervousness. He was in for a fight. But he was up to the challenge.

All her warning systems went off at once. Too late. Standing at the dresser, her back to the mirror, Pauline felt the surging power of his presence reach out to her from across the room, where he filled the doorway. It seemed as if the oxygen had been suddenly siphoned from her bedroom, and she had to remind herself to breathe.

Growing whole again would be even more difficult with Marcellus fulfilling a dream come true; she had never really expected him to come after her. In a way, his arrival smacked of a nightmare, for her power to resist him had already been tested and found fallible.

The first man ever to set foot in her bedroom, he seemed

quite at home. Feeling fuddled by longing, her misgivings increased by the second as he invaded her private domain.

"I like it," he said, walking around as he spoke. "It reminds me of my big sister's room when I was little. Not too girlie, but feminine. I always felt a sense of welcome," he said, with melancholy in his expression. "You never met her," he said, fingering the lacquered jewelry box on the dresser. "But you will," he said, glancing at her side-long with cryptic certainty.

Strolling past her to the bathroom, he said, "You know, I see a lot of changes in you in this room. Calm and reassuring, as always." Disappearing into the bathroom: "Must be the nurse's training." Reappearing: "And you always had a quiet strength about you that I liked. But now I see a self-confidence in you that wasn't there before. Yeah, there's still that wee bit of vulnerability about you, but it seems as if you're not afraid to show it now." Sitting at the corner foot of the bed, inches from her, he said, "I like your hair, too. Not that I didn't like it long, you know I did, but this style adds character, a sophistication that wasn't there before. In a way, it scares me," with a self-derisive expression, lips twisted in a bemused set.

Though impressed by his keen insight, Pauline pretended otherwise. Ignoring his eyes, she picked up the wine from the dresser with casual indifference. The trembling, two-handed grip around the glass as she raised it to her lips revealed the tenuous hold she had over her emotions, giving her away. But she had no intention of falling under his spell again. Feeling his gaze on her, she thought he seemed to be enjoying her struggle for composure.

"Marcellus, what are you doing here?" she asked in an impatient, agitated tone.

"If you thought I was going to let you nurse this misunderstanding all night long, you made a mistake," he replied, smiling at her with a look of lazy indulgence.

"I only made one mistake," she replied mockingly.

Undaunted by her nastiness, he spoke in a voice as smooth as silk. "Well, I'm here to make sure you don't make another one."

"I'm sure there will be others," she replied coolly, "but they won't be with you."

He chuckled, finding humor in her seemingly unaffected demeanor. It galled her, but she hid her frustration with an indifferent shrug. Two could play at his game. Swallowing the wine in one gulp, she set the empty glass on the dresser and walked away from him, to the other corner of the bed nearest the door.

As if prepared to stay indefinitely, Marcellus leaned against the dresser, folded his arms across his chest, and crossed his legs at the ankles.

"Don't run from me, Pauline," he said. "It's too late. I'm not going to let you get away this time. I was a fool before, but not this time."

"You're right about one thing," she retorted, "it *is* too late. And while we're on the subject of time, you better leave."

"In good time," he replied, pushing himself off the dresser to approach her.

Though barely perceptible, Pauline shifted from one foot to the other. Her instincts warred in her, screaming for her to run, yet ordering her to hold her ground. He walked by her, then she felt him behind, towering over her, like a warm cloud. She felt her heart skip again and again. Swallowing hard, she lifted her chin and boldly met his gaze in the mirror.

"I know now we should have hashed it out, said the ugly words out loud, then it would have been over and we could have been having an argument over something else," he said.

Pauline stared, hypnotized by their reflection. She saw a staggeringly successful and accomplished man, coveting her, a simple woman, with his eyes. Though he did no more than look, the woman in her awakened as if from a deep sleep, her body aching for his touch. As the tense silence stretched, a vague sense of unreality came over her, and locked in her burning gaze was the afterimage of shared passion between the handsome couple in the mirror.

"You see it, too, don't you?" he asked. "We belong together."

She shivered imperceptibly at the husky tone of his voice, shaking her head in denial. "Marcellus . . . "

He backed away from her to amble across the room. He took a position in front of the cherry chifforobe stationed between the twin closet doors. "Remember when the three of us . . . you, me, and Don . . . went fishing one day? You snagged a bull red. In fact," he added with a chuckle, "you caught most of the fish. Don gave up fishing within hours after we started. Do you remember what he started doing?"

Pauline closed her eyes momentarily as if she could no longer stand the distant sight brought near in the mirror before her. Marcellus was still at her back, his reflection squared in front of the tall dresser, lessening its visibility with his magnificent expanse and height.

"He took pictures," he replied when she didn't. "I had forgotten all about them. Until Sarah showed them to me tonight. They weren't in their original form, of course," he continued conversationally. "But I guess that, as the artist, he's allowed."

"What are you talking about?" she asked, spinning to face him headlong, her curiosity too great.

"Had you not run out, you would have seen the sketches and remembered. The sketches were drawn from the pictures Don took that day. Only he took me out of the shots to draw you."

A look of awareness crossed Pauline's expression, and

relief sighed through her. But knowing the origin of the pictures used to damn her didn't change the way things were between them, she thought bitterly. "Well, that's settled," she said in tone of indifference.

Marcellus snorted, amused. He walked toward her with stalking intent in his gaze. Pauline had nowhere to run. Her only defense was to give him her back. The shadow of him was complete in seconds. He stood behind her, over her, his breath fanning her hair. She gulped.

"I don't want to hear any more denials from you," he said, his breath fanning her hair. "You promised me, and I'm going to hold you to it."

"I didn't promise you anything," she replied stiffly, holding herself rigid under the dynamic vitality he exuded.

"Oh, yes, you did," he replied. "It was sealed in my bed, remember. You let me hold you"—slowly running his hands from her shoulders to her buttocks and back again—"and smell you"—lowering his head to rub his nose against the side of her neck—"and touch your heaven." He pulled her into him, and a shuddering sigh escaped her lips. "Lady, you're mine. And you know I don't like losing things."

"I'm not a thing," she said, jerking away from him to stand at the dresser. Her hands were shaking so hard that she gripped the edge of the dresser to still them.

"No, you're not," he said, lowering his head to caress her ear with his whispered breath. "But let's not argue semantics. You know what I mean."

Determination faltering, she exclaimed in a low, tormented voice, "Marcellus, don't do this to me."

"Don't do what . . . want you like I do? Too late. I've wanted you since the moment I first laid eyes on you, and I don't believe I ever stopped. In fact, I know it for certain. Call it my precious memory, if you will."

With dark, snappy eyes reflecting in the mirror, she replied sharply, "How dare you?" She spun around to face him headfirst, her hands placed belligerently on her hips. It hurt just to remember his distrust—her vision shaded in gloom with the memory—but she plunged on. "You have a lot of nerve, claiming you have all this affection for me, all the while believing I've been sleeping with your best friend. You've got a lot of nerve, you bastard," she spat out in hurt-singed anger.

"I never believed Sarah," he said succinctly in a gruff tone. His expression bordered on bitterness. "The reason I was so angry was because you continue to speak with forked tongue. When you see the sketches, you'll see exactly what I'm talking about.

"Now, you can go on and call me a bunch of dirty names because I did believe you aborted our child. Well," he added, "I convinced myself that you had. My ego could handle that a little bit better," he said with a self-derisive chuckle in his voice. "But, on your part, you let me believe. Encouraged it, even."

Tears squeezing from the corners of her eyes, Pauline didn't hear much beyond his admission that he hadn't fallen for Sarah's fable. She wanted desperately to believe that it was true. He grabbed her by the shoulders, turning her to face him.

"You think I came all this way to lie to you . . . for what reason? What would I have to gain by baring my soul to you if I didn't need you in my life? I'm not blind or stupid to the fact that other men, my best friend included, would be attracted to you. You're a beautiful woman, Pauline."

"But Don is . . . "

"Don is what . . . white? And you think that makes a difference? That that would somehow make you less attractive to him? Hell, he's still a man, and you're still a desirable woman. When are you going to get that through your

head?'' With more than a hint of frustration and desperation, he let his instincts lead him. ''I hope you're not
equating me, what's happening between us, with what your
parents did. I'm not going to abandon you, and, if I hurt
you, it will be because of my own stupidity, and something
you'll have to correct. But it won't be intentional. Never
intentional,'' he said with emphasis. ''It's just me and you,
Pauline. And I know you want me.''

''That's your libido talking; go take a shower. The only
thing between us is a convenient release of physical
desire,'' she argued weakly, eyes lowered. ''That's all it's
ever been between us.''

''Uh-huh,'' he replied in a singsong rhythm. ''Showers
won't help either one of us.'' Stroking her bosom, his voice
dipped into a seductive register. ''Look . . . see how your
body responds to my touch. Can another man make you
feel the way I make you feel?''

''I'll find one,'' she said tightly, her defiant tone marred
by breathless desire.

''I don't think so,'' he replied confidently, ''or you would
have found him by now. But rest assured, there will never
be another man for you.'' His silky voice contained a threat,
a hint of jealous possessiveness.

As if blithely ignoring the truth of his words, she said,
''As for what I feel . . .''

He cut her off, taunting, ''Oh, so you admit to feeling
something? That's a start.''

''Don't flatter yourself. What I feel is only a natural
response to a physical stimulus,'' she said stubbornly.

''Then I'll take that,'' he replied, lowering the straps of
the gown. ''For now.''

''No,'' she replied, crossing her chest with her arms. He
pried them apart, pinning them behind her back. Struggling against the steel band of his possession, she
exclaimed, ''No, damn you, don't pull your macho stunt
with me.''

Loosing his hold, but not freeing her, he cajoled, "Then come to me, Pauline. Stop running away from me . . . from us."

He was looking at her with desperate, deep longing in his eyes, wearing her down with words she wanted to hear and heady sensations that sent fire through every nerve in her body.

"Damn you," she said with capitulation in her voice.

"Yes," he replied, his lips searing a path down her neck, her shoulders, "damn me all you want, as long as you come back to me. And I want to hear it, Pauline. Say you want me, too . . . want to build on what's between us that won't go away," he commanded in a raspy whisper.

She was conscious only of his nearness, his lips. As another wave of warmth traveled along her pulse and want flooded her soul, she could barely speak. "I . . ." she said.

"Say it," he implored her with his voice, his look.

With tremors of rapture in her throat, she said fiercely, "Yes." In a crevice deep in her mind, she knew a kiss could not absolve the hurt feelings between them. But her mouth and her soul clamored for his kiss. It was that need that lifted her to her toes, wrapped her hands behind his neck, pulled his face to hers. *I love you,* she thought, the vow screaming through her senses. But it stayed silent on her lips.

"Yes, I want you, heaven help me," she whispered. It took only a feather-light touch of his mouth on hers. Rhyme and reasoning fled, and memory took over.

Wordlessly, though volumes spoke in his eyes, Marcellus pulled the gown over her head, then swept her up in his arms. After placing her in bed, he peeled the shirt off his back and stepped out of his pants.

Feeling cocky and arrogant, among other lusty emotions, he stood at the foot of the bed like a conquering hero,

staring down at his warm-blooded prize. Pauline was looking up at him with hunger blazing in her eyes, her lips
parted invitingly.

He was in no hurry to possess her; he had the rest of
their lives to prove to her she wasn't making a mistake. In
fact, he was determined to remove the word in connection
to his name from her vocabulary. He meant what he had
told her; there would be no other man for her. She would
never want of his loving, in or out of bed.

Setting out to brand her his irrevocably, gently, he
grasped a slender ankle in each hand to make room for
himself between the parting of her legs. He started with
a big toe, licking his way up her body. From her silken
belly, up to her stomach and ribs. His tongue caressed her
sensitive swollen nipples, while his hands searched other
pleasure points.

When he reached her face, he could tell she was eager,
desperate even, to have his mouth on hers. Taking perverse
pleasure in heightening her anticipation, he stalled, trail-
ing a path along the side of her cheek with his tongue,
then retreating to the moist hollow of her throat.

While he cajoled her with his unlimited seductive arse-
nal, she tempted him to hurry, sending currents of desire
through him. Her hands were everywhere, never still, making heated paths up and down his body and applying tanta-
lizing pressure to his buttocks. She rocked her hips from
side to side beneath his and parted her lips in invitation.

Still restraining his ardor, he finally granted her desire
as his lips met hers in a gentle drugging kiss. Their tongues
sought each other out and danced together in a silent
melody. Demanding more than a kiss, he felt her hand
sliding down his side to reach his hardness, which was
slapping against her thigh. He caught the naughty hand
and pinned it over her head, capturing her other hand as
well. He felt her smile in his mouth.

Methodically, he worked his way back down her body,

his tongue warm and moist against her soft flesh. Attuned to her hot desire and his destination, he dipped his tongue into the center of her universe, hidden beneath the wiry black hairs between her thighs. He was aware of her writhing on the bed, frantically clutching at the sheets and whimpering his name over and over. But he would not be hurried. He drank of her essence leisurely, with savoring and purposeful delight. Her reaction was like an ambrosia, a challenge to his control. The more he stoked the fires of her passion, the hotter his own grew. With the blood pounding through his heart, his head, he hoisted himself over her. Buried in her softness, a mutual shudder ran along their lengths. He wrapped his arms around her waist and pressed his mouth to hers.

Controlling the tempo of their movements, he was like a conductor, leading the soloist through an intricate piece of music, and her body understood his rhythm. With each trusting the other to do justice to an age-old score, it was divine ecstasy. Their bodies were in exquisite harmony with one another as low, measured thrusts and arched hips gradually quickened to a fever-pitched intensity.

With molten shafts of sensation flowing through him, Marcellus began to rise higher, to thrust deeper into her body. Pauline met each powerful stroke with an equal force of her own, caressing him with the instinctive movements of a woman who knows how to please her man. With passion growing to explosive proportions, the bed rocked under the weight and thrashing movements of the lovers. They talked to each other in arduous sighs, as a burning sweetness raged through them both.

Abandoning herself to the spiraling climax, a hard moan of erotic pleasure burst from her lips. Feeling as if he were shattering into a million pieces, groans of satisfaction shook through his body as he spilled his love into her.

Trembling from the world of wondrous sensations, they held each other tight. Unburdening her of some of his weight, Marcellus kissed her on the mouth. It was a light kiss, but a tender, lingering one. Tears of pleasure spilled from her eyes, and he licked them from her cheek.

She captured his mouth for the sweetest kiss he ever had, engraving a vow of love on his soul. Rolling over, he tucked her curves neatly into his own contours, a hand on her breast moving gently. With contentment and peace flowing between them, they succumbed to the numbed sleep of satisfied lovers.

Hours later, Marcellus stirred. He looked down at Pauline; she was still asleep in the crook of his arm. Sometime earlier, he had awakened to pull the covers over them and turn off all but the bathroom light. He didn't know what woke him up this time.

The clock on the bedside table showed the time to be five minutes after midnight. He felt a little queasy in the stomach, possibly due to the half-eaten fast-food dinner.

As he swung his feet to the side of the bed—"Boom!"— there was an unbelievably loud blast that ripped through the house like a roar of thunder. The noise was deafening, powerful. Awakening instantly, Pauline cried out as Marcellus fell onto the bed, rolling into her.

She asked, in a soft, frightened voice, "Marcellus?"

Listening, he scanned the room automatically. "Is there another way out of here?" he asked with an alarming sense of urgency in his voice.

Shaking her head, "No."

"Stay here," he commanded, crawling off the bed away from her. He hobbled about the floor in a rush to put on his pants. "I'm going to check it out," he said, zipping his pants, as he headed toward the door.

"Marcellus!" she cried with choking apprehension in

her voice. But he was gone. She got out of bed, looking around the floor for her gown. As she pulled it over her head, a second explosion rocked the house.

Stumbling over the bed, arms flailing the air, she screamed, "Mar-cell-us—!"

Chapter Sixteen

It was after two in the morning when Pauline finally set the alarm behind the door of Marcellus's home. She had just completed a meeting with Clay, CSI Security Chief, to apprise him of the latest incident and put him on the alert.

Rubbing her eyes with the balls of her hands, she sighed wearily. She had to get up in a few hours. After finding out what Dottie was able to accomplish, she was going to bed.

Walking through the family room on the way to the kitchen, she noticed the green sketchbook sticking out from the sofa table behind the couch. Curious, she picked it up, and a small white envelope fell out from between the pages. She bent to retrieve it, and read the words scribbled on the back aloud. "Deal with this." Her expression screwed itself into a frown. She read the love note next and shook her head. What a weak piece of evidence Sarah was using to convict her, she thought: anyone could have written it.

She returned her attention to the scrawled words on the

card. Biting down on her bottom lip, she wondered what was meant by the message. Did the anonymous love note have anything to do with the reminder? And what made Sarah think she had written the love note?

Opening the sketchbook, she felt the shocking truth of Marcellus's claim that even she wouldn't be able to deny the proof of her feelings for him. Only someone with a warped perception would, she thought, staring captivated at the subject of Don's artistry. She didn't know what constituted good art, but she was duly impressed with his skill, capturing her face in a myriad of moods that bespoke warm emotions.

Closing the sketchbook, she recalled what Marcellus said about the possibility of Don finding her attractive. Was it possible Don had written the note for her, but never mailed it, realizing it was improper? Did the scribbled note refer to his taboo emotions for her?

"Oh, God," she groaned, leaning back against the couch. Now Sarah had her suspecting herself.

She stared mindlessly up at the ceiling. But the tragic events ever since she started at CSI, leading up to now, nudged through her thoughts. Just when she felt certain nothing worse could happen, it did, she snorted.

At least this time the killer wasn't successful, she thought, filled with memories of the explosion.

The blast woke up the entire neighborhood. Curious onlookers poured onto the street, most wearing their pajamas. Some thoughtful person called the fire department and a truck arrived promptly, accompanied by an ambulance. Firemen sprayed a white foam on the inflamed vehicles in the driveway, while the ambulance rushed Marcellus off to the hospital.

She wanted to accompany him, but had been forced to stay behind to answer questions from the fire inspector and the police officers who showed up later. Speculating it was the work of an arsonist, the inspector guessed that someone doused the car or cars—he wasn't sure of the order or number—with gasoline, then lit a match. The explosion was inevitable. The front of her house, the garage, living room, and part of a small bedroom were blown away.

The policemen dropped her off at the hospital, where she called Marcellus's parents and Dottie. After treatment for superficial cuts, abrasions, and bruised ribs, Marcellus was released. He was upstairs in bed now, being attended by his parents, who had driven him home from the hospital. She had ridden with Dottie, fearing she would unleash the hysteria she had contained until that point.

They had been fortunate, compared to what could have happened, she mused, looking toward the stairs. But it was too soon to start counting their lucky stars. The killer had tried once. He or she might try again.

With a tremulous sigh, Pauline got up, returned the sketchbook to the sofa table, then walked into the kitchen. Dottie was sitting at the table, using her fountain pen as a drumstick to beat on her legal pad.

"Any luck?" Pauline asked, dropping into the chair across from Dottie.

Setting the pen on the pad, Dottie replied, "Your guard will be here first thing in the morning. He's good. I've used him before."

Pauline had asked Dottie to help her secure a private guard. Though Clay seemed trustworthy, she refused to risk Marcellus's life in the hands of someone whose hands were already full. "Thanks, Dottie," she said, yawning.

"I aim to please," the attorney replied. "Now, what about you?"

Pauline read the message in Dottie's expression. "No one is trying to kill me," she replied.

"We don't know that," Dottie said, folding her arms on the table. "Both cars were blown up at your house," she said emphatically.

"Only because he was at my house, and his car was parked right next to mine in the driveway," Pauline countered. "My only tie-in to CSI is through Marcellus and Donald." On her fingers, she counted off, "I possess no company secrets, I barely understand the work they do, and I make no decisions about money."

"You seem to have given this a lot of thought," Dottie said.

"Sitting in the waiting room at the hospital, I didn't have anything else to do but think," Pauline said somberly, thinking: mostly about Marcellus. Mindful of what had transpired between them before the explosion, he had been right about so many things, she thought. Yeah, she had changed her outward appearance, yet so little on the inside had changed. She was merely an old book with a new cover. She had never stopped loving him, either.

"I sense something else going on here," Dottie said questioningly.

After a brief pause, Pauline said plainly, "I love him, Dottie." But was it enough? Briefly, she squeezed her eyes shut as if to block out the questioner, knowing from where the question derived.

"That may seem like a revelation, to you, but I assure you it's not," Dottie replied.

Pauline chuckled thoughtfully, then her face tightened with memory of the explosion. With her lips trembling, she said in a barely audible, choking voice, "I almost lost him tonight." Clamping her hands over her mouth to imprison a sob, tears bordered her eyes.

"Go ahead and cry if you have to," Dottie said, "get it out of your system, but don't dwell on what could have been. The worst is over."

Brushing away tears, Pauline snorted with skepticism. "I keep telling myself that, but something always happens to make it a lie."

"Well, we can hope," Dottie replied, reaching across

the table to take her hands. Squeezing them affectionately, she said seriously, "I still think you need to take some precautions. I don't think going back to CSI is a good idea."

"Why? It's been proven that, if someone wants to get you, it doesn't matter where you are," Pauline said flippantly. She folded her hands in her lap. "Besides, we're probably safer there than anyplace else."

"Ann-Marie wasn't," Dottie retorted quietly.

Pauline returned Dottie's concerned look with one indicating her mind was firmly made up.

"Since I can't talk you out of it," Dottie said resigned, "maybe I can get you to go up and get some rest. It's going to be a long day for you. Probably longer than you can imagine. And I'm sure Marcellus is not going to make it any easier when you introduce him to Rufus."

"I know," Pauline said in an introspective voice. But she wasn't concerned about Marcellus's reaction to having a bodyguard. Rather, she was pondering whether she had done the right thing by contacting Clay; whether she should have consulted Marcellus. If she trusted the wrong person, her best intentions could backfire on them both.

"Go," Dottie said, gesturing with her hand for Pauline to get up. "Right now. Let Barbara take care of Marcellus while you get some sleep."

"Are they spending the night?" Pauline asked, leaning on the table as she slowly got to her feet.

"Do you think Barbara is going to leave her baby boy now?"

"Yes, she is," Malaby replied, sauntering into the kitchen, a portable phone in his hand. "They've been like two rams, butting heads ever since they got upstairs."

Chuckling, Dottie said, "Marcellus is nothing but a big spoiled baby. I bet the nurses were glad to see him leave the hospital."

"Pauline, don't worry about your house," Malaby said.

"I've got some men there now, boarding it up. Right now, you better get upstairs. Send my wife down. Dottie, you staying?"

"No, sir," Dottie replied.

"Well, what are you waiting around for? Go tend to your patient," Malaby ordered Pauline with a smile.

"Thanks, Mr. Cavanaugh," Pauline said, kissing him on the cheek.

It was with reluctance that she headed up the stairs to play nurse. She still wasn't sure she was ready to face Marcellus, for there was still unfinished business between them. Though the sketches of her and the note were damning evidence, he still should have had more faith in her than to believe such a relationship with Don was even possible.

Midway up the stairs, she met Barbara coming down.

"Thank goodness you're here," Barbara said. "He's only grown more stubborn in his old age. I couldn't get him to do anything. He's in pain, but he won't take his medicine."

"Don't worry, Barbara," Pauline replied. "I'll let him stew a little bit longer while I bathe, then he'll be more than ready for something to ease his pain."

"Good for you," Barbara said with a conspiratorial smile. "Don't let him run you ragged," patting Pauline's hand affectionately. "Malaby and I are probably going to get out of here, so I'll talk to you later."

She watched Barbara descend the stairs, but her gaze held the memory of the pre-explosion interlude between Marcellus and her. He was definitely more persuasive than she had the power to resist, she thought. But it only meant they were weak for each other in the vicinity of a bed. Great sex was only one aspect of a solid relationship: if not built on a foundation of trust, there was nothing to build on between them.

Drawing a deep breath of courage, Pauline tiptoed into Marcellus's room and stood at the foot of his bed. Though

he lay still—sprawled on the bed under a tangle of burgundy linen, a bare knee sticking out from the sheet—
she could tell he was only pretending to be asleep. A small
band-aid covered a spot above his right brow, and his
bronze chest was wrapped in white gauze. Neither of which
marred his attractiveness, she smiled to herself, a stream
of warm sensations coursing through her.

Suddenly, the smile jelled into an expression of terror,
as she caved in to the frightening possibility that she could
have been standing over a cold, lifeless body as a result of
his heroics. Paralyzed by the dark premonition, she realized they must never relax their guard, for whoever had
tried to kill Marcellus wouldn't stop trying until caught or
successful.

With her jaw clamped tight in a grim, determined set,
she strode off to shower. After drying off, she put on a
pajama top from his drawer and sauntered into the bedroom, buttoning the shirt.

"It's about time you got here," Marcellus said in a
grumpy voice, his eyes still closed.

"I knew you were faking," she accused teasingly.

Opening his eyes, he replied, "I thought you were my
mother, returning to harass me."

"She's gone," she said. "Ready for that pain-killer yet?"

"No," he replied, shaking his head from side to side on
the pillow.

His ingenious eyes never left her face, pinning her with
a long, silent scrutiny. She returned the look, her eyes
moving into his, seeing nothing except love brimming in
the depths of his gaze. Biting down on her shy, smiling
lips, she felt like a breathless girl of eighteen.

"Well," she said, unconsciously wetting her lips with her
tongue, "is there anything else I can get you?"

Raising himself on his haunches as if to get a better look
at her, he eyed her, up and down, covetously, before he
spoke. "If there is, can I have it?"

"What kind of question is that?" she asked. "You know you can."

"Then I need something," he replied.

Noting his expression, a sparkle in his eyes as though he was playing a game, she asked suspiciously, "What?"

A slow, secret smile spread across his features. "You can't give it to me until you get over here."

The scorching intent of his gaze, the budding ache in her loins: she was ripe for passion. With a slight sway of her hips, she sashayed the short distance to the head of the bed. Leaning over him, she could almost smell his excitement.

"What do you need?"

His arm snaked out around her waist, and before she realized his intentions, she was tumbled onto the bed on top of him. He groaned, clutching at his ribs.

Laughing, she said, "Serves you right."

"Stop nagging and kiss me."

Smothering her last words with his lips, Marcellus groaned, not with pain but from the thundering delight in his heart. That explained why he refused to take the pills; they would not only ease the pain, but deaden his sense of feeling when he so desperately needed to feel . . . pain and all.

Ever since the explosion, he had thought of nothing but Pauline, realizing what a lonely existence he had been living until she came back into his life. She gave him a reason for living greater than his own instincts of survival. If it were possible, he loved her even more. A profound need to build a new history between them consumed the trilogy of his essence.

"We still have a lot of things to talk about," he whispered when she removed her mouth from his.

Pauline rolled next to him and propped the side of her

face on her hand to gaze at him before she spoke. "I know. But not tonight. You need to get some rest. Is there anything else you need?"

"Oh, I have a long list of needs," he replied.

With her mouth twisted in an amused set, she asked innocently, "What did you have in mind?" A splendid sibilant seeped past her lips when he slipped a cool hand under her pajama top to fondle one of her breasts. "Hm," she muttered winded. "That's nice, but it will have to keep," she said. "Your ribs need to mend."

Marcellus stared at her, his black eyes sparkling like polished diamonds in the dark room. He wanted her. He wanted to control and be controlled by her, to get under her skin as surely as she was under his.

With his hands at the collar of his pajamas, he pulled her closer to him, then gave the fabric a quick, hard yank. As the top parted down the center, several buttons popped loose. She gasped, staring at him with amazement and the laughter of pure feminine delight in her throat.

"No pain, no gain," he replied, brushing his lips against hers before he reclaimed her mouth.

Feeling a happy ditty whistling in her heart, Pauline neither looked nor felt like a woman who had gotten only three hours of sleep as she walked out the back door into the following morning. A light breeze blew, causing a mild ripple in the pool and stirring the plants and bushes surrounding the patio. The threat of rain added another shade of color to the late sunrise.

With a bounce of purpose in her stride, she crossed the patio to the detached three-car garage and manually raised the door to reveal the Corvette in the center space. Thinking about all that horse-power under the hood of the sporty black car, she looked back at the house, her bottom lip pinched between her teeth in debate. Maybe she should call Clay to send a vehicle for her. She had never mastered shifting before.

But what the hell, she decided with a shrug.

With stuttering starts and stops, and gears screeching painfully, the car jerked out of the drive. It was a good thing Marcellus was asleep.

Before going to CSI, the first order of business was a stop at the hospital, where she had already confirmed Sarah's presence. She intended confronting Don's wife, believing Sarah knew more than she was telling. Her behavior up to this point indicated a guilty conscience, Pauline thought. She meant to find out the reason behind it.

Minutes later, Pauline stepped off the elevator at the third floor of the hospital. The morning shift was well underway. A familiar nurse was sitting behind the desk at the nurse's station, her head bent over mounds of paperwork.

"Good morning," Pauline said to get the nurse's attention.

"Oh, good morning, Ms. Sinclair," the nurse replied. "Haven't seen you in a while."

Pauline let the remark pass without comment. "How is Mr. Wellsing this morning?" she asked instead.

"There's been no change, Ms. Sinclair," the nurse replied somewhat sadly.

With a nod indicating she had suspected as much, Pauline asked, "Is Mrs. Wellsing in her room?" pointing down the hall.

"No," the nurse replied. "We needed that room, so we had to kick her out. But she's here at the hospital. I saw her a short while ago with Dr. Hawse. They may have gone down to the cafeteria for coffee."

"Thanks," Pauline replied. She retraced her path to the elevator. While she was waiting for a car to arrive, Detective Collins turned the corner of the corridor she had just come from, heading her way.

"Ah, Ms. Sinclair," Detective Collins said as if pleased to see her.

"Detective Collins," Pauline replied in a flat, emotionless voice.

"Without Mr. Cavanaugh this morning?" Detective Collins asked, with a slightly raised brow.

"I have a feeling you already know the answer to that, Detective," she replied.

Holding up his hands, wrists together as if cuffed, he replied with a chuckle, "Caught me." Dropping his hands, "Heard about the bombing at your place." He explained, "I got a call from an officer with the Houston Police Department. He's going to fax me the details along with the preliminary report from the Fire Department."

"So I guess now you're going to accuse me of blowing up my house," she said snidely.

"No, Ms. Sinclair, people who take other people's lives usually go out of their way to ensure their own safety," he said, as if finding humor in the situation. "I don't believe you blew up your own place. But I do believe you know more than you're telling."

Did that mean he no longer suspected her? she wondered. Unwilling to trust his word or his friendly manner, she kept her feelings of relief from showing.

"Then I don't know what else to say, Detective."

"Just don't say it to the wrong people, Ms. Sinclair," he replied. "You probably already have."

"I'm afraid I don't understand," she replied.

"Somebody went out of his way to warn you, Ms. Sinclair."

An elevator car arrived; the doors sprung open. Assaulted by a terrible sense of curiosity about the detective's remark, Pauline let the car go.

"Warn me?" she asked, swallowing thickly. Her ears were burning with Dottie's advice to watch her step.

"Yes. The way I figure it, that explosion was a warning

to you. The killer could easily have broken into your house and gotten rid of you. Maybe he's following you right now."

By painting a picture of peril and her ultimate demise, Detective Collins was trying to scare the wits out of her. She wondered if it were one of those tactics used by TV detectives to frighten victims into confessing. She had a feeling Collins no more believed what he said than she did.

"Well, if that's what you believe, why aren't you trying to do something about it?" she asked, shooting him a challenging look.

"I am," he replied. "But you won't help."

"I've told you everything I know," she replied.

"Then you better search your memory a little harder," he said.

I intend doing more than that, Pauline said to herself as she watched him walk away. He paused mid-stride, as if agonizing over a decision, then spun around, facing her.

"Did you know that Ann-Marie Johns wanted to be a writer?" he asked.

The sneaky detective was full of surprises. In her interviews with some of the CSI staff, she had learned of Ann-Marie's hobby, probably as he had. Wondering what he was up to this time, she stared at him with a look of ignorance.

Returning to narrow the distance between them, Detective Collins said, "Well, she did. Seems she had shared some of her short stories with her ex-boyfriend before they broke up."

"Get to the point," Pauline said.

Staring at her with a sidelong, pondering look, Collins replied, "Yes, the point. One of her stories was very interesting," he said unhurriedly. "If I remember correctly, it was called, 'One Way Love.' Quite unimaginative if you ask me, but I'm no writer. The story is about a woman who falls in love with her married boss and plans to kill off the wife. It's a very common plot in my business."

"How does the story end?" she asked, controlling her anger. It seemed she was still his prime suspect.

"Well, it seems the wife was having an affair and wanted a divorce anyway," he replied in a bored tone of voice. "I suspect that Ms. Johns was just too much of a softy to kill anybody off, even on paper. That's what I call having a happy ending. Unfortunately, real life seldom does. Be careful, Ms. Sinclair."

According to Marcellus, Pauline recalled, Leonard Coombs was in love with Ann-Marie. He was married. Was that the basis of Ann-Marie's story? If so, that triad could only be completed by Leonard's wife, who would have a motive for murdering Ann-Marie.

Still, what did that have to do with Donald?

Unless, she thought, taking the next elevator car, Sarah Wellsing was involved in an extramarital relationship, and to alleviate her own guilt, had accused Don of violating their wedding vows.

With rote memory, she strode to the cafeteria. From just inside the wide entry, she scanned the crowded room carefully. Business was brisk, as the morning patrons had converged for breakfast.

Sauntering toward the center of the room, she spotted Sarah and Dr. Hawse at a back corner table near the sliding glass doors. The patio beyond was filled with smokers, who were not allowed to light up in the hospital.

Making her way through the maze of small square tables and gold-cushioned chairs, she silently rehearsed the words she wanted to say. She needed answers she felt certain only Sarah could provide. Though they say the wife is always the last to know, she felt that that was not the case this time. Detective Collins's recent storytelling fueled her belief.

Dr. Hawse looked up as she neared. A smile broke out on his face as he got to his feet, extending a hand in greeting. Following his gaze, Sarah stared headlong at Pauline. With fear glittering in her eyes, she shifted uncomfortably and began to look around as if seeking a place to escape.

"Pauline, it's good to see you," Dr. Hawse said sincerely.

"Hello, Dr. Hawse," Pauline replied, shaking his hand. "It's good to see you, too." Turning, she said, "Sarah."

"Pauline," Sarah muttered, her lips barely moving.

"Why don't you join us?" Dr. Hawse asked.

"I came to talk to Sarah," Pauline said with a smile on her lips that didn't reach her eyes.

Looking back and forth at the women with a question mark on his face, Dr. Hawse said, "I think I'll take this opportunity to get in a puff before I'm called back. I may not get another chance today. Pauline . . . maybe I'll see you later," he said with a hopeful expression.

"Maybe," Pauline replied.

Dr. Hawse walked off, and the last vestige of tolerance left with him, leaving a decided chill in the atmosphere between the women.

Pulling a chair from the table, Pauline said, "Sarah, we have to talk."

"We don't have anything to talk about," Sarah replied with belligerence in her tone.

"You were more than eager to talk to Marcellus," Pauline retorted as she sat down. She licked her lower lip, managing to quell her temper. She wanted Sarah's cooperation, not trade angry quips with her.

With her back becoming ramrod straight, Sarah shot Pauline a cold look. Wordlessly, she picked up her purse from the floor on the side of the chair, then stood up.

Pauline stood, as well. With her eyes flashing a firm warning, she said in a low voice, "If you want a scene, I'll give it to you. And it won't end here." Sarah covered her ears with her hands, and Pauline leaned toward her. "You'll be in court facing a slander suit for spreading your vicious lies," she said in a quiet, ruthless tone. "Then the whole world will know of your fear . . . that you were incapable of satisfying your husband." Desperate, she latched onto the first idea that came to her. "And to cover up your inadequacy, you put the blame on someone else so you would look like the poor, victimized, loving wife," with mocking in her voice. "Is that what you want?"

Letting her purse fall onto the table, the strap still clutched in her hand, Sarah glowered at Pauline. She dropped back into the chair as if the weight of the world was on her shoulders.

Pauline hated pouring salt in Sarah's wounds, but she had no choice. The time for pleasantries was over. Sitting down, she cut to the quick. "Who told you Don was having an affair with me?"

With her eyes lowered, and defeat in her profile, Sarah studied her hands before she spoke. "No one had to tell me," she said as if the fight had been drained out of her. "The evidence was all over the place. Those sketches he drew of you, the note. I only found one, but I'm sure there were more."

"The note was typed, Sarah; anybody could have typed it," Pauline pointed out.

"Then you appeared at CSI," Sarah said. "To be close to him, I assume," she said with a sarcastic snort.

Wordlessly, Pauline stared intensely as Sarah opened her handbag to pull out a tube of lipstick and a compact. Looking into the mirror, she spread lip-gloss to her mouth with trembling hands, then tossed the tube and compact back into the purse.

"Sarah, what are you guilty of?" Pauline asked.

"I don't have anything to be guilty about," Sarah snapped.

"Don't you realize you have given yourself the best motive there is for attempting to kill Don?" Pauline replied. "You," she said with emphasis, "suspected him of having an affair. Maybe he told you he was leaving you."

"He never said any such thing," Sarah exclaimed. "I'm

going to have his baby." Shocked at what she had blurted out, she stared at Pauline with wide-eyed embarrassment, covering her mouth with her hands.

Taken aback, Pauline didn't know what to say. Finally, she said, "Congratulations."

"He doesn't want it." Sarah gulped and a big tear formed in the corner of her eye.

"What?" Pauline replied in a loud whisper of amazement. "Sarah, I'm confused."

"What's to be confused about?" Sarah replied sarcastically, sniffing. "Having an affair is his way of punishing me. But I won't get rid of it. I won't."

"Sarah, I refuse to believe Don would want you to get an abortion," Pauline replied, thinking they couldn't be talking about the same man. "Did he ask you to get rid of it?"

"No," Sarah replied weakly, shaking her head. "I hadn't gotten around to telling him I was pregnant. But I already know what his reaction would be."

Trying to make sense of Sarah was like putting together a two-thousand piece puzzle and every piece was black, Pauline thought, a confused frown on her face. The guilt Sarah harbored for getting pregnant had made her delusional and paranoid. Sarah needed professional help or, better still, for Don to recover and set her straight. But of course she was in no position to offer counsel, she reminded herself.

"Sarah," Pauline said hesitantly, "about me and Don, we're only friends, nothing more. I'm definitely not the person who assaulted you. I don't know where you got that from."

"Your perfume," Sarah said, succinct and sure.

Realizing it was useless to argue the point, Pauline moved on. "Those sketches were done from snapshots Don took a long time ago, and I have no idea whatsoever who wrote the note. Or even if it has anything to do with me. It could be from one of your friends, for all I know." Noticing Sarah's eyes darken with thought and wrinkles spread across her forehead, she asked eagerly, "What?"

With a wave of her hand, Sarah replied, "Nothing. It's nothing."

"Come on, Sarah," Pauline implored. "What you're holding back could be vital to finding out who's responsible for changing the lives of possibly three people now."

"Three?" Sarah asked.

"Someone poured gasoline on Marcellus's car in my driveway last night and set it afire," she said, looking at Sarah with every emotion she felt about the matter—anger, fear, concern—shining in her eyes.

"Oh, my God!" Sarah replied. "Is Marcellus okay?"

"Yes, he's fine," Pauline assured her, with relief in her voice. She folded her arms on the table. "Now, tell me what you know."

"I don't know anything," Sarah replied, shaking her head. "I swear!"

"But you were about to say something a second ago," Pauline countered.

"I . . . I was just thinking," Sarah stammered in musing tone. "I called the office one day, and Amy said something about Don acting like a man who had been jilted. She didn't mean anything by it, of course"—talking with her hands—"you know how she is . . . tactless and talkative, but harmless."

Pauline jumped on the disclosure. "So Amy told you he was having an affair?"

Sarah shook her head side to side in a negative gesture. "No, no. She didn't know Don and I were . . ." She paused, fumbling for the right words, then seemed to give up and said instead, "The honeymoon was over, so to speak. But Amy didn't have anything to do with my suspicion. Don did. I caught him in a couple of lies about where he was going, or where he had been. That Thursday before . . .

before he got sick, he went out and didn't get back until real late. He refused to discuss it," she ended on a lengthy sigh.

"Sarah," Pauline sighed, struggling to keep a neutral tone, "even if Don had been acting out of character, it doesn't necessarily mean he'd been seeing another woman. One: you've been married barely a year, and two: he works all the time," she argued reasonably.

"I know, but . . ." Sarah said, her assumption waning.

"But what?"

"He found me at CSI. There's nothing to say he couldn't have found someone else," Sarah admitted softly, her vulnerability clearly evident in her expression.

Pauline's shoulder slumped in utter frustration. Talking with Sarah was another blind alley, and she was running out of places to look for answers. She looked at Don's wife helplessly. "I don't know what to tell you." Getting to her feet, she sighed. "Hopefully, you and Don will get the opportunity to work through this misunderstanding. I'm sure that's all it is. He probably has a very good explanation."

Sarah forced a smile through her worried look as she gazed up at Pauline. "Have you and Marcellus worked out your misunderstanding?"

Forced to answer that, Pauline knew she wasn't being completely honest when she replied, "Yes." At least, the tender thread weaving through her, just thinking about Marcellus, was utterly genuine.

Sarah nodded, with wistfulness shadowing her expression.

With the warmth of her smile echoing in her voice, Pauline echoed softly, "Yeah."

Chapter Seventeen

"Rufus Tolliver?" Marcellus asked groggily, sitting on the side of the bed.

Wiping the remains of sleep from his eyes with the back of his hand, he squinted and shook his head, then tried again to read the note. It had been left on the empty pillow next to him by Pauline.

It was ten-thirty, according to the clock on the bedside table. He had no idea what time Pauline had left this morning. The last thing he remembered—after they made love, he recalled with a look of subconscious wonder on his face—was that she had given him a pill and some water. Then nothing but sweet dreams that not even the horrors of the explosion could tarnish, followed.

Itchy, he scratched at his bandaged chest, then pushed himself up to his feet. He slipped into his robe at the foot of the bed, deciding he'd better find out what this note was all about now, even though Pauline had promised to call him around noon.

Walking into the kitchen, Marcellus's eyebrows drew

together in an agonized expression. He was instantly cautious, but unafraid, as he examined the stranger. A bald-headed man with a berry brown complexion, the size of a Viking, was sitting at the table in his kitchen, drinking his coffee and reading his newspaper. A dark gray blazer was hanging over the back of a chair; on top of it was a big black leather holster with an equally big silver gun.

"I guess I'm to confirm that you are indeed Rufus Tolliver," he said matter-of-factly.

Of indeterminable age, the giant stood to a seemingly endless height past his own. He was awesomely muscled.

"At your service, Mr. Cavanaugh," he replied in a voice in contrast to his size, a tenor.

"Want to tell me what are you doing here, Rufus?" Marcellus asked. He decided to reserve judgment, though he had an uneasy feeling about this. Holding up the note, "This only says that I'm to expect company. I assumed it was you, but there's no explanation as to why you're here."

"Yes, Ms. Sinclair did say that she didn't go into details in her note," Rufus replied. "I work for the Timbuktu Security Agency. Ms. West contacted the agency last night on Ms. Sinclair's behalf. I'm your bodyguard, Mr. Cavanaugh."

"Don't you have something else to do, Clay?"

"Nothing more important than what I'm about to do," he replied.

Pauline thought she'd detected a smile on his face, but it was so transitory that she couldn't be sure. They were riding up to the third floor. Clay had met her as soon as she walked into the lobby of CSI where a security guard, rather than a receptionist, had been placed permanently.

After leaving the hospital, she made several stops in preparation for the memorial service tomorrow before returning to CSI. It was shortly after noon, and already she was tired. Snatches of the conversations she had had with Detective Collins and Sarah bandied about in her head, striving for clarity. Neither conversation had been very helpful in figuring out the identity of the killer or the motive. She was beginning to think that two different agendas had been set into motion. But, of course, that would mean two killers, and that didn't make sense, either.

"You haven't talked to Mr. Cavanaugh by any chance, have you?" she asked, wondering if Clay's presence was Marcellus's way of getting even with her for hiring a body-guard for him.

"No, ma'am," he replied. "I spoke with Mr. Tolliver."

"Did he say anything about Mr. Cavanaugh?" she asked, smiling to herself.

"No, ma'am. He reported that everything was fine."

Ever the consummately tight-lipped, close-to-the-chest chief of security, Pauline thought amused. She would never get any information from Clay.

The doors opened, letting them off on the third floor. With Clay shadowing her steps, they headed to the clinic. Mentally, she sorted out her thoughts about what was still left to be done. What she'd rather be doing intruded, and she had to catch the delectable sigh that nearly escaped her throat.

Clay preceded her into the clinic. He looked about the front room, then strode to check the adjoining opened area and returned. "Everything looks in order, Ms. Sinclair," he said. He handed her a card, explaining, "My pager number, if you can't reach me by phone."

With an amused suspicion that Marcellus had a hand in Clay's behavior towards her, Pauline replied, "Thank you, Clay."

"Yes, ma'am."

Pauline stared after him as he marched from the room. She looked down at the card, then headed to the desk. The phone rang. Pauline set her briefcase on the floor alongside the desk, then moved to pick up the receiver. She paused momentarily, wondering how to answer. Finally, she picked up. "Pauline Sinclair."

"Good afternoon."

It was Katherine's cheerful voice. Smiling mirthfully, Pauline replied, "Who says?" She sauntered around the desk and dropped into the chair behind it.

"Now, now," Katherine admonished, a smile in her voice, "it's too early for that kind of attitude. You've got a ton of work to do."

"Don't remind me," Pauline replied.

"And, of course, the word is out that you're the high authority today," Katherine replied.

"With all the gossip going on around this place," Pauline remarked, "it's a wonder anybody gets any work done. Have you heard from Marcellus?"

"A dozen times already," Marcellus's secretary quipped. "As I understand it from him, he's been unable to even bribe the man. And when that didn't work, he resorted to childishness. He said, and I quote: 'If you can get Ms. Sinclair to call off her guard dog, then I'll come to work and make some executive decisions. But if she won't, and I can't buy this sucker off, then take the problem up with her. Let her make the damn executive decisions!' End of quote."

"Just for that, I won't call him anytime soon," she said, pretending to pout.

"He told me what happened last night," Katherine said, her tone grave.

Exhaling a bemused breath, Pauline said, "I don't know what to say. If Detective Collins doesn't hurry and find the killer . . ." her voice trailed off to silence. She nibbled at her bottom lip. "I'm afraid, Katherine," she said quietly. For his life *and* for them, she added for herself, conscious that the latter thought was becoming more pronounced.

"That's understandable," Katherine replied. "I'm a little scared myself."

"Well, worrying about it is not going to solve anything," Pauline said.

"No, it's not," Katherine agreed, her tone game. "You take care."

Ending the call, Pauline fingered the card from Clay, then put it in the top drawer of the desk. She rose and walked the room to stare out the window. It looked dark out, like a late evening; the promised rain from morning had arrived. The sky's tears fell as the rain slapped against the thick panes of the windows.

A wistful cloud settled over her gaze. It was a perfect stay-in-the-bed day, or to lounge with one's lover.

"My goodness, Pauline," she chided herself laughingly. Then mirth faded entirely from her visage again and melancholy outlined her expression.

What on earth was she going to do when the baffling events at CSI were solved and she was no longer needed? She didn't doubt he wanted her now. But was that enough to sustain them during better, less life-threatening times? Besides, wanting and loving were two different matters, and neither meant eventual marriage. She wasn't even sure that was what she wanted.

With a feeling of having to hold close to herself, not to let go, she wrapped her arms around herself. She almost dreaded discovering the killer who had brought them together. Aware of what that meant, guilt pricked at her innards.

Exhaling a frayed breath, she returned to the desk and pulled back the chair. Before she sat down good, a tepid knock sounded at the door. She looked up. "Dr. Kent," she said, surprise in her tone.

"Yes. May I speak with you a moment?"

Pauline merely nodded as she settled in her seat, trying to prepare for this unexpected visit. Dr. Kent closed the door behind her, then looked for a chair to pull in front of the desk. Examining the African American woman, she noted the scientist possessed her standard studious air, but there appeared a chink in her usual snobbish manner today. A handsome woman, her heart-shaped face was tastefully made up using warm shades of color that highlighted her brown-sugar complexion. Pearl earrings made a perfect mate to the smoky gray dress under her long white lab coat.

She looked gussied for a man, Pauline speculated. As usual, however, every strand of the black hair on her head was in place, twisted in a ball. Dr. Kent sat and folded her pampered hands, with clear polish on her nails, in her lap.

"What can I do for you?" Pauline asked. Even had they met under different circumstances, she knew instinctively that the two of them would not have become friends. Ironically, she and Sarah stood a better chance of forming a friendship.

"Well, first off," Dr. Kent began, gesturing with her hands as if indecisive, "I owe you an apology."

Pauline felt her eyebrow arch over her taken-aback expression.

"The other day . . . when you asked if I'd sought you out, I lied," Dr. Kent admitted chagrined. "I didn't want Dr. Chin to know of my plans. I'm sure Marcellus has told you about my vacation request."

Despite the obvious commonality of their African heritage, Dr. Kent's brown eyes seemed cold and calculating even when she tried to be friendly, Pauline thought. She wondered about the wounds to her ethnic sister's soul . . . the kind of person that existed beneath the layers of education and studied poise.

"No. He hasn't," Pauline replied. While she was curious as to where this conversation was headed, she also wondered if Dr. Kent was capable of murder.

"I put in for it ages ago. Before this mess with Don and Ann-Marie." Dr. Kent paused to take a deep breath.

Pauline's mind conjured scenes featuring the scientist: hitting Ann-Marie over the head with a barbell, stuffing the body in a closet then later, pouring an excessive amount of chlorine in the pool and dumping the body in it.

"I figured that's why he hasn't approved it yet," Dr. Kent continued. She paused; her expression asked if her guess was correct.

Pauline remained silent, a stoical look on her face. She could smell the chlorine, hear the splash of the body falling in the pool, as if actually present during the commission of the crime.

Dr. Kent resumed talking. "I know some people around here would take offense to my leaving. But I've already booked my travel plans and hotel accommodations. I really don't want to cancel them. I need this vacation," she added imploringly.

Pauline breathed a restorative sigh, releasing herself from the nightmarish daydream. "Dr. Kent . . ."

"Call me J.T.," Dr. Kent cut in to offer.

Pauline placed her arms on the desk and folded them. "Okay, J.T. I don't understand what you want me to do."

Dr. Kent scooted to the edge of her chair, placing her hands on the desk. "I know I don't have the right to ask, but I want you to talk to Marcellus . . . get him to approve my vacation."

Jolted, Pauline sat with her back against the chair. Shock was too tame to describe what she was feeling—it was shock compounded by a high degree of wariness and suspicion. She released the breath she didn't realize she had been holding.

"Well." Pauline spoke at last, wetting her lips with her tongue. "I, uh, I don't know . . ."

"Like I said, I know I haven't been especially, uh, cordial." Dr. Kent seemed to snatch the word from the air.

"It would seem more appropriate to take this matter up with Marcellus directly." Pauline spoke her mind. "Why don't you?"

"With all the finger-pointing going on around this place, every little action is looked upon suspiciously," Dr. Kent replied, disdain flitting across her features. Then her expression changed completely. "I heard there was an accident . . . that Marcellus is recuperating at home. Is that true? Truth seems hard to come by around here lately."

"He suffered a few bruises," Pauline replied, not wanting to divulge too much. "He should be in tomorrow."

A second of silence passed before either woman spoke. Pauline spent hers trying to digest this situation. She decided that it was nothing more than her own dislike of Dr. Kent that had prompted the image of murder in her mind. But she held on to her caution about Dr. Kent's motive for seeking her out with this particular request.

"Well, think about what I asked," Dr. Kent said. "And, if the opportunity presents itself when you see Marcellus . . . Well, think about it."

Oh, she would definitely do that, Pauline thought.

The lights flickered as thunder cracked the sky. Marcellus looked up from his reading. The lights held steady. He was sitting at a table in the dark, archival Texas Room of the Houston Public Library. Since he couldn't get rid of his bodyguard, Rufus was sitting across the table from him, reading today's newspaper.

The paper in Marcellus's hand was an article copied from the *Houston Chronicle Newspaper,* bearing the date of Thursday, September 15, 1995. *Justice Department Scrutinizes NASA Sting* was the headline caption.

Pauline had been right: if he thought about it long enough, he would remember. And he had, Marcellus mused. Leonard may have been on to something that he, in hindsight, should have known about.

Year before last, it had become public that the Justice Department had launched an investigation into alleged fraud in the NASA contracting community, as well as among NASA employees. The undercover probe was called *Operation Lightning Strike* and resulted in the prosecution of a dozen individuals and two companies. One company escaped prosecution by paying a $1 million settlement— and no doubt by squealing on the other guys, Marcellus chortled as he read. While this particular article detailed a subsequent investigation by the FBI into alleged impro- prieties by the Justice Department and the U.S. Attorney General's office related to the 20-month undercover sting, it offered another meaning to Leonard's rambling.

Did lightning really strike twice? he wondered, laying the copy down before him. He and Don had been securing finances for CSI when the first operation was occurring. But he could think of another dozen scenarios that could help clarify the current strange and deadly events at CSI. Namely, the attempted theft of *Project Ba.*

With pondering etched on his face, Marcellus decided not to approach Trent Ringnald with his theories, although he was certain the NASA security chief knew something. Since it was obvious that Rufus put a cramp in his snooping style, maybe he'd get Dr. Chin to do some checking with his associates in the science community . . . see if he could find out if any of them had heard anything in the way of an undercover investigation.

He'd also give Clay a call, he mused. "Have him bring Donnie to the house," he whispered aloud to himself. Folding the news clips to slide them in his raincoat pocket, he said, "One more stop to make, Rufus, then we can head home."

* * *

Standing almost in the center of the large lab, Pauline searched the faces of the researchers passing her by as if she were invisible. She was looking for Dr. Chin. Her curiosity had gotten the better of her after the meeting with Dr. Kent. She didn't know what she hoped to find out—maybe confirmation that Dr. Kent had overexaggerated. Two white-coated scientists walked in her direction. She stopped them. "Excuse me. Have you seen Dr. Chin?"

"Chin?" the taller of the two men echoed as if he hadn't heard her correctly.

"He's not here," the other replied. He spoke rapidly, but clearly and distinctly. "Left early, won't be back today."

With a curse in her thoughts, Pauline muttered a disgusted breath. "Okay, thanks," she said to herself with disappointment, for they had already walked off. She wondered what to make of Dr. Chin's absence as she headed for the exit. Reaching the large opened space of a door, she nearly bumped into another researcher. With a clipboard against her chest, she was a pretty black woman who looked more like a Girl Guide than a scientist. Donnie was at her side.

"Excuse me," Pauline said.

"Pauline! Pauline! Pauline!" Donnie exclaimed.

"Hello, Donnie," Pauline said, blushing embarrassed by the robot's excited greeting, knowing Don was responsible for it.

"Well, you must be somebody special," the woman said. "I've never seen him act like that before. Why don't you greet me like that?" she asked the robot with a teasing pout in her voice.

Staring down at the robot, the questions she had returned, full-blown. If Don programmed Donnie to recognize her, maybe he programmed the robot with a clue as to what was really going on at CSI.

The young researcher extended her hand. "Hi. I'm Dr. Elizabeth Savannah, but you can call me Liz. I gather you're Pauline."

Shaking hands, Pauline replied, "Yes, I am. Nice meeting you." Trying to mask her curiosity, she inquired, as casually as she could, "You said Donnie doesn't normally act like that around people?"

Laughing, Liz replied, "No. He's usually all business. I guess Don must have programmed him to respond differently to you."

Looking up from Donnie, she caught Liz staring intently at her. Pauline asked, "Why are you looking at me like that?" There was a hint of humor in her voice; she felt an unusual affinity toward this woman.

"You're Marcellus's woman," Liz replied matter-of-factly.

Her lips trembled with the need to smile, and then Pauline couldn't help laughing at the young doctor's candor. "Yes," she admitted.

"I thought so. Good catch. Well, see you later," Liz said, about to walk away.

"Wait," Pauline said, halting her. Liz raised a questioning brow. "Two questions."

Clutching the clipboard to her chest, Liz said, "Shoot."

"What's the deal with Dr. Chin?" she replied. "I've been told he left early. Is he sick or something?"

"No, he got a call from the boss," Liz replied nonchalantly.

Pauline's eyebrow shot up in surprise. "A call from Mar . . . I mean, Mr. Cavanaugh?" she smiled embarrassed. At Liz's affirmative nod, she wondered what Marcellus was up to. She'd tried reaching him, but had gotten no answer.

"What's the other one?"

Reminded of her original purpose, Pauline replied, "Is it possible to remove Donnie from the building?"

Déjà vu marked Marcellus's steps. He remembered having had this feeling of apprehension once before. He didn't like not knowing—especially Pauline's whereabouts. The question was making him crazy, wondering why hadn't she arrived yet when Clay phoned hours ago to inform him of her departure from CSI? He had been prowling the house from the front door to the back ever since.

"What time is it, Rufus?" Marcellus called from his family room into the kitchen, where Rufus was downing a can of soda.

"Not even sixty seconds past the last time you asked, Mr. Cavanaugh," he replied. "Six-fifty-three."

His anxiety was forcing him to rethink the explosion. It had been assumed that he was the intended victim; yet, in hindsight, he couldn't help wondering if that assumption was off base. After all, he had been out-of-pocket when things started to change at CSI. Don must have hired Pauline because he had known or sensed that something was amiss. Since they now knew Don had been poisoned, it stood to reason that the killer might have suspected that Don had confided in Ann-Marie, causing her death. Pauline would have been a surprise to the killer, but when it became known that Don had hired her, the killer would have to consider her a threat, as well. Collins may have been right to target Pauline, he thought, but for the wrong reasons.

Marcellus buried his fingers in his hair, then dropped his hands to his sides, exhaling deeply. At least Clay had thought to put a tail on her. If anything happened, he would know about it right away. Relaxing was out of the question until she walked through the door, but knowing about Clay's precaution eased his anxious mind a bit.

Absently, Marcellus rubbed his chest as he sauntered into the kitchen to sit at the table. "This is your line of work, Rufus; what are your thoughts about today's excursion?"

"I've never seen a rock that big in my life," Rufus replied.

"That's not what I was referring to," Marcellus said laughingly, "but, since you mentioned it, think she'll like it?" Selecting an engagement ring for Pauline was the last stop they had made today.

"If she doesn't, I'll marry you," Rufus said.

"You're joking, but you don't know Pauline Sinclair like I do," Marcellus replied, smiling privately into space.

He didn't know how he had lost control, but he had. And the truth of that was never more evident than his granting her permission—over Clay's strenuous objections—to remove the million dollar man, Donnie, from the building, he chided himself teasingly. He was witness to a Pauline he had never met before, or even suspected existed. She seemed to have grown into this incredibly strong-willed, assertive woman right before his very eyes. Or maybe it was he who had grown, an inner voice told him.

Though he didn't know what the future held—except Pauline in his life—he was certainly making some startling discoveries about himself. If someone had told him four weeks ago that he would relinquish control over his life to anyone, he would have denied it vehemently. Even the semblance of such an attempt on anyone's part would have been met with a fight to the bitter end.

It just showed that you couldn't predict how you would act, given a set of atypical circumstances. Don and Sarah were a prime example of that, he reminded himself, his lips set in a wry twist. He would have sworn they were the most loving, devoted couple in the world. Yet, Sarah suspected Don of the worst kind of deceit.

It didn't make sense, he thought, for her behavior was the antithesis of what love was all about. No trust, no love.

Could there be one without the other?

He knew better than to judge Sarah harshly: he was not wearing her shoes, he reminded himself. He only knew for certain that he was clear and strong in his feelings for Pauline. It was love, pure and simple.

He shuddered to think about his reaction if she were to tell him to take his ring and shove it—again. It could come down to trust, he feared, wondering whether Pauline trusted him as much as he trusted her.

But she had to have known it, for why else would she have the free rein she enjoyed at CSI, a company that he, *Marcellus*—not another Cavanaugh in sight—helped build from the ground up. Granted, Clay and Katherine kept him informed of her activities, but he supported her decisions.

As if gleaning a new insight, he smiled, recalling that that was exactly what his father did for his mother. He felt pleased with himself. "I hope I got it right this time," he said, unaware that he'd spoken aloud.

"I don't know 'bout right, but it sure seems like you got it bad," Rufus said jokingly.

Smiling to himself, Marcellus said, "Yeah, I do, don't I?"

The doorbell rang and, in his rush, Marcellus nearly knocked Rufus over to get to the front door.

"Wait a minute, Mr. Cavanaugh," Rufus warned, hurrying to precede him. "I wish you would have let me change that bandage. If that's Ms. Sinclair, she's not going to be pleased."

"Will you just check the door, Rufus?" Marcellus replied with his urgency showing.

Rufus peeked through the opening, then looked over his shoulder at Marcellus. "It's not her."

Marcellus's expression collapsed into disappointment as Rufus opened the door. "Yes? May I help you?"

"I'm here to see Mr. Cavanaugh. I'm Dr. Kent. I work at CSI."

What an interesting development, Marcellus thought with wonder. Rufus looked at him for permission to allow her to enter, and Marcellus gave it with a brief flick of his wrist. "J.T.," he said, "what a surprise."

"I came to talk to you directly," she replied, dripping water on his marble foyer floor. "I tried taking this matter up with Ms. Sinclair, whom you left in charge," she said with restrained scorn, "then I decided to talk to you myself."

He'd been informed that Dr. Kent had left CSI in a huff—in the same call he'd learned that Pauline wanted to remove Donnie from the building—but he never would have guessed that she'd come straight to him, he thought, mulling over the reason for her presence.

"But I didn't know you had company," she said, flicking a raised eyebrow at Rufus.

"Oh, this is my, uh, cousin, Rufus. He's visiting from . . ."

"Chicago," Rufus supplied. "I thought I'd find friendlier weather down here."

"I keep telling him to wait awhile," Marcellus said, knowing the dawdling banter must be driving J.T. up the wall. Her look of impatience didn't disappoint him. "We'll talk in my study," he said, pushing the door closed. "Uh, Cousin, do you mind entertaining yourself for a few minutes?"

"Leave the door open," Rufus replied.

Dr. Kent looked at them strangely, Marcellus noticed as he ushered her down the hall to his study. He offered no apologies for the mess: papers littering his desk, as well as the coffee table.

"May I take your coat?"

"No, I won't keep you long. I heard about your incident.

Don't you know enough to stay away from explosive devices?''

Marcellus couldn't tell whether she was serious or jesting, the latter of which would have been uncharacteristic. He decided to let it pass, and indicated she should take a seat on the leather couch. He sat in an adjacent arm chair. "Now, what's the problem?"

"My vacation request," she replied, running her fingers through her hair. Her hands came away damp and she brushed them together. "As you know, I was planning to leave town tomorrow. And, after speaking with Ms. Sinclair, I do realize how it looks for me not to be present, especially with the memorial service and all. But, as I explained to her, I made my plans long before any of these . . . these bizarre things started happening at CSI." She glanced sidelong toward the door, where a reflection of Rufus's shadow revealed his presence. She leaned toward Marcellus, her hands clasped together on her knees.

"What's *really* going on, Marcellus?" she asked in a conspiratorial whisper of concern. "I think I deserve to be told."

Chapter Eighteen

Mere seconds ago, Pauline had been teeming with rage when she walked through the door. It had taken her less than a minute to sense Marcellus shed his coat of anxiety, to see the covetous glimmer in his black eyes and, then, to be drawn next to him for this. . . . His warm lips on hers, his tongue in her mouth . . . her fury was shattered by the insouciant timbre of his drugging kiss filling her with celestial joy.

Though not now—with ecstasy absorbing her—she knew remorse would come later. As for now, he was kissing her with such mastery and command, she felt a heavy liquid sensation bubble in her loins.

Her hands entwined behind his neck, her knees were still wobbly when he lifted his mouth from hers. With her eyes closed, she gazed up in the direction of his face, smiling like a sensual lush. "You missed me, huh?"

"Like the dickens," he replied.

"I missed you, too," she said softly, opening her eyes.

"Oh, you mean a big-time executive like you had time to think about me?" he replied teasingly.

"It's amazing I thought of anything else." Indeed, it had been, she mused, laughing at herself; then sound faded from her voice as she simply stared at him. She could feel her heart pounding in her bosom as surely as she felt the string of want threading through her and between their gazes.

"Stop that," he growled, tugging her against him playfully, "or I'll never let you out of my sight again."

Pauline shivered imperceptibly at the promise of permanence in his words. It seemed so unfair that the fates had gone through so much trouble to bring them back together, only to have doubts conspire against them now, she thought, a cold sense of unease disrupting her warm emotions.

Rufus interrupted the moment. "What do you want me to do with him?" he inquired, nodding at Donnie in his arms.

"Just set him down, Rufus, thanks," she replied. The three of them were in the kitchen. She was damp from the rain that had began to pour down shortly before she arrived. "Marcellus, we have a lot to discuss," she said, realizing too late that he would misinterpret the subject matter she meant.

"I'll say," he retorted decisively. "What took you so long to get home? It's after eight o'clock. I almost sent out the Marines to look for you."

Leaving CSI, she'd driven all the way back home, eighteen miles out of the way to Houston, she recalled. Just for the hell of it, and to think. It had been cute for a while, having Clay keeping tabs on her all day, knowing it had to have been on Marcellus's orders. But when she left the building and noticed the car follow her from the parking lot, it ceased to be humorous. What did he think she was going to do . . . steal his company's precious robot who was riding with her in his own car? One part of her brain— the part that wasn't muddled with concern over their relationship—considered that it might have been for her protection. But another question lingered more prominently: whether the action was just another indication of the tepid trust Marcellus had in her.

"What's the matter?" Marcellus asked of her sudden disquiet.

"Nothing," she replied, shaking her head, forcing a smile.

The doorbell rang. Striding toward the front of the house, Rufus announced, "Pizza's here."

"Help yourself, Rufus," Marcellus said, his gaze riveted on Pauline. "I'm going to take Ms. Sinclair up to get out of these wet clothes."

"Yes, I like the idea of changing," she said, pulling at her damp dress.

His hand on the small of her back, he lowered his head and added in a whisper, "Into something more pleasing to my eyes."

"Behave," she chided, giggling.

"That's what you get for sneaking out of here this morning and not waking me up," he retorted. He picked up her tote and dress bag in one hand and, with the other, guided her from the kitchen.

"You were sleeping so peacefully, I didn't want to disturb you."

"That's the kind of disturbance I want," he replied.

"You have enough disturbance at CSI to last you a lifetime," she said soberly.

"Don't worry; we'll get through it," he replied with staunch determination in his tone.

Her doubt which refused to go away, betrayed Pauline. "Will we?"

Suddenly, she pulled up in the middle of the hallway, a burning, faraway look in her gaze. Her eyes did a slow slide up into his expectant gaze. "Sarah's pregnant," she announced in a whisper.

"Yes, I know," he replied matter-of-factly. He gently propelled her forward to the master bedroom. "She told me the other night."

Though she knew it paled in significance to what really bothered her, it was another secret between them. "You didn't tell me," she said somewhat accusingly.

"I forgot," he said, setting the tote and dress bag on the bed. "Besides, it wasn't the most important thing on my mind at the time," he said. "If you remember correctly . . ." he added with a lecherous grin on his mouth, prodding her memory.

"Oh, I do," she said fondly, before the memory played itself to completion with the explosion. "I'll never forget it the rest of my life," she shuddered.

"I want you to know we have not concluded our discussion," he said, his voice lowered as he arched a warning brow at her.

"I know," she replied hesitantly. His expression altered marginally; a shadow of annoyance crossed his face. She feared he would press the issue, but he wouldn't like her answer any better now than he had night before last. "Can't we postpone a little bit longer?"

"All right," he relented, his tone somewhat gruff with his displeasure. "But you're running out of time, lady." Switching subjects, he said, "Let's get back to your day." He sat on the side of the bed and folded his arms across his chest.

"Okay, the beginning," she said relieved, stepping out of her shoes. As she shimmied out of the dress, revealing her black one-piece teddy, she said, "Dr. Kent came to see me."

"Put on a robe or something," he said.

Propping her hands on her hips, she asked curtly, "Why?"

"Because I want to be able to concentrate on what you

have to say, that's why," he said, grabbing for her with both hands.

Laughing, she scooted out of his reach. "Can't you control your libido, Mr. Cavanaugh?" sauntering toward the closet, deliberately swaying her hips.

"Not when you're around," he replied. "And especially when you're prancing around in nothing, Ms. Sinclair."

She liked this feeling, as if a hand of joy had wrapped her in its wonderful clutches, Pauline mused . . . before melancholy veiled her emotions. Standing in the closet, she slipped into his long silk black robe. As she wrapped the folds and tied the belt at her waist, she pondered telling Marcellus how she really felt. Debating how to begin without appearing to be making a demand, she realized she was prevaricating again. She stepped out and into his view.

"That's a little better," he declared with a smile that didn't reach his eyes.

With a breath trembling in her chest, she guessed at his thoughts. Hastily looking away, she started toward the bathroom, eager to escape the scrutiny of his watchful gaze. "I need to change your bandage."

"Later."

She swallowed as she came to a dead halt. "Okay, where was I?" she asked, facing him reluctantly.

"Dr. Kent," he replied, adding before she could speak, "You should know she told me about her meeting with you. She's agreed to stick around another day. At least, until after the memorial service."

"What?" she exclaimed. "After going through that big show about her plans, and not wanting to cancel them? Not to mention that she can be civil when she wants something," she added in a hands-on-your-hips tone of voice.

Marcellus smiled amused. "J.T. can be charming when she wants to."

"Like a snake," Pauline rasped. "What is she up to?"

"I don't know, but I want her to stick around until I find out," he replied.

"Marcellus," Pauline said with grave concern, "her whole behavior strikes me as very peculiar." She wet her lips. "I've tried not to let my dislike of her interfere with my judgment, but now knowing about her two faces, I can't help thinking she had something to do with poisoning Don. And even Ann-Marie's murder."

"That's your imagination," he replied. "J.T. may be a liar, even a hypocrite, but a killer?" He shook his head in disbelief.

"How do you know?" she pressed. "How can you be sure? I hope you're not just being chauvinistic about this. Women can be just as deadly as men."

"Point taken." He stared at her intensely for a fraction of a second before he spoke. "I went to the library today and did some checking. That something in the back of my head about Leonard's mumbling about lightning paid off."

"What did you find out?"

"A couple of years ago, the Justice Department launched an investigation of fraud involving NASA and some of its employees and subcontractors."

Pauline frowned quizzically. "What are you saying . . . that there's another investigation going on now and it involves CSI? Is that something Don could have known or found out about?"

"If he did, I'm sure he would have contacted me in D.C. Besides, murder is an extreme measure to keep that a secret," he explained. "If the information was leaked, then the Justice Department would be the one with egg on its face. I can't see any other consequence that would make sense if that was the case. But anything is possible," he sighed, weary of his guesses. "I was hoping to have heard from Dr. Chin by now," he said, as if speaking to himself.

"Is that project Don was working on worth killing for?"

"Only if he completed it," Marcellus replied, his expression grim. Abruptly, his expression and demeanor changed to an almost casual indifference. "Tell me about Donnie."

Clapping her hands together as if suddenly remembering the robot, she said, "You should have brought him up with us." When he showed no sign of moving, she proceeded. "I went to the lab looking for Dr. Chin, and ran into Dr. Elizabeth Savannah."

"Oh yes, our young protégé," he said with a pleased look, bobbing his head.

"But Dr. Chin was not there, as you well know," she said, treating him to a sidelong arched brow.

"After restoring my memory about that federal investigation," he said, "I called Dr. Chin. Since I couldn't very well do my own checking with Rufus shadowing my every move, I asked Dr. Chin to do a little snooping around with his scientist associates." At her astonished look, he added, as if to ease her mind, "You should know that Clay and I had already had him checked out. He's clean."

"Okay? What did he say?"

"Well, unfortunately, he hasn't called back, so I still don't have any answers. I'm hoping Donnie can tell us what's going on. I assumed you reached the same conclusion," he said with an affectionate smile alight in his eyes.

Pauline smiled back before she spoke. "Remember when I first met Donnie, and he acted as if he and I were old friends? Well, he did it again today in front of Liz. It would appear that Donnie only goes haywire around me. It made me think that Don had somehow installed some information in him."

"Great minds," Marcellus declared. "I'll get him right away," he said, springing from his seat.

As Marcellus sprinted from the room, Pauline sauntered off to the bathroom to return shortly, carrying a box of gauze and a roll of tape in her hands. He could have let

Rufus change his bandage, she shook her head in amused scolding. For all his virility, he could be such a big baby, she thought, a well-known surge of desire streaming through her. "And possibly not the only one in your life," a little voice inside her head spoke aloud. She would make an appointment with her doctor later this week, she decided calmly. But it was difficult, keeping her excitement at bay, and equally hard stilling the nagging thought in the back of her mind.

She sat on the couch in the sitting area of the bedroom and buried her face in her hands. She wanted guarantees, even knowing there were none, she chided herself. But she couldn't avoid a look at Sarah and Don: two people who claimed to love one another—yet, the harmony between them had been broken. She couldn't help suspect that their whirlwind courtship contributed to their present predicament. She dropped her hands to her thighs and lifted her head, her face cloudy with uneasiness. She feared she and Marcellus were on that same rocket path.

If only she knew for sure whether this insatiable desire between them was love . . . and whether, this time, it was for real.

"Here we are," Marcellus said, carrying Donnie into the room. He set the robot on the floor in front of the couch, "Do you know how to start him up, or shall I?"

Forcing animation to her countenance, she sprang up happily, "Yes." She kneeled in front of Donnie. "Simply do this," she said as she reached under his right arm and pressed a button.

Slowly, Donnie came to life, like a human waking at the crack of dawn, stretching his arms and yawning. While he was performing a series of circuit-system checks, the lights on his face blinked off and on, then a whirling sound like a disconnected telephone emitted from the mechanical man: Donnie was functional.

"Donnie?"

"Pauline! Pauline! Pauline!" the robot squealed.

Marcellus rolled his eyes to the top of his head at the robot's response to Pauline. "Hello, Donnie," he said.

"What's happening, dude?" Donnie replied.

"You're what's happening," Marcellus replied laughingly. "Do you have a message for me?"

"Code word! Code word!"

Looking up at Marcellus, Pauline said, "I guess he wants the code word. I don't know it. Do you?"

"Touchdown," Marcellus said.

With a smile turning up the corners of her lips, Pauline mouthed, "Touchdown?"

"A little history between friends," Marcellus replied as Donnie analyzed the information fed him, performing another series of checks.

"Password?" Donnie asked in his automated voice.

Marcellus stared at him nonplussed. "There's only one code word, Donnie."

"Password. Password," the robot demanded with stubborn insistence.

Guessing, Pauline said, "Try my name again."

"Oh boy, now I've got to deal with your ego, too," Marcellus rasped teasingly. "Pauline."

Still, nothing from Donnie, except another demand for the password. Pauline and Marcellus flashed curious glances at each other, then at the robot.

With a peeved stare at Donnie, Marcellus exhaled deeply. "All right," he said in a grouchy voice, "Pauline Yvette Sinclair."

"Please wait for your message," Donnie replied.

Staring open-mouthed, hands on her hips, Pauline whispered, "I didn't know Don knew my middle name."

In seconds Donnie stilled, and a human voice coming from a speaker inside him spoke. "What's happening, dude?"

"That's Don's voice," Pauline said with amazement widening her eyes.

Well, old buddy, I hope you appreciate all the hard work I put into meddling in your life. Ha! Ha! By the time I figured it would take you to sort through my actions, I plan to be on a boat trip, sailing the Nile River with my lovely wife, finally giving her that well-deserved honeymoon. Boy, will she be surprised. Accept my anticipated congratulations . . . unless you and Pauline could not reach an understanding.

Pauline and Marcellus sat frozen, absolutely stunned, as Don's taped message continued in the vein of revealing the conspiracy he had put in motion to bring them together. He even revealed what had once been her secret from Marcellus about losing their child. She chewed on her lower lip and stole a glance at him. He was sitting ramrod stiff, his emotions concealed in the utterly black look on his face.

"I've been throwing passes—even Katherine tossed a few—but you kept on missing the ball."

Pauline couldn't help interrupting the message to ask, "What does he mean by that?"

"It goes back to when we played football in college," he replied, his voice neutral, his mind intent on listening to the message.

Pauline felt she had to sheath her inner delight upon hearing Don's disclosure. He couldn't stand by any longer, watching Marcellus drown himself in work, dating women who posed no threat to his equilibrium. He also admitted he knew his wife was pregnant, but hadn't said anything to Sarah, waiting for her to tell him. She had been somber and skittish around him, he explained: *"That will teach her to try and hide something like that from me. Doesn't she realize I know her body as well as I do Donnie's circuitry?"*

Marcellus whistled. "I can't believe it," he whispered at last, amazed. "All this time, and I thought . . ." his voice trailed to silence.

Resuming control of his system, Donnie said, "This is the end of this message."

Pauline's heart was thumping madly in her chest, wondering about Marcellus's reaction. As casually as she could manage, she asked, "Well?"

"Well, what?" Marcellus looked at her headlong, his eyes focused and clear.

"Do you believe him? What about the other things that have been happening at CSI? It sounded as if Don didn't have a clue about what we suspect now."

Marcellus covered his face, as if embarrassed, then dropped his hands. "I should have seen this. Dr. Chin told me, but I was so intent trying to find out what he knew about the project that I didn't pay attention to the signs. I even saw the vacation request."

"What are you rambling about?" Pauline asked.

Marcellus shook his head, a cryptic grin on his face. "All along it was nothing but an elaborate scheme Don concocted to get us back together. I bet Katherine was in on it, too."

"He didn't mention receiving love letters," she stated with a question mark in her tone, though it wasn't the priority on her mind. Her heart was beating anxiously, thinking about the unvoiced question.

Marcellus sighed at length before he replied. "No, no, he didn't. But he has had to handle such a situation before. So, it wouldn't be the first time."

Pauline nodded, remembering being told about the woman Don had had to fire. Deciding to take the plunge, she asked the question echoing in her heart. "Do you mind that he interfered in your private affairs?"

Marcellus merely looked at her . . . as if he couldn't believe what he'd heard. Or worse, searching for the right words for a diplomatic answer that would let her down easy. With heaviness growing in her heart, she wished she could take the question back.

From the stillness, he moved suddenly, and it took her completely by surprise. Leaning toward her, Marcellus cupped the back of her head, his palm and fingers warm as they splayed to encompass the back of her neck, as well, and he pulled her face to his.

"What do you think?" he asked, his breath against her flesh before pressing his lips to hers. The touch was soft and sensitive as his mouth moved over hers with exquisite tenderness. She opened her mouth with a small whimper, granting, inviting the entry of his tongue for a kiss that propelled her toward new sensations—something to think about. There was passion in the kiss, but also the facsimile of a deep emotional commitment. She shuddered in breathless wonder, as if this was their very first kiss.

He released her lips to kiss her forehead with a featherlike touch, then moved back to look at her. "I love you, Pauline Yvette Sinclair."

He loved her! Pauline thought with unadulterated excitation. No contrived tones, no lustful looks, no hesitation, just plain-spoken. *Marcellus loved her.* She wanted to shout, but joy clogged her throat, and she could only return his look, with love shining steadfast on her face.

"Marcellus, are you sure?" she finally managed, her eyes tearing. "I mean . . ."

A glow of affection was in his dark eyes, and a correlating smile curled on his lips. "Come here, woman," he commanded gently, drawing her even closer to him. He draped an arm around her shoulder and pulled her legs across his thighs in a familiar position. "Do I have to . . . ?"

"Excuse me," Rufus said from the doorway.

Not now! Pauline wanted to scream at him, not while her emotions were in ecstasy, and primitive yearnings stirred her blood. Neither budged an inch from their intimate place together.

"What is it, Rufus?" Marcellus asked, his voice tight with restraint.

"Mrs. Sarah Wellsing is here to see you," Rufus replied.

Pauline sighed, matching the sound of frustration Marcellus uttered as he took his eyes from hers to look at Rufus. No time to bask in the revelation.

"Tell her we'll be right down," he said as if weary. After Rufus left, Marcellus ran a hand across his head. "I wonder what's the problem now. I don't know how much more of Sarah's insane behavior I can put up with."

"Be patient," Pauline said. She felt generous now, knowing that what she had to do would be easier when they returned. "She's pregnant and feels guilty because of it. And it's possible she's here for some other reason."

"Should we tell her that Don knows about the pregnancy?" he asked.

With a shrug, Pauline replied, "I think so. It won't hurt anything, and it might even make her feel better. Get rid of some of the guilt she's been carrying around. Don ought to be ashamed of himself."

"If she's been acting like a crazed woman all this time, she deserves it," he retorted. "Let's go," leading Pauline from the room, down the stairs.

Reaching the landing, they saw Sarah sitting on the couch in the family room. Although she was styled and dressed, an improvement over her unkempt appearance of late, she looked pathetic and small; misery was etched on her face. Puddles of tears were in her eyes.

"Sarah, what's the matter?" Marcellus asked. Seeing how badly she had deteriorated in temperament, he felt guilty for his remark. No one deserved this kind of wretchedness. Kneeling in front of her, he took her hands in his. "Is it Don?"

Sniffing, Sarah replied, "They, uh . . ." The words died on her lips as she struggled to control her voice. Drawing a deep breath, she said brokenly, "The doctors said . . .

the longer Don remains in a . . . a coma . . . the less likely
he is to recover.''

Marcellus and Pauline exchanged a knowing look. He
felt a hard fist of pain choke off his breath. Pauline sat
next to Sarah and draped an arm across her shoulders.

''And if he does recover,'' Sarah continued in a slightly
stronger voice than before, ''the chances are great that he
will be nothing more than a vegetable.'' The tears began
a continuous stream down her face, choking her voice.
''They want me to consider turning off the life-support
system,'' she said in a rush. Staring at Pauline and Marcellus
as if seeking answers, she said, ''I don't know what to do.''
She yielded to the compulsive sobs that shook her.

Marcellus sat on the other side of Sarah and began
rubbing her back with comforting strokes, creating a somber threesome. Neither knew what to say; all felt powerless.

He wanted to deny Sarah permission to end Don's existence, even knowing it was not his decision to make. Don
was his best friend. He couldn't imagine not having him
around anymore. ''Sarah, you can't,'' he blurted, then
flinched in self-flagellation.

''Marcellus,'' Pauline chided softly. ''Sarah,'' she said
calmly, ''I know it's not easy. It never is. But there's no
hurry to make a decision. You'll have to live with whatever
you decide, so take your time and be as sure as you possibly
can.''

The light caught the diamond and twinkled in the semi-
darkness where Marcellus sat, holding the engagement
ring perched on the tip of his index finger, Don's sketch
pad in his lap.

It was late, and the house was quiet. Not wanting Sarah
to attempt to drive home in the condition she'd been in,
Pauline had insisted she stay the night. The three of them
had sat up drinking beer and eating pizza like old friends

catching up on each other's lives—careful not to mention Don's name, though each had felt his presence. Pauline had passed out shortly after Sarah, which had fit in nicely with Marcellus's plans for the rest of the night.

He was already dressed and ready to go out, save for a phone call. Sitting behind the desk in his study, he flipped the pages of Don's sketch book. They were damned good. Particularly this one. An unconscious smile twinkled in his eyes as he stared at Pauline's profile as she looked off the page with the most angelic expression he'd ever seen. Don had managed to see what he had failed to, he mused, thinking that his ego had gotten in the way.

He caressed the page, traced the fine features of her charcoal face then, mindful of staining the picture, he snatched his hand away. He turned to another page. His partner was quite talented . . . in more ways than one.

He was feeling incredibly humbled. And even more determined to ensure the well-wishes his best friend had for him. Just thinking of the trouble Don had gone through on his behalf, he felt blessed by their friendship.

In one of those short bouts of disconnected thoughts, he recalled that he used to suffer the illusion that he didn't need anybody to get what he wanted in life. His parents had ensured that he got the best of everything they could provide—education, contacts, and the strength of character to succeed. But they hadn't taught him how dissatisfying success was when you didn't have anyone with whom to share it.

It was a lesson he had had to learn for himself. And with a little help from his friends, he smiled softly.

Don didn't have an inkling of the pending disaster that would strike their company, he recalled, his thoughts doing a curious form of double-think. The love note and Don's subsequent handwritten reminder to deal with it also apparently had no bearing on CSI.

Unfortunately, while playing Cupid, Don had inadvertently put Pauline in jeopardy, for there was indeed a conspiracy of a sinister nature underfoot.

Had he and Pauline not been sidetracked by Sarah's arrival, he would have elaborated on his suspicion. But she was asleep now, and he wouldn't dare wake her. Tomorrow, he mused, his thoughts skipping ahead to the memorial service Pauline had planned for Ann-Marie Johns. It seemed probable that CSI's nemesis would make their move then, he anticipated, deciding upon a course of action.

The phone sounded, and he snatched the receiver before the bell had completed its first ring. "Yeah? . . . Okay. Heard from Dr. Chin? . . . I don't want to wait. . . . No, you don't need to pick me up; Pauline got me a bodyguard, remember," he added, mirthful. "Yeah; I'll meet you there in—" he looked at his wristwatch "—say ten minutes. . . ." He replaced the receiver, then returned the engagement ring to its velvet case and dropped it in the top drawer.

"You wouldn't be trying to sneak out of here, now would you?"

He looked up across the room to the doorway. "Rufus," he said, "I was just about to come wake you up."

"I'm not asleep," Rufus replied, strolling into the room. "You'll want to enlighten me."

"We're going out," Marcellus replied, getting to his feet. He picked up his raincoat from the back of the chair. "You can even help us put the extra camera in place."

"Do you know what time it is?" Rufus asked with some equivalence of calm in his tone.

Marcellus consulted his wristwatch. "One-forty-two," he replied correctly.

"Do I get to know where we're going?"

"Since you're driving," Marcellus said, slipping on his coat, "we're going to CSI." Before Rufus could inquire why, he explained, "To catch a thief. And maybe a murderer, too."

Chapter Nineteen

A shaft of morning light peeked into the room from an opening in the curtains. Pauline knew it was time to get up, but the bed was so cozy and warm and full of life that she didn't want to move. Feeling rested, she'd had the best night's sleep she'd had in weeks—months even . . . 18 of them in fact, she mused.

Opening her eyes, she propped her hands under her head and stared at the ceiling. The memorial service for Ann-Marie was today. Her heart skipped an anxious beat, and she thought fleetingly that it was a forewarning.

Glancing sidelong at her lover, a contented expression on his sleeping face, the dark moment passed. It was just nerves. She and Marcellus had come too far to be thwarted by any obstacle. The fates would not abandon them, she mused, feeling elevated by her new objectivity.

Moving as not to disturb him, she felt a delightful joy just watching him. Which she did with savoring, her mind rehashing decisions and thoughts she'd postponed too long. Far too long, she told herself. It was easier suspecting his motives than dealing with her own insecurity, she reflected. There was only one question, and it was not what he wanted of her.

Her courage was fueled by the direction of the conversation they started last night, not to forget his professed assurance of love. She could admit to herself that she wanted Marcellus: her need for him was more compelling than sexual fulfillment. He'd already given her—in action—the words she craved. She realized now that it had been her own insecurity that warped their sincerity with unrealistic expectations: Life guaranteed nothing except what one made of it. Now, she had only to reciprocate in kind with words, for her deeds already reflected those of a woman insanely in love.

"Like what you see?" Marcellus asked, his eyes still closed, a smile tilting up the corners of his mouth.

Feeling more sure of herself than ever before, Pauline grinned out of an overflow of well-being. When she spoke, it was with unrestrained emotions, as she looked at him with eyes that saw no faults. "Uh-huh."

Opening his eyes, Marcellus matched her reclining stance: lying on his side, he hunched on his elbow to stare back at her. "I do, too," he said, his eyes lazily appraising her face.

Her body reacted instantly to his sultry look, his caressive voice still ringing in her ears. Hungering for his touch, she felt the eager tremors of desire spreading through her limbs. She reached out to stroke the side of his face, and he trapped her hand on his jaw, rubbing it across his mouth. With his eyes still on hers, he dipped his tongue in the center of her palm, and the tingling effect spread through her like wildfire.

The phone rang.

Closing his eyes, Marcellus groaned his umbrage with the intrusion, and dropped back into a lying position.

"I'll get it," she said, crawling over him to answer the

phone on the bedside table. "Good morning, Cavanaugh residence," she said as they resettled in their new positions. Cutting a sidelong glance at him, she said, "Hold on, Barbara, he's right here. Oh?" she said with surprise. "Yeah, sure. No, I'm moving in slow motion this morning. . . . Yes, it's today, ten o'clock. . . . Lunch? I'd love to. . . . All right, I'll see you then," she said, ending the call. "That was your mother."

"I gathered as much," he replied, tugging her to his side. "Pauline, I want you to stay close to me today."

"Is that another version of not wanting me out of your sight?" she asked with teasing, loving laughter in her voice.

"I never want that," he began in a tone that matched the intent in his eyes. Stopping to place a kiss on her mouth, "but . . ." the ringing of the phone interrupted him, and he bit off a curse. "You might as well get that; it's for you. I knew this would happen," he said, with a combination of impatience and resignation in his voice as he passed a hand across his head.

"You knew *what* would happen?" she asked as the bell rang again, her hand on the receiver.

"I take you out in public, and everyone becomes so enamored of you that they want to consume your time," he quipped prosaically.

"Jealous?"

"Damn right; I want you to myself."

Though his tone was rough, there was no displeasure in his expression. Just the opposite, in fact: he looked rather pleased with himself, Pauline noted with a shiver at the endearing admission.

"Answer the phone," he barked, laughing, as he rolled across the bed to get up.

She watched him head for the bathroom, with a dulcet sigh sibilating through her and her eyes love-glazed as she picked up the receiver. "Hello."

* * *

From the back wall of the stage, innocent brown eyes stared out from the blown up picture of Ann-Marie Johns, framed by dark blue velvet curtains. Pink carnations, dozens of them in whites vases, lined the stage floor across the front of the color photo. Soft piano music, a program of melancholy tunes, mingled with the hushed tones of people piling into the auditorium at CSI.

Marcellus felt as if he'd been injected with a shot of adrenaline. Two opposing reasons explained this excitation, but the main one was at his side. He and Pauline were standing in a far isle next to the brown-paneled walls, out of range of being overheard.

He found himself studying her soft, dark-skinned profile. Her chocolate-tinted creamy complexion glowed. He was like a glutton, as if his spinning senses were not satisfied by her nearness alone. She wore a pencil-slim dress in a rich royal blue. Her neck looked warm and inviting in the low, square-necked collar; a wide kinte belt framed her narrow waist, drawing attention to her firm bosom and the shapely flare of hips. Any red-blooded man would follow the natural progression of her attractiveness to ogle her fine filly legs in sheer stockings of a neutral shade, then scout up to see how the face matched the body. He would not be disappointed, he thought, with feelings of fire kindling in him. She was a provocative study of black womanhood—and she was his woman.

She looked up to catch him looking at her: he would make no apologies for his expression, a dead giveaway to macho pride stamped on his face, and desire coursing through him.

He sensed a difference in her this morning. It was inside, invisible to the naked eye. He couldn't decide if that was altogether good or bad. He only knew they couldn't go on indefinitely living like roommates—one of them hesitant to make a commitment, and, for his part, almost willing to accept any crumb of hers that she was willing to give, as long as she didn't reject him outright. But tonight, whether the trap set to end his company's troubles worked or not, they were going to conclude the unfinished business between them.

"What happened between you and Mrs. Johns?" he asked. It was from Katherine that he'd learned of Mrs. Johns's deliberate absence from today's presentation. While she wasn't able to elaborate, she had given him her best guess of a rift between Pauline and Ann-Marie's mother, based on Mrs. John's vehement refusal to be present, and a terse tone when Pauline's name was mentioned.

Pauline drew a short breath, and ran her tongue across her lips before she replied. "A misunderstanding."

Marcellus frowned. "That's all you have to say about it?"

Bobbing her head up and down, she looked at him resolutely, adding, "It's no longer important."

Then she flashed him one of those mysterious looks he'd seen on her face when she thought he wasn't looking or was too preoccupied to notice. Though always accompanied by a smile when caught, it went deeper than the physical manifestation of affection.

Marcellus knew not to worry over Pauline's refusal to give details. Whatever happened, she had made her decision. Since she was impervious to impetuosity, he knew she had given it a lot of thought. "All right," he said, but she had already averted her attention to the crowd.

He wished she'd make a decision about them. He could have forced time between them, he thought, recalling all the postponements he permitted. But he hadn't. In part because he feared losing her if he demanded a formal commitment from her. Still, her ambivalence about their future together maddened him. But she was who she was, and he wouldn't change her for all the space in the universe.

He felt, then saw, her tugging at his coat. She nodded discreetly toward the audience, asking, "Who is that with Mr. Coombs?"

Looking out, he sighted the glamorous-looking woman, one of her possessive arms entwined with one of Leonard's, whose coffin face was eclipsed in extreme grief. "That's Leonard's wife Joan."

"That's his wife?" Pauline echoed in an astonished whisper. "She's beautiful."

"Never judge a book by its cover," he replied, lifting his brow sardonically.

Misery stamped on her face, Amy headed in their direction. She carried Pauline's black medicine kit in one hand, while squeezing the starch out of a handkerchief with the other. Her eyes were already liquid with tears.

"Oh, good, she thought to bring my kit," Pauline said. "I meant to bring it down with me."

"Think you'll need it?" Marcellus replied.

"I hope not, but you can never tell," she replied.

"You left this upstairs," Amy said, passing the bag to Pauline. "I thought you might want it, just in case, you know, so you wouldn't have to go back for it."

"Yes, I did, thank you," Pauline replied. "How are you holding up?"

Amy shrugged her shoulders limply and attempted a smile before she spoke. "I'll be okay." She started to walk off, then changed her mind. "Oh, I almost forgot." She folded the wrinkled handkerchief, and pulled a crumpled pink slip of paper out of her pocket. "This call came for you just as I was locking up the office."

"Oh," Pauline said, "okay." She read the message.

"Is anything wrong?" Marcellus asked.

Still staring at the message, a frown line across her forehead, Pauline replied, "No. The insurance company wants me to drop by the office to discuss what I want to do about the damage to my house, that's all. Thanks, Amy,'' she said, slipping the paper into her dress pocket.

That was the kind of thing he was referring to, Marcellus thought, mildly exasperated. If Pauline had firmed up her decision about them, she would take the insurance money and simply walk away from that house. He started to tell her that, too, after Amy walked away to take a seat on the front row next to Katherine, who sat dry-eyed and stoic. But he held his tongue.

The minister, a tall, white-haired man from a nearby church with ties to CSI, was standing slightly off-stage on the right behind the podium. He was consulting his notes, which included information that had been provided to him about Ann-Marie.

"What are they doing here?" Marcellus asked quietly, nodding in the direction of his parents and Dottie, taking seats near a back row.

Following his gaze, Pauline replied in a like tone, "Oh, good, Dottie was able to make it. She wasn't sure when I talked to her earlier. And your mother and I are going to lunch afterwards," Pauline replied, smiling up at him cheekily.

"And I thought you got dressed for me," he replied, feigning hurt feelings. "What is my dad going to do, keep Rufus company while he shadows me all day?"

"I'm sure you guys will think of something," she replied with mirth in her voice. "Where is Rufus, by the way?" she asked, looking across the auditorium. "He's supposed to be at your side at all times," she said in a slightly piqued tone of voice.

"Don't worry, he's seen to that already," Marcellus replied. Though CSI's security staff had been given high-alert instructions, he didn't want to take any chances. "You remember what I told you this morning—stay close. Don't leave without telling me."

"Yes sir," she responded, her attention divided between his conversation and the program activities.

"I'm serious, Pauline," he added, his expression solemn. "We didn't get to talk last night. Things are not ironed out to my satisfaction, but we'll do that tonight for sure. Meanwhile, stay alert. I think today might be the day."

She looked up at him curiously. "What are you talking about?"

Before he could reply, the sudden silence seized their attention. The pianist stopped playing, and the minister stepped up to the microphone. He cleared his throat, and the sound carried throughout the room.

"I'll tell you later," Marcellus whispered in her ear. "Just stay close."

"We are here today," the minister began, "to pay our respects to a very dear friend and colleague . . . Ann-Marie Johns." The coffin of grief opened; a dirge-like atmosphere held the room in mournful containment. "And I want you to know," the minister continued, "that in spite of the sinful way in which Ann-Marie was taken from us, she is not in any suffering now. She's in good hands."

Several "Yes, Lords" and "Amens" floated from the assembled. Eyes misted and lips trembled with the promise of tears. With her head bobbing up and down, Katherine rocked gently in her seat. Amy was sobbing softly into her handkerchief. A pitiable wail escaped Leonard Coombs's throat, and his wife shot him a disdainful look. He sucked in a deep breath and pressed a fist against his mouth, biting back his sorrow.

As the minister continued the memorial homage, Amy's lamentations grew louder. Unable to contain her grief any longer, she bolted from her seat and hurried up the center aisle and out of the auditorium.

"I'll be right back," Pauline whispered to Marcellus before making her way quietly from the auditorium.

Signaling one of the security guards with a look and a

pointed finger at Pauline's departing back, Marcellus noted a significant absentee from the gathering. Before he could give it another thought, he saw Dr. Chin slip into the auditorium from one of the far end doors. What really piqued his interest was the scientist's companion. *What's Wanatabe doing here?*

With the bag in her hand, Pauline walked into the ladies' room. "Amy?" she called out, "Amy, are you in here?"

In the center of the room, she looked around. It was apparent that no one else was in the room. Backing out the door, she retraced her steps to the lobby. With a hand on her hip, she searched the area with a curious gaze. A security guard stood posted in the corridor.

"Is everything all right, Ms. Sinclair?" he asked.

"I was trying to catch up with Amy Bridgewater," she said, her gaze sliding toward the elevators. The lighted number caught her attention; the car stopped at the lab floor.

With a curious mutter, she wondered who could be going up to the lab at a time like this. All the offices were closed until noon today.

There was only one person who possessed the audacity to ignore common courtesy, and that was Dr. Kent, who apparently had had a change of heart about attending the memorial service. *The nerve of that woman,* she thought to herself. She jabbed the button on another elevator.

"Wait a minute, Ms. Sinclair," the guard said. "I don't think Mr. Cavanaugh wants you to leave the floor."

With Dr. Kent's insensitivity occupying part of her thoughts, the other part was wondering where Amy had gone. Pauline replied, "Well, you can tell him where I've gone."

The doors of the elevator opened quickly, but the guard

prevented her entry, indecision in his expression. "I don't know about this, Ms. Sinclair."

"Well, you can come with me if you want to," she said, thinking that Marcellus's concern was touching, but unnecessary: after all, he was the one in need of protection. "I'm just going to run up to the ninth floor to check on Amy," she said. Even though she wasn't sure it was where Amy had gone, it was the only place she could think of that she would go to be alone with her grief.

He pulled opened the walkie-talkie strapped to his hip and spoke into it. "One-C, to Nine-A," he said. The person called responded, "Nine-A, here." Pauline enacted a series of impatient gestures—rolling her eyes and sighing impatiently—as the guards conferred. "Ms. Sinclair is on her way up." "Gotcha, One-C," the person called replied. "All right, Ms. Sinclair," the guard said, stepping aside to allow her entry onto the elevator.

"Thank you," Pauline said exasperated, as the elevator doors closed. Sticking her free hand in her pocket, she felt the crisp paper and pulled out the message Amy had given her. She would have the house fixed up, then put it on the market for sale, she decided. After all, she and Marcellus needed only one residence, she thought, smiling to herself.

Folding the message to return it to her pocket, her gaze caught small drawings—circles looped together like a horizontal figure eight with slanted lines drawn from one loop—on the back. The doodling was vaguely familiar.

The elevator doors opened. Shoving the message back into her pocket, she stepped off. Another guard met her.

"Did you happen to see which way Amy went?" she asked.

"Amy Bridgewater?" he replied. "Amy didn't come up here."

Pauline frowned, bewildered. Where else would Amy

have gone? The clinic, maybe? "Okay," she said lightly, as she reentered the elevator.

"Ms. Sinclair . . . ?" he insisted, as the doors were closing.

"I'm going back downstairs," she replied, seconds before the elevator began its descent.

Suddenly, the elevator jerked and, instinctively, Pauline reached for a side wall to steady her balance. The car came to a dead halt. With a heartbeat thumping light and fast in her ears, she wondered what was happening. Just as she was about to press the lobby floor button again, the car rattled, gearing to descend. She held her breath in anticipation, eager to reach the ground floor.

But the elevator didn't deliver her there, as she had hoped. Rather, it stopped at the research floor. She felt apprehension like a second skin, and tried to brace herself for the unexpected.

The elevator doors opened, but no one stepped on. She peered curiously out into the semi-dark, empty corridor. As the doors threatened to close, she hopped off: she didn't want to be on the elevator in case it got stuck. She could find an exit and walk down to the lobby, she decided, uneasiness making her impulsive. The doors closed, taking light and sound with it, leaving her in a silhouette of silence.

"I guess I'm not cut out for spying."

The admission came from Dr. Chin, but no one reacted to his attempt at humor. Marcellus examined the official shield in its leather pouch, his thoughts scampering as if in a race to reassemble pieces of a puzzle.

"You're not Ken Wanatabe, but Ken Kotetsu. You don't work for a Japanese cartel, but for the Justice Department," he said, returning the ID holder to the American-born Japanese.

They—Marcellus, Clay, Dr. Chin and Ken Kotetsu—
were in CSI's camera room, where security monitored the
activities of the employees. Rufus stood just outside the
partially cracked door.

"Yes," Ken Kotetsu nodded.

Word had gotten around that Dr. Chin was asking questions among his associates and it had reached Ken Kotetsu.
Suspecting Chin of being an accomplice in the conspiracy
to steal from CSI, Kotetsu took him in for questioning. It
explained why Dr. Chin had never gotten back to Marcellus.

"Lightning strikes twice," Marcellus said thoughtfully.

"But never in the same place," Ken Kotetsu added, a
hint of a smile on his thin lips.

"Though I have a feeling I know the answer, why don't
you tell me who at CSI you're after," Marcellus said.

"Dr. Jacqueline Kent."

"Looks like you guessed right, boss," Clay interjected.
"We let her in the building as you instructed."

"Aren't you going to stop her?" Dr. Chin asked.

"Not until we catch her in the act," Marcellus replied,
a bittersweet chuckle in his voice.

"Hello."

Startled, Pauline pivoted sharply to face the owner of
the greeting, her heart jumping in her chest. "Amy," she
said, a hand at her bosom, "you startled me."

Amy merely stared wordlessly at her. The tension
between them increased with frightening intensity. The
smirk of a smile on Amy's reddish-orange painted lips
suddenly looked grotesque. Feeling the hairs on the back
of her neck stand up, Pauline stepped back instinctively.

"I thought you might need something from my little
bag here," she said, trying to keep the nervousness from

her voice as she displayed the medicine kit. "That's why I came looking for you."

"And I was counting on it," Amy said.

"But what are you doing here in the lab?"

"I couldn't get to the ninth floor, as if you didn't know," Amy quipped. "Security is stationed on every floor except this one. I just had to wait for you to find that out. It was a gamble, hoping that when the elevator came down from nine, it would have you on it. If you hadn't showed up, I don't know what I would have done," she said in a voice dripping with false helplessness.

Searching anxiously for the meaning behind the words, Pauline grew more uncomfortable under Amy's wild-eyed, fixed stare. She felt an urge to drop the kit and run; instead, she stuck her free hand in her pocket. As her fingers touched the crumpled message, she sensed a grave error, too late to correct it. Unexpectedly, Amy's presence was replaced by a montage of seemingly unrelated pieces of recollections, snatches of seemingly irrelevant conversations at the hospital. Images—Don gasping for air, the decomposed body of Ann-Marie Johns floating in the pool, the smoky debris of car remains in her driveway—flashed across her mind like a series of clips from a movie.

"I made a boo-boo and gave you the wrong one," Amy said, cutting into the drama in her head. "I meant to give you this one."

Pauline accepted the pink message slip, puzzled. She looked it over carefully, front and back. The message from her insurance company was the same. However, the new note contained no doodling. She looked up at Amy, her heart pounding like a drum corps beating in her bosom.

With deliberate languor and a sinister grin spreading on her mouth, Amy brought both hands from behind her back and lifted them simultaneously into a firing position. Facing the barrel of a silver gun, Pauline sucked in a deep breath, like a diver about to plunge into icy waters. The medical kit hit the floor with a dull thud.

"Surprise," Amy said in a giggling Valley-girl voice.

The elevator bell emitted a short ring, announcing another passenger about to debark. Amy bit off a curse, glancing up at the lighted numbers above the elevator, while keeping an eye on Pauline. Galvanizing into action, she kicked the kit aside, then snatched Pauline into position, facing the elevator.

"Not a word," she whispered, holding the gun on Pauline squarely, with a steady-handed grip. She pressed her back against the wall between the two elevators out of the brightest path of light.

Swallowing the lump that had formed in her throat, Pauline nodded obediently. She would have been impressed by Amy's wit if she weren't so damn scared.

The doors opened, and Dr. Kent walked off the elevator.

"Oh," Dr. Kent exclaimed, surprised to see Pauline. Regaining her composure, she said snidely, "Well, well, well. What are you, the welcoming committee?" sauntering off the elevator into the corridor. At Pauline's utter silence, a look of uneasiness crossed her expression. "I only came up to get some notes I forgot to take with me yesterday, then I'm going to run back down to the service," she said, attempting appeasement.

Dr. Kent never knew what hit her. Stepping out of the shadows, Amy clobbered her on the back of the head, and she swooned to the floor in an unconscious heap. Containing the scream clawing at her throat, Pauline covered her mouth with both hands, her eyes as wide as saucers, shocked by Amy's capacity for cruelty.

In that flashing instant, she concluded Amy was sick, and on the heels of that realization, came acceptance of her own precarious hold on life.

Chapter Twenty

"She's going up now," Clay announced.

"Good," Marcellus said pleased. The men had reassembled in the lobby and stood together as if in a huddle. "Dr. Chin, I suggest you stay here. Mr. Kotetsu, I can't stop you from tagging along, but this is our show." With purpose in his long strides, he headed for the elevators: Mr. Kotetsu, Clay and Rufus matched his steps. "Have you seen Pauline?"

"I thought she was in the auditorium," Rufus replied.

"No," Marcellus said, pressing a summoning button on the wall. "She left to see about Amy."

"They're probably in the ladies' room," Clay said. "Want me to have someone check?"

With his brow tilted, Marcellus looked with uncertainty toward the lobby. Pauline probably had her hands full; she didn't need him begging for attention, too. But it sure was taking a long time.

"Marcellus?" Rufus prodded.

Rubbing his chin, Marcellus looked back and forth at

Rufus and Clay before he spoke. "Rufus, why don't you stay here just in case she comes out looking for me?" He added, "If this takes longer than I think it will, tell her not to leave until I finish."

"Gotcha," Rufus replied, giving him a thumbs up.

Marcellus stepped on the elevator where Clay and Mr. Kotetsu were waiting. As the doors were closing, two hands grabbed each side and pulled them apart. It was a CSI guard.

"Three monitors went down in the store," he said winded, trying to catch his breath. "One in the corridor, two in the main lab."

Reaching the glass-encased, off the gym-size lab, breathing laboriously, Pauline propped the dead weight of Dr. Kent against the wall. Staring as the body slid to the floor, she rubbed her sore arms. Dr. Kent looked as if she was merely taking a nap.

From the entry way, Amy said, "Now stand over here." Waving the gun, she guided Pauline to stand in front of the desk.

Complying, her gaze still on Dr. Kent, Pauline felt assaulted by terrible regrets. With time to ponder missed opportunities in her lifetime, she wondered if Ann-Marie had felt what she was feeling. Squeezing back the hot tears threatening to fill her eyes, she wished she could have back the time she wasted denying her feelings for Marcellus. She never got the chance to say *I love you*. If it hadn't been for her foolish insecurity, more than one bedroom in that big, rambling house would be filled with children.

Suddenly, she clutched at her stomach. Even without proof, she felt certain she was pregnant, and it brought out her worst thoughts. An autopsy would reveal the truth. Marcellus would be left alone with the knowledge that he had been robbed of another child. She couldn't let that happen, she told herself, summoning courage in the face of her fear.

"Don't get sick on me," Amy said. She sauntered alongside Pauline and rubbed the barrel of the gun across her cheek. It was cold on her warm skin, and Pauline winced slightly as if her flesh had been nipped.

"You like?" Amy asked in a girlish voice. "Her name's Nancy. Don't you think that's a nice name for a .38 special?" she asked, backing from Pauline to the desk. "I thought so."

With her gaze riveted on the revolver with the wooden handle, Pauline felt and heard her stomach growl as if hungry. She wondered where it got the nerve, believing she was using up every nerve in her body with fear.

"Put your hands behind your back," Amy said, her hand inside a drawer of the desk.

"What for?" Pauline asked, watching Amy pull a roll of metallic string from the drawer in the desk. With adrenaline kicking in, she saw an opportunity coming that she dare not pass up, believing Amy could not tie her up and keep the gun on her at the same time. Hope leaped to her chest, the desire to live canceling out the fear in her.

"I can't have you reaching for the gun, can I?" Amy replied. "Turn around. Now," she shouted when Pauline was slow to move.

Though she felt hope abandoning her, Pauline said, "You'll never get away with it."

"Famous last words," Amy retorted.

From a sidelong glance, the end of the gun was a silver blur, and Pauline realized Amy was not about to relinquish the weapon. Fear and tenacity became battling opponents inside her. She wetted her lips nervously and eased a foot foreword. At the sound of the hammer cocking into place, she froze.

Pressing the gun hard against Pauline's temple, Amy said, "Don't try it."

Pauline tasted defeat in the sigh she exhaled. She stiffened as Amy looped the string around her wrists, one at a time, tying them behind her back. She grunted as Amy pulled the string, tightening it. The wiry rope was stronger than it looked; the more she twisted her hands, the tighter it grew, cutting into her flesh.

"That will definitely hold you," Amy said chuckling, "it's been dipped in titanium. You learn all kinds of neat little science things around this place . . . you can become a *McGyver.*"

"Why, Amy? Why?" Pauline asked, turning to face Amy. She would not be beaten by this insane woman, she told herself with haunting persistence. Just because she couldn't use her hands didn't mean she couldn't keep her head. She just had to be patient and ready for the slightest lax in Amy's guard.

"Why?" Amy echoed. "That's simple," she said, hips perched on the edge of the desk, legs crossed at the ankles. "Not only did he reject me as a woman, he was going to fire me."

"Oh my God," Pauline whispered introspectively, her gaze bright with understanding. "Now, I see," she said more to herself. "You sent him those love letters. But he already has a wife. Or had you forgotten?"

Amy snorted. "Sarah? She's so gullible." Laughing, "She called to ask me about the love note she'd found. Can you believe it? By the time she would have realized she no longer had a husband, he would have been mine," she bit off confidently. "He sent me flowers," she said defensively, as if her actions were justified. "For my birthday in February." Her expression grew wistful, a wee smile turning up a corner of her mouth. "A dozen red roses," she said softly with affection. "That's when I knew he felt something for me. But then," her features hardening, "after he guessed my signature, he confronted me, and just did a complete about face," she concluded outraged.

"The doodling," Pauline thought aloud, memory clouding her eyes. "That was your signature, the drawings that almost looked like a bee."

"I'm not as good an artist as he was," she replied in a So-what? tone of voice. "I laid my feelings out to him, and you know what he said? That he was going to have to think about what to do with me," she quoted in a nasty tone of voice. Her expression metamorphosed into utter disbelief. "He told me to take the day off, and I find out later that Ann-Marie was going to be my replacement." As if her thoughts suddenly veered, she said, "I didn't know about his plans to hire you. I had to think quickly and figure out how to use you to my advantage. Only you worked out too well and stayed longer than you should have. I thought I had timed the release of the crushed pills in his juice just right. He was about dead when I called you to come up. I figured by the time you got there, it would be too late. Instead, you saved him," she said as if ticked off.

"It was your mother's medication, wasn't it?" Pauline asked, but she felt certain of her guess. She was stalling, trying to distract Amy and buy herself some time. "What about Ann-Marie? Why did you kill her?"

"I couldn't afford to take the chance that somebody would take her ideas seriously," Amy said, gesturing with her gun hand. "She got to rambling on about her stupid story, and how she was going to capitalize on the situation. That's when I knew she would have to be dealt with before she told anyone else her story."

"She did," Pauline interjected, recalling her conversation with Detective Collins. "She told her boyfriend."

Amy shrugged. "It doesn't matter. He can't prove anything."

"So you convinced her into going to the gym with you," Pauline said. Careful not to move her shoulders, she twisted her wrists behind her back, trying to wiggle them free of the knot.

"The place pretty much cleared out after the ambulance carted you and Don away to the hospital. People were all upset. Or pretended to be so they could go home." She laughed wildly with her memories. "I even fooled Katherine with my little act. And you know hardly *anything* gets by her. Only, I didn't leave," she admitted flippantly. "We had the gym to ourselves, Ann-Marie and I. There she was on that exercise bike, her legs pedaling away as she ran off at the mouth about her story," she said, shaking her head amazed. "She got carried away . . . didn't hear when I walked up behind her and cracked that bar across the back of her head." She chuckled, satisfied. "By the time she realized she'd been hit, it was too late. One more swing was all it took."

"But she was your friend!" Pauline said with protest, though she knew it would do no good.

Laughing with mockery, Amy quipped, "All's fair in love and war. Best friends or not, no one was going to get in my way."

"You've taken a mighty big risk for nothing," Pauline said solemnly, realizing the rope hadn't given an inch of space behind her.

"You still don't get it, do you?" Amy replied with a sarcastic rasp. "I would have thought that you, of all people, would understand. You're like me . . . a nobody! But you landed probably one of the most eligible bachelors around, and one with money to boot. Don . . ." She said his name intimately. "Don was my chance. The risk was well worth it, I'd say."

"But nobody guessed it. Nobody had a clue," Pauline said with emphasis.

"Nobody but you," Amy quipped. "You were too close. I tried to warn you off, even tried to implicate you in that so-called assault on Sarah. But when the cops released you, you came right back. And then, unfortunately, everybody got the wrong impression when both cars blew up in your driveway. Everybody, including you, thought Mr. Cavanaugh was the target.''

Pauline knew it was useless denying it; even though, she hadn't put the pieces together then. But it was easy enough to see that Amy was paranoid, and no doubt delusional, as well.

''Then, today, when I got careless, I knew that I couldn't afford to wait any longer,'' Amy said. ''I had to do something in a hurry. You should have left when you had a chance. Now, everybody believes you're off consoling me, and they'll think that until your body is discovered in that space ship over there,'' she said confidently, nodding to the other side of the glass partition. ''Only, you won't be wearing a suit. No suit, no oxygen. It's a fantastic simulator,'' she boasted, ''with all those little colorful gadgets and stuff. Don let me go in for a demonstration right after they built it. You'll like it . . . for about three minutes, then you'll lose consciousness. And five minutes later, it will be all over,'' she said, with a nonchalant shrug.

''How do you want to handle it?'' Clay asked, his expression as tight and serious as Marcellus's.

''There's only one other way in,'' Marcellus replied as if speaking to himself. ''I'll go up,'' he said. ''Take the other car to two, then walk up. Give me a walkie-talkie. I'll be in touch.''

Alone in the car now, Marcellus rode up to the ninth floor. He raced to his office, locked the door behind him and headed straight for the bathroom. He disengaged the floor length mirror from the door, revealing an opened elevator shaft that had been installed largely to provide easy access for Don. He stepped on, pulled the door closed behind him and stabbed the down button with his thumb.

Pressing the speaker button on the walkie-talkie, he said, ''Clay.''

"Still here," Clay acknowledged shortly. "Where are you?"

"I'm on my way down," he replied.

Holding the walkie-talkie down at his side, he closed his eyes, drawing a mental image of the lab, trying to remember which piece of equipment he could use as a shield once he got off in order to catch Dr. Kent red-handed. The console that controlled the space ship occupied that corner of the lab. A sliding door fronted the elevator. If he squatted, then he could get off unnoticed.

The elevator stopped with a jolt. Clutching the walkie-talkie, he crouched slightly as he put his hand on the handle of the door facing him. His heart was beating a mile a minute as if he was the hunted instead of the hunter. Slowly, he slid open the door. It creaked, and he flinched.

He could see nothing at floor level except consoles, with the largest one located near him. A silver ladder stood alongside the space ship that sat atop its own separate platform, looking as if it was suspended from overhead.

Getting down on all fours, he crawled out onto the lab floor. Stealthily making his way to the console about five feet away, he heard shoe heels clicking on the tile floor. Not one pair of women's high heel shoes, but two, and they were coming his way.

"You don't have to keep looking back here. I'm not going anyplace, and no one's going to save you."

With his face wrinkled severely in a frown, he identified the voice as Amy's. His brain seemed to malfunction with this new disclosure. Scooting down to lie on his belly, he peered around the corner of the console and spotted Pauline, walking hesitantly, her hands behind her back.

As his stupefied gaze spread to Amy, focusing on the revolver pointed directly at the back of Pauline's head, his chest felt as if it would burst. Beads of perspiration popped out across his forehead, and the craziest thought sprang to mind. He never got around to telling Pauline how much he appreciated the trouble she was going through to impress his mother. Even though he never cared what or how his mother felt about Pauline, he wanted her to know that. Now, he just wanted the future.

In his nervous haste, he bumped the walkie-talkie against the console, and the noise was no more subtle in the sound-proof room than the discreet rattle of a rolling cart. He sat frozen with a grimace on his face and a prayer on his silent lips.

Pauline stared intently in front of her; there was no movement, not even the whisper of sound, but she knew she heard it. And so did Amy. Feeling Amy's hand gripping her shoulder, she halted. She cursed herself silently for stopping, believing it was partly her hesitation that clued Amy to the intrusion as they stood in a path between two small console boards with large black knobs.

"Who's there?" Amy asked sharply.

"I didn't hear anything," Pauline said, trying to play it off. She wondered if Marcellus had stumbled upon them, while praying it wasn't him.

"Shut up," Amy commanded, placing the gun to the side of her head. "I said, who's there?" she repeated with emphasis. "If you don't show yourself, I'll blow her brains out right now."

When Marcellus stepped out, Pauline emitted a startled cry. With frightful alarm prominent in her eyes, she wanted to plead with him to go back, even though she knew it was too late. She felt fate was conspiring against the good guys.

"Aw, the lover to the rescue," Amy said mockingly.

Despite the bravado of her words, Pauline could tell Amy was not in as control as she tried to appear. Her hands were shaking ever so slightly now.

"Give it up, Amy," Marcellus said coolly. "You'll never

make it out of here alive. There are several guards on the other side of the door."

"If I don't make it, neither will you," Amy retorted. "I've got nothing to lose now." She shifted nervously, looking over her shoulder warily, the gun an extension of her hands.

"You can lose everything by killing us," Marcellus said, slowly advancing. "If you let us go, I'll see to it that you get the best legal advice around. I promise you, Amy," he said with heartfelt sincerity.

"I said stop," Amy shouted. "Stop, or I'll kill her," she promised, shifting the gun back on Pauline.

"No, no, you don't understand," Marcellus replied as if pleading with a temperamental child, shaking his head as he continued toward them. "I can't let you do that. If you kill her, that means you kill me, too. And I just can't let that happen."

"Marcellus," Pauline cried, with pleading, tears streaming silently down her face.

"I said stop," Amy said between gritted teeth, switching the gun back to Marcellus with a shaky, two-handed grip.

Watching Amy's finger crook around the trigger, Pauline didn't think. She threw her weight onto Amy, and both women tumbled over the console, then rolled onto the floor.

Pauline hit her head on the corner of the console. She felt the wind knocked out of her, and a sharp pain blasted down her body. She groaned as Amy crawled over her in a stampede to reach the gun that had clattered to the floor. Barely conscious, she heard a rustle of frantic activity; grunts and cries drifted in and out of her head. The gun went off. The cannon-like boom was followed by the long, tortured wail of an entrapped animal.

Pauline whispered, "Marcellus." White lights impaired her vision, then the world faded to black.

Chapter Twenty-One

Pauline felt hands on her body—big hands—on her head, neck, shoulders, arms, everywhere, examining her. The gentleness of the touches soothed, rather than frightened her, for she could identify those hands under any circumstances.

She smiled, or rather, an attempt was made as her eyes fluttered opened to focus on Marcellus's face. His eyes were fixed on her in a tender vise, a soft and loving curve on his lips. Her heart reacted immediately to his radiant visage. She tried to sit up, and a hot pain shot up her body. But those big hands weren't about to let her move, holding her still gently by the shoulders.

She relaxed between the hard floor at her back and his comforting nearness above her. "Am I dead and you're my angel from heaven?" she asked groggily. Though her eyes were closed, she was certain now that the smile found its way to her mouth.

"Oh, no, baby," Marcellus replied, flashing his pearly white teeth in an ebullient grin. "You're very much alive, and I'm your angel on earth," he said in a deep voice that simmered with emotion.

Pauline saw the thoughts change in his eyes, now wide with the half-laugh that comes from experiencing fear. She reached up to caress the side of his face with her hand, and with an affected groan, Marcellus held it trapped next to his flushed skin.

"I want to get up," she said, trying to lift herself on her haunches.

"Hold on," Marcellus said, taking control. With tender care, he lifted her off the floor and snuggled her in the cradle of his arms, next to his warm chest.

"My head is killing me," she said, fingering the bump at the back of her head. He pushed her fingers aside and began to gently rub the spot.

"I thought I had lost you," he said into her hair, a faraway look in his eyes.

"Me, too," she replied. "I thought I'd never see you again. God, Marcellus, I'm so sorry."

"You have nothing to be sorry for," he assured her. With remnants of fear affecting his voice, he said, "I've never been so afraid in my life."

"I kept thinking of all those wasted months, the baby we lost, and how we could have had at least two more by now," she said, her hands touching his face with gentle caresses.

"Shh," he said, crushing her to him. "The most important thing is that we have today and many tomorrows," he said, as he lowered his head to her face and kissed her lingeringly on the mouth.

A small sound of wonder came from Pauline's throat, as she wrapped her arms, solid and strong, around him. Hearing a loud "harrumph," Pauline and Marcellus parted reluctantly to look up and see Detective Collins hovering.

"Seems like I missed all the action," he said.

"Where's Amy?" Pauline asked, sitting up to look about anxiously. She spotted Clay conferring with two uniformed police officers in the glass cubicle across the way; a yellow strip of plastic was stretched over the entrance into the lab. "Marcellus ... the gun ... I heard ...," she said excitedly, her hands frantically examining him.

Shushing her, Marcellus pressed a finger to her lips. "Amy's fine. A little sick in the head, but otherwise okay. Rufus took her down to the clinic to wait for you," he said to Collins. Pointing, he said, "Since you're so into evidence, the bullet hit that console."

"Good," Pauline replied relieved, sagging back into the comfort of his embrace.

"You'll have to wait to get a statement," Marcellus said to the detective in a tone that brooked no arguments. "I want to get Pauline checked out first."

"That's understandable," Detective Collins replied agreeably. "I've already stopped down at the clinic and had a brief chat with Ms. Amy Bridgewater. I suspect she'll get a good lawyer, but I'm fairly certain we'll get a conviction for premeditated murder on Ms. Johns." He rocked back and forth on the heels of his shoes, hands in his coat pocket. "I, uh, I guess I owe you an apology, Ms. Sinclair."

"You guess?" Marcellus replied, lifting a fractious brow.

"I do," Collins corrected. "And I am sorry, but only because I let things progress as far as they did. I did try to warn you."

"You were right about that," Pauline said musingly. "Amy said as much herself."

"Before I go," Detective Collins said, "I thought you might like to know that Mr. Wellsing is going to be all right."

"What?" Marcellus and Pauline asked with simultaneous excitement in their faces.

"Yeah," Collins replied, smiling as if he'd had something to do with it. "That's why I missed the action. He came around. It took a while, but putting together what he knew with my suspicions, we were able to piece the puzzle together and figure out Ms. Bridgewater was the culprit all along. He said he had been feeling fine until a couple of hours after he drank the juice she'd brought him from the cafeteria. She must have dumped the heart medicine in the bottle and shook it up pretty good. He didn't start having cramps until he left you, Ms. Sinclair, to return to his office. She was watching him when he doubled over, clutching his stomach." He shivered. "Gives me the creeps just thinking about how cruel that woman was."

Pauline interjected, "She was in love with him."

"I'd hate for somebody to love me that much," Detective Collins quipped.

"Plus, she believed Don was going to fire her and give her job to Ann-Marie," Pauline added.

"No, he wasn't going to fire her," Collins corrected. "He said she was a damn good secretary. But he was going to transfer her to another division in the company and reassign Ann-Marie to his office. He never realized the danger of his executive decision," he added thoughtfully, staring at Marcellus. "Said that was more your area. Well, I guess I'll see you later. Mr. Cavanaugh, Ms. Sinclair," he said as if tipping a hat. "Good luck."

Pauline clutched Marcellus's arm. "What happened to Dr. Kent? Is she all right?" she asked anxiously.

"She's safe in the government's hands right now," he replied sarcastically, displeasure drawing his brows together in a frown. "She returned planning to break into Donnie. She hadn't been able to find Don's notes on *Project Ba* anywhere else she had looked."

"But Donnie's at home."

Marcellus smiled wickedly. "She didn't know that."

Pauline wrapped her arms around Marcellus and snuggled next to his chest. "What a strange set of coincidences, don't you think . . . one company facing J.T. Kent and Amy Bridgewater at the same time?''

Marcellus shook his head, disagreeing with her assessment. "Not coincidence. Everything in life has a purpose. I believe what happened here, both within the company and its leadership, was nature's way of forcing us to get our houses in order . . . here and at home," he added, looking at her significantly. "Don and I had been so intent on making a success of the company that we lost sight of the fact that the people who work here are the company. All of them weren't happy, and we failed to see that. The oversight carried over into our home lives, as well. Next time, we'll do a better job of taking care of business."

"Think it's over?"

Smiling down at her suggestively, he said, with promise in his voice, "Oh, but the best is yet to come."

Hospital rules were definitely being violated in Don's room, with laughter-filled voices raised in joyful celebration. A nurse opened a crack in the door, stuck her stern face inside, and the din dropped to soft giggles.

Amid good-byes, promises to return, and hugs and kisses all around, Dottie, the senior Cavanaughs, and Katherine took their leave. Sarah, who never strayed far from Don, was standing at his bedside. She took his hand in hers. Pauline sidled alongside Marcellus; her eyes matched his in affection as they smiled at Don.

"We shouldn't overstay our welcome," Pauline said softly to all, but to no one in particular. "Don will tire us out if we do."

"Not yet," Don said in as emphatic a tone as he could manage. He was still weak: Each of them knew what it cost him just to lift his head off the pillow. His chuckles were deep and hoarse-sounding, and when he spoke, his speech was slow and slurred. His eyes, however, were sharp and clear with his feelings about being alive. "Dr. Kent. Where is she?

"Locked up for the time being," Marcellus replied. "I had a feeling she was going to try something today while everyone would be preoccupied with the memorial service."

"So you knew it was her all along?" Pauline asked with surprise in her expression and tone.

"No, I just had a strong suspicion. It wasn't confirmed until Dr. Chin arrived with the federal agent. You remember Wanatabe from the Shishumi Corporation?" he asked of Don. After a head-bob from his partner, he continued, "As it turns out, his name is Ken Kotetsu, and the company he works for is the U.S. Justice Department." Don attempted to whistle, but only managed a dull whoosh of air. "A follow-up of Operation Lightning Strike set off by Jacqueline Kent herself. She mentioned a secret project we were conducting to Jason Ringnald, who didn't want to be implicated by association. So to cover his you-know-what, he contacted the Justice Department, who sent Koketsu to investigate. When he got nothing from either of us, he went after her with a ten-million-dollar offer." Pauline whistled. "She agreed to steal the specs on a project she didn't even know the name of," he concluded, shaking his head, amazed.

"She's going to be in jail a long time," Sarah said softly.

"It depends on who she hires to defend her," Marcellus said. "The set-up reeked of entrapment, and if her attorney can sell that, she may only get probation, a whopping fine. A light sentence would be a bonus. As for Amy . . ."

"Can't figure," Don stammered, ". . . how Amy got key to lab?"

"She used your key," Pauline replied. "She had to have gotten it the day you were rushed to the hospital."

"Feel . . . sorry . . . for . . . her," Don said.

"She doesn't get my sympathies," Marcellus quipped.

"Or mine," Sarah added. "Pauline, Marcellus," she continued softly, a look of shame on her face, "I can't tell you how sorry I am for the things I said . . . the horrible accusations I hurled around like a crazy woman. I . . . I can't believe it of myself," she said with a self-derisive short laugh. "I'm truly sorry . . ."

"You ought to be," Marcellus quipped.

"Yeah," Don got out thickly.

"Forget it," Pauline said.

"I hope you'll forgive me."

"Do we get to be godparents?" Marcellus asked.

"I'd like that very much," Sarah smiled.

"Hey, look, old buddy," Marcellus said, "Pauline and I are going to get out of here and let you get some rest."

"No," protested Don in his husky voice, "not tired."

"I know you're not tired, but I am," Marcellus replied with a chuckle.

"And so am I," Pauline echoed. "I want to go home and sleep for a week."

Marcellus leaned over the side of the bed to whisper in Don's ear. When he straightened, Don's heavy-voiced laughter mingled with his.

"What are you two up to?"

Marcellus winked. "Man talk," he said, then laced his hands with Don's. "You hurry up and get well, so you can take that trip."

"What trip?" Sarah asked.

"Tell you later," Don replied, exchanging a conspiratorial look with Marcellus. "A long way," he added cryptically.

"Yeah. Asante, my friend."

The air vibrated with the sounds of passion. The crescent-shaped moon threw a tip of light into the bedroom, silhouetting the driving strength of Marcellus's body possessing Pauline's, as she reciprocated in kind.

Fevered groans filled the air the moment ecstasy exploded from them. The earth fell away, and she went with him to that place of rapture. The hunger they had for each other was finally satisfied. Again.

Marcellus leaned over Pauline to kiss her tenderly on the mouth. "I love you," he said.

Holding his face close to hers, she replied, "I love you, too," and kissed his lips.

Marcellus slid an arm under her, drawing her nearer to him. "Feel all right?"

Laughing, Pauline replied, "I do, if you do," earning a chuckle from him. "You tired?"

"Why? Are you ready for more?"

"Are you up to it?"

He laughed as if the idea were outrageous. "Give me a few minutes to recover first," he replied, squeezing her affectionately.

Marcellus sighed at the warm feelings in his heart. He smiled in the near dark, remembering what he had told Don at the hospital earlier tonight. Or was it last night already? he wondered with only a fleeting interest in time.

It hadn't been a joke between men, as he told Sarah and Pauline. He just didn't want them to know how anxious he was about proposing to Pauline. He felt pretty sure that she wouldn't refuse him this time, but his insides quivered with a nervousness that he believed was natural under the circumstances.

"Why did you come back?" Marcellus asked, breaking the balmy silence.

Pauline didn't pretend ignorance. "Have you forgotten you badgered me, played on my sense of guilt?"

"Yeah, but that never worked before," he retorted.

Pauline laughed before she spoke, then the amusement left her voice. "At first, I was convinced it was because

of Don. He had been there for me when you and I we**nt**
our separate ways. Then, after he was hospitalized and
you made such a big speech about how he must have
needed me for some reason other than what he told me,
I thought . . ." she paused, a melancholy smile flirting with
her features, then she cleared her throat, "I thought it
made sense."

"I see," he replied dryly, not pleased by her answer. He
was about to demand a little honesty from her when she
brought his hand to her lips and kissed it gently, then held
it cradled between her bosom.

"All right," she said, grudgingly, "I thought it was a
chance for me to prove to you that I wasn't the type of
person you obviously believed was capable of killing her
own child. Is that what you wanted to hear?"

"Is it painful to say?" he replied.

Chuckling to herself, she replied, "No. I guess not. Not
anymore. It's part of our history we can't deny."

He nodded his head in agreement. "I feel the same way.
It's embarrassing as hell to remember my stupidity then,
but I needed that lesson for now."

She sat up on an elbow to look at him; her eyes twinkled
in the half-light and her mouth was curved in a smile. "I
thought all you wanted to do was punish me."

Marcellus feigned outrage with a snort. "Punish you?"

"Don't even go there," she warned. "You know exactly
what I'm talking about."

"Yeah, I know," he said sheepishly. "I was a bastard."

"Yes, you were, my darling," she leaned over to kiss him
on the mouth. "You went out of your way to drive me
crazy, making me feel like a four-year-old who didn't know
her mind from one minute to the next."

He sighed at length. "I never stopped wanting you. Even
when I thought you'd done something horrible. That was
scary."

"Why . . . because you felt as if you'd lost control?"

"You know it," he retorted.

"Yeah, I do," she admitted. "There were times when I didn't know what I wanted."

"You think it didn't scare me, not knowing what to expect of you, when I loved you and wanted you so much for so long?"

"We put each other through so much," she said softly, a wry smile on her face.

"In a way, I'm glad it happened. And it probably had to happen the way it did, because of who we are. The experience has taught me a few things about myself," he said, taking her hand to place a kiss in her palm. "I always felt I knew exactly what I wanted. And most times that's been true. But sometimes, a person needs more than a sketch of what he wants; the outline has to be filled out. And you can't do it in a hurry and expect to have everything fall into place as if the world evolved around your dreams and wishes."

"What are you trying to tell me, Marcellus?" she asked, somewhat anxious.

Believing Pauline suspected something, Marcellus thought maybe she thought she knew him a little too well. "What do you think?"

"I think you're taking a long route to tell me that maybe we need a little space between us," she replied falteringly, toying with the bed linen.

The features of his face contorted into a complicated set of wrinkles. In a near shout, he said, "What?"

"I can understand if you need more time, you know," she said, her voice quivering, "to think through whether we're right for each other. I mean," she said, talking with her hands, "we were brought together by an unusual set of circumstances, and now that that's been cleared up, maybe we need to see if we feel the same about each other without having a crisis to deal with."

"Jesus Christ!" Marcellus replied, slapping his forehead

as he fell back onto the pillow. "You make about as much sense as Sarah."

Defensively, she replied, "I just don't want you . . . us to be uncertain, that's all."

"Pauline," he said, sitting up to face her headlong, "there is nothing uncertain about my feelings for you, or us."

"There isn't?" she asked.

"In fact," he said, as he reached to the head of the bed to turn on the light. "This is just to give you an idea of just how certain I am."

Shielding her eyes from the light, Pauline complained, "What are you doing?"

After seconds of fiddling in the bedside table, Marcellus faced her, his hand outstretched. Sitting in his palm was a gray velvet jeweler's box.

Pauline's mouth dropped open in utter surprise, and he was pleased. She looked up into his face, where a lop-sided grin was etched into his expression. She sat up, holding the sheet against her nakedness.

Marcellus lifted the top of the box, revealing a ring with delicate stones of purple amethyst circling a big diamond on a yellow gold band. "Pauline Sinclair, will you marry me?"

Pauline's mouth was still open in surprise. Tears of pleasure found their way to her eyes and clogged her throat. She couldn't speak; she bobbed her head up and down. As he put the ring on her finger, a joyous sob escaped her throat.

"Yes," she said, leaning over to kiss him gently on the cheek. "Yes."

Dear Readers,

Asante Sana (thank you, very much) for your wonderful reception to Sydney Webster and Perry Mason McDonald in *Indiscretions*. I hope you will have an equally favorable response to Pauline Sinclair and Marcellus Cavanaugh as they sort through the maze of intrigues—both of the heart and man—in *CONSPIRACY*.

I love hearing from you, so please keep writing me at the address below. Again, thanks for supporting me and Arabesque.

Sincerely,

Margie

Margie Rose Walker
3030 South Gessner
Suite 260
Houston, TX 77063

ABOUT THE AUTHOR

Margie Walker has enjoyed writing since she was a little girl. After graduating Magna Cum Laude from Texas Southern University, she married her college sweetheart, then returned to school to earn a Teacher's Certificate and a Master's degree in Speech Communication. She worked in radio and as a journalist while raising her two sons. Margie Walker is in six year residence with Writers In The Schools, a program which places professional writers in the classroom. *CONSPIRACY* is her fifth romance novel.

Look for these upcoming Arabesque titles:

May 1997
SOUL DEEP by Monique Gilmore
INTIMATE BETRAYAL by Donna Hill
MAMA DEAR, A Mother's Day Collection

June 1997
RHAPSODY by Felicia Mason
ALL THE RIGHT REASONS by Janice Sims
STEP BY STEP by Marilyn Tyner

July 1997
LEGACY by Shirley Hailstock
ECSTACY by Gwynne Forster
A TIME FOR US by Cheryl Faye
THE ART OF LOVE by Crystal Wilson Harris

LOOK FOR THESE ARABESQUE ROMANCES